I0687536

Exodus:
The House of Silence
Volume 1

J.A. Jaken

ForbiddenFiction
www.forbiddenfiction.com

an imprint of

Fantastic Fiction Publishing
www.fantasticfictionpublishing.com

THE HOUSE OF SILENCE, VOLUME 1
A Forbidden Fiction book

Fantastic Fiction Publishing
Hayward, California

© J.A. Jaken, 2012

CREDITS
Editor: Rylan Hunter
Cover Design: D.M. Atkins
Cover photo: Paul Prescott and valuavitaly - Pixmac
Production Editor: Erika L Firanc
Proofreading: JhP323

SKU: JAJ-000001-02
ISBN: 978-1-62234-084-2

Published in the United States of America

Reiji saw the direction of his gaze

and covered the bruise on his arm with one hand, scowling. "So the client last night got a little excited. So what?"

Danny stared at him. "You're saying a customer did that to you?" Was that why he was in such a bad mood today?

"You sound surprised." He laughed at the dumbfounded expression on Danny's face. "That's the benefit of being new, I suppose; Charon isn't going to risk chasing you away by giving you the really fun clients, now is he?"

The accusation made Danny's face heat. It was true he'd only been an employee in the House of Silence for a couple of months, but he didn't think of himself as that naive about how things worked here. "You're lying. Charon would never let any of the guests hurt us. We're too valuable to him for that."

"You really are an innocent. Charon has his own reasons for doing what he does that have nothing to do with us." He sounded bitter when he said it. Turning away, he kicked at one of the broken pieces of pottery with his toe. "Your turn will come eventually. Just wait and see."

Also recommended...

You may also enjoy these other ForbiddenFiction works:

Pathfinder by J.A. Jaken
Shai discovers he is a pathfinder and is desperate to find a genetically suitable partner to prevent his extrasensory talents from running amok. Unfortunately those talents make him a target for the brutal crime lords and other violent denizens who inhabit the city of Nhil-Rhar. Shai needs to learn how to use his pathfinder senses—no matter how much they terrify him—before he's trapped in a partnership that will enslave him for the rest of his life.

http://forbiddenfiction.com/library/story/JAJ-1.000012

Don't... by Jack L. Pike
"Don't... open me." Three simple words that tease Jack, taking him places from his dark past. For Jack, BDSM is a way to resist his worst impulses. Yet, the stranger calling himself The Unknown seeks to use that to seduce him. As Jack slips further down into the abyss, two men hold the power to save him. Will it be Gray, the Master who knows Jack's every secret? Or Jan, the first man to give Jack a reason to hope? With deadly ghosts coming out to play, Jack may lose everything, even his life. (M/M)

http://forbiddenfiction.com/library/story/JP2-1.000134

DISCLAIMER

This book is a work of fiction which contains explicit erotic content; it is intended for mature readers. Do not read this if it's not legal for you.

All the characters, locations and events herein are fictional. While elements of existing locations or historical characters or events may be used fictitiously, any resemblance to actual people, places or events is coincidental.

This story depicts fictional BDSM; it is not intended to be used as an instruction manual. It contains descriptions of erotic acts that may be immoral, illegal, or unsafe. The characters are not models for the Safe, Sane and Consensual forms embraced by most current practitioners of BDSM. The author takes license with the use of BDSM for dramatic effect. Do not take the events in this story as proof of the plausibility or safety of any particular practice.

This book is dedicated to all of my friends and readers from fandom, who provided such steadfast support and encouragement for my writing over the years.

Contents

Chapter 1

Ander

There was something to be said for winter. The all-encompassing quiet of it, the darkness, the way it wrapped around the woods like a blanket, fog frozen in delicate filigree patterns on the bare limbs of the trees. All of that blemishless white covering the hills like a shroud—as if the land weren't merely sleeping, but dead, and the world were holding its breath in silent mourning.

Ander Delacroix held the collar of his coat closed at his throat and looked out over the familiar contours of his family's land, hunching his shoulders against the bite of the wind. He tried to remember playing here as a child, but the image wouldn't come. Surely he had played here somewhere? This land had been his home for his entire life, but the thought brought no comfort with it. Like himself, it had passed its prime, and the memories caged within it were cold and barren things.

A low crackling of ice caught his attention, and he lifted his head, turning. The sight of the large grey wolfhound that emerged from under the shadow of the forest made him smile faintly. "Is it dinnertime already, Dram?"

Dram lowered his shaggy head and whuffed softly, tall ears pricking forward at the sound of his master's voice. His frosted breath plumed in the air; Ander glanced down at his hands and realized they were nearly blue with cold, his fingers stiff from exposure to the evening wind.

"I suppose it *is* time we headed back," he said with a sigh, giving the woods a final, lingering glance. Scratching Dram once behind the ears, he turned in the direction of home.

1

The sun was just beginning to dip below the horizon, touching the branches of the trees with an edge of burnished gold. The sky was aglow with color, from rose to plum to peach to crimson, vermillion spreading like a stain across the clouds in reaching streamers of fading light. It reflected off the front of the house as it came into view, turning each window into a wisp of shimmering flame, brightening the shadows that stretched across the front courtyard in advance of the coming dark.

Home. Again the thought rose that that knowledge should bring some manner of emotion with it, some spark. But there was nothing. It had meant something to him at one time; that was for certain. Back when his parents had still been alive, when he had been the heir and not the lord of the estate. He hadn't been irresponsible in the way of his brother, but he'd known how to enjoy his life. And Sara....

The image of her rose up in his mind's eye; a fey-eyed child running wild across the hills without a care for the scratched palms and skinned knees such adventures inevitably brought with them, urging him with breathless excitement to follow where she led. Her blond hair hung loose around her shoulders; she was a woman grown now in his memory, but her eyes were the same, wide and blue and laughing, laughing.

Gods above, he missed her.

Theirs had been a marriage of convenience, arranged by both their parents, but he had been fond of her. He'd always been a serious child, aged beyond his years by the burdens that being an eldest son brought with it, and she had been a breath of fresh air. He hadn't been displeased to learn that she was to be his wife.

"I'm glad you're back, my lord." Eli bowed slightly as he ushered Ander inside, reaching for his overcoat. He, too, was getting on in years; he hadn't been young when Ander was a boy, although he looked as sharp as ever in his freshly pressed slacks and long-tailed coat. "The weather is getting worse."

Ander surrendered his coat and unwound the thick wool scarf from around his neck, catching a glimpse of his face in the mirror on the foyer wall. The face that looked back at him was nearly that of a stranger—a man almost forty years of age, with a thin face that spoke of his aristocratic heritage, brown hair hanging past the tops of his shoulders. But there was grey in the brown now, and there were creases in the skin at the eyes, the pinched-down corners of the mouth.

"The weather doesn't bother me," he said, giving Dram's head a last absent pat. "Make sure the dogs are fed?"

Eli turned from hanging Ander's coat in the hall closet. "Of course. And you?"

Ander shook his head. "I'll just have some cognac in the study."

He could feel Eli's disapproval following him as he left the room, but didn't let it bother him. There was so much for Eli to disapprove of lately. The long walks he took in the woods each day, heedless of the weather or his health, the loss of contact with his friends... his propensity for skipping meals seemed the least of the old retainer's worries.

The thought made Ander smile wryly as he pulled open the cabinet at the study's far wall and reached for the decanter inside. Fire crackled in the fireplace, sounding not unlike the crackle of ice on the pond outside. He poured himself a drink and moved to sit in one of the high-backed chairs in front of the hearth, leaning close to the fire to stay warm. Outside the window, wind whistled mournfully through the eaves as the last of the daylight bled away.

"The mail, my lord." Eli appeared at his side and set a pile of letters on the small end table beside him. "Soup is warming in the kitchen in case you change your mind about dinner."

Ander nodded his thanks and took a sip of his drink as Eli left him alone again. Not for the first time, he wondered what the point of it all was. All of those years sacrificed to learning how to manage the Delacroix lands and affairs, and for what? What did he have to show for it? Just this dusty old house with its echoing, empty halls, and the frozen lands outside. He was alone here now, except for the dogs and his servants. While their loyalty to him was unbreakable, he found their company wearing. They were a reminder of all that his life had become, this silk-lined cage, and all that he'd lost.

He thought about Antoine, his younger brother, who was out and about in the world somewhere, free of these obligations. Antoine had always been a playboy at heart, without the seriousness or dedication required to run their family's affairs. Ander had scorned him for that ever since they were children, thinking him weak, but now he wondered if Antoine hadn't had the right of it all along. What use were lands and prestige if he had no one to share them with? What was the point of any of it?

One of the letters in the pile of correspondence Eli had left for him caught his eye. Turning his head, he pushed the letters on top of it aside to see a dark burgundy envelope with a seal in the shape of a closed eye, the words on it written in gilded gold ink. It was addressed to him—Lord Ander Delacroix—with no return address.

He stared at the envelope for a moment, taking another slow sip of his drink. Then he gave in to the pull of curiosity and reached for it, breaking the seal with one finger to pull out the letter inside. It was a single sheet of crisp white parchment on which a simple message had been penned in elegantly scripted calligraphy:

Lord Delacroix,

Your presence is requested for an evening of entertainment at the House of Silence.

His initial impulse was to throw the letter into the fire in disgust. He knew what the House of Silence was; a high-class bordello on the Khatar border in which men catered to the fantasies of other men. It was a favored topic of discussion among people of Ander's social class—for its forbidden nature, for the veil of secrecy that surrounded it, and for the fact that it seemed beyond the reach of the government. The House had earned its name with a reputation that whatever encounters went on inside its walls were never spoken of in the outside world; men of all rankings and social strata were said to be clients there, with no one on the outside being the wiser.

He took another sip of his drink, frowning into the fire.

Why in hell's name would anyone send him an invitation to such a place? He was not the type of man who frequented brothels of any kind; he never had been, not even before his marriage. He'd always been too serious for that, too focused on the demands of his station and upholding the honor of the Delacroix name. His brother, on the other hand.... But no, that was *his* name on the envelope and no mistake, etched in glistening gold ink.

It wasn't as if he'd never *thought* about the bordello, especially in his younger years. Any man with blood in his veins who said dif-

4

ferently would be a liar. The allure of secrecy, of fantasy, of pandering to one's darkest dreams. The House of Silence was a neutral zone where men could go to indulge in their fantasies and be someone else for a day — or to be more truly themselves than they could ever be in the normal day-to-day world they inhabited. But he'd never seriously considered....

The image of Sara rose in his mind's eye, and for a moment his hand shook so that he could barely hold onto the letter. But she was nearly eighteen months dead now. It would never have been her wish that he lock himself away inside this house and wait to die; she would want to see him happy, or at the very least at peace. He thought about this silent house with its empty halls, the memories that hung like tattered ghosts throughout every inch of its lands. He wondered how long he would spend wandering these halls before he became a ghost himself... just another memory in the Delacroix family line.

Maybe it wouldn't hurt to be something less than responsible, just this once. To lay aside the burdens of his station and indulge in something for himself.

Maybe.

His first impression of the House of Silence was that it was enormous. It had two long wings that were each three stories high, with a round, tower-like extension toward the back that raised it up even higher. Broad steps rose from the drive to the tall double doors, which were made of sturdy polished wood and inlaid with panes of stained glass. The front portico stretched across the entire front of the building, with tall fluted columns holding up the beveled roof.

It was all a little ostentatious for Ander's tastes. He frowned uncomfortably, wondering what on earth had possessed him to come here. He'd driven himself without letting Eli know where he was going; his car was even now in the skilled hands of the valet who'd greeted him at the foot of the drive without asking for so much as his name. He gazed after it longingly, thinking that it wasn't too late yet to turn back.

The thought of returning home again stopped him. For good or for ill, he was *here*, so he might as well see what the place had to offer. He wasn't entirely sure there would be anything here that would interest him, anyway. Just a quick peek inside, and he could go home then if that was what he decided to do.

Pulling the hood of his overcoat further down over his face, he started toward the building's front stairs. His boots crunched in the snow that blanketed the gravel-strewn driveway, but thankfully there was no ice. The doorman standing watch at the front door dipped his head in silent greeting and opened the door for him, ushering him inside.

It was much warmer within than it had been without. Ander looked around with interest, seeing a tastefully decorated lobby with wide, twin staircases sweeping up the far wall like a pair of bird's wings to intersect with the hallway upstairs. A glittering chandelier hung from the ceiling two stories above, coating the foyer floor in soft golden light and muted shadows. Several wooden doors opened off from the lobby into other rooms, each of them luxurious but surprisingly modest in their decoration.

"Lord Delacroix, welcome." Ander glanced up in surprise to see a tall, dark-haired man coming down one of the staircases toward him. He was dressed simply in dark slacks and a white button-down shirt, with a midnight grey waistcoat that matched precisely the silvering hair at his temples. His face was strangely ageless, clean-shaven and lean.

Ander frowned. "And you are?"

The man smiled. "Forgive me. My name is Charon Marque." He said it with an odd accent; Mar-*kay*. "I'm Master of the House and the owner of this establishment."

Ander considered him thoughtfully. Despite his unassuming appearance, there was something about this man that was disconcerting. Perhaps it was the self-assuredness of his movements, a languid grace that was almost feminine and spoke of absolute self-control. Or maybe it was his eyes. There was something odd about them, like they didn't blink often enough; or perhaps it was that they saw too much of what Ander would have preferred to keep hidden.

"Ander Delacroix," Ander said belatedly. "But then, you already seem to know that."

"Of course." Marque touched a hand lightly to the back of Ander's shoulder and guided him into one of the lobby's adjoining rooms. "You received our invitation?"

"Yes." He pulled back his hood once they were in the smaller room, feeling much less exposed now that he was no longer in public view. "Although I'm still not certain...."

Marque nodded in understanding, gesturing for him to sit down on the low couch in front of the window. Outside, the night pressed up like a void against the frost-rimmed glass. "It's perfectly natural to feel hesitant about visiting us. You'd be surprised how many of our guests feel that way when they first come here."

The observation surprised Ander. He'd been thinking that his hesitation was something out of the ordinary, unique to his situation.

He sat down at one corner of the couch and watched in silence while Marque poured him a drink from the wet bar in the corner. He accepted the glass with a nod of thanks when it was handed to him and tasted it politely, wetting his lips. It was very fine liquor, at least the equal of what he had in his estate back home.

"So tell me, Lord Delacroix." Marque sat down in the chair across from him and leaned back comfortably, taking a sip from his own drink. "What is it the House of Silence can do for you this evening?"

Ander swirled the drink in his hand absently, listening to the way the ice clinked against the sides of the glass. "I...." The heat that rose in his face at the question was profoundly annoying. "I'm not sure."

Marque observed him carefully for a moment, as if taking a measure of him. There was a glitter in his eyes that reminded Ander uncomfortably—for a passing moment—of Dram.

"Let me explain to you what we do here." Marque's gaze was intent. "We are in the business of fulfilling fantasies, of answering the deepest wishes of a man's soul—even," he said with a small smile, "those that our guests might not be aware of themselves."

Ander shivered without knowing why. The room was warm, and he was still wearing his overcoat. "I don't know what you mean. I'm not even sure why I came here tonight."

Marque looked at him weighingly for a moment longer, then stood up and went to a small intercom panel to one side of the room's door. He touched a button on it and spoke softly into its speaker before returning to his seat.

"Sometimes it's a challenge pairing up a guest with an appropriate Companion." Marque took another sip of his drink. "But I think in your case, the choice is a simple one."

Ander realized his hands were sweating. He could still say no to this, he told himself firmly. There was nothing keeping him here if he decided he wanted to leave.

He looked up anxiously when the door opened again, admitting a slim, dark-haired boy wearing black trousers and a sleeveless dark green top. The boy closed the door quietly behind himself after he entered and stood there silently, waiting.

"I believe Danny might be to your tastes this evening," Marque said, eyeing Ander over the rim of his glass.

This wasn't at all what Ander had been expecting. He observed the boy in silence, considering. The boy was slender and undeniably beautiful, with dark, haunting eyes and a winsomeness that seemed out of place in this kind of establishment. His hair was just a bit too long, falling over the line of his dark brows and curling slightly against the sides of his face. He looked ridiculously young to be employed here; he couldn't be a day over eighteen, and that was pushing it. It made Ander feel oddly protective of him.

"How do you do, sir?" Danny said, moving forward to sit beside him on the couch. His voice was soft, with an accent so subtle Ander couldn't place it.

"Hello," Ander responded automatically, too conditioned by courtesy to allow his uneasiness in the boy's presence to show. After a moment, he said, "My name is Ander."

Danny smiled at that, and the expression transformed his face from beautiful to absolutely breathtaking. He reached for Ander's hand and held it. "It's a pleasure to meet you, Ander."

Ander's heart was pounding. After a moment's hesitation, he curled his hand around Danny's fingers, feeling the slender warmth of them press against his palm. How long had it been since anyone had touched him? Had he truly been alone that long?

When he looked up again, Marque was smiling. "Well?" Marque said. "Would you like Danny to be your Companion this evening?"

For a moment, Ander couldn't find the breath to speak. This was a line right here, and if he crossed it, there would be no going back. Accepting Marque's offer would mean that he had finally accepted Sara's death, that he had made the decision to take something for himself that had nothing to do with the duties of his station. It would mean that he was going on with his life.

He saw Sara's face in his memory, there and then gone; she was smiling. She wouldn't want him to be alone, wouldn't want him to continue punishing himself for things he couldn't have changed. Drawing in a deep breath, he forced himself to meet Marque's gaze and nodded.

"Yes."

Chapter 2

Stepping Into the Unknown

Marque set his glass aside, looking pleased. "I'm sure you won't be disappointed. If you'll come with me, we'll take care of the financial arrangements."

Ander nodded and stood up, pulling his long coat closed around himself. He followed Marque to a small writing table against the far wall, where Marque began to draw up an official-looking document that amounted basically to payment for services rendered. Ander closed his eyes briefly when he saw the price but didn't comment on it. He filled out the necessary information when asked to do so, signed the document with his personal seal, and the transaction was complete.

"Very well." The smile Marque gave him was pleased. "I'll leave you in Danny's capable hands, then." He bowed slightly and left the room.

Ander started when Danny's hand slipped into his again, slim fingers tightening around his own. "Shall we go upstairs?" Danny asked, smiling up at him.

"Er, yes." Ander hated that he felt so out of his depth here. He wasn't used to any kind of physical closeness, and the prospect of giving in to this winsome boy's allure was a daunting one. But the allure was definitely there; there was no denying that. Aside from his physical beauty, there was an underlying sweetness to him, almost a shyness, that Ander found intensely appealing.

He followed in silence while Danny led him out of the room and toward the large staircase leading upstairs from the lobby. The upper hall was wide and thickly carpeted, with several tall oak doors leading off from it to either side.

"How long have you worked here?" Ander asked. His eyes followed the line of the bare arm that brushed against his own; it was long and shapely, ending in a delicately boned wrist and a slender hand. The boy looked so young. Ander thought he should feel like a monster for what he was about to do, but all he felt was a kind of low-burning anticipation. That seemed wrong to him; he was old enough to be the boy's father, after all. But despite his youth, there was a world-awareness — a world-weariness? — to this boy that made him seem somehow older than his physical years.

"About two months." Danny opened one of the doors and gestured for Ander to go inside.

"And how did someone like you come to be here?"

Danny's head bowed slightly at the question. After a moment, he said, "No one talks much about their past here. We are who we are inside the House, and anyone we once were outside these walls...." His mouth curled slightly. "Well, the past is best left to the past."

The expression on his face wasn't bitter, but it was close. Sad, perhaps? Rueful? Just how *had* this boy come to be an employee here? Ander was consumed by curiosity, but chose not to pursue the matter further.

"So long as you're here of your own free will," he said. That was the one thing he was sure of; as appealing as Danny's company was, he had no interest in securing it through force.

This time the look Danny gave him was mischievous. "Given all the choices in the world, I wouldn't choose to be anywhere else." There was something in his tone that made Ander believe him. His fingers slid around Ander's hand again and squeezed, tugging lightly. "Come inside and sit down."

The room was a suite, decorated in somber shades of maroon and dark mahogany. The paintings that hung on the walls looked quite expensive; if nothing else, the House of Silence did quite well for itself from a financial standpoint.

Ander lowered himself onto one end of the long couch when he was bade to do so, unable to relax despite his best efforts. Danny's presence was unassuming, completely nonthreatening — which was precisely what Marque had had in mind when he'd chosen him to be

Ander's Companion, no doubt—but still, Ander couldn't shake the feeling that he was on the cusp of something dangerous. His chest felt tight, and his hands were sweating.

Danny divested him of his coat and scarf with practiced ease and hung them on the stand beside the door, then settled beside him. There was a gilded platter sitting on the low table in front of them. Danny removed the lid with a flourish and turned to him with a small smile. "You must be hungry."

The platter was filled with all manner of sliced fruits, wedges of cheese, small crusts of bread. Only after seeing the food did Ander realize how very hungry he was; he hadn't eaten at all that day, gathering up his courage to come here.

"I...." He wasn't sure what to say. It was almost amusing how tongue-tied he was, he who had been trained in court graces from such a young age. "I am hungry, yes. Thank you."

Danny reached for a slice of fruit on the plate and held it up to Ander's lips. After a moment, Ander closed his eyes and accepted the offering, soaking up the heat of the boy leaning against his side.

"Is it good?" Danny's breath was warm against Ander's cheek. Ander shivered, not sure why such an unremarkable gesture should seem so intimate. It had been so long since he'd experienced any kind of closeness with another human being, physical or otherwise.

"Yes," he said. His mouth was very dry despite the fruit, which was delicious. When Danny offered him a glass of wine, he accepted it gratefully.

It seemed so simple a thing, to eat and drink, or to experience the company of another person. It had been an age, however, since he had found enjoyment in any of those things. It felt jarring somehow, like feeling pleasure of any kind was a betrayal of sorts. That, more than anything else, told him just how far gone in grief he'd become over the past year.

"Have you eaten yet tonight?" he asked, curling his hand in his lap to keep it from shaking. He gestured toward the platter of food self-consciously. "You can eat something, too, if you'd like."

The smile Danny rewarded him with for that made something deep inside Ander tremble. "Thanks. I was hoping you'd ask." He reached for a cube of cheese and popped it into his mouth, closing his eyes in visible pleasure as he swallowed. The sight made Ander smile inwardly. Here was an individual who had the ability to take pleasure in the simplest of things, much as Sara had. The comparison crossed his mind before he could censure it, overshadowing his enjoyment of the meal.

Danny's eyes flickered when they saw Ander's face. "Is anything wrong?" he asked, sounding honestly concerned.

Ander shook his head, chastising himself for his preoccupation. He'd come here to *forget* such worries, not ignite them further. "No. I suppose I just wasn't expecting this kind of... of service. I was expecting that we would...." He trailed off, unable to make himself finish the sentence.

Danny smiled slightly. "Inside the House of Silence, all of our guests' needs must be seen to—including such mundane needs as food and drink." He regarded Ander thoughtfully. "And there are other, more subtle needs to be seen to as well."

Ander felt his face heat, although he had the impression Danny hadn't been talking about sex just now.

Something in Danny's smile softened, and he reached out to hold Ander's hand again, folding their fingers together. "Will you trust me? Just for tonight?" His eyes—round and dark—held Ander's gaze.

Trust him? Ander thought about the reasons he'd come here tonight. If he was being honest with himself, it wasn't just sex he wanted. So what *did* he want? Warmth, companionship, someone to take his mind off of his troubles for a short while. Danny was offering him all of that, as if he'd seen inside Ander's soul to know precisely what it was he needed.

He didn't know whether to be impressed or terrified that Marque had been able to read him so easily.

"Yes," he said, closing his eyes.

He drew in a sharp breath when Danny leaned in to kiss him. The feel of the boy's mouth on his was startling; it was warm, and soft, and not demanding at all. In fact it seemed almost hesitant, as if Danny weren't sure his advances would be welcomed, or that Ander would want him.

Again that surge of protectiveness flared up in Ander, and he curled his hand around Danny's arm, deepening the kiss. Danny made a soft sound against his mouth and leaned into it, so that Ander could feel the low vibration of the heartbeat in the chest pressed against his own.

Danny pushed his head back into Ander's hand where it cupped the back of his neck, arching like a cat. His eyes were half-closed. "It feels good when you do that." His voice was little more than a sigh.

Ander felt like some part of him was going to break inside. "Danny...."

"I like the way your hands feel when they touch me." Danny lifted Ander's hand and kissed his palm, brushing the skin there lightly with his tongue. "*Will* you touch me, Ander?"

Ander's breath fell out of him entirely at the question, his heart racing. He stared wide-eyed as Danny reached down and lifted the edge of the dark green shirt he wore, pulling it off gracefully over his head and tossing it aside over the arm of the couch.

Danny's mouth curled in a small smile. He took hold of Ander's hand and lifted it toward his chest, sliding it lightly across the bared skin there. "It's all right," he said.

The feel of warm skin under his fingers hit Ander like a physical blow, making him shiver. He pressed his hand forward without thinking, feeling the subtle thrum of a heartbeat that wasn't his own underneath his palm.

"That's it." Danny's breathing was deepening now, his eyes falling half-lidded. He had such long lashes, giving him a sultry appearance that somehow failed to detract from the aura of innocence around him.

Ander clenched his teeth, again reminding himself that this was a boy he was fondling. Just a boy, and he'd never been the type to lust after youth of any kind. But there was no denying that the desire to continue with this was strong; Danny had at least the semblance of willingness, which was apparently enough to appease his libido. His skin felt tight and hot with the desire to feel more of that slender warmth pressed up against him.

"It's okay." Danny's voice was a whisper now. He slid one hand underneath Ander's hair to cup the back of his neck and leaned in to kiss him.

Impossible not to respond to that, to meet the hunger of the kiss

14

with his own steadily increasing appetite for physical touch. His arm slid without his conscious volition around Danny's waist to pull him forward, and Danny gave in eagerly, nearly straddling his lap as his arms moved around Ander's shoulders to hold him close. Ander pressed a thumb over the boy's nipple as they kissed, his chest seizing when Danny's breath hitched at the touch.

"Does it feel good?" Danny asked. His breath panted across Ander's face, long fingers twining through his hair.

Ander laughed softly, not quite sure how to answer the question. He felt dizzy, lost, like he was tumbling down a vast chasm and losing all sight of the sun. But at the same time he felt freer than he had in a very long time, like a bird soaring high above the petty troubles of the world beneath it.

"You're trembling," he whispered, pressing his cheek against Danny's shoulder.

Danny's breath fluttered across his brow. His fingers stroked slowly through Ander's hair, making him shiver. "Does it disappoint you? That I'm not as jaded as you thought I'd be."

Disappoint him? There was nothing about Danny that was disappointing. There was something pure about him despite his line of work, something that Ander felt irresistibly drawn to. There was nothing at all pretentious in him; the honesty of his reactions was invigorating, the way he truly seemed to enjoy having Ander here with him.

Ander closed his eyes and sighed, letting Danny hold him. If he was being truthful, it felt good to be embraced like this, to be close like this. He'd forgotten what it was like. Maybe it *was* all an illusion, an act, bought and paid for by his not inconsiderable fortune... but what could it possibly hurt to give in and allow himself to believe in it, just for this one night?

Danny seemed to sense the capitulation in him. He smiled as he reached for Ander's hand and drew him slowly to his feet, leading him inexorably into the adjoining bedroom. Ander closed his eyes when they got there, a vision of sumptuous furnishings and tasteful luxury flickering briefly around him before Danny moved in again, eclipsing his awareness of the room.

He stood as if in a dream as his clothing was removed, Danny's lips trailing soft kisses like brands being burned into his skin. Such a sweet mouth this boy had, so very warm. Ander held the back of his head in one hand, not protesting as the last of his physical defenses was peeled away from him.

In the bed now, naked skin to naked skin, and *oh*.... Danny's body felt hot against him, burning him as they slid together underneath the sheets. His fingers closed hard around Danny's wrist, holding that slender limb down against the mattress beside their heads; Danny's eyes were wide as they looked up at him, his lips parted. Ander couldn't help but kiss him then, and Danny opened to him with such eagerness it made his chest ache. As hesitant as he'd been at the start of the evening, now that it had come down to it, he wasn't sure he could stop if he tried.

"It's okay," Danny whispered to him again, cupping one hand around the back of Ander's head to hold him close against him. "It's all right, Ander. I'm not going anywhere."

Desire sizzled underneath Ander's skin as he touched the boy, feeling all of that tender strength surging against him, urging him to take what they both knew he wanted from it. He could feel that Danny was hard against him; no matter what other circumstances there were surrounding this joining, Danny wanted him, too. Ander clung to that fact as he accepted the vial of oil Danny handed him and moved to prepare the body beneath him for what was to come.

"That's it," Danny breathed. He smoothed Ander's hair back from his face with one hand, pressing a tremulous kiss to his cheek. "I'm yours tonight. You can do whatever you want to me."

The words seemed to break something open deep inside of Ander's chest. With a shudder, he coated his fingers liberally with oil and reached down between their bodies to touch the humid crevice between the boy's legs, fingering the opening there. It felt hot to his touch, quivering, like it both dreaded and anticipated what was to come.

Ander moaned softly as he felt Danny's body give way around his fingers. So hot, so very smooth.... He hadn't done this for a very long time—not like this, not with a man—not since long before he'd married. He'd always thought of it as a kind of senseless indulgence, this kind of sweaty coupling between men, but right now it felt as necessary as breathing to him.

So exhilarating as he slid his cock inside. The pleasure of it was so intense it stole his breath away, whiting out the world around him. He held Danny tightly as they moved together, hearing nothing but encouragement in the sounds the boy was making and telling himself that made it okay.

A stab of self-directed derision twisted through Ander, making his stomach tighten. It wasn't enough suddenly to take his pleasure this way, to make use of this boy's body for his own selfish gratification. Resting his weight on one bent elbow, he groped down between their bodies with his other arm and took hold of Danny's slender cock, hissing through his teeth as the heat of it seared against his palm.

Danny made a wounded sound, curling against him. The honesty of the reaction made the flare of protectiveness Ander had felt earlier return in force; clearly the boy wasn't used to having his own needs paid attention to in this way while he was servicing clients. Ander pressed a kiss to his shoulder, trying to soothe him as he squeezed the hard flesh in his hand. He caressed the boy slowly from root to tip, sliding down to feel the weight of his balls briefly before going back to stroking the hard cock in earnest. Danny clung to him fiercely for a moment before giving in with a whuffling sigh, his body relaxing as he allowed Ander to pleasure him.

There was an inevitability to the way Danny's body opened to his, the way the boy's legs wrapped around him and held him close as their hips rocked together, finding the rhythm that would bring them both to ecstasy. Ander shuddered at the feel of fingers sliding through his hair, slim arms hugging tight around his shoulders as Danny's voice panted breathlessly in his ear. Such a wanton boy, so very needy.... Ander felt like a dirty old man as he touched him, used him, but there was no shame in the thought anymore. There was only desire, and the indulging of it.

When it came, his climax felt like it ripped something vital out of him, leaving him hollowed out and shaken in its aftermath. Danny's cry as he came was as sweet as Ander had imagined it would be, full of life and joy and heady intoxication. His voice broke when he said Ander's name, making something buried deep inside of Ander shatter.

Through it all Ander held him, and soothed him, and tried to tell himself that it would all be okay in the end.

Afterward, they lay together in the large bed, wrapped around one another without speaking. The feel of fingers stroking through his hair was something Ander felt he could easily become addicted to.

"What happens now?" Ander said at last. He wasn't quite sure of the etiquette involved in these kinds of encounters, or of removing himself from them once they were ended.

Danny's eyes were impossibly dark where his head lay on the pillow next to Ander's. He was still breathing hard from the orgasm Ander had wrung out of him.

"You should get some sleep," he murmured, curling his hand under his cheek. He smiled slightly.

The knowledge that he wasn't going to be chased out immediately after coupling made Ander relax slightly. Tentatively, he slid an arm around Danny's shoulders, holding him close. Danny leaned in against him with a sigh, one hand groping for Ander's underneath the bedsheet and twining their fingers together.

Despite the weariness tugging at him, Ander lay awake for a long while. He wondered when he was going to start feeling something about all of this; he had betrayed Sara's memory, after all, by giving his body to another. More than that, he'd violated a boy half his age—however world-wise and willing he might have seemed. He expected to feel disgust at himself, anger, scorn, but he felt nothing. That seemed wrong, somehow.

He wondered if Sara would be happy for him that he'd managed to find comfort in this boy's arms, that Danny had been able to lift the veil of darkness in his heart, however briefly. Humans weren't intended to go through life alone, after all, not even after suffering such a great loss. It was a new thought, and one that he would have to consider carefully in the days ahead.

"I'm glad I came here tonight," he whispered, pressing a soft kiss above Danny's ear. The admission made something loosen within him.

18

Danny's arms tightened around him briefly. "Me, too."

Smiling to himself in the darkness, Ander considered the fact that right here, for right now, that would have to be enough.

Ander ducked his head as he wound his scarf around his neck, pulling the ends of his hair out from underneath the thick wool with one hand. His long coat was wrapped heavily around him, giving him some degree of anonymity as he approached the House's front doors. Fortunately, there were no other guests in the lobby at this early hour.

"Lord Delacroix." As Ander passed by, Marque emerged from the office, dressed in the exact same clothes he'd been in the previous evening. Ander guessed he must have been working all night, monitoring the guests who arrived at the mansion. "Are you leaving us so soon?"

Ander wondered fleetingly whether it was common for the owner to personally see off guests the morning after their engagements, or if that was a benefit reserved solely for first-time visitors to the House.

"It's time for me to return home now." Not that anyone there would be expecting him, but he couldn't shake the feeling that he'd overstayed his welcome in this place. Even so, he couldn't regret his decision to come here.

The look Marque gave him was weighing. "Was Danny's company to your liking?"

The image of Danny's face rose in Ander's mind, in all of its beauty and youth and vulnerability. "Yes," he said after a moment's hesitation, unable to answer that question with anything but the truth. "Very much so."

Outside the tall windows, the morning was grey and overcast, heavy with the promise of further snow. The sun had barely risen. The thought of going out into that dank, dreary chill wasn't in the least bit appealing, making him think longingly of the bed upstairs where he'd left Danny sleeping. He wondered if it was cowardice or gallantry that had prompted him not to wake the boy when he'd gone.

"Of course, you're welcome to return whenever you wish,"

Marque said.

Ander tightened his hand around the end of his scarf. "Thank you, but this was an aberration for me. I don't intend to ever return." Now that morning was here—now that the darkly seductive dream that was the House of Silence was ending—he couldn't wait to return to the sane and familiar world he was accustomed to.

Marque bowed his head. "I'm sorry to hear that. I hope that—at the very least—you received what you came here to find."

Had he? The question disturbed him. He'd learned a lot about himself during the evening he'd spent here, but he didn't know enough to guess whether he'd be better or worse off now because of it. Maybe it would have been better to have gone on the way things were, as painful and futile as it had been. Instead, he'd opened himself up to the possibility of change. And change, at its very heart, was a terrifying thing. He wondered what was going to be born from the chrysalis of this evening, and just what further changes it would provoke in him before it was through.

"Good day, Mr. Marque." Bracing himself against the cold, he pulled open the door. He didn't meet Marque's eyes as he stepped outside.

"So," Charon said, leaning one hip against the stair railing. "What did you think of our Lord Ander?"

Danny considered the question seriously. "He's extremely sad about something," he said at last. "Innocent," he amended, thinking that would be a better word to describe him. Of all the clients Danny had serviced since he'd come to work here, Ander had without a doubt been one of the gentlest.

"He certainly seemed satisfied enough with you." Charon sounded amused.

"Of course." Danny shrugged.

"Because you weren't the brazen whore he was expecting?"

Danny gave him a narrow look, irritation tickling through him. "You know I don't like that word."

Charon looked contrite. "I know." Sliding one hand over the back of Danny's neck, he looked down into his eyes. "You can still blush after everything you've seen here," he said, running a thumb over Danny's lower lip. There was undeniable fondness in the gesture.

Danny cleared his throat and looked away. "Will he come back, do you think?" he asked, deliberately changing the subject.

Charon smiled. "Oh, yes. Undoubtedly."

Danny was surprised. "You sound so sure of that."

Charon's smile took on a rueful cast. "Did you see the look in his eyes? That's a man on the edge, Danny. He's lost, even if he doesn't know it yet. He's drowning, and he's looking desperately for something to hold on to. Last night, that something was you."

Danny looked thoughtfully toward the front door where Ander had disappeared. "So you think he'll be back to save himself. To keep himself from drowning."

"I think he has to."

Danny nodded, accepting this. It was true that while the doors of the House of Silence were never locked, the majority of those who lived inside these walls were here because they had nowhere else to go; they had no other choice but to be here, one way or another.

Why should Ander be any different?

Chapter 3
Danny

Danny rolled over in bed, squinting his eyes against the streamers of light that slid in around the edges of his bedroom curtain. No matter how hard he tried, he could never arrange it so that it blocked out the sunlight completely. For someone whose chosen vocation required him to catch what sleep he could during the daytime more often than not, that was turning out to be quite a problem.

It took him a moment to realize that there was a body in the bed beside him. Propping himself up on one elbow, he stared down at the tousled brown head lying on the pillow next to his.

His eyes narrowed. "Tam. *Tam*. Wake up."

Sleepy hazel eyes blinked open and looked up at him, crinkling at the edges once they registered the annoyance in his expression. "Good morning, Danny. Did you sleep well?"

Danny rubbed at his eyes and resisted the urge to sigh. Tam Temetria was his senior in the House of Silence, his elder by a handful of years, yet his behavior prompted Danny to think of him as a child more often than not. He very rarely took anything seriously, least of all himself, which meant that the ire of those he managed to exasperate tended to slide right off of him.

"We've talked about this before." It was an effort to keep his voice even; his privacy inside this room was pretty much the only possession he had that was worth anything to him. He didn't appreciate having it taken away from him. "I've told you not to sneak into my room without permission when I'm sleeping."

Tam made an annoyed face and rolled up into a sitting position, swinging his legs over the side of the bed. The sheet slid down to pool around his hips with the movement, but it shifted enough for Danny to guess that the other man had opted to sleep naked.

"You're no fun at all." Tam linked his fingers around his opposite wrist and stretched, rolling his shoulders forward to ease the kinks out of them. His bare back was pale beige in the filtered sunlight that trickled in around the curtain's edge, glowing with a healthy tan. He was taller than Danny was, and longer-limbed, but without Danny's innate slenderness. He liked to work out and it showed, but not to the extent that it took away from the lean lines their customers found so appealing.

This time Danny did sigh. "Just don't do it again, all right?"

The answering grin Tam gave him was impish. "Whatever you say."

Right. Danny reached for the shirt tossed over the corner of the bedside table and stood up, shrugging into it as he made his way toward the adjoining bathroom. The air of the room felt cool against the bare skin of his ass; Tam wasn't the only one who preferred to sleep naked. He could feel Tam's eyes on him as he went, but refused to blush under the scrutiny.

By the time he finished showering and brushing his teeth, Tam was gone. Absently sliding a brush through his hair to smooth the snarls out of it, he selected a pale blue shirt and dark trousers from the drawers of his bureau to wear. As he did so, he caught a glimpse of his reflection in the tall oval mirror sitting on top of the bureau and frowned, regarding himself with a critical eye. He knew what the customers saw when they looked at him; a boy of uncommon beauty who looked even younger than his age, delicate in a way that reminded him uncomfortably of the china dolls his stepmother used to collect when he was a child. There were days when he thought he was no different than they were; a possession to be admired, carefully used and carefully kept, and somehow just as fragile.

Shaking off the dark mood, he left his room and headed downstairs in search of breakfast. The kitchen inside the House of Silence was open at all hours of the day, because the cooks understood that the House's employees worked odd hours that could leave them with precious little time to eat, and they were often left with the need to grab their meals whenever they could. Even when there wasn't a formal meal prepared, there were always leftovers available in the over-sized refrigerator that could be scrounged through at any time of the day or night.

Fortunately, Madam Mirian seemed to be in residence this afternoon, judging by the mouth-watering smells that wafted up from the stairwell as Danny descended into the House's lower level. His stomach growled faintly as he rounded the corner into the cavernous room; the previous night's customer had been demanding, and he'd collapsed exhausted into bed that morning as soon as the opportunity presented itself without bothering to find anything to eat.

Madam Mirian was the undisputed master of the House's kitchens, a tall, rotund woman who had a preference for pale dresses with lacy frocking and fancy-stitched embroidery. Her hair was black and held up around her round face with a variety of lethal-looking bobby pins, giving her a severe look that was completely contrary to her motherly demeanor.

"Danny! How nice to see you." She didn't look up from the large silver pot she was stirring over the stove, leaving him to wonder if the rumors were true that she had the ability to see out of the back of her head. Newer House members who attempted to take advantage of her seeming preoccupation by sneaking desserts before eating a healthy dinner quickly discovered that nothing went on inside the walls of her domain that she was not aware of. "Come in and sit down. I'm just cooking up some elk stew for dinner this evening, but I think we've got some leftover haunches from last night that could be served up as cold cuts for you. Elle, be a dear and slice some bread for the boy, would you?"

Elle was Madam Mirian's exact opposite in many ways, blond-haired and slender and only a couple of years older than Danny, with the harried look of someone asked to do too many demanding tasks at one time. Her movements were fluid, however, as she turned away from her current chore to pull a half-loaf of bread from the bread cupboard and started to expertly carve it into thin slices.

Danny wandered over to the refrigerator to pour himself a tall glass of milk. By the time he sat down at the long table tucked away in the corner of the room, Elle was setting a plate filled with sliced meat and bread down in front of him. He looked up at her with a smile.

"Thanks."

She blushed straight down to the frilled collar at the neck of her dress and looked away, which never ceased to charm Danny. She was new to the House's kitchen staff, but even so, she seemed ridiculously shy for someone who worked in a brothel. "Y-You're welcome, Danny."

Leaving her alone to return to her duties, Danny turned his attention to the food in front of him. It was delicious as only food eaten after a couple of missed meals can be, filling places in him that he hadn't even realized were empty. He drained his milk down to the last drop and was just considering going back for more when he heard raised voices in the hallway outside.

Curious, he went to investigate. The sound of something shattering made him quicken his pace, a trickle of foreboding moving through him. Outside the kitchen at the base of the stairs, two figures were standing over the remains of a broken vase that covered the lower steps.

"Idiot!" Reiji Kendo's fists were balled into fists at his sides, tension strung throughout his wiry frame. He was shorter than the man he faced, but there was something in the way he carried himself that made it seem as if he were taller. He was maybe twenty years old, with dark red hair cut in dramatic angles at either side of his face and hard, dark eyes. His body was lean with a dancer's grace, and much stronger than it appeared at first glance.

"You're the one who bumped into me." The other man's voice was calm.

Vincent Michaelis had long black hair that glistened almost blue in the overhead light, surrounding a face that looked as if it had been chiseled by a master artisan. He was a rare beauty, but without the same delicacy of features that Danny had. He would have been absolutely breathtaking to look at if not for the black velvet eyepatch that covered his left eye, and the hint of scarring that could be seen in the skin along its lower edge. However, for reasons that Danny could never adequately explain, that one imperfection in his face made him seem even more appealing.

Danny flinched when Reiji swore and lashed out, hitting Vincent hard across the face. Like he really needed to deal with this this afternoon. Checking a sigh, he hurried forward to grab Reiji's hand before he could strike the other man again. "Hey! Break it up."

Reiji glared at him, wrenching his wrist free of Danny's grasp with no apparent effort. There was a rumor that he practiced a martial art of some kind in his free time, and incidents like these made Danny think it wasn't such a farfetched notion. "What the hell do you care?"

"I care because Charon's going to be pissed if you mark up his face before the customers get here tonight." Danny's heart was pounding; Reiji was more than capable of kicking his ass if he was of a mind to, and he seemed to be in a particularly foul mood today. "Besides, you know he's not going to fight back." It was true; picking a fight with Vincent was like kicking a puppy.

"It's all right, Danny. Really." Vincent's visible eye was a searing blue, dark as sapphire. "I'll go get something to clean this up." He gave Reiji a dark look and then turned down the hall toward the storage closet where the brooms were located.

Danny released the breath he'd been holding, turning to give Reiji a wary look. Frowning, he took a close look at the other man for the first time. Reiji was wearing a sleeveless top that showed off the subtly defined musculature of his arms to good advantage; Danny's eyes widened when he noticed the bruises at his wrists, on his upper arm, an inflamed puffiness at the corner of his mouth as if he'd been struck there. Something about the placement of the bruises made Danny think they hadn't been won in a fight; the marks on his arm looked disturbingly finger-shaped.

Reiji saw the direction of his gaze and covered the bruise on his arm with one hand, scowling. "So the client last night got a little excited. So what?"

Danny stared at him. "You're saying a *customer* did that to you?" Was that why he was in such a bad mood today?

"You sound surprised." He laughed at the dumbfounded expression on Danny's face. "That's the benefit of being new, I suppose; Charon isn't going to risk chasing you away by giving you the really fun clients, now is he?"

The accusation made Danny's face heat. It was true he'd only been an employee in the House of Silence for a couple of months, but he didn't think of himself as *that* naive about how things worked here. "You're lying. Charon would never let any of the guests hurt us. We're too valuable to him for that."

"You really are an innocent. Charon has his own reasons for doing what he does that have nothing to do with us." He sounded bitter when he said it. Turning away, he kicked at one of the broken pieces of pottery with his toe. "Your turn will come eventually. Just wait and see."

The conversation with Reiji stuck in the back of Danny's mind through the rest of the day, like a burr snagged in the fabric of his thoughts that he couldn't quite shake. It was true that some of the clients he'd serviced had been less than gentle with him, but none of them had ever made him feel threatened in any way. He'd assumed that was because he was an important resource, a valuable piece of property belonging to the House of Silence, and Charon would never allow harm to come to something he valued, even if it was purely for the object's monetary potential.

Even so, he knew there were things that went on inside the rooms in this House that he wasn't aware of, and could hardly guess at. The House was in the business of fulfilling fantasies, and not all fantasies were innocent, now were they? What happened when a client with a darker bent came knocking on the House's doors? Admittance into the House of Silence was by invitation only, but surely there had to be some individuals among its vast and varied clientele who were looking for something other than what could easily be found in the mundane world outside the House's walls. Danny was disturbingly certain that Charon wouldn't turn such customers away.

Charon summoned Danny to his office that evening, and Danny felt his first real misgivings as he obediently went to meet with him. The Master of the House was sitting behind his broad mahogany desk when Danny arrived, head bowed over the mound of paperwork in front of him. He didn't look up when Danny entered the room.

"Sit down, Danny." Charon gestured absently in the direction of the leather armchair in front of the desk, his mouth pinching down in a frown as he picked up a sheet of paper and perused the lines of miniscule text on it with steadily growing irritation. He looked as if he'd been neck-deep in financial documents and administrative paperwork for quite some time. "How are you this evening?"

"Fine." Danny sat down as instructed, glancing up at the paintings that adorned the walls. The office was expensively decorated in a way that would appeal to the clients who came here, with a somberness that emphasized the House's dedication to its mission of fulfilling dreams. To a boy who'd grown up in a rural farming town, it was all a bit grandiose; and yet there was something intimidating about it as well. He always felt somehow smaller when he was in this room.

"That's good to hear." After another few moments, Charon signed the document with a flourish and set it on top of the stack of similar papers at his elbow, finally looking up to give Danny his full attention. "I have a special request for you this evening, if you're up for it."

"Of course."

"Excellent." His eyes glittered in the soft golden light of the desk lamp as he smiled. "We have a party coming in from Aechestan, three young men from one of the local families there. I want you to take care of them."

Danny glanced down at the hands folded in his lap, swallowing thickly. He tried to hide his displeasure, but nevertheless, he couldn't help thinking that Charon knew full well how much he disliked serving multiple partners. If so, it certainly didn't stop him from giving Danny these kinds of assignments.

"Unless there's some kind of problem with that?" One of Charon's eyebrows rose slightly.

"No, of course not." He looked up quickly. He wasn't in a position to choose his partners when he was working; that was the nature of the job, after all. If he thought otherwise, then he was just as naive as Reiji had accused him of being. "Just let me know where to meet them."

Charon's smile deepened. "Good boy. I knew I could count on you."

Chapter 4
Pushing the Edge

The customers were already in the Blue Room when Danny went to join them. He paused outside in the hallway with his hand on the doorknob, taking several deep breaths to prepare himself before opening the door.

"Good evening," he said as he stepped inside the room. "I'm Danny, and I'll be your Companion tonight."

The Blue Room was one of the more ostentatious suites available in the House of Silence, decorated in vibrant shades of azure and cobalt and sapphire. Gold fringes hung from the edges of the tall lamps, matching perfectly the gold leaf on the tables and the gold braid on the low couches and chairs.

The three men seated around the room looked up with interest when he entered. They were dressed with a careless elegance that suggested they were rich enough to take it for granted, but stylish enough to reflect their youth and their awareness of current fashion trends. Young lords, Danny guessed, from a rather well-off family. Spoiled and irresponsible, without anything much to do with their time other than spend the fortunes their parents had earned for them.

He could tell from their expressions that they liked what they saw in him. The predatory sharpness of their gazes made his skin crawl, but he hid his discomfort with practiced ease as he moved to stand in front of them.

The eldest of the three was maybe thirty years old, with thick blond hair and a slightly rounded face that was clean-shaven except for a thin moustache. He leaned forward, propping his elbows on his knees, and fixed Danny with an appraising stare. He whistled low through his teeth in appreciation. "That Marque sure knew exactly what we were in the mood for tonight. It's almost scary how well he can read us sometimes." He grinned, showing a flash of white teeth. "I'm Eri. These are my cousins, Marc and Louis."

"It's nice to meet you." Danny bowed his head slightly, noting the empty bottle of wine that sat on the table in front of them. Apparently they'd already imbibed a fair amount of the House's more liquid pleasures that evening.

"So polite, isn't he?" The one Eri had indicated as Marc was red-haired in a way that reminded Danny of Reiji, although this man's hair had more of an orange cast to it. He was the stockiest of the three, with a square frame and large hands.

"Of course. They train them that way, don't they?" Louis was blond like his older cousin, but thinner, with an almost feminine cast to his features. His eyes were eager as they swept over Danny from head to toe, evaluating his physical qualities with a frankness that made Danny have to fight the urge to blush.

Eri laughed out loud at that. "True enough." He snapped his fingers commandingly. "Danny, was it? Come here and let's get this thing started."

Danny swallowed hard and moved forward to obey. He kept his gaze down as he sank to his knees in front of the low couch, positioning himself between Eri's spread thighs. His hands were steady when he reached to unfasten the young lord's belt and open his trousers.

"Mmm, yeah." Eri's fingers clenched hard in the hair at the back of his head, pushing Danny's head downward. Danny forced himself to relax under the rough treatment, his mind already making the familiar disconnect from his body that allowed him to perform these acts without losing any part of himself in the process.

Eri's erection was large enough to make Danny hope he would be content with oral sex this evening and not require actual intercourse, although he didn't have much hope that he would be so lucky. He closed his eyes as he took the thick member into his mouth, wincing only slightly when the hand on the back of his neck tightened in unvoiced appreciation.

It wasn't as if he had any illusions that he was anything other than an object to be used by them this evening, but still, it was disconcerting to hear the three of them continuing to drink and talk amongst themselves as if he weren't even there. The hand on his neck slid up to pet at his head occasionally, thick fingers sliding through his hair with a possessiveness that made him shiver straight down to his toes. He thought longingly of Lord Ander from several days before, remembering that man's quiet courtesy and gentle nature.

Despite himself, his mind began to wander. The past wasn't something he enjoyed dwelling on, but there were times he couldn't avoid thinking about the events that had brought him here. He was used to being looked down on, after all; he was the youngest son in the Bordelain family, a halfblood bastard from an affair his father had had with another woman. His real mother had died when he was still very young. He barely remembered her, although memories of her tended to surface and comfort him from time to time.

After his mother's death, he had gone to live with his father and his father's family in the farming village of Rochefort. His father's wife hated him and made no effort to conceal her dislike of him, or the favoritism she felt for her son Michael. It was made clear from the outset that Michael was to be the heir to their family's lands and business; she felt threatened by Danny's existence, even though Danny had never shown an interest in taking over anything.

It hurt most because he and Michael had been close once. But Michael's mother poisoned him against Danny over time, until Michael's fondness for him turned to petty cruelties that grew worse day by day. Their father died not too long after that, and Danny's existence in the house quickly became unbearable. Without their father's calming influence to temper her hatred of him, Danny's stepmother took to beating him for every imagined transgression. Unable to bear it any longer, he ran away from home and, after a great deal of wandering, eventually wound up at the House of Silence.

At first he'd been hesitant about the idea of sharing his body with strangers, having avoided prostituting himself by a narrow margin when he'd been living on the street, but he truly had nowhere else to go. Charon had been quite effusive in his welcome, offering him food and a steady income and the security of a well-furnished roof over his head. Danny, who had nothing and absolutely no one to call his own, had eagerly accepted.

The truth was that Charon had been kind to him when no one else was, and although Danny recognized that as Charon's typical psychological manipulation, he was grateful for it nonetheless. Even if it meant he had to put up with customers like these three lords, whose cruelty lay in the sheer indifference they felt for him. It was a far cry better than being actively hated.

Eri finished with a low groan, filling Danny's mouth with a bitter flood that left him gasping. His fingers tightened in Danny's hair hard enough to bring tears to his eyes. When he was done he slumped back in his seat with a satisfied sigh, his thighs splaying open bonelessly.

"Hot damn," he said, petting appreciatively at Danny's head. There was a low undercurrent of amusement in the words that made Danny's face heat. "You're rather good at this, aren't you?"

The question seemed to be rhetorical, so Danny didn't bother trying to come up with an answer. He kept his gaze down as the red-haired man — Marc? — moved in from one side, reaching down to take a firm grip on his hair.

Eri looked up at his cousin with a lazy smile. "Let's move this party into the bedroom."

Danny shivered as he stood up and moved with them into the adjoining room, trying to ignore the feeling of foreboding that fluttered through him. It was only sex after all; demeaning sex, maybe, or arduous sex if he was particularly unlucky, but still it was just sex. It was nothing he hadn't done before. He wasn't an innocent by any means, no matter what people might think when they looked at him. He could handle whatever these spoiled lordlings could dish out.

He *could.*

"Strip," Eri said offhandedly as he stepped into the room, taking a sip from the glass of wine he'd carried in with him. A half-empty bottle hung loosely from his other hand.

Danny swallowed hard and reached down to lift the edge of his shirt, pulling it up over his head. The air of the room felt cool on his bared chest, making him shiver.

"Fuck, yeah," the other blond one said, dropping into a chair next to the bed. He looked to be the youngest of the three, but there was something in the bald intensity of his gaze that made Danny distinctly uncomfortable. He leaned forward to rest his elbows on his knees, his eyes glittering as they followed Danny's movements.

Just sex, Danny reminded himself. He deliberately kept his gaze down as he reached for the button of his trousers. He lowered the zipper and slowly pushed his clothes down over his hips, his skin prickling as he felt the gazes that crawled over him.

Marc was sitting on the edge of the large bed now, fumbling at the waist of his pants. "Come here," he said once he had them open, gesturing for Danny to come toward him.

Checking a sigh, Danny obeyed. He climbed up onto the bed as Marc scooted back to lean against the headboard, stretching out on his stomach so he could take the older man's erection into his mouth. Marc's fingers closed over the back of his skull, shoving his head downward without preamble.

Not choking took all of Danny's concentration for a moment. Jaw aching, he tried to relax and let his body be used. Tears prickled behind his closed eyelids as he did his best to pleasure the thick cock in his throat, telling himself it was all going to be over with quickly.

"So good," Marc panted above him, fingers gripping his shoulder with enough strength to bruise. Danny curled over him, trying not to squirm too noticeably.

"I think this is one of the best we've had." Louis's hands were cold where they slid along the insides of Danny's thighs, urging his legs to open. Danny made a sharp sound of surprise when he felt a finger dip into his ass, jabbing inward forcefully.

"He's an angel, all right." Eri loomed in Danny's vision, shirtless now with his trousers hanging open at the waist. The backs of his fingers slid along Danny's cheek briefly before pushing him inexorably back to lie against the pillows.

"Eri," Marc protested, sounding like a child complaining over having a favorite toy taken away. "I wasn't finished yet."

"Shut up. Just hold him down, would you?" The heavy buckle of his belt brushed against Danny's arm as he reached for something on the bedside table.

Dizzied by the change in position, Danny drew in his breath sharply when he felt Eri straddle his hips, knees pressing firmly against his ribs. He raised his hands instinctively only to feel strong fingers close around them, pushing them down to the mattress at either side of his head.

"What...?" He blinked up at Eri, who was looking down at him with an expression of naked hunger. Danny shuddered and tried to free himself from the hands that held him, without success.

"Just relax, boy." Eri's mouth curled slightly as he held up the white beeswax candle he'd taken from the nightstand. The flame at its tip flickered ominously, drawing Danny's eye.

Danny's heart was pounding. He wasn't sure what was happening, but he could sense that the evening's entertainment had spiraled somehow out of control. He glanced to one side, saw Marc's intently attentive expression, looked to the other to meet Louis's disturbingly eager eyes. Both of them looked more than ready to go along with whatever Eri had planned.

"Relax," Eri said again, smoothing the hair back away from Danny's face with one hand. With the other, he tilted the candle sideways, causing a fat drop of melted wax to fall onto the middle of Danny's chest.

Danny let out a strangled cry, his back arching. He wasn't sure if it was more from pain or surprise at the unexpectedness of it, but damn, that fucking *hurt*. His hands curled into fists inside the grips that held him, nearly succeeding in wrenching free.

"Damn, Eri." Louis's voice was breathless. "Look at him move."

"Yeah." Eri grinned, white teeth flashing, and then tipped the candle again, laying down a trail of melted wax from Danny's breastbone to just above his navel. The white beeswax stood out vividly against the backdrop of his flushed skin, turning the skin immediately surrounding it a deep, searing pink.

"Shit! Stop it!" Danny clenched his teeth and groaned, trying futilely to twist away. Unshed tears made his vision blurry as the sheer helplessness of his position came crashing in on him. There was no way he could defend himself against all three of them, no matter what they planned to do to him.

"Shh, it's all right." Eri's tone was patronizing. He dripped more of the wax onto Danny's stomach, carefully intersecting the previous line he'd laid down, his brow furrowing in concentration as if he were creating an intricate piece of artwork. He caught his lower lip briefly between his teeth as he moved back up to Danny's chest.

Fury welled up inside of Danny until he thought it was going to spill out of him. "Stop," he hissed, yanking so hard on his wrists that he almost managed to pull free.

Eri's hand on his stomach held him down. "Uh-oh, see there... be careful." A nail scraped at the skin just below Danny's navel, brushing away a fleck of cooling wax. "Don't struggle so much; if you mess up the design I'm making, I'll have to clean it all off and start over again."

Danny squeezed his eyes tightly shut, willing the nightmare to be over. Each time the wax touched him it felt like the sting of an insect, sharp and piercing. The pain from the small burns seemed to roll through him, combining one with the other until it set up a kind of dull glow underneath the surface of his skin, warming him from the inside out.

"That's it." The sound of Eri's voice consumed the entirety of his focus now, sinuously intruding into his every thought. "Such a good boy. That doesn't feel so bad, does it? Ohhh...." His voice dropped a register as a drip to Danny's nipple made his unwilling captive yowl in protest, trying again to twist his body away. "Does that hurt, angel?" The sarcasm in his voice made Danny want to hit him, but the fingers clasped around his arms were inescapable. "You're only making it harder on yourself by trying to move away."

"I want to hear him scream, Eri." Louis looked up at his cousin with shining eyes, a smile curling his thin lips. When he noticed Danny looking at him, he pressed a fluttering kiss across the inside of the wrist he held, the corners of his eyes crinkling.

"Is that so?" Eri sounded amused. He smoothed a hand over the inside of Danny's thigh, nudging his legs apart. The glance he cast down at Danny was playful. "Come on, angel. Open up for us, will you?"

Danny tried to resist, but between the three of them they managed to get his legs open despite his efforts to fight them off. His struggles stilled when Eri leaned down over him, propping his weight on one arm next to his head. Curling his hands into fists, Danny glared up at him, panting.

"This is so hard for you, isn't it?" Eri smoothed the hair back from Danny's eyes with the back of one hand. His eyes were amused. "You really are cute, you know that? This truly isn't as bad as you're making it out to be."

Danny squeezed his eyes shut, his heart racing. He bit back a whimper when Eri leaned back again, sitting back on his heels.

He opened his eyes again quickly when he felt fingers lift his flaccid cock, squeezing the head of it lightly. Eri was gazing down at Danny's genitals with a thoughtful expression, rubbing one thumb contemplatively over the skin behind his balls.

"Don't," Danny whispered, staring up at him in naked entreaty.

The first drip of wax that hit his balls made his back arch off the bed with a strangled cry, agony arcing up through his groin to impact with his spine. Danny's breath left him in a rush when the next drop fell, trailing a line up over his sac to the base of his cock.

Fucking *bastards*. He was crying now, for the first time crying, damn them all to hell. He jerked his head away reflexively as a hand curled underneath his chin, holding his head immobile as Eri continued to torment him. An open mouth pressed against the side of his face, tasting his tears.

More wax, and he couldn't think of anything now except that he wanted it to be *over*. No part of his balls were left untouched as the candle dipped perilously close over his groin, coating him with a meticulously applied layer of hardening wax that seemed to drag at him, weighting his balls down even as it seemed to lift him high above himself, pain singing underneath his skin.

"Gods, that's beautiful." Impossible to tell which one of them was speaking now. Another splash of wax, this time on his cock, laying down a line of purest agony up the underside of it all the way to the tip. *That* made him jerk and twist away with a ragged scream, his entire body clenching tight to try to get away from it. But there was no escaping it, no escaping *them*, no matter how much he wished for it.

It took him a few moments to realize it had ended. Breathing hard, he fought to regain his composure through the furious pounding of his heart. "Fuck, Eri." The voice was a low buzzing next to his ear, impossible to focus on. "I've never seen anything like this one."

Danny lay rigid with his eyes squeezed shut, shaking violently. His entire body felt sensitized, exhausted and tingling, like a million ants were crawling over him. Whether that was a result of the burns or the wax slowly cooling into hardness on his skin, he couldn't be certain.

"Gods, you're so sexy." Eri bent to kiss him, tongue stroking demandingly into his mouth as their teeth clicked together. His fingers clenched hard in Danny's hair, holding him motionless when Danny would have turned away.

Rough hands cupped the undersides of his thighs, tilting his hips upward as Eri slid back to kneel between his legs. Danny curled his hands into fists and held his breath when Eri drove his erection into him, too excited, apparently, to bother preparing him more than he'd already been.

It hurt, but there was something relieving even in the pain. This, at least, was familiar. Danny turned his head to the side and pressed his face against the side of his upraised arm, holding his breath as Eri thrust into him again and again and again. His body bent nearly double under the force of it, the muscles of his thighs and back aching under the strain. He did nothing to fight it, however, knowing intuitively that submission was the quickest way to get through this stage of the fantasy.

Eri swore viciously when he came, in a voice that spoke of nothing but heartfelt appreciation. He lay shuddering over Danny's body for a moment before pulling out, his breath falling out of him in a ragged sigh as he flopped backwards onto the bed.

Danny barely had time to catch his breath before Marc moved to bend over him, sliding eagerly in to take his cousin's place. Dropping his forearm over his eyes, Danny clenched his teeth and tried not to whimper too loudly when hard fingers closed over his hips to hold him steady while Marc pushed into him.

It was just sex then, hard and hot and sweaty, with the added discomfort of the wax seething over his skin. Fortunately, his own pleasure was neither expected nor desired, which freed him from the trouble of pretending that he was enjoying it. The low, rhythmic grunts Marc made as he rutted sounded somehow obscene, making Danny's stomach clench. Fortunately he finished quickly, leaving room for his younger cousin to move in and take his fill of what Danny's body had to offer.

Danny flinched when Louis leaned down to lick at his nipple, tongue skirting the edge of the circle of wax that had hardened over it. He closed his eyes when sharp teeth nipped at his sensitized skin.

"You really are a gorgeous little whore." Louis's voice was thin and breathless with excitement. His fingers splayed wide over Danny's thighs, pressing deep handprints into his skin.

Danny's ass was already wet and stretched from the other two men's cocks, so Louis slid inside easily. It still hurt, however, more so than the other two because Danny was already feeling a bit raw from overuse. He wondered dimly what he would do if any of them decided they wanted to go for another round, or if he was fooling himself to think he even had a choice in the matter.

Louis shoved into his body with hard, jerking thrusts that seemed designed to make him as uncomfortable as possible. The small cries Danny couldn't suppress seemed to inflame him, urging him on to even greater heights of brutality as he fucked him, his hips slapping with bruising force against the underside of Danny's thighs. Danny turned his face to the side and squeezed his eyes shut so he wouldn't have to look at him, wouldn't have to see the almost childlike glitter of excitement in the man's eyes as he drank in his pain.

"How does it feel?" Louis panted, fingers digging bruises into Danny's hips with every movement he made. A bead of sweat fell from his brow to land on the bridge of Danny's nose. "Does it hurt, you fucker? Does it feel *good*?"

Finally he finished, his hips snapping forward a final time as he emptied his passion into Danny's body. Danny bit back a sob of relief, feeling as if his ass were going to break in two. A hand clenched tightly in the hair at the back of his head, pulling his chin back as teeth dragged hard up the side of his neck to the hairline behind his ear, biting down firmly while Louis whimpered through his orgasm.

When it was over, Danny felt as if he'd been through a beating. Tears still clung to his lashes, and his throat was raw both from the oral sex he'd performed earlier in the evening and the cries he'd been unable to suppress while they were tormenting him.

"You really are a sweet one." Eri's voice was a low purr of satiation as he smoothed a hand over Danny's stomach. Danny winced when he worked a thumbnail underneath one of the thick droplets of hardened wax there, peeling it slowly up from the skin.

"Please," Danny whispered, folding his arms over his eyes. He was rewarded by the feel of lips brushing against his side, trailing an open-mouthed kiss over his skin.

He could feel Eri's chuckle vibrating up through his ribs. "I think we're done with you for tonight."

Danny didn't have to be told twice. He rolled off the bed and reached for his clothes, shrugging into them without bothering to brush off the rest of the wax. Part of him worried that his customers would be annoyed he wasn't providing more in the way of conversation, but they seemed to have already forgotten his presence as they moved to refill their glasses from the wine bottle they'd brought in from the adjoining room, laughing coarsely together. He kept his gaze down as he snatched up his shoes and padded barefoot toward the door.

"We'll see you again, angel." Eri's voice trailed behind him as he let himself out of the room.

He didn't allow himself to think about much of anything as he started in the direction of his private room, arms crossed defiantly over his chest. He felt numb, his heartbeat refusing to settle down even though the night's engagement was over. For a moment he considered going to Charon and telling him what had happened, but memories of his conversation with Reiji earlier that day stopped him. He was afraid that Charon really wouldn't care, that he'd say it was just a part of the job and that he needed to stop complaining about the duties his chosen vocation entailed. That fear kept him silent as he climbed the stairs toward the upper hall.

At this time of night the halls of the House were nearly deserted, with most of its residents either sleeping or engaged in the various acts of their trade behind closed doors. It left him feeling safely anonymous as he opened the door of his room with a trembling hand and went inside.

He shed his clothing and showered quickly, hissing low through his teeth as he scraped away the last of the hardened wax that covered him. That bastard Eri had marked just about every part of him, turning his body into some kind of obscene display of exotic art. It was a small relief that the burns underneath the wax appeared to be mild, for all that they'd pained him. This was the first time he'd had to bed anyone with any kind of sadistic impulses; it wasn't an experience he was looking forward to repeating any time soon.

Finally, scrubbed nearly raw and aching both inside and out, he collapsed exhausted onto his bed. The room was warm despite the winter night outside, but even so, he couldn't shake the chill that gripped him. He lay on his back staring up into the darkness that hid the ceiling from view, too shaken and numb to even think of actually being able to fall asleep.

He wasn't sure how long he lay there before he heard the door-knob to his room turn. There was something covert about it, as if the person turning it were trying hard not to wake him. He supposed he should have been more alarmed than he was, but there was only one person who seemed able to breech his room's locks on a regular basis.

He continued staring up at the ceiling as the door opened and then closed again, still with that same air of guilty furtiveness. After a brief shuffling the mattress dipped, and a body slid underneath the sheet beside him.

"Can't sleep?" Tam said after a moment, his voice so soft it barely carried through the darkness of the room.

"No." He didn't say anything further, not feeling particularly inclined toward conversation.

Tam seemed to sense his mood and didn't say anything else. After a while he reached for Danny and tentatively closed his arms around him, stroking lightly at his hair.

Danny rolled onto his side and curled into the embrace, wondering why he wasn't chasing Tam out of his bed. Hadn't he been protesting against this kind of intrusion just the other day? But if he had to be honest with himself, it felt good to be held right now. There was something soothing about it, like it was somehow managing to gloss over his memories of the past few hours.

For the first time, he wondered if the reason Tam snuck in to sleep with him so often was because he was trying to forget his own client encounters. Had he ever been paired with a customer who pushed him past his limits, making him feel as lost and abused and unsettled as Danny felt right now? Maybe Danny wasn't the only one seeking comfort here, who was hungry for the balm of a reassuring touch.

Danny wrapped an arm around Tam's shoulders and squeezed him tightly, pressing a kiss to the hair at the side of his head. He felt Tam tense up at the hug, surprised by the unexpected welcome when before Danny had only tolerated his presence if not actively trying to shoo him away. Neither of them said a word, however, as they relaxed again in stages into the blanketing darkness.

Closing his eyes, Danny thought that this time, he might actually be able to fall asleep.

Chapter 5

Vincent

Vincent's favorite room in the House of Silence was the Winter Garden. It was a wide, cavernous conservatory situated at the heart of the building, at the base of the large tower that contained the House's central corridors. The floor of the garden was tiled in interconnecting rings of green-veined marble, with elaborate frescoes decorating the walls and ceiling. There was a feeling of vast space to the room, despite the fact that it was filled with scattered copses of trees from foreign places, dark green ferns, thick bushes sporting blossoms of pale blue and white. Tall windows covered its slightly curved rear wall from floor to ceiling, looking out over the expansive hills behind the estate. Far beyond the frozen grounds of the House's rear courtyard, the dark line of an evergreen forest stood a stark contrast to the unbroken white of the snow.

He liked it because it was quiet here, and because it was easy to lose himself in the humid heat of it and pretend that the rest of the world had ceased to exist. The trees in particular reminded him of the country he'd been born in, with a subtle spiciness and rich, earthy scent that would always remind him of home. Looking out the windows, it was easy to imagine that the landscape he saw out there was only slightly more real than a picture painted in a child's fairy tale, as if *it* were somehow the object that was carefully kept and mounted on display behind a pane of frosted glass—instead of the other way around.

"You look pensive today."

The unexpectedness of the voice intruding into his sanctuary made him frown. Turning around slowly, he saw Tam Temetria perched insouciantly on the edge of the white stone fountain that sat at the center of the room, dressed with his usual flair in expensive wool trousers and a high-collared red sports coat. Pale grey ruffles showed at his sleeves and at the collar of his vest, the golden thread embroidered into their edges glittering in the muted overhead light.

For all the man's flamboyant gaudiness, he could move quiet as a wraith when he wanted to. Vincent's frown deepened. "What do you want?"

The skin at the corner of Tam's eyes crinkled, giving Vincent the annoying impression that he was being laughed at. "You're a very blunt person, aren't you? Would it kill you to at least say hi when people talk to you?"

Vincent didn't see the point in offering any word of greeting, particularly since he didn't welcome Tam's presence here. "I'm not sure what you want me to say."

"Anything. Everything. We never really get the chance to talk, you and I."

"And what makes you think I want to talk to you?"

Tam's expression flickered at that. "That's kind of rude. I'm hurt."

Vincent rubbed his forehead with the fingers of one hand, groping for patience. "What do you want?" he said again.

Several seconds passed while Tam seemed to consider the question. Finally, he looked up at Vincent with a small smile. "You don't like me very much, do you?"

Vincent shook his head. "I don't like you or dislike you. But I don't understand you."

"Oh?" Tam raised one eyebrow quizzically. He held his arms out to either side. "I always thought I was rather an open book. What you see is what you get."

Vincent regarded him curiously for a moment before saying, "I don't understand why anyone who has somewhere to go back to would choose to work here."

Tam glanced away at that, looking out toward the tall windows and the meticulously sculpted landscape beyond. Vincent felt an immediate flash of contrition for having broached the subject, since the unwritten rule of the House of Silence was that no one—absolutely no one—talked about the past. That was what allowed all of them to keep their sanity despite the many varied paths that had brought them each here.

He was just opening his mouth to apologize when Tam turned to him again, giving him a smile that didn't quite reach his eyes. "We all have our reasons," he said.

No doubt. Vincent leaned against the trunk of one of the tall date trees that dotted this end of the room, considering what he knew of Tam Temetria. Not much came to mind; he was an affable sort of the kind who made it a point to get along with everyone he met. Such amiability made Vincent mistrustful. Plus it was obvious that Tam came from money. It was more than just the way he dressed; it was the way he moved, the way he spoke, the familiarity he had with the various workings of this grand estate. More than anything else, Tam seemed *comfortable* here, and that was unusual enough to draw note.

The rumor was that he was from some venerable old family that desperately wanted him to return to them, but that for some inexplicable reason he'd chosen to remain here. The story was far-fetched enough that Vincent didn't seriously consider it, but still, it left him wondering. Curious as he was, he made no further mention of the life either of them had had before they'd come to the House of Silence. Such inquiries were bound to turn attention to his own past, and that was something to be avoided at all costs.

"I came here to be alone," he said pointedly, crossing his arms over his chest and turning away. He wished Tam would give up on his misguided attempts to befriend him.

There was a lengthy bit of silence after that, as if Tam were regarding him intently. It made Vincent nervous, because for all that Tam came across as a frivolous dolt at times, there were other times when he seemed to be uncommonly perceptive.

Finally, there was a low shuffling as Tam stood up from the fountain's edge. "No problem, Vincent. I'm sorry I bothered you."

He sounded like he honestly meant it, which made the whole thing worse. Vincent clenched his jaw and waited impatiently for him to leave.

Alone again, he let out the pent-up breath he'd been holding and turned toward the windows. The chill of the landscape outside seemed to reach inside of him, touching him deeply in a way that even the familiar balm of trees and greenery could not entirely warm. He struggled against it for a moment longer before giving it up as a lost cause and turning to go. Whatever fragile peace he'd been able to find when he first came into this room was gone.

He left the garden and made his way upstairs to his private room, crossing paths with Danny briefly as he rounded the turn in the upper hall. He said hello to him in passing, feeling stung as he remembered Tam's accusation that he was a rude person. He could be courteous when he chose to be, so long as it was toward someone he didn't find objectionable. He liked Danny; the boy was young and refreshingly earnest. Plus he never intruded where he wasn't wanted or asked uncomfortable questions.

In his room at last, he made a point of locking the door and leaning back against it, letting out his breath in a heavy sigh. He reached up to remove the dark ribbon he'd used to tie back his hair that morning, letting the long strands fall loosely around his shoulders. After a slight hesitation, he removed the eyepatch he wore as well, massaging gently at the scarred skin where his left eye used to be.

It had to be his imagination when the eye still pained him. The injury was years old, a part of a past that he preferred not to dwell on for any length of time. Any ability it had to hurt him was long gone, swallowed up by time and by his steadfast determination not to let it have any power over him whatsoever. Inside the sheltering domain of Charon Marque, the past was little more than a specter, a shadow without any tangible form or substance.

A memory of fire rose up in his mind's eye, the heat of remembered flames beating fiercely against his skin. Black smoke, acrid, bitter, choking the breath from his lungs. A stampeding thunder of horses' hooves, strident jingle of harness, animals screaming in terror as they bolted from the flames. Laughter, coarse and biting, as strong hands shoved him down, pain of hard fingers gripping him, hitting him violently as he struggled. Anguish, helplessness, choking on his blood, his fury, and through it all the piercing wail of his sister's screams....

No. *No.* The past had no more ability to hurt him.

Not here.

45

Not now.

Not ever again.

Loosening his hands from the fists they'd curled into, he went to prepare for work.

His customer that night was a longstanding client who tended to request Vincent by name during his infrequent visits to the House of Silence. He was a man by the name of Francois Aburon, an impeccably dressed, well-mannered businessman of high breeding who had a number of preferences that Vincent was particularly qualified to see to.

Aburon was an exceptionally tall man, broad in the shoulders underneath his expensive tweed sport coat. He was muscular enough to make Vincent feel small and insubstantial standing next to him, with unusually piercing eyes that were the color of old stone. His face was square with a kind of rugged appeal to it, although he could never be mistaken as handsome. His head was clean-shaven, making it difficult to accurately say what his age might be. Late thirties, Vincent guessed, or early forties. Despite the physical intimidation inherent in his appearance, Vincent liked the look of him; there was something about being with him that was vaguely comforting.

Vincent let his breath out slowly and leaned back into the overstuffed armchair in front of the fireplace, tucking his bare feet up comfortably underneath himself. He shivered under the feel of stiff bristles moving through the long strands of his hair; for whatever reason, Aburon liked to brush it for him, as if he found the repetitive motion of it somehow soothing. Vincent considered it a harmless affectation, although he did find it curious. It was one of the more tame fetishes his various customers displayed.

"You're so beautiful." Aburon's hand slid underneath Vincent's chin, tipping his head back to make him look up at where the taller man stood behind him.

Vincent looked away sharply. "No. I'm not."

The corner of Aburon's mouth curled upward as he released Vincent's chin and smoothed a hand over the side of his head. The gesture was reminiscent of a tolerant owner petting a favored pet. "You're too hard on yourself." His fingers lingered at the edge of the patch covering Vincent's eye. "You think this scar takes away from your beauty, but you're wrong. It only makes you more alluring."

Vincent shivered again, more deeply this time. He had no illusions about his physical appearance; he knew he was disfigured, that whatever physical beauty he might once have had was now irretrievably gone. If anything, he knew he had a kind of exotic appeal to his customers. He knew he looked foreign, with his dark olive skin and his sharply defined features, and his accent that was reminiscent of the eastern regions near the sea. He'd tried hard to lose the accent since he'd come to the House of Silence, but he'd never quite been able to manage it entirely.

Rising up onto his knees, he twisted smoothly around in the chair until he faced Aburon and leaned in to kiss him. Aburon opened to him instantly, tongue stroking deeply inside his mouth as a wide hand applied subtle pressure at the small of his back, holding him close.

"Beautiful," Aburon said again, breathing out against Vincent's lips. Then, more softly, "Take your clothes off."

Smiling inwardly, Vincent obeyed. His hands were steady as they unwound the belt of the wraparound vest and shrugged out of the stiff weight of it, then went to work on the buttons of the full-sleeved shirt he wore underneath. He kept his gaze down, not particularly caring to see the naked appreciation that shone in Aburon's eyes as his body was exposed. His build was slender, lissome, which was desirable to the vast majority of his customers. Aburon had never made any secret of the fact that he found Vincent's body to be an intensely exciting plaything.

"On the floor," Aburon said. Despite the gentleness of his tone, the note of command in it was unmistakable. "You know what to do."

Yes. Vincent knew what to do. Keeping his gaze lowered, he moved to stand in front of Aburon and sank down to his knees, wincing slightly at the rough scrape of the carpet against his shins as he settled into a comfortable position. Taking a deep breath to steady himself, he moved his hands behind his back and held them there.

The feel of leather cuffs sliding closed around his wrists made him breathe in sharply. No matter how many times he went through this, he could never quite let go of the fear as he waited for it to begin.

His heart was beginning to pound fitfully now despite his best attempts to keep himself calm.

"Relax." Aburon's voice was a low rumble behind his ear. A hand stroked down the back of Vincent's neck, heavy and possessive. "Just breathe."

Breathing was something Vincent could do. He focused his whole being on it, lifting his head into Aburon's palm as the man gave his head a last lingering pat and moved around to stand in front of him. From there it was easy to lean forward and close the distance between them, his mouth opening instinctively as he nuzzled the other man's crotch.

Something inside of Vincent went still and quiet as he gave worship to the body in front of him, rubbing his face against Aburon's steadily firming erection through the stiff fabric of his trousers. With his hands bound behind his back, he had to rely on his innate sense of balance to keep himself upright as he slid his lips down to mouth at the heavy balls underneath, his tongue pushing hard against the fabric of the pants. The scent of the man was everywhere around him, warm and musky and strong and masculine. It made his mouth water, made him wish that Aburon would consent to open his clothing so Vincent could taste him directly.

Aburon's fingers clenched hard in his hair briefly before releasing him. "That's enough," he said. His voice was hoarse. "Go into the bedroom and stand at the foot of the bed."

Vincent rose gracefully to his feet and obeyed, moving with an unhurried stride into the adjoining bedroom. The bed in this suite was large and canopied, with a heavy white curtain held back at the corners and tall, elaborately carved wooden bedposts that were polished to a deep cherry shine. The fire here was lit, too, the warmth of it bringing a wave of gooseflesh to his skin as he moved into position at the foot of the bed, his back to the room.

He stood where Aburon had left him and waited, his thoughts buzzing at the back of his head. He felt a bit off-center this evening, his focus strained. It made him jump slightly when he felt Aburon's fingers close around his forearm, massaging lightly at the skin above the cuffs.

"You're distracted tonight." There was no censure in the words, just honest observation, but they made Vincent flinch regardless. He bit hard on his lower lip as Aburon's fingers moved over the cuffs that bound him, undoing the small metal clasp to separate them so his arms could fall loosely down at his sides.

Neither of them spoke while Aburon lifted Vincent's left wrist to the tall canopy post beside him and attached the cuff to the thick metal D-ring embedded there. He slid his hand heavily down Vincent's arm to his shoulder, petting him languidly, before moving to do the same with the other hand on his other side. Vincent let his breath fall out of him in a long sigh, allowing the familiarity of the motions to roll through him. This was something they'd done before on several occasions, oftentimes in this very room. Aburon liked to start their evenings together with a certain amount of ritual, especially when they hadn't seen each other for a long time.

Bound spread-eagled now, facing the bed, Vincent felt more naked than just the loss of his clothing could justify. The room swam in front of him unexpectedly, making him momentarily dizzy. He curled his hands around the bedposts, concentrating on forcing his tightly clenched muscles to relax; this was going to be a lot harder on him if he was tense when it happened.

Aburon gathered up the heavy fall of Vincent's hair in both hands, laying it carefully forward over his shoulder where it wouldn't obstruct access to his back. The feel of the ends tickling against his nipple made Vincent shiver.

"Are you ready?" Aburon's voice was soft.

Vincent drew in a deep breath and then let it out slowly, tightening his hands around the bedposts. "I'm ready."

The first strike of the whip against his back made him bite back a sharp cry, more from surprise than at the pain of it. It was the cat this time, the one with the braided tails. Aburon wasn't wasting any time this evening.

"Good?" Aburon asked, touching his bowed head lightly.

Vincent squeezed his good eye shut and nodded. "Yes," he whispered.

"Yes?"

"Yes. More, please."

The next blow struck the other side of his back, slashing like claws across his shoulder blade. He could feel a slow trickle of blood make its way down the side of his ribs.

"Again, please," he said, without opening his eye. His breathing was ragged. "Another."

Aburon hit him with the whip again, and then again, spacing the blows out along his shoulders and upper back, catching him along the underside of one arm unexpectedly. Vincent curled his hands into fists inside the cuffs that bound them and opened himself up to it, letting the pain move into and through him until he felt his entire body must be glowing from the white hot intensity of it.

"Come on, Vincent." Aburon was breathing hard now, his tone wheedling. "Stop being so stubborn."

The whip licked across Vincent's ass without warning, making him choke back a scream. He knew Aburon wanted to hear his voice, but it was a longstanding contest between them for him to try to hold out as long as possible. Almost too quick to follow, another blow caught him along the side of one hip, the tips of the braided tresses wrapping around to strike dangerously close to his groin.

Among his many other redeeming qualities, Aburon was a virtuoso at the art of whipping slaves. Vincent felt nothing but respect for the man, and heartfelt gratitude. So many of his customers only pretended at dominance, looking for Vincent to play a role in a game they didn't truly understand. But Aburon understood the true heart of what dominance was in a sexual setting — it wasn't bullying, wasn't a childish insistence on having his orders obeyed. It was about conquering the soul of a slave, overcoming the barriers of will and want and desperation that stood between them, until at the end they were one being, one will, one purpose focused together on the path he was directing them toward.

Vincent was shaking now, his entire body alive with anticipation as the pain crawled through him, seething under his skin. He saw Aburon move out of the corner of his eye and tensed involuntarily, biting back an aborted cry when the whip landed hard over his chest, barely skirting his nipple. Then another blow hit the backs of his thighs, feeling like nine serpents wrapping around to sink venomous fangs into the side of his leg.

Vincent's spirit soared.

Chapter 6

An Affinity for Pain

The beating continued until Vincent staggered under one of the blows with a broken sob, clinging hard to the bedposts to steady himself as he pitched forward.

"That's enough, I think," Aburon said thoughtfully.

It wasn't enough, damn it. It never was. Vincent felt a flash of resentment that he would end it so soon, but swallowed the emotion forcefully, reminding himself that this was for the customer's enjoyment, not his own.

He flinched when Aburon moved around to stand beside him. When a few moments passed and nothing happened, he raised his gaze reluctantly to see the other man staring down at him with a probing expression.

"Why do you need this so much?" Aburon said.

Vincent pressed his lips together and looked away. Providing answers to those kinds of questions wasn't a part of what he was getting paid to do this evening.

Aburon smiled slightly. "Keep your secrets, then." His thumb traced the edge of Vincent's cheekbone, wiping away the tears that dampened the skin there. "We all have them, don't we?"

Vincent thought that was rather a curious comment to make. He wondered briefly what kind of a life Aburon lived outside the walls of this House, if the people he worked with and lived with on a daily basis had any idea what kind of thirst this man had for domination, for subjugation, for drinking in the pain of others. Aburon was one of the purest sadists Vincent had ever come across. For him, the infliction of pain wasn't about cruelty, or ego-boosting, or play-acting; it was about sexual gratification, pure and simple.

He couldn't help feeling disappointed when Aburon reached up to release his wrists from the bedposts, carefully lowering them to hang limply at his sides. He didn't remove the cuffs, though, which made Vincent grateful.

51

He shivered when Aburon's lips brushed across the side of his face. "I need, pretty one," Aburon whispered, pushing downward gently on his shoulders.

Vincent immediately lowered himself to his knees, his breath stuttering at the pain of the movement. There was a low rustle of fabric as Aburon opened the front of his pants, never looking away from Vincent's face. Vincent barely had time to open his mouth before fingers clenched in his hair hard enough to make him cry out, yanking his head forward to meet the turgid erection that was shoved into his throat.

"I love how much you love it when I hurt you," Aburon said breathlessly, thrusting inwards. Vincent whimpered low in his chest and rode it out, squeezing his fists closed so tightly his nails bit into his palms. The welts on his body were starting to sting now as his sweat mingled with the blood there, making his breathing quicken. His arms ached from being bound earlier; he knew he was going to have some excruciatingly vivid bruises on his wrists from the cuffs in the morning.

But pain was an old friend. Vincent felt it, accepted it, and took it into himself, drawing strength from it. He knew that his eager reception of whatever Aburon chose to do to him was what made the other man keep coming back to him. In a way, the two of them were a perfect match. Their time together was always intense, no matter how long or short a time Aburon spent on him.

Aburon pulled out of his mouth abruptly, closing one hand around his chin. "Not like this," he panted. There was a hint of desperation in his eyes that made Vincent feel a twinge of pride, knowing he was the one to affect him that way.

Vincent was disappointed, but he understood why Aburon had stopped him. This client generally preferred to take his release inside of Vincent's body, after Vincent had been thoroughly broken for him. They weren't there yet, not by a long shot, but the night was still young. The thought of it made Vincent shudder in something that didn't bear much resemblance at all to fear.

Aburon left Vincent on his knees while he removed his clothes, folding them and laying them carefully on top of a chair beside the bedroom door. Vincent watched him covertly, admiring the hard, rigidly defined lines of him. Aburon was a powerful man, both physically and mentally, and it showed in the self-confident way he moved. He had absolutely no self-consciousness at being naked; his body language was relaxed, his cock hard and thick, arcing up over his stomach in a palpable display of the desire he felt.

When Aburon returned, he trailed a finger over Vincent's cheek in a caress that seemed to have real affection in it. "Up on the bed now," he said, smiling slightly.

Vincent climbed onto the bed without needing to be told twice, lying down cautiously on his back. The wounds from the whipping seemed to scream at him as he settled himself against the white sheet, making his breathing shallow. His hands clenched into fists at his sides.

"You're so beautiful like this." Aburon took hold of his wrist in a firm grip and bent down to trail his mouth across Vincent's stomach, licking at the blood beading at one of the scores on his lower chest. Vincent drew in his breath sharply and tried to stay motionless under the sensual assault. He couldn't hold back a whimper when Aburon's teeth grazed his nipple, one hand lifting his wrists up to the headboard and attaching the cuffs securely to the metal ring over his head.

Perversely, being bound always made Vincent feel comforted, as if the loss of control over his body somehow managed to set his mind free. He couldn't hold back a moan when Aburon's hand moved down to his groin and urged his legs to open.

He held his breath dizzily when Aburon's fingers skirted around his rather obvious erection and closed around his balls, the grip tightening into something that wasn't quite pain. The threat of it was there, however, making him shudder. He stared up into Aburon's eyes, his entire body trembling. "Please," he whispered, not sure what it was he was asking for.

The hand on Vincent's balls tightened briefly before sliding down to finger at his hole. "You feel so empty inside, don't you?" Aburon's voice was soft against Vincent's cheek as he bent to kiss the side of his face. Vincent made a small sound when the tip of Aburon's finger slipped into his body's opening, teasing him. "You want me inside you?"

Yes. Pride kept Vincent from saying the word aloud. It surprised him sometimes that he could have any pride left after the things he'd seen and done in his lifetime, but there it was. Sometimes he thought pride was the only thing he had left of the person he used to be.

Aburon smiled slightly, his eyes glinting in the firelight as he dragged a thumb over the side of Vincent's face, wiping away the drying tears there. "Not yet," he said, giving Vincent a contemplative look. He pressed an almost chaste kiss to Vincent's lips before turning to reach for something on the bedside table.

Vincent stared up at the ceiling, willing his heartbeat to settle. The worst part of this job was the uncertainty of not knowing what the client was going to do next. But this was Aburon, so he trusted that whatever was going to happen to him would be good. He was so hard he ached, so hard his body *sang* with it, and Aburon hadn't even touched him there.

"Mmm." Aburon's hands were between Vincent's legs now, startling him with a cool swipe of lube between his asscheeks. Vincent's breath caught in his throat when something hard and blunt brushed against his opening, pushing its way inside.

The dildo was a large one, cool to the touch and gently rounded. Aburon slid just the tip of it inside him before stopping, one hand massaging gently at the inside of Vincent's thigh.

"I know how much you love these things." There was a smile in Aburon's voice now. He dragged his nails over Vincent's hipbone once before dropping his hand down again, rubbing at the muscle just beneath his groin.

Vincent's hips trembled as he fought the desire to push down on the dildo, forcing it inside his body. Doing such a thing without being told would end in nothing but punishment, and not the fun kind; he knew that from personal experience. Worse than that, it would make Aburon disappointed in him, and that he could not bear. His toes curled against the bed sheets, his legs shaking.

"That's it." The words were approving. "Just lie still and feel it." The tip of the dildo pushed in just a bit further before sliding out again. Vincent couldn't hold back the protesting groan the loss of it dragged out of him.

Aburon kissed the inside of his thigh in reward for his obedience. The dildo came back, pushing gently against his entrance without

54

breaching it. When several seconds passed without any further movement, Vincent had to clench his jaw to keep from screaming in frustration.

Chuckling softly, Aburon nipped at the curve of his hipbone. "All right," he said indulgently, his lips curling against Vincent's side. "You want it that badly, then take it."

Given permission at last, Vincent stretched out his body, pushing his hips downward to nudge the dildo inside. He couldn't hold back a small whimper when he did it; the whipping he'd gotten from Aburon had been quite thorough, and any movement at all was painful because of it. But it didn't seem to matter; or rather, the pain made it feel even better when the hard silicone plug finally slid into him, filling him in the way he needed to be filled.

"That's it." Aburon's voice was deepening now, arousal blurring the edges of his words. "Keep moving just like that."

Vincent bit hard on his lower lip and flexed his hips, taking as much of the dildo inside of himself as he could before pulling back, then pushing down again sharply, fucking himself on it in a steadily undulating rhythm that made his head spin.

"Fuck, Vincent, you're magnificent." Aburon's free hand splayed across Vincent's waist, holding him steady while he kissed his way up his stomach to his chest and finally to his face, taking possession of Vincent's mouth with a deep kiss that left them both breathless.

Vincent felt like he was flying when the dildo was finally shoved inside of him, filling him up completely. His hands moved inside the cuffs restlessly as Aburon leaned away from him, leaving him feeling cold despite the heat of the fire. It wasn't the largest plug they'd ever used by far, and while the feel of it was enjoyable enough it left him distinctly wanting.

It was a surprise when he felt Aburon's hand close around his erection, drawing his attention to that part of his body abruptly. He hissed softly when Aburon pinched the tip of it, fingering the slit there.

The smile on Aburon's face wasn't comforting in the least. Vincent watched him warily as he dipped a finger into the jar of lubricant on the bedside table and then returned to the cock in his hand, smearing a generous dollop of it over the tip.

Vincent clenched his teeth and stared up at the ceiling again, his entire body going taut. His heartbeat thundered in his ears. Aburon ignored his reaction, sliding the lube around with his fingertip briefly before working it into the slit of Vincent's cock, pushing it down inside of him.

"Just keep breathing," Aburon said, sounding distracted. His entire attention was focused on the task at hand.

Vincent's thighs were trembling by the time Aburon leaned toward the bedside table again, this time reaching for a long, thin piece of metal he'd laid out there. Vincent's breath caught in his throat when he saw it; it was an ingenious little toy known as a sound, which, when inserted into a man's urethra, would make it impossible for him to come until it was pulled out again. He couldn't help watching while Aburon smeared even more lube over the length of the thing, then moved back to take hold of his erection.

"Relax," Aburon said, his voice calm. He held Vincent's gaze as he fingered his slit again, moving the tip of the sound into place. "We've used these before, yes?"

Yes, they had, and it was always a mind-blowing experience. Vincent lay still and shook for him, not understanding the signals his body was sending him. He couldn't tell if he was dreading this or longing for it. His cock was still hard, perverted and hopelessly needy as always, but the feel of Aburon's hand on him could hardly be called pleasure. It was just *sensation*, pure and intense and threatening to drive him overwhelmingly, inescapably mad.

But this wasn't about what *he* wanted. That was the fact he clung to as the end of the sound slipped inside of him, making his hips lift off the bed. It burned, but it was a good burn, flaring out to the base of his spine and turning his thighs to rubber. His hands clenched and unclenched inside the cuffs that bound them, wishing desperately for something to hold onto.

Aburon purred low in his chest, stroking the base of Vincent's cock with his other hand. He gave the sound a little twist before sliding it in further. "I wish you could see yourself right now."

Vincent turned his face away, panting. He didn't want to hear about how wanton he looked, or how beautiful Aburon thought he was. He didn't want to think. He only wanted to *feel*, to experience what Aburon was making him feel.

Another twist, and this time he couldn't hold back the cry that fell out of him. Aburon caressed his thigh lightly before he let go of the sound, letting gravity pull it the rest of the way inside.

"Gods," Vincent whispered, sweat plastering his hair against his brow.

Aburon leaned down to kiss him. "Yes," he whispered against Vincent's lips. He stretched out beside him on the bed, half-covering him, the inexorable weight pressing against Vincent's sensitized skin an agony of its own.

The kiss went on for a very long time, hard hands closing around Vincent's arm and side to hold him down when he would have struggled. Vincent felt his mind begin to go blank under the onslaught of it, his frantic thoughts fading to a low buzz of white static before disappearing entirely.

"That's it, you lovely boy." Aburon's voice was low and husky, heavy with lust. "Just lie still and feel it." He nuzzled the underside of Vincent's arm, biting down hard with his teeth. The thought that he was going to be wearing Aburon's marks tomorrow — all of his marks, both visible and not — made Vincent's chest swell with a yearning that brought a sob to his throat. Because he *wanted* that, wanted this man to mark him, claim him, free him from the prison of his thoughts until there was nothing, absolutely nothing left but the things his body could feel.

"So," Aburon said, mouthing at the curve of his shoulder. "Are you ready to have me inside you now?"

"Yes," Vincent said without hesitation, too caught up in the sensations rolling through him to even think of being embarrassed over the admission. "*Please.*"

He gasped, pressing his face against the shoulder in front of him when Aburon grabbed the base of the dildo inside his ass, giving it a hard twist before pulling it out about halfway. Vincent's hips shook as Aburon fucked him with it for a bit before pulling it out of him entirely.

Yes, this was it, *finally.* Vincent wrapped his legs around Aburon's waist and breathed out slowly when he felt the thickness of a warm cock slide into him, pushing inward with inexorable pressure until the other man's hips were settled firmly against his ass. The feel of being filled was always a bit uncomfortable for him, but there was something exhilarating about it as well that he couldn't adequately describe. Offering himself up to be used in this way seemed like the ultimate act of submission, more abasing even than bending under the whip. Not pain, but something deeper than pain, that touched him in places inside where he'd almost forgotten he knew how to feel at all.

"Amazing." Aburon's fingers tightened around Vincent's hips as he pulled slowly out and then pushed in again, once, twice, before setting up a steady rhythm that made Vincent moan softly in time with the thrusts. There was nothing gentle about it; Aburon was a man who knew what he wanted and wasn't afraid to take it. Vincent opened himself to it, offering himself up for whatever Aburon might choose to use him for.

He flinched when Aburon leaned down to cover him, broad chest pressing his abused body deeper against the sheets. The steady movement of the cock in his ass didn't falter.

"Does it hurt you that much?" Aburon whispered, breath tickling Vincent's ear. "But you're so hard." As if to prove the point, his hand moved down to close around the erection sitting heavily between Vincent's spread legs, squeezing it tightly.

Vincent made an inarticulate sound of protest. The weight of the body leaning over him was oppressive, stifling, making it difficult to breathe. The pressure against the wounds on his back was agonizing, the metal sound a sliver of molten heat inside his cock.

"I know you hate it when I do this." There was a faint note of amusement in Aburon's voice now. His hand slid up Vincent's erection and then down again, cupping his balls briefly before moving back up to stroke him again. "You're not too fond of pleasure, are you? But this is a part of it, too. I want you to come for me, Vincent."

Vincent lay there panting, tears burning in his one good eye. He blinked them away angrily. Pleasure seemed to radiate out like shards of broken glass from the place where Aburon stroked him, mingling with the pain he felt until he could no longer tell one from the other. His skin crawled, alive with sensations he couldn't describe. He no longer knew if he loved it or hated it, needed it or was crumbling under it, if he was burning up under the heat of it or transcending some-

58

how into something that soared above the limitations of the physical body he inhabited.

Aburon's fingers grasped the small metal ball at the end of the sound and pulled it out abruptly, making Vincent's back arch off the sheets. It was purest torment when he came, the sensations exploding through him so forcefully it ripped a scream from his throat. Aburon clutched him tightly and thrust into him, hard, as if he fully intended to split Vincent's body in two. A few more of those and he was coming, grunting low in Vincent's ear as he shook from the force of it, the power of his orgasm transferring into Vincent's captive body until it left them both shaking and breathless.

Afterward, he carefully eased Vincent's legs down onto the bed again and unclasped the cuffs at his wrists. Vincent's arms fell down to his sides numbly, his hands tingling as sensation slowly returned to them.

Vincent bowed his head when Aburon closed his arms around him, holding him close. The feel of a hand gently stroking his hair made him shiver.

"Sleep with me tonight," Aburon said, pressing a kiss against the hair above his ear. He ran his tongue lightly over the strap of the eyepatch there. "I don't have to be back at work until late tomorrow."

Vincent nodded. He was familiar enough with this particular client to know how the rest of the night was going to play out. They would shower together in a little while, then move back into the bedroom where Aburon would kiss the bruises on his wrists, the wounds on his back, offering subtle worship to this proof of the suffering he'd inflicted while simultaneously ensuring that the pain of them would linger. It was a more subtle torture than the branding of the whip, but equally satisfying in its way for both of them.

Before morning they would have sex a second time, less violently than the first, more sensuous, perhaps with Vincent's hands bound again as they moved against the blood-smeared canvas of the sheets. It would be less an act of achieving pleasure than an act of claiming, of submission, a reaffirmation of their respective roles of owner and owned. In the end Vincent would be left without the slightest doubt of whom he belonged to, at least for this one night.

"Yes," Vincent said, and smiled.

Chapter 7

Tam

Tam knew when he woke up that morning that it was not going to be one of his better days.

On the whole, he preferred to keep a positive outlook on life, choosing to focus on the good in things and pretty much ignore the bad. It was a worldview that had helped keep him optimistic and relatively sane in a line of work that habitually ground less stalwart souls into dust. Nevertheless, there was something in the feel of the air as he made his way downstairs for breakfast that made him cautious, as if he were some kind of small prey animal that could scent danger on the wind.

The sight of his brother standing in the middle of the House lobby when he came downstairs confirmed it.

For a moment, he considered turning around and heading straight back upstairs. He wasn't sure why it should surprise him that Aaron had found him here; and it didn't, not really. The Temetria family had one of the most extensive intelligence networks in the country. His was a noble lineage, ancient and renowned, with its roots sunk deep in the mercantile commerce, social structure, and government of the southern provinces. In their home territory, they were regarded much like royalty. This far north, however, very few had heard of them, which provided Tam with a welcome blanket of anonymity to hide under. Or at least it had, before Aaron had shown up here.

"Tam." Aaron's mouth turned down at the corners when he saw him. The stiffness of his posture eloquently proclaimed just how uncomfortable he was in this place. It must be difficult for a man of his social standing to step inside a brothel like this in such a public fashion; something serious had to have happened to bring him here.

Tam forced his hand to unclench from the stair railing and stepped forward to meet him. "Hello, Aaron. It's been a while."

"Three years." Aaron was taller than Tam despite being two years his junior, with a narrow frame wrapped tight in a luxurious long coat of fur-lined leather. The brothers' coloring was nearly identical, from the hazel eyes they'd inherited from their mother to the sand-colored hair that could never be entirely convinced to fall into place no matter how ruthlessly it was styled. Aaron was lankier, however, more angular, with none of Tam's unconscious grace.

"Has it been that long?" He glanced around distractedly. Thankfully, the lobby was deserted at this hour of the morning, but there was no telling how long that would last. "I don't think you want to have this conversation in public. Let's go into another room where we can talk."

"By all means." Aaron gestured sardonically for Tam to lead the way. The leather gloves that covered his long hands were made of butter-soft calf's skin and had doubtlessly been custom made.

"Where's your driver?" Tam asked as he held open the door to a large study that opened directly off of the lobby, closing it firmly behind them once they were both inside. He didn't suppose Aaron would appreciate knowing that the House's employees often met with first-time clients here.

Aaron made a small sound of disbelief. "Waiting outside in the car. You don't honestly expect me to bring him in here, do you?"

"Perish the thought." Tam crossed his arms over his chest, groping for patience. "It wouldn't do to let the hired help find out what the family's eldest son has been up to."

"No. Of course it wouldn't." The words were crisp. "Really, I don't understand you at all. Why in hell's name would you choose to be here? Are you *trying* to disgrace our family? Do you hate us that much?"

"Not everything is about you, Aaron."

Aaron glared at him, anger evident in the stiff line of his lips and the belligerent flash of his eyes. He calmed himself with a visible effort. "I didn't come here to argue with you."

"That's good to hear." Tam moved to one of the room's large

windows and stared out at the snow-covered hills. Frost clung to the edges of the windowpane in delicate starburst patterns. It was a small consolation that his brother was probably miserable here for more than just the obvious reasons; Aaron hated the cold. "I'm surprised it took you this long to find me."

"Don't be idiotic. Of course I knew where you were almost as soon as you arrived here; I just didn't see a reason to come after you until now."

"Really?" The thought of Aaron knowing where he was and choosing not to do anything about it made him uneasy. "And what made you change your mind?"

There was a heartbeat's pause, so slight he almost missed it. "Our father is dying."

Tam's throat tightened. "Dying?"

"Yes. Of inoperable cancer."

Tam stared out the window without saying anything. His fingers felt cold where they gripped the edge of the windowsill.

"Well?" Irritation was creeping into Aaron's voice again. "Don't tell me you have no response to that."

"I don't know what you want me to say."

"This isn't a damn game, Tam!" Glancing at the closed door uncomfortably, he lowered his voice. "I've come to bring you home with me. He's asked to see you."

That made Tam turn away from the window, staring at him incredulously. "I think his wishes on that matter were made very clear the last time I saw him."

"Things change. Your presence is needed. You're the heir whether you want to be or not."

Tam fought down the surge of panic that rose in his chest, threatening to choke him. For a moment, he couldn't have spoken if his life depended on it.

"Does he know what I've been doing these past couple years?" he asked once he got his voice under control again.

Aaron's expression darkened. "Of course not. Do you think I'd tell him? It's bad enough that *I* know what kind of depravity you've fallen into. He'd never outlive the shame of it if he knew."

Being told he was a source of shame to his family was nothing new to Tam. The corner of his mouth curled upward slightly. "I didn't exactly fall into it, you know. It was more a kind of jump. Or maybe a slide...."

"You are a disgrace to our family, and you always have been." Rage sharpened the words, colder than the winter air outside. "It was a fluke that made you the eldest, when by all rights it should have been—"

"Then take it!" The past several years of frustration exploded in his chest, making him dizzy. "I never wanted any of it. Everyone knows you're the favorite son, that you're the brightest, and the best suited to running the business. No one will object if you're the one who takes over after he's gone."

"You know full well that formally disowning you would bring just the kind of attention down on our family that we're trying to avoid." Again, he visibly brought himself under control. "Besides, I don't have any objection to the way things currently stand. I have my own share of the inheritance, and it's sufficient for my needs. We both know I'll be the one to run the family business, anyway."

The annoying part of it was, Tam believed he was telling the truth. Aaron didn't have an ambitious bone in his body; he already had everything he could ever want in life, and didn't see the point in troubling himself to grasp for more. He was a true son of the Temetria family, with a full appreciation for the centuries of tradition and privilege that went with it. Tradition dictated that Tam be the heir, and that was good enough for him.

Aaron's expression softened slightly. "Come home with me, Tam. Whatever it was that brought you out here, whatever drove you to it, it doesn't matter anymore. This might be your last chance to see him, and he did ask for you. That has to mean something, doesn't it?"

Tam dropped his gaze to the floor, his chest tightening. "Yeah," he said reluctantly. "It means something."

He had a feeling he was going to regret this when all was said and done.

Charon was in his office when Tam went to find him. He looked up from his desk as Tam stepped into the room and, after a moment's contemplation, got up to move to the wet bar by the bookshelf.

"I hear we had a visit from the younger son of the Temetria family," he said, pouring a splash of brandy into a glass and holding it out.

Tam accepted the glass, sipping from it gratefully despite the earliness of the hour. Aaron would be mortified to know that his presence here had been noted by the Master of the House, although Tam wasn't surprised. Not much went on inside these walls that Charon didn't know about.

"I'm afraid so." Tam's gaze moved to the window. "He's asked me to go back home with him."

"I see." Charon finished fixing his own drink and turned around to face him, leaning one hip against the edge of the desk. "Are you planning to go with him?" His tone was completely nonjudgmental.

That was the question, now wasn't it? "I don't want to. But he says our father's dying."

"Ah, the venerable Lord Markov." He didn't sound surprised, which made Tam wonder just how much he followed events that transpired in the world outside this House.

To Tam's knowledge, Charon was the only one who knew about the past he was doing his best to run away from, although several others inside the House might have guessed. Tam had heard most of the rumors; how he was the only son of some once-affluent family that had fallen on hard times and he was trying his best to support them, how he was some kind of missing heir who was being desperately sought after by the family that had lost him, how he was a murderer guilty of patricide hiding out inside the House of Silence in a last-ditch effort to evade the law. Each rumor was more colorful than the last, although they were rarely spoken to his face. In this instance, the House's unwritten law about not discussing one's past was particularly welcome.

"Yes. Our family physician is with him now, doing what he can to make him comfortable."

"Hmm." Charon took a sip of his drink, regarding him closely. "So what exactly is it you came here to ask me?"

Sometimes this man's perception was frightening. "I suppose... I suppose I came here to ask your permission to go."

Charon's mouth curved slightly. "There's a reason the House's doors are never locked, Tam. Everyone here is free to go whenever they please."

"I know that. It's just...." Frustration was making his head ache. "I guess I just need to know... to know that I...." He trailed off, unable to find words to describe just what it was he was asking for.

Charon held his gaze consideringly for a long moment. "You'll always have a home here, Tam. No matter what happens."

Yes. Those were the words exactly.

Tam let out a breath he hadn't even known he'd been holding. "I shouldn't be long. Maybe a week, tops."

"Take as long as you need."

Charon Marque was many things—and Tam had his suspicions about some of them—but loyal to those he chose to employ was definitely at the top of the list. Relaxing for the first time since he'd seen his brother that morning, Tam finished the last of his brandy. "Thanks, Charon. I mean it."

"Don't mention it." The glint in Charon's eyes turned wicked. "Let me know if you want me to send Reiji out to greet your brother properly to our House."

The image that brought to mind made Tam laugh for the first time in what felt like ages.

Chapter 8
Family Obligations

Tam shifted uncomfortably as the limousine pulled into the long, winding drive leading up to the Temetria family estate. Tall trees lined both sides of the road, the thick canopy of their branches interlocking overhead to form a tunnel of green-tinged light as sunlight filtered down through the leaves.

It was all very picturesque, but he was far too anxious to appreciate the view. He frowned when they paused at the front gate, a towering monstrosity of black iron and aged red brick. The gate opened for them almost instantly, and the car moved ponderously forward again.

"You look nervous," Aaron commented. "Don't be. Whatever the two of you fought about before you left, it doesn't matter anymore."

To whom? Tam thought resentfully, but kept the comment to himself. "I hate it here," he said bluntly, watching dispassionately as the main house came into view. "You'd think the fact that I left would be some kind of clue as to how I feel about the place."

Aaron looked annoyed. "Look, whatever it is you've been doing these past few years...."

"It's called whoring."

Aaron's eyes flickered apprehensively toward the front of the car, but the soundproof partition that separated them from the driver was firmly in place. "You will not use that word in front of our father."

"Aaron—"

"You will *not*." The cold fury in his voice made Tam glance at him in surprise. Aaron tended to lose his temper with him fairly regularly, but never like this. There was a wild light in his eyes as he held Tam's gaze. "I don't know what possessed you to do the things you've done, or what kinds of things you've allowed those men to do to you, but you will *not* vilify our home or our family with any mention of—"

"I can describe those 'kinds of things' to you if you'd like." He wasn't sure what made him say it. He usually tried so hard to get along with people, but there was just something about his brother's casual denigration that drove those kinds of peacemaking habits clean out of his head. "I'm sure it would be quite educational. I can draw pictures if that would help...."

For a moment he seriously thought Aaron was going to try to hit him, and boy, would *that* have been interesting. Tam's muscles tensed, poised to defend himself, but his brother got himself under control with an effort. Tam wasn't sure if he was relieved or disappointed.

The wheels of the car crunched over the paved stone driveway as they came to a stop in front of the house's main doors. Aaron stared out the window for a moment, his jaw rigid, before pulling his coat closed tightly around himself and stepping outside. He didn't look in Tam's direction again.

Tam sighed heavily and raked a hand back through his hair. Just what the hell was he doing here? He'd known from the start that it was an incredibly bad idea to come, but he couldn't very well ignore what might be his father's dying request, now could he?

He somehow found the courage to climb out of the car. Aaron was already halfway up the stairs leading inside, clearly having had enough of conversation with his estranged brother for the time being. Tam didn't blame him. Sometimes he found his own company a bit wearing, too.

The Temetria estate wasn't quite as large as the House of Silence, but it was close. The front doors were towering arches of polished oak, monstrous in their proportions, as if they'd been designed with the specific intention of making those who passed through them feel somehow smaller as they went inside. It was a phenomenon Tam had noted when he was a young boy, and the effect didn't seem to have diminished any over time.

Winters here were milder than they were up north at the border where the House of Silence was located, but it was still chilly enough to make Tam's hands numb as he moved to go inside. He tucked his fingers under his arms as he climbed up the broad stairs that fronted the house, glancing briefly at the carved rams' heads that decorated the wide landings to either side.

Aaron was waiting for him in the foyer inside. "This way," he said shortly. The sharp-edged narrowing of his gaze said clearly that he considered the subject closed about what was and was not appropriate conversation to have in front of their father.

He needn't have worried. Baiting his brother was a pastime Tam engaged in with considerable pleasure, but he was still overwhelmingly intimidated by his father. It pissed him off how intimidated he was by him, because it had to do with more than just the man's virtually god-like status as the head of the Southern Mercantile Cabal. It had to do with the fact that he was Tam's father, and that even after all these years, Tam still wanted to win some scrap of the man's approval.

The house hadn't changed at all since Tam had last been here. It still had the same hollow, echoing quality he remembered, as if he were walking through a museum, or a tomb. Briefly, he compared it to his memories of the House of Silence. Even when its halls were at their emptiest, the House of Silence felt warm and lived-in to him, filled with the tenacious heartbeats of individuals doing their best to survive in a world that had more often than not tried its damnedest to drive them into the ground.

And that was the true appeal of the life he lived there, even if it was an appeal he could never find words to describe to his disapproving brother. Every single person who lived in the House of Silence, from Charon to the working boys to the lowliest kitchen maid, were family. It wasn't a family joined by shared blood, but by shared experiences, shared suffering, and even if they didn't share the details of those trials with one another, the understanding was there. No one judged each other, no one claimed to be better or greater or more deserving. They were all screwed up in their own ways, and somehow in the midst of it, they'd found contentment.

Aaron stopped in front of a closed door at the end of the hallway, breaking Tam from his thoughts. "He tires easily," he said brusquely, "so don't upset him." He gave Tam a meaningful look before pulling the door open.

There was always something about entering into his father's presence that made Tam feel he should be kneeling and offering obeisance of some kind. It amused him that even in the midst of illness, the Temetria patriarch's regal aura hadn't diminished. The bed where his father lay was huge and situated where it provided a clear view of the gardens outside, surrounded by various racks of medical equipment.

Markov Temetria didn't look ill at all to Tam's eyes; he had the same strong features, the same square jaw, the same thinning grey hair cropped close against his temples. The cords in his neck might be standing out a bit more than Tam remembered, his hands knotted with a bit more arthritis where they curled against the top of the white sheet, but other than that, he was exactly the same as the last time Tam had seen him. When his eyes slitted open to see who was coming into the room, they had the same concentrated, burning fire.

Those eyes widened slightly when they saw his two sons approaching. "*Tam?*"

Tam drew to a stop several feet away from the bedside and forced himself to smile, his heart knocking against his ribs. "Hi, Dad."

His father stared at him for a moment longer, as if doubting the evidence of his senses, before turning toward Aaron. "Leave us alone to talk."

Aaron stiffened slightly at that, but nodded. "Of course." He gave Tam a last unfathomable glance before turning to leave the room, latching the large door firmly behind him.

Tam half-believed he had forgotten how to breathe. "It's been a long time."

"Too damned long, son. Come here where I can see you." More than anything else, Markov's voice gave evidence of the trauma his body was undergoing. It used to be deep, robust, powerful enough to carry across the length of the grounds when he was in a particularly towering rage. There was a rasping quality to it now, an unaccustomed fragility, as if he were having difficulty drawing enough breath to speak.

Obediently, Tam moved forward to stand beside the bed. Despite his best efforts to make himself relax, his hands were curled so tightly at his sides he could feel his nails pressing into his palms.

His father regarded him in silence for several moments before saying, "It's about time you came home."

Tam couldn't help smiling a bit wryly at that. "I seem to recall you being quite clear when you told me to get out."

Markov snorted. "And would you have stuck around even if I hadn't lost my temper and said that?"

It was impossible to be anything other than honest. "No. I wouldn't have."

"Well, then." He gazed up at Tam with a probing expression, as if he could peel away his son's thoughts to get at the heart of what lay beneath. Tam shifted uncomfortably under the scrutiny.

"I'm not going to ask what you've been up to all this time," Markov said at last. "Or how you've been surviving. I know for damn sure you didn't touch any of your accounts, or contact any of our business associates." His gaze said he was curious, but he had too much pride to ask. Tam kept silent. "In any case, you're here now and that's what counts. No matter what shameful choices you made in the past, all that matters is how we go forward from here."

Tam's jaw tightened. "I don't recall doing anything while I was here that I would be ashamed of."

Everything had started to go wrong about four years ago, when he had been told rather unceremoniously that he was to prepare to meet the woman who was to be his future bride. That had been quite a shock to him, especially considering the fact that he'd never made any particular secret of the fact that he was gay. He'd never flaunted it, but he hadn't been ashamed of it, despite his family's rather antiquated views on the matter.

Markov frowned, his eyes narrowing. "You were young and irresponsible before, Tam, but I hope you've grown up a bit since then. You have responsibilities to this family that you have to uphold."

Damn it, why did he ever think he should come back here? All these years had gone by, and absolutely nothing had changed. "I don't have any intention of getting married."

"So you still...?"

Several possible responses came to mind, but Tam settled for saying, "Yes."

Markov remained silent for quite some time. "I see."

The fight the two of them had had when Tam refused the arranged marriage had been explosive. Aaron tried to play peacekeeper, but his efforts had been hampered by the fact that he was completely flummoxed by his brother's preference for his own gender and disgusted by the thought of men having sexual relations with other men. He thought Tam was being deliberately difficult just to spite their father and said so, which prompted Tam to ask if he really thought he'd stoop so low as to take it up the ass just as an act of delayed teenage rebellion. The whole debacle had devolved very quickly after that.

Tam had a lover in the city at that time, but they hadn't been particularly serious and were more sex friends than anything else. When things finally came to a head and he was offered the choice between accepting the marriage proposal as his father wanted or leaving the house, he'd had no hesitation about packing his bags and taking off for parts unknown.

It had been more than three years since then. Even now, Tam didn't regret leaving. "I don't understand why it's such a problem," he said, staring down at the floor in front of his feet. "You have another son. Aaron's as straight as they come; he shouldn't have any problem finding a nice girl to marry and start producing viable heirs."

"That isn't the point, Tam." There was anger in his father's voice now, giving it a semblance of its former strength. Tam flinched under the sound of it. "You are my eldest son. My heir. The entire community is going to look to you when I'm gone, and I will *not* have you doing anything that will dishonor our family name."

Tam closed his eyes. "I'm not trying to dishonor anyone."

Markov sighed. "I know you're not. But there comes a time when you have to start making decisions for the good of the family, instead of for yourself. It's something we've all had to do, son."

Tam wondered what kinds of sacrifices his father had made for the good of the family over the years. Strange that it had never occurred to him to wonder before. While their country was technically a monarchy under the rule of a queen, the power of the royal family had been waning for the past few decades. The real power in this modern age lay with the businessmen, in particular with those who commanded the powerful merchant cabals. The Temetria family was one of the oldest of its kind, with footholds in virtually every corner of the country's economy. Those who controlled the flow of commodi-

71

ties controlled the money, and those who controlled the money had all the power. And power, no matter what its source, was always a jealous master.

Tam wanted no part of it.

"I know you're not going to let me down." Markov sounded tired. He lay his head back against the pillow, his gaze moving to the window. "You're here now. You've come back to us. No matter what kind of shame you've brought to us in the past, you still have a chance to make things right."

Tears pricked at Tam's eyes. Angrily, he blinked them away. "I'm sorry you're still disappointed in me." When Markov didn't say anything further, he turned to leave the room.

Aaron was waiting in the hallway outside. "Well?" he prompted once Tam had shut the door.

Tam scowled. "To paraphrase: I'm a shameful son, but all will be forgiven if only I give up this pesky 'being gay' nonsense and settle down with a woman so I can start making tons of babies who will be able to continue the soul-crushing horror that is our family tradition."

"You're being unreasonable."

"*I'm* being unreasonable? How would you like it if I asked *you* to find a nice guy to settle down with? Believe me, that feeling of heebie-jeebies you just got... I get the same feeling every time I think about marrying one of Dad's upper-crust, social-ladder-climbing, perfectly pedigreed vipers."

For a moment, Aaron looked honestly lost. "I don't understand you. I've never understood you... or the choices you've made." He let his breath out in a heavy sigh, rubbing his eyes. "But I do understand that this is important to you. I'll try to talk to him, okay?"

Tam's gaze drifted to the closed door. "How much longer does he have?"

"It's difficult to say. Dr. Ericksen says that the cancer's fairly well established in him, although right now it's confined primarily to his lymphatic system. His immune system's weakened, so he has to be careful whenever he goes outside. He's doing his best to fight it. Some days it doesn't even seem like he's ill, but other days he gets tired so easily. It's been... difficult."

"Yeah." Tam felt tears prick his eyes again, only it wasn't from anger this time. No matter what disagreements he'd had with his father in the past, the man was still his father.

The look Aaron gave him was contemplative. "You're not going to stay here, are you? No matter what he agrees to."

Tam glanced up at him. He hadn't really thought about it, but.... "No. I'm not."

Something like pain flashed across his brother's eyes, there and then gone. "May I ask why not?"

Why, indeed? Tam let out his breath in a heavy sigh, looking around at the grandly furnished hallway that surrounded them. "I don't belong here, Aaron. You don't need me to tell you that. You're the one who's going to take over the family business; you'll be the one to wear the metaphorical crown no matter what 'tradition' dictates. There's nothing for me here."

Aaron absorbed that in silence for a moment. He didn't look happy about it, but neither did he seem able to come up with an argument to refute it.

"Where will you go?" he asked at last.

Tam smiled ruefully. "I'm going home."

He parted ways with the car at the base of the hill and climbed on foot up the tall drive to where the House of Silence waited, a single strap from his backpack thrown over one shoulder. It was later in the day than he'd intended it to be when he got here, and it had snowed again while he'd been gone, but for some reason it was important to him to make this last leg of the journey alone. For a moment, he flashed back to a similar scene nearly two years ago, when he'd made the trek up this hill for the very first time.

The doorman standing on the front landing bowed his head in greeting when Tam approached, pulling the door open for him with a gesture of welcome. Tam smiled at him in passing, feeling warmed by more than just the extensive heating system the House boasted as he stepped inside.

The first stop he made was to Charon's office.

73

"Welcome back, Tam." Charon pushed back from his desk when Tam entered and came around the front of it to greet him.

"You look surprised to see me."

"To be honest, I wasn't sure you would be returning." His smile was wry. "I know Lord Markov can be very persuasive."

Tam chuckled and shook his head. "He doesn't have anything to offer me. Nothing I want, anyway." His father's approval, no matter how much he might ache for it, was not something he was likely to be offered in this lifetime. "The House of Silence is the only home I have anymore."

Something in the way Charon's eyes glinted said he'd been expecting this answer. Disregarding Tam's trail-worn appearance, he reached out to clasp him on the shoulder and pulled him close, dipping his head down to kiss him. Tam tensed at the unexpectedness of the movement, but Charon didn't hesitate, prying Tam's lips open with his own and then dipping inside with his tongue.

Tam shivered down to his toes at the feel of it; there was nothing compromising about the kiss, nothing passive, nothing that suggested at all that this was an act deserving of shame, and *yes*, this was exactly where he wanted to be. More than that, it was where he needed to be, and as his father was fond of saying, that was what really mattered.

"Welcome home," Charon said with a small curl of his lips. His forehead brushed against Tam's, warm breath tickling his cheek. "Now why don't you go upstairs and get showered, so you can get back to work."

Tam grinned at him, feeling lighter inside than he had in a very long while. "Yes, sir."

Chapter 9

Aburon

The man known inside the House of Silence as Francois Aburon liked his life to be free of surprises. He preferred things to be predictable, readily foreseeable, perhaps even mundane. He liked to operate within the confines of an established schedule, without unanticipated incidents of any kind. Not that life cooperated with his wishes at all frequently.

But that was the nature of the world, and as much as he disliked unpredictability, he didn't consider it worth the energy to get aggravated by such trivialities. He was by nature a very staid, levelheaded personality, and very few things ever managed to unsettle him.

Charon Marque was one of those things.

Not that the House's Master had ever done anything unanticipated. On the contrary, he behaved exactly as Aburon would have predicted every time they met, with an unfaltering courtesy and gentle humor that one would expect in the owner of such an internationally renowned establishment.

It wasn't anything Marque did that made Aburon uneasy; instead, it was the man's general demeanor, his bearing, the way his eyes seemed to see straight through surface appearances into the heart that lay underneath. He was a master at psychological appraisal, at the very least. His reputation for pairing up guests with an appropriate Companion was legendary, and as far as Aburon knew, he'd never once been wrong. Such ability to see into the soul of a man was uncanny, and Aburon didn't trust it.

All of which Aburon might have forgiven if Marque hadn't been as opaque as painted glass himself. As talented as Marque was at seeing into the minds of others, he kept his own thoughts carefully caged away behind sharp-eyed glances and practiced smiles.

"I apologize," Marque said, looking honestly repentant, "but Vincent is otherwise engaged this evening."

No matter how hard Aburon tried, he could read nothing but sincerity in the other man's gaze. Nevertheless, he couldn't help thinking there was something lurking behind the professional smile that he couldn't quite see.

"It's not surprising that he'd be unavailable on occasion. It's not as if I'm his only customer."

"No," Marque agreed. He held out a glass of dark red wine, which Aburon accepted. "But I'm sure we can find another Companion that will be to your liking this evening."

The wine had a rich, fruity sweetness, with a fleshy aftertaste that burned at the back of his mouth when he swallowed. Definitely one of the House's better vintages. "What about that dark-haired boy I saw on the stairs? He was certainly striking enough."

"Danny?" Marque considered. "I don't believe he would be suitable to your tastes."

Which meant the boy wasn't trained to play the kinds of power games Aburon preferred. He wondered how Marque would react if he pressed the issue, saying he wanted that one and none other this evening. Briefly, he considered it, just to catch a glimpse of the inner landscape Marque kept so carefully hidden. Would the Master of the House hand the boy over to appease his customer's whim? Or would he deny the customer to protect his employee?

But if the boy truly weren't suited to Aburon's kind of play, then it wouldn't be a very enjoyable evening. And for the amount of money he was paying to be here, he had no interest in indulging in anything other than the best the House had to offer.

"I think perhaps a Companion with more experience," Marque said, taking a sip of his own drink. "More seasoned, with a dynamic quality you would find appealing."

"Just make sure he's not the kind to break easily," Aburon said. Despite everything he'd said, he *was* irked that Vincent wasn't available. Whatever Companion he was given was likely to feel the brunt of that tonight.

Marque seemed to consider the request seriously for a moment. "I have just the thing," he said at last, straightening with a decisive air. He crossed to the intercom on the wall and touched a button on it lightly, murmuring brief instructions before turning around. "The Rose Parlor is one of your preferred rooms, I believe? Your Companion will be waiting for you there."

"You seem confident that I'll approve of him."

A slight smile touched Marque's face, there and then gone. "If you're at all dissatisfied with him, I trust you won't hesitate to let me know."

Count on it, Aburon thought grimly, although he didn't have much fear that he was going to be disappointed. Despite his mistrust of the House's owner, he'd never once left the House of Silence feeling anything less than perfectly satisfied.

The Rose Parlor was an intimate, elegantly furnished room at the end of the east wing. He assumed it had gotten its name from the stylized rose pattern on the dark red wallpaper, although the decorator had taken the liberty of including long-stemmed roses in glass vases on the end tables tonight as well. The air had the lingering sweet scent of freshly cut flowers, with a faint undertone of woodsmoke from the smoldering fire in the hearth.

A young man with sandy brown hair was perched on the edge of the bed when Aburon entered, leaning back on both arms in a casually indolent posture. "Hi," he said, tipping his head back to give Aburon an appraising look. "I'm Tam."

Aburon smiled as he closed the bedroom door behind himself, latching it firmly. This one wasn't as poignantly beautiful as Vincent was, but there was something appealing in the trimly muscular lines of him that Aburon definitely found attractive. There was an air of subdued challenge in the young man's gaze that made Aburon's chest tighten in anticipation.

This was going to be *fun.*

He moved forward to stand at the side of the bed, looking down into Tam's upturned face. He was impressed when the other man didn't look away; most people found his physical presence intimidating, both because of his size and because of the self-assured way he tended to carry himself. Tam's relaxed expression didn't change, although there was an edge of watchfulness in his eyes that he couldn't quite hide.

That was good. Aburon would have been disappointed if the boy thought there wasn't anything for him to be anxious about.

"My name is Aburon," he said, keeping his voice low. "You may refer to me as Mr. Aburon, or 'sir' if you prefer. Do you understand?"

Tam nodded. "Perfectly, sir."

There was a note of wryness in his voice — very faint but still unmistakably there — that they would have to do something about. Aburon's smile deepened. "You may begin by removing your clothes."

Without any perceptible hesitation, Tam moved to obey. He was wearing a loose-sleeved white shirt with a wide collar and tight black trousers. He bowed his head forward as he pulled the shirt off, revealing a tanned expanse of finely sculpted chest. Very nice, indeed.

Aburon sipped from the drink he'd brought upstairs with him, his eyes tracking his Companion's every move. A flash of red at the man's ear as he bent to remove his socks drew Aburon's attention to the fact that he was wearing an earring. Aburon was hardly an expert in such matters, but it looked like a real ruby.

The discarded clothing was folded with a fair amount of care and placed aside on a chair next to the bed. Naked, Tam turned to face him. Aburon took a moment to drink in the sight of him, all smooth lines and lean muscles, eyes following the faint dusting of sand-colored hair on his chest where it swept downward to join the thicker thatch of brown hair at his groin. His cock, hanging heavily between his legs, was impressively sized.

"Not bad," Aburon said, stepping forward. He took the other man's cock in hand and squeezed it lightly, feeling a flash of amusement at the sharp intake of breath the action caused. He stroked the heavy flesh once, twice, until he felt it begin to harden in his palm.

"Turn around," he said, "and face the wall." He watched with hooded eyes as Tam obeyed, moving to the wall beside the bed and placing the palms of his hands flat against it at about shoulder height. Someone had certainly taken the time to train obedience into *this* one; Aburon wasn't sure if he was pleased or disappointed at how easy this was turning out to be. He thought fleetingly of the dark-haired boy he'd seen earlier that evening — Danny, he thought Marque had said his name was — and wondered what it would be like to train a new pet who had never known a master's touch before.

The tall wooden cabinet against the far wall opened easily, and inside he found all of the many toys he was used to finding there. The House of Silence was well-stocked with a variety of different tools to satisfy a broad range of possible entertainments. After a few seconds' perusal, he selected a handful of them and then returned to where his Companion was waiting.

Tam's head was lowered, a thin line of tension in his shoulders revealing the rising anticipation he was feeling. He was nervous, although he was doing his best to hide it.

Aburon regarded him thoughtfully. "Do you like pain?"

The tension in the other man's shoulders grew more pronounced. Aburon could see the effort it cost him not to turn his head around to look at him.

"Not particularly," Tam said after the barest of pauses.

Impossible not to smile at that, just a little. Such bald honesty was commendable, but there was a fine line between frankness and impertinence. Before the night was out, this man was going to understand the difference between the two.

Aburon reached out to cup his hand over the back of Tam's neck, relishing the way the muscles there flinched when he touched him. He felt the warmth of the skin there for a moment before sliding his hand down, fingertips tracing the line of the other man's spine until they reached the delightfully smooth patch of skin directly beneath the small of his back.

A small pause as he applied a dollop of lube to his fingertip, and then he slid his index finger into the crack of Tam's ass and pushed inside. He watched in appreciation as Tam's back arched at the unexpectedness of the intrusion, his hips jerking slightly as he shifted to adjust his balance against the wall. "Fuck," he breathed, so softly Aburon almost missed it.

Insolent little brat. Aburon grinned, pushing his finger in deeper. His heart was starting to beat faster now, excitement stirring up a dull buzzing underneath the surface of his skin. He was beginning to appreciate the full value of the Companion Marque had chosen for him. While Tam was familiar enough with the motions of dominance games, having doubtlessly bent himself to other men's wills countless times, there was no true submission at the heart of him. And that was a challenge that Aburon just could not resist.

"Easy," Aburon soothed, knowing that someone with this man's pride would take the comment as patronizing. He watched with pleasure as Tam's jaw tightened, his head dipping lower against his chest as he leaned forward more heavily against the wall.

Such a delightful toy. Aburon removed his finger and reached for the dildo he'd selected, applying a liberal dose of lube to the end of it. Using one hand to hold open the cheeks of Tam's ass, he guided the dildo into place with the other and began to ease it inside.

Tam sucked in his breath slowly once he realized what Aburon was doing. His eyes closed briefly, then opened again, his fingers curling where they pressed against the wall. His feet shuffled further apart, making the adjustment to maintain his balance.

The dildo went in without any noticeable difficulty, and Aburon wiped his fingers clean on the soft white towel he'd brought with him from the cabinet. It wasn't the largest dildo he'd found there, but it wasn't the smallest, either. Big enough to feel, certainly, without distracting him from anything else Aburon might choose to do to him.

"Mmm," Aburon said, admiring the hard line of the back in front of him. "How does that feel?"

For a moment, he didn't think Tam was going to answer him. Then, "Cold. A bit uncomfortable, actually."

His hand was knotted in the back of Tam's hair before he was fully aware of his intention to move. A sharp jerk downward, and Tam hit the floor hard on his knees, an aborted cry of surprise catching in his throat as Aburon yanked his head back.

"I think," Aburon said, looking down at him, "that you meant to phrase that a bit differently."

He could see Tam's throat move when he swallowed. The eyes that looked up at Aburon were wary now, having lost their edge of casual indifference.

"Cold," Tam said again, more cautiously this time, "sir."

Aburon smiled. "Very good." He trailed his knuckles across the younger man's cheek.

Now that Tam was on his knees, it seemed a shame to waste the position. Aburon released his hair and gestured for him to turn around away from the wall, his hand reaching to unhook the buckle of his belt. He'd been half-hard ever since he'd first heard the insolence in Tam's voice, and the undimmed challenge in the man's eyes was only intensifying the low burn of arousal he felt.

He pressed his thumb against Tam's lower jaw to open it as he moved in, using his other hand to steady the base of his erection. Tam's eyes slid closed, but he opened readily enough, taking Aburon into his mouth obediently.

Ah, that was it right there. Aburon rocked forward gently, enjoying the feel of slick pressure that engulfed him. Tam was quite talented at this. His tongue slid along the underside of Aburon's erection in a long glide as he sucked him further in, lips molding around the hardness of him. His hands were curled tightly on top of his knees, which were spread just slightly. The edge of tension in him was still there, faint yet still noticeable, leaving Aburon to wonder if he disliked giving head as much as he disliked pain. The thought amused him.

Damn, the kid was good at this; it was going to be over far too soon if they continued for much longer. Grabbing the hair at the back of his head, Aburon pulled Tam off of him, sliding his cock out of his mouth with a wet pop. There was a flash of resentment in the glance Tam flickered up at him, gone almost as soon as Aburon saw it. Apparently, Tam did not like being manhandled.

"That pride is going to be your undoing one day," Aburon said, quite seriously.

Tam gazed up at him without saying anything. His expression was placid, his posture relaxed. There was nothing overtly challenging in him at all. Yet there was a subtle edge of defiance in the line of his jaw that drew Aburon's eye, so slight it would have gone unnoticed if he hadn't been looking for it.

Aburon slapped him.

Tam rocked to the side with a low grunt of surprise, and yes, there was the telltale tensing of his muscles that suggested he was making a conscious effort not to fight back. This one was not used to sitting still and taking abuse, although he clearly considered it within his job's purview to do so.

"Are you going to beat me?" Tam said in a soft voice, without raising his head. He sounded only mildly curious. "Sir."

"I think your previous masters have been much too soft on you." Aburon's hand twitched at his side, aching to hit him again. Instead, he reached for the ball gag he'd taken from the cabinet earlier. He grabbed hold of Tam's lower jaw and pulled it open, pushing the gag unceremoniously inside his mouth. Tam's eyes widened slightly, his nostrils flaring as Aburon pulled the straps of the gag around to the back of his head and cinched them closed, making sure they were well tightened.

That was better. The ball of the gag was a large one, and stretched Tam's jaw in what had to be a fair amount of discomfort for someone who wasn't used to wearing it. The sight of the black straps lying across the flushed skin of his cheeks was unexpectedly appealing; this man looked good in bondage. Briefly, Aburon considered binding his wrists as well, but then he discarded the notion.

He was having too much fun watching Tam force himself to submit to make it any easier on him.

Chapter 10

Castigation

Aburon perused the arrangement of other tools he'd laid out on the bed before reaching for a heavy leather flogger. He made sure Tam got a good look at it before he moved around to stand behind him, deliberately positioning himself out of direct view.

"You're arrogant," he said, enjoying the way Tam's shoulders tensed at the sound of his voice. Clearly, he was trying not to anticipate the blows he knew were coming, but he was just as clearly being unsuccessful in the effort. Delicious. "And you're willful. You pretend to submit, but it's just an act to you. That might be sufficient to appease other masters you've had in this place, but it isn't good enough for me."

Tam's back seemed to be glowing in front of him. There was a faint tracing of markings on the smooth skin, so faint they were almost invisible. Tam had certainly engaged in play like this before, although it had obviously been a while for him.

Aburon gave no warning before he unleashed the first blow, not holding back any of his strength. Tam's body jerked forward under the impact as he caught himself on both hands on the floor in front of him. The strangled cry he made was more surprised than pained, although there was plenty of pain evident in the sound as well. Aburon had no doubt he would have been cursing if he hadn't been gagged.

He waited while Tam straightened, moving tentatively back into an upright position and settling his hands into place again on top of his bent knees. He was breathing more heavily now, and there was a fine tremor visible in the taut lines of his shoulders and arms. The dark knob of the dildo in his ass looked obscene where it filled the

83

entrance of him.

"Don't try to anticipate," Aburon said, running his fingers contemplatively over the flogger's flails. The scent of leather was thick in the air, overpowering the scent of the flowers. "Just accept it. It's only pain, nothing special. Like pleasure, it's just another sensation."

He lashed out with the flogger again, twice in quick succession. Tam's back was awash with red splotches now, blood rushing angrily to the surface of the skin. Aburon barely waited for him to straighten this time before hitting him once more.

"Lean forward," he ordered sharply. "Hands on the floor."

Tam shuddered once and obeyed, dropping his head forward against his chest. In this position, he could absorb the strength of Aburon's blows without losing his balance. Aburon took full advantage of that, working over one side of his back and then the other, the flogger setting up a rhythmic tempo as it thudded against his skin.

Aburon was starting to sweat now. He shrugged out of his suit jacket and tossed it aside, opening the first few buttons on the collar of his shirt. The back in front of him was a solid shade of vivid red now, the raised welts from the flogger's lashes creating a patchwork of paler outlines on the skin.

Beautiful.

He put the flogger aside and reached for another whip, this time selecting a single-tailed beauty that coiled snake-like against the coverlet of the bed. He allowed the long tail to unfold sinuously as he picked it up, noting the way Tam's head twitched when he heard the subtle susurration of leather.

Aburon crouched down behind him, touching one hand lightly to his hip. The skin there felt hot to the touch. "Don't forget to breathe."

As much as Aburon enjoyed torturing slaves, he was always attentive to the slave's needs during their time together. He had no intention of committing lasting harm, just as he had no interest in forcing himself on an unwilling partner. The joy for him lay in the slave's choice to submit to him, and in the mutual exploration of the bond that existed between them, even if it was just for a single night.

There were tears on Tam's face. Slowly, the tension drained out of him, and the hip under Aburon's hand lost its frantic trembling. Aburon slid his thumb over the smooth skin there and leaned in to kiss the side of his neck, mouthing hungrily along the line of his shoulder until he could press his tongue against one of the welts there. Tam moaned faintly at that, making Aburon's heartbeat quicken.

"Pretty little slave," Aburon murmured, pressing lightly with his teeth. He slid the hand on Tam's hip downward until it found the knob of the dildo and pushed on it gently, relishing the way Tam gasped when the hard rubber plug moved inside his body.

Satisfied, Aburon stood up again and lifted the whip. This was a nastier implement than the flogger had been, and would leave more lasting marks. The thought excited him.

The first lash made Tam's entire body jerk, a muffled scream making its way past the constriction of the gag. A perfectly etched stripe of purest white appeared across the flushed red of his back, a razor-thin line of blood decorating the length of it. Aburon admired the sight for a moment before lashing out again, and then again.

Tam was sobbing openly now, all hint of defiance gone. Whatever inner core of arrogance had caused him to resist Aburon's mastery earlier had completely burned up in the purity of the pain he was feeling. He was a creature of pure sensation now, aware of nothing but the torment he was suffering and the fact that Aburon was the one inflicting it on him.

Unable to resist any longer, Aburon dropped the whip and stepped around Tam's huddled form to stand in front of him. He bent to grab Tam's chin, lifting his head upward. Tam responded instantly to the direction without a trace of hesitation, his eyes squeezing shut as Aburon unclasped the straps of the ball gag and removed it, trailing a line of saliva down his chin. His mouth opened before Aburon could prompt him to take Aburon's erection into his mouth.

Fuck, yes. Aburon closed his eyes, basking in the feel of the throat muscles that closed around him, pulling him further in. Tam's tongue felt hot, slick where it pressed against him, massaging the underside of his cock. Aburon clenched his hands in the other man's hair and held on tightly, unable to resist thrusting his hips forward.

"Enough," he gasped, and Tam released him instantly, sitting back on his heels. His eyes were dazed.

Aburon removed the rest of his own clothing hastily, his skin itching now with the desire for copulation. He held himself in check, however, enjoying the urgency that thrummed through him in time with his rapidly beating heart. The sight of Tam's pleasantly bruised mouth, his downcast eyes, was nearly overwhelming him with lust. Tam was completely open now to whatever Aburon wanted to do with him, the shadow of hard-won humility evident in every curve of his trembling form.

Tam rose unsteadily to his feet when Aburon urged him to do so, but still with evidence of that unconscious grace Aburon had noted in him at the start of the evening. It was breathtaking the way this man moved, even when his limbs were trembling from pain exhaustion.

Aburon stepped forward to kiss him, cupping his jaw in one hand to hold him steady as he plunged his tongue deep into his mouth. Tam opened to him readily, making a small noise in the back of his throat when Aburon reached down to fondle the dildo.

"That's it," Aburon said, pulling the dildo out maybe half an inch before pushing it in again. Tam's hips jerked forward against his at the movement, bumping their erections together. Aburon chuckled deeply, and did it again.

"Ah," Tam said, turning his head to one side. His expression looked pained, although Aburon was reasonably certain it wasn't pain he was feeling right now.

"Does that feel good?" Aburon whispered, bending down to nuzzle the hair above his ear. He continued to play with the dildo, moving it in small in-and-out motions that kept Tam's hips moving. He settled his other hand firmly at the small of Tam's back, holding him in place. His thumb brushed the edge of one of the welts there.

Tam's hands moved aimlessly for a moment before closing around Aburon's upper arms, squeezing tightly. "Please," he breathed, bending his head forward against Aburon's chest.

That was exactly the kind of surrender Aburon had been waiting for. He pulled the dildo out in one long slide that left Tam gasping and tossed it aside onto the towel he'd thrown over the end table next to the bed. Reaching down, he replaced it with two of his fingers, pushing them in up to the knuckles as he bent to ravage Tam's mouth with a kiss.

"Get on the bed," he said, and Tam obeyed him instantly, arranging himself face-down over the coverlet and lifting up slightly onto his knees. Aburon climbed up onto the bed beside him and, after a moment's contemplation, rolled the other man over so that his tortured back pressed against the sheets.

The expression on Tam's face was desperate as he stared up at him, his eyes wide. Clearly, the position was painful for him, but it didn't diminish the erection that was framed prominently between his spread thighs.

"You're beautiful." Aburon bent down to trail a kiss across his collarbone, taking Tam's erection in hand and stroking it a couple of times to encourage it to remain attentive. He smoothed his hands along the insides of Tam's thighs, easing them open and lifting them off the mattress. He reached for Tam's hands and coaxed them to grasp ahold of the undersides of the thighs where Aburon had just held him, gripping firmly to hold his knees up against his chest.

So nice, seeing a recently whipped slave holding himself open and offering his body up so willingly in this way. Aburon drank in the sight of him, his eyes lingering on the hard cock briefly before moving to the shadowed crevice further down. The puckered opening there twitched slightly as if it were aware of the scrutiny, shimmering with a faint sheen of lube.

Aburon shuddered deeply and decided that anticipation was all well and good, but enough was enough. Leaning his weight forward onto one arm next to Tam's shoulder, he steadied his erection with one hand and moved into position.

He watched Tam's face closely when he eased inside of him, enjoying the flickers of emotion he saw there. Pain, as the movement jarred the injuries on his back. Physical effort, as he strained against the superior weight pressing down on top of his own. Concentration, as he tried his best to bend into the position that Aburon required of him. And heartfelt relief, because despite his initial resistance, his body was well-trained and wanted desperately to be filled.

There was something raw about the rhythm of sex that Aburon never tired of. No matter how many times he did it, no matter how many different partners he shared the act with, there was something new and fresh about it each and every time. It was more than just a riot of sensations hissing underneath his skin, more than just bodies moving together. It was a kind of sharing, a connection, that he couldn't experience with another human being in any other way. Even when it was with whores like this one, it was a transcendent experience each and every time.

Tam's body was bent nearly double underneath him, his face screwed up in an expression that wasn't quite pleasure and wasn't quite pain, but was probably a bit of both. Aburon was firmly of the belief that masochism could be taught, with the right motivation. Taking pleasure in one's own suffering, one's own degradation; that was what he liked to see in the slaves he played with, no matter what other qualities they might possess.

It was what made Vincent stand out among the others, because he had never needed to be taught. Vincent craved pain the way he craved air to breathe, and had intensely committed and unfeigned devotion for the one who was able to give it to him. Being the focus of that kind of worship was heady, addicting, as Aburon could well attest. Yet there was something charming about this kind of joining, too, with one he had to work at bending to his will.

His climax seemed to burn at the base of his spine before it hit him, gaining in intensity as he drove faster and harder into the willing body beneath him. Tam made a strangled sound as Aburon leaned over him without bothering to rein in his strength. This Companion was a flexible one, more so than many of the others, and Aburon had no intention of taking it easy on him now.

Aburon groaned deep in his chest when he came, closing his eyes against the explosion of sensation that rocked through him. He gripped Tam's body tightly, his hips jerking as he emptied his passion inside of him. So good.... He bit Tam's shoulder, not gently, and smiled through the shudders that wracked through him when Tam whimpered at the feel of it.

When he opened his eyes again, he saw Tam staring up at him with desperation shining in his eyes, his mouth open and panting. His cheeks were flushed, his hair dampened with sweat where it curled against the sides of his face. It was most definitely a good look on him. And yes, Aburon was well within his rights to leave him hanging in this state, however... he was feeling merciful tonight.

Tam choked back a sob when Aburon's hand closed around his erection, engulfing it completely. His fingers curled against the mattress to either side of him, his back arching in silent entreaty. Aburon wondered if he had any inkling of how very slutty he looked at that moment, and supposed he probably did. But they were past the point where pride had any meaning in what went on between them. The time for shame would come later, after their bodies' passions had been appeased and they had the opportunity to catch their breath, when Tam finally had a chance to start distancing himself again and taking stock of what had happened to him.

Aburon was looking forward to it.

But for now he concentrated on stroking the thick flesh in his hand, taking in every twitch and sigh Tam made as his body was expertly aroused. Tam's eyes squeezed tightly shut, a thin whine escaping him as Aburon stroked him faster, bringing him closer to the climax he was so desperately reaching for.

He stopped right before the end of it, earning a strangled cry that brought Tam's body arching up off of the bed. Tam's eyes slitted open, and *there* was that light of defiance again, a deeply burning resentment that demanded to know just what the hell he thought he was doing. Aburon grinned, deeply enjoying himself. He was half-tempted to leave him like this for the rest of the night, just to see more of those lovely expressions cross his face—and to have more to punish him for—but this being their first time together, he really did want to find out what this man looked like when he came.

Aburon bent down to touch his lips to Tam's ear, tonguing lightly at the earring there. "Who do you belong to tonight?" he whispered, squeezing the base of the other man's cock tightly.

Tam made a strangled sound, almost a growl, that sounded more bestial than human. He muttered something that Aburon couldn't quite hear but that was probably less than complimentary.

Aburon's grin broadened. He tightened his grip even more, feeling gratified when the answering yelp Tam made had more than a fair bit of pain in it. "Who?" he prompted, giving the flesh in his hand a long, slow stroke that he knew would be more aggravating than pleasurable in Tam's current condition. He closed his teeth over the lobe of Tam's ear, biting down firmly.

Tam hissed at him, anger evident in the sound of it, but in the end need won out over pride and he said, "*You*, all right? You."

Which wasn't anywhere near the heartfelt declaration Aburon would have preferred, but for a first time together it would have to do. He shifted to cover Tam's mouth with his own, stroking deep with his tongue as he moved his fist fast over the slickened cock in his hand, bringing Tam to a swift and shattering climax.

The relieved cry Tam made echoed in the air of the room long after he was done. Aburon propped his weight on one elbow and looked down at him, still stroking the other man's cock absently as the shudders that moved through him lessened and eventually died out altogether. Closing his eyes, Tam sighed and half-rolled onto his side away from him. The sheets underneath him were stained red with spots of blood from the scores on his back.

Aburon let him catch his breath for a few moments before reaching for him again.

"We're going to go into the shower now," he said once he was sure he had Tam's attention, "and you're going to show me just how good you are at getting the both of us clean. Then we are going to return to this room, and we are going to work on this persistent willfulness of yours."

Disbelief shone in Tam's eyes, shimmering through the sheen of his tears. Had he honestly believed his service tonight would be ended once they'd had sex together just the once? Aburon wasn't a master who could be appeased by anything quite so simple, as Tam would quickly learn.

Aburon smiled slightly, feeling a touch of pity for him. Cupping a hand underneath Tam's chin, he forced the other man to look at him when he would have turned away. "You didn't think we were done, did you? I paid for your services for the entire night, and there's still a lot we can do before morning." Once again, it was uncanny just how well Marque had been able to read him. Had he known that with Aburon's favorite currently unavailable, he would be craving the challenge of breaking in a new slave? Had he known that this particular Companion's surface compliance but core of pride would be just the combination to enflame and intrigue him?

Honest fear shone in Tam's eyes, but that was a part of it, too. There was always fear in the beginning, before the slave learned how rewarding true submission could be. Not submission of the body alone, but of the mind, the heart, and finally the soul. Aburon didn't fool himself into thinking they'd reach anything near that level of communion during this first night together, but he was willing to take it as far as he could.

Rolling up and off of the bed with a satisfied air, he strode toward the bathroom, trusting that Tam would follow.

Chapter 11
Reiji

The door to Charon's office was closed when Reiji walked up to it, which was a rare enough occurrence to draw note. Curious, he pressed his ear against it, hearing a low murmuring of voices coming from inside. The door, regrettably, was too thick for him to make out any of the words.

He flinched back when the door opened unexpectedly. Taking several quick steps backwards, he tried to look like he hadn't just been eavesdropping as Charon appeared in the doorway, ushering out a nervous-looking blond boy ahead of him. Reiji's eyes narrowed, focusing on the unfamiliar face. The boy looked maybe fifteen, fine-boned and slender, with clear blue eyes and a kind of anxious air that reminded Reiji of a mouse.

"Working rooms are on the first and second floors, employee quarters are on the upper floor, and the kitchen is on the lower level, toward the back of the stairs." Charon's hand settled onto the kid's shoulder, squeezing firmly in reassurance. "If you're ready, Keiss will show you around."

"Um, sure." The boy's gaze flickered toward Reiji and quickly moved away.

"This way, sport." Keiss was one of the senior working boys, tall and lanky with elbow-length brown hair styled in intricate braids around a long face. His affable, easy-going nature made him a popular choice to introduce new employees to the estate. He grunted as he lifted the kid's backpack up onto his shoulder. "This all you brought with you?"

"Uh, yeah. That's all I have."

"No problem. Let's head upstairs and get you settled in your room, then we'll take the grand tour. The tower's off-limits without special permission, but other than that, you pretty much have the run of the place...." He was still chattering good-naturedly as he rounded the corner toward the stairs, the blond kid trailing attentively behind.

Charon watched them go with a kind of distant satisfaction. When he turned to look at Reiji, his expression was amused. "So you've added spying to your list of hobbies?"

Reiji scowled at him. "I wasn't spying. I was... observing. Covertly."

Charon laughed aloud at that. Shaking his head, he held the door of his office open. "Come inside."

Reiji went into the office and appropriated a corner of the large desk to sit on, arranging his legs cross-legged underneath himself. "Who the hell was that, anyway?"

"A new employee." Charon sat down in the high-backed leather chair behind the desk, leaning back to gaze up at him. "His name's Damien."

"He looks like a fucking virgin."

Charon shrugged. "Virginal types have their appeal to the right kind of customer."

Reiji couldn't dispute the statement. Glancing down at the bowl of hard candies sitting beside him on the desktop, he reached for one and popped it into his mouth. "Have you fucked him yet?"

Charon gave him a censuring look. "Reiji. You know one of the rules here is that I don't discuss personal information about the employees."

Reiji resisted the urge to roll his eyes. "Come on, Charon. It's not a secret that you like to try out new boys when they get hired. That's one of the perks of being the boss, isn't it?"

The line of Charon's mouth tightened slightly. "I'm sorry you feel that way."

The truth was, Reiji knew Charon *did* sample each of the new employees when they first arrived, just to get a feel for them and the kinds of customers they might appeal to. It was all done with a kind of clinical detachment, although he was never anything less than respectful with them. But he never slept with them more than once; that was one of his infamous rules, too.

"So." Charon folded his hands together and assumed an attentive expression. "What can I do for you today?"

There was something in the businesslike tone of the words that Reiji found irritating. "Ever since Nat left, I haven't had anyone decent to spar with," he said with a scowl. "I was hoping you might think about hiring someone with some kind of fighting experience."

"You want me to hire you a personal trainer?"

"If that's what it takes." It wasn't like the House didn't have the money for it.

Charon regarded him consideringly. "Surely one of the bouncers...?"

Reiji frowned. Bouncers were full-time security guards who patrolled the estate during working hours, whose job it was to look after the boys and make sure the customers were behaving themselves. While Charon was always meticulous about screening clients before entering into a contract with them, there was always the chance that you could end up tied and gagged by the wrong kind of customer, unable to call for help, and find yourself in hell.

But those were the risks you assumed when you were in this kind of business, or so Reiji believed. They were none of them going to live long lives, anyway, most likely.

"No offense, Charon, but most of them couldn't fight their way out of a wet paper bag."

Charon's mouth curled slightly. "You might be surprised."

Reiji didn't feel like arguing the matter. "So I take it this means no sparring partner?"

"I'll see what I can do."

Whatever that meant. Cupping his hands over the edge of the desk, he hopped down and headed toward the door. "Let me know what you decide," he said curtly, without looking back.

Seriously, dealing with that man was more trouble than it was worth sometimes.

The Den was a luxuriously furnished communal area toward the middle of the west wing where many of the House's customers liked to spend the early parts of their evenings. Reiji looked around when he entered, the hard bass rhythm of the music from the corner speakers vibrating in the backs of his teeth. The room was dimly lit, arranged in numerous intimate niches formed by long couches and tables where the customers could lounge in varying degrees of formality to partake of the House's more carnal pleasures.

There was a boy kneeling naked on the floor at the feet of his current night's master, collared and leashed, while another with hair dyed a lustrous sapphire blue gave head to a customer in the corner. Other boys moved around the room offering various services, mostly of the oral variety, while their customers laughed and drank and generally enjoyed the festive atmosphere at their playthings' expense.

A boy in the back corner of the room caught Reiji's eye, pressed face-first against the wall while one of his clients thrust into him forcefully from behind, groping him lustily in a kind of drunken slump. The boy's wrists were being held against the wall at either side by the man's companions, who looked on with shining eyes, no doubt impatiently waiting their turn to try out this particular amusement park ride. The boy caught Reiji's eye as Reiji passed by and curled the corner of his mouth upward, rolling his eyes toward the ceiling in a long-suffering kind of way. Reiji snorted and moved on.

A pair of boys who looked enough alike to be brothers were stretched out naked together on a long table toward the center of the room, kissing and fondling each other while the group of men seated around the table laughed coarsely and looked on with openly leering expressions. While Reiji watched, one of the men held out his glass of champagne and poured it over the two boys, then leaned down to lick the spilled drink up off of their skin. Both boys continued with their enthusiastic rutting without giving any indication that they'd noticed.

Further into the room, a smooth-skinned boy who looked young enough to be actively illegal was curled up in the lap of an older customer, eating the grapes the man fed him with a small, private smile and nuzzling his gratitude against the man's chin. Another boy with sensual eyes sat wrapped around his customer from behind, one hand sliding under the open buttons of the man's shirt while another moved down to open the front of the man's trousers and slipped inside. The client bit his lip in obvious enjoyment and tipped his head back over the boy's shoulder, his eyes closing.

While the faces changed each night, it was all business as usual to Reiji. He moved forward, feeling the weight of the gazes that had moved shark-like to focus on him as soon as he'd stepped into the room. That, too, was what he had come to expect. He knew he had a dramatic appearance, lean and wiry, with his dark red hair and deceptively fey-like features. Tonight he was dressed in a sleeveless black mesh shirt that stopped just above his navel, where a gold ring winked provocatively in the dim light. His pants were tight and rode low enough on his hips to show the sharp jut of his hipbones, outlining the toned muscles of his ass and thighs.

Ignoring the rapt gazes that followed him, he moved onto the dance floor. The music was louder here, with a hard-edged urgency that caught pleasantly in his chest, making his heartbeat quicken. There was something exhilarating about the press of bodies around him, writhing together frantic and sweaty. He'd always been fond of the club scene before he'd come to work here.

Closing his eyes and breathing in deeply, he began to dance. Even without looking, he knew everyone's eyes were on him. He moved easily to the music, sliding a hand up underneath the front of his shirt to pet at the skin of his stomach. He grinned when he felt a body step up behind him, hands pulling his hips back suggestively as they moved together. Another body appeared in front of him, grinding against him, a leg sliding between his. Reiji wrapped his arms around narrow shoulders, tipping his head back as a tongue licked the side of his neck.

He could have any or all of these bastards if he wanted them; it occurred to him rather suddenly that he was bored as hell with the whole sordid thing. It was all the same thing night after night, and how long had it been since there was a point to any of it? He knew what all of these men wanted from him and couldn't help feeling contemptuous about it; sex had been a job to him for so long now, he'd forgotten what it was like to do it just for the fun of it.

He extricated himself from the bodies around him abruptly and left the dance floor, ignoring the grasping hands that tried to get him to stay. Glowering, he snatched a glass of champagne from the tray of a passing waiter and drank deeply from it.

His eyes fell on a young man sitting at a corner table, who was chatting amiably with his friends and sipping at a glass of wine. The man's suit was slightly rumpled, but his hair was neatly styled and his face was handsome, almost angelic when it smiled. Not bad at all. If Reiji had to choose a client to put out for tonight, he could certainly do worse than that one.

Having made his choice for the evening, Reiji moved forward to meet him. He had taken only a few steps when he was stopped by a voice from the table next to him. "Reiji *Kendo*? Is that you?"

Eyes narrowing, Reiji turned around. Lounging at the corner of a plushly stuffed armchair was Haruno Eches, a member of Reiji's former street gang. Tall and gangly, he had the same close-cropped brown hair and casually dangerous air that Reiji remembered. He had a leg thrown carelessly over the chair's overstuffed arm, the fingers of one hand twined tight in the hair of the whore currently bent over his groin.

"Gods, how many years has it been?" Haruno straightened, his eyes focusing incredulously on Reiji's face.

"Not enough," Reiji said sourly.

He had abandoned his gang several years before and was still firmly convinced that doing so had saved his life. Not that there hadn't been a kind of rugged appeal to the life he'd shared with them — living by their own rules, defending their territory, and making damn sure that absolutely no one dared to fuck with them. Of course the flip side of that was the absolute poverty they'd lived in, bothersome entanglements with law enforcement officers of varying levels of corruption, and near-constant battles with rival gangs that left them beaten, scarred, and oftentimes dead.

Still, they'd been the only family Reiji had ever known at the time. He never knew who his father was, and his mother was a common street whore who had better things to do with her time than bother with the child she'd given birth to. He'd been raised primarily by one of the charity-funded orphanages before he was old enough to set out on his own. Reiji had learned from an early age that the world was a cold and vicious place that would chew him up if he let his guard down for so much as a second.

"You haven't changed at all." Haruno's eyes glinted with amusement. He shoved the whore off his lap and stood up to face Reiji directly, absently pulling up the zipper of his pants. "Still such a cold bastard, aren't you?"

Reiji glared at him. "What the fuck do you want?" He couldn't begin to guess how Haruno had been able to afford to come in here; he must have fallen into some serious money during one of his various criminal enterprises.

"Ouch." Haruno winced, although there was still that godawful glint of amusement in his eyes. "Is that any way to talk to a paying customer?"

"Fuck off," Reiji said, enunciating each word distinctly. He was in no mood to deal with this kind of shit tonight. While the thought of selling his body to various nameless strangers had never bothered him unduly, he was not prepared to yield to this man in any way, shape, or form. Haruno was a bottom-feeding asshole of a user and always would be. Despite appearances to the contrary, Reiji did have his pride.

The amusement in Haruno's eyes took on a dangerous edge. "I thought you must have been lying dead at the side of the road somewhere. Someone with an attitude the size of yours doesn't last long, you know? But who would have fucking thought you would've found your way into this place. You really work here?" He grinned, clearly tickled by the idea.

Reiji glanced away, his jaw clenching. "If you'll excuse me, I'm supposed to be working."

Haruno whistled low through his teeth. "Wow, they've certainly got you whipped. I'd like to meet the guy who managed to tame you. He must be one awesome son of a bitch."

Reiji reminded himself that Charon wouldn't be very happy with him if he broke a guest's jaw, no matter how much the bastard deserved it. "Maybe I'll introduce you someday. But I really do have to go now."

He had half-turned toward his previously selected conquest when a hand around his elbow brought him up short.

"What's the hurry?" Haruno said, his voice low.

Reiji shook off the hand without stopping to think about it. "Don't touch me again."

The light in Haruno's eyes turned positively wicked. "Why not? You're a whore, aren't you? And I'm a guest of this exceptionally fine establishment. That means if I asked you to bend over for me, you'd have to do it. Right?"

Reiji glared at him, a dull roaring starting up in his ears. Haruno never had liked him very much; he'd been too smart, too quick, and far too skilled at street fighting for Haruno to feel at all comfortable around him. Haruno was the type who liked to find someone bigger and stronger than he was to hide behind, and Reiji had never been interested in playing those kinds of games. In Reiji's world, you either stood up for yourself or you got out of the way.

"Wrong," he said, leaning in close to Haruno and dropping his voice so the word only carried between the two of them. "Because no matter who you stole from to get into this place, you're still an insignificant, small-time thug who wouldn't know good taste if it came up and bit you on the ass. You're a nobody, Haruno, and you always will be."

He could tell by the tightening of the skin between Haruno's eyes that he'd scored a hit. Feeling vaguely triumphant, he started to turn away.

"Fucker," Haruno spat, and swung a fist at him.

Reiji reacted reflexively, dodging the blow and catching Haruno's wrist in his hand. In a sudden moment of clarity, he knew full well that he could diffuse the situation and walk away if he chose to, leaving Haruno behind to nurse his wounded pride in peace.

That didn't seem like a very attractive solution, as he thought about it.

Chapter 12
A Clash of Wills

Pulling hard on Haruno's arm to unbalance him, Reiji punched him. Haruno moved instantly to defend himself, but he was untrained and off-center, and Reiji had been spoiling for a fight for days now.

Reiji had trained in a variety of martial arts styles since he was a kid, begging for lessons wherever and whenever he could. He'd offered everything he could in trade for it—money, booze, drugs, his body, whatever he had at his disposal—and had found a number of very capable teachers over the years. Even now that he was gainfully employed and it wasn't so much a life-or-death matter to be able to defend himself, he still kept up with it because it had become a habit, one that was as much a part of him as his preference for hard rock music.

Haruno might be a world-class loser, but he was a scrappy little punk. There was a loud crash as the table behind them bumped and skidded against the wall, sending the glasses on top of it flying. The sound of shattering glass filled Reiji's ears as he dodged a knee aimed at his groin and grabbed a fistful of Haruno's hair, cuffing him once across the face and sweeping a leg behind his ankle to send him pitching to the ground.

He was just pausing to catch his breath when he felt a hard hand clamp onto his shoulder, squeezing tightly. Glancing up indignantly, he found himself looking into the face of one of Charon's bouncers. Reiji vaguely recalled that his name was Jeremy, but that was all he knew about him. Like all of the other bouncers, he was stylishly dressed in an elegant dark suit, his broad shoulders stretching the expensive fabric as he bent down to help Haruno to his feet.

"Excuse me," Jeremy said, in a voice that was impeccably courteous. "You seem to be disturbing the other guests."

His expression was mild, although the grip he kept tight on Reiji's shoulder had a weight of authority to it. Reiji shrugged it off angrily.

Haruno's eyes were furious. "Did you see what this asshole of a whore did to me?" He swiped at the corner of his mouth with the back of one hand; the skin came away dotted with blood.

"Yes. I saw everything that happened. If you'll come with me, please?" Again, his tone was faultlessly deferential. He dipped his head in polite apology, although the look in his eyes when he glanced at Reiji said clearly that it wasn't a request.

Well, hell. Glowering, Reiji took off in the direction of Charon's office, not needing to be told where to go. He felt like a damn school kid being called in to the principal's office. Once there, he pushed the door open without bothering to knock and went to stand against the wall, crossing his arms over his chest.

Charon looked up from his desk with wary curiosity as the rest of them entered. "Hello, Reiji," he said.

Reiji glared and didn't say anything.

Succinctly, Jeremy explained that there had been an altercation, describing the events that had occurred in brief yet surprisingly precise detail. Charon remained silent throughout the entire recital, his eyes moving from Reiji to the silently fuming Haruno and back again.

"I see," he said once Jeremy was done. He steepled his hands in front of his face and considered the matter in silence for a moment. "Who threw the first punch?" he asked at last.

Jeremy indicated Haruno, causing Reiji to cast him a triumphant glare.

"Now wait just a—" Haruno spluttered, clearly incensed, but a glance from Charon silenced him.

Charon stood up from his desk and walked around the front of it where he could face them more directly. "Mr. Eches, I trust you realize that the services you paid for this evening did not include assaulting one of my employees or damaging my property. You are clearly in violation of the contract you signed."

Haruno's eyes widened. "But—"

"You will be billed for the cost of the damages to the room," Charon said coldly, cutting him off, "in addition to any medical care my employee might need due to your assault on his person. In addition to that, you will not be welcome inside this House again until it is made clear to me that you have better control over yourself. Is that understood?"

Obviously, Haruno's backbone was only capable of carrying him so far. Dropping his gaze to glare at the floor, he nodded, face flaming.

Reiji chortled inwardly, feeling more than pleased at the way the situation had been resolved. He was just beginning to relax again when Charon turned to him.

"And you, Reiji." The disappointment in his voice was a thousand times worse than any trace of anger would have been. "You should know better than to fight with a guest while you're on duty. You can't tell me that you didn't have the opportunity to walk away before the situation progressed to that point."

Something ugly coiled in Reiji's chest. He held Charon's gaze with an effort, unable to refute the statement.

Charon's mouth turned down at the corners. "I want you to go to Mr. Eches and pleasure him before he leaves. With your mouth or your body; it's your choice."

Reiji stared at him, his throat constricting. "Charon—"

"Don't test me in this, Reiji." And *now* there was anger in his voice, cold and brittle. The look in his eyes said clearly that he would not accept any rebellion.

Feeling numb, Reiji turned to look at Haruno. Haruno's eyes were wide, full of surprise but with a dawning pleasure that made Reiji's stomach tighten. Fists clenching tightly at his sides, Reiji walked stiffly toward him.

He deliberately didn't think of anything at all as he lowered himself to his knees. Humiliation made his skin feel hot and prickly, but that was really nothing new, now was it? Plenty of guests enjoyed playing humiliation games, and for those who were willing to pay for it, he was more than happy to play along.

But this wasn't about payment; this was because he'd fucked up, and he damn well knew it. He closed his eyes as he opened the front of Haruno's pants, trying to ignore the knowledge of Charon watching with attentive interest, of Jeremy standing with detached curiosity at the other side of the room. This was punishment, pure and simple. Putting the upstart whore back in his place.

He'd never tasted Haruno's cock before, and gods willing, he'd never have to do it again. Haruno's thighs quivered as Reiji took him into his mouth, sucking hard to try to bring him to the edge as quickly as possible. After a few moments, fingers wound their way into Reiji's hair and held on tightly. He had to resist the urge to bite down at the feel of it, reminding himself that his boss was watching.

Haruno was ridiculously easy to please. After only a couple of minutes, his grip on Reiji's hair tightened so strongly it brought tears to his eyes, and his hips thrust forward sharply as he came. Reiji swallowed with ease and then rocked back onto his heels, wiping at his mouth with the back of his hand. He glared up at Haruno with bitter eyes, daring him to say anything.

"I think," Charon said softly, "that ends our contract with you. Jeremy will show you the way out now."

Reiji stared hard at the floor as Haruno moved to follow Jeremy out of the room. He remained on his knees even after the sound of their footsteps had faded away down the hall.

The feel of a hand on his head made him tense up slightly. The hand, after a moment's hesitation, moved down to stroke the back of his neck.

"You did good, Reiji."

"Yeah. Whatever." He stood up without looking Charon in the eyes and walked out of the room.

He didn't know if he was relieved or disappointed when Charon didn't call him back.

One of Reiji's favorite places to hide out was on the railing at the corner of the second floor balcony. It was situated in the shadow of an overhanging archway and was hidden from the view of just about every other point on the floor, but still provided a near-unobstructed view of the entire lobby below.

He seriously felt like going out and beating the crap out of someone, but the only one he saw was Vincent Michaelis, wandering down the stairs in the direction of the kitchen for breakfast. Taking his anger out on Vincent wasn't any fun because he didn't react to physical abuse the way a normal person would; he actually seemed to *like* it when people beat up on him.

Gods, they were a fucked up bunch of bastards in this place. Every fucking one of them.

Pulling his knees up to his chest, Reiji hunched his shoulders against the curve of the wall and glowered. He wasn't sure how long he sat there before a shadow flickered at the corner of his vision, resolving into a familiar sandy-haired shape.

"Morning," Tam greeted.

"Go to hell," Reiji said, without any heat. He didn't move his gaze away from the lobby below.

Tam leaned one shoulder against the wall beside him. "I hear you caused quite a stir in the Den last night."

"What the fuck ever. That bastard started it; I was only defending myself." He turned to meet Tam's eyes, saw nothing but open curiosity there, and felt his defensiveness fade slightly. "And Charon completely fucked me over because of it. Made me blow the asshole right there in his office." He scrubbed at the back of his head with one hand, glowering. "Fucking pissant didn't deserve to be here, anyway."

Tam considered for a moment. "Did you ever realize that your language takes a significant turn for the worse when you're pissed off?"

The comment startled a laugh out of him. Shaking his head, he turned back to look down at the lobby. "I don't know why I hang around this place, anyway."

"Hmm." Tam didn't say anything else for a while. Then, "You do know that there's probably one person in the entire world you would have humiliated yourself like that for?"

Reiji continued to stare straight ahead. It was true; if anyone else had told him to blow Haruno Eches of all people, he would have told them in precise detail what they could go do with themselves. But it had been Charon who asked him, and for whatever fucked up reason he had, it was important to him not to disappoint that man.

The memory rose up in his mind's eye of himself at a much younger age, scrawny and bedraggled, all elbows and knees and fierce, violent personality. It had been raining on that night; he hadn't eaten for days, and his temper was shorter than usual because of it. He'd spotted Charon from a distance and followed him, his attention snagged by the expensive long coat and sharp suit that suggested this was a man with a great deal of money. Long coats tended to have deep pockets, which could sometimes be picked if he was particularly quick and particularly lucky.

He hadn't been particularly quick or lucky that night. Charon had caught him with insulting ease in the act of attempting to steal from him; only instead of turning him in to the cops, he'd brought him into a local diner and bought him dinner instead. Reiji had been mistrustful of him at first, but hunger was a powerful motivator and he'd eventually caved in and allowed himself to be fed. From there it was a simple slide into engaging in an actual conversation, as Charon talked to him about things like comfort and security and the near-impossible promise of three square meals a day.

In the end, it hadn't been the promise of food that had convinced Reiji to go with him. It was the fact that Charon had been kind to him, had treated him like an equal. There had been something in that strong, handsome face that Reiji felt irresistibly drawn to. Sincerity, perhaps. Honesty. No matter what else Charon Marque was, he was a man who cared deeply about his chosen profession and the responsibilities that came with it.

"You know," he said, without looking in Tam's direction, "when you're poor, it's like the entire world's your enemy. You don't have anything, and you don't have anyone, except for what you can fight for and manage somehow to hold on to. And then when someone comes in and says he can take you away from all that, and offers you the keys to a world you never even knew existed...."

"Yeah," Tam said, sounding as if he honestly understood. And then, apropos of nothing, "It's a shame he refuses to sleep with his employees more than once, isn't it?"

Reiji turned to glance at him, his eyes narrowing. "What the hell is that supposed to mean?"

Tam smiled slightly. "Nothing." He peeled himself away from the wall and stretched, light glinting on the earring at his ear. "I'm going to head downstairs for breakfast. You coming?"

"No. I'm gonna stay here for a while longer."

"Suit yourself." Whistling tunelessly to himself, Tam started in the direction of the stairs.

Reiji watched him go, feeling hollow inside. He wondered again why he put up with all of this, and just what it would take to push him over the edge completely. But they were all in this together, whatever "this" was, and wherever it was going to take them, they were taking the journey together. There was a kind of comfort in that, however twisted.

"Fucking idiots, every one of us," he said with a scowl, and settled back to watch the day come in.

Chapter 13
Brand

Brand Chamberlain stood in the circular driveway in front of the House of Silence, looking up at the gothic façade of the estate with a frown.

Whoever the architects had been, they'd been fond of elaborate archways and intimidating sweeps of carved grey stone. There was something haunting about the building, almost menacing, but in its way it was darkly beautiful as well. The myriad windows were dark this late in the morning, most of them with the curtains drawn. This was a place that enjoyed its privacy, apparently.

Not that that was surprising, given the nature of the business that went on there. Tearing his attention away from the physical structure, he moved toward the stairs leading up to the broad front doors. A doorman in a sharp black suit stood sentry on the portico, wrapped snugly in a long coat with pristine white gloves to ward away the morning chill. Doubtlessly, he was there to see off any stragglers among the House's clientele from the previous evening.

"I don't have an appointment," Brand said, putting a note of authority in his voice. "But I'm here to see—"

"Of course, sir," the doorman said, bowing slightly. "The owner should be in his office."

The easy invitation left Brand feeling a bit off-center. He'd expected it to be far more difficult to gain entry into the place. The doorman pulled open the door with a welcoming gesture, his face a mask of practiced courtesy that completely hid whatever he might really be thinking. After a moment's hesitation, Brand went inside.

The lobby was as grandly appointed as he would have guessed

from seeing the outside of the building. The twin staircases sweeping toward the upper floors were elegant and streamlined, designed to draw the eye. The chandelier hanging from the ceiling two stories above was impressively huge; the light that filtered through its gem-cut crystal contours was diffused, casting little prisms of color over the marbled floor below.

"Excuse me," he said, stopping a casually dressed young man in passing. "I'm looking for the owner's office." He regarded the kid narrowly, wondering if this was one of the prostitutes the House employed. The thought made him uncomfortable; the boy looked awfully young to be in this line of work. But then youth was probably a selling point to a lot of the customers in this place.

The kid gave him a wary look. "Down that hallway, on your right," he said, pointing.

"Thank you." The wariness in the kid's gaze didn't lessen, despite Brand's careful attempts at courtesy. The thought made him sigh; while he'd foregone wearing his uniform this morning, there had to be subtle signs he couldn't hide that he was a law enforcement officer. At the academy, his fellow recruits had teased him for looking too much the part—tall and athletic with long legs designed for running, dark blond hair cut short around a strong-jawed face, and eyes that were an arresting shade of greyish-blue. He'd been told in the past that his eyes could sometimes be intimidating, too intent when he was focused on solving problems that puzzled him. It was something he'd been working on toning down, with limited success if this kid's reaction was anything to go by.

Rubbing a hand ruefully over the back of his neck, he started in the direction the kid had indicated. None of the doors he passed looked as if they opened into anything resembling an office, until he got about halfway down the hall. Then he found himself at his destination, looking into the office of the infamous Charon Marque.

The room was dominated by a large mahogany desk, with deep bookshelves lining most of the walls. The sparse decorations were tasteful but clearly indicative of the wealth their owner enjoyed. This was unmistakably a space devoted to the conduction of business, although a small wet bar in the corner suggested that Marque enjoyed a bit of liquid relaxation on occasion while he was working. Broad windows looked out over the snow-covered hills outside, providing a breathtaking view of the grounds behind the estate.

Marque was seated behind the desk, head bent over the mounds of paperwork in front of him. He looked up when Brand appeared in the doorway of the room, one eyebrow rising in silent inquiry. "Hello," he said, smiling politely. "May I help you?"

There was something striking about Charon Marque that Brand couldn't quite define. He'd noticed hints of it in the man's dossier pictures, but it was even more apparent in person. His hair was dark black with a dusting of grey at the temples, giving his refined features a distinguished appearance that most men of his age didn't achieve. His posture was perfectly straight, but his movements were languid, almost drowsy, with a kind of leisurely gracefulness that suggested he had no great need to hurry in anything he did. On the contrary, his expression was sharp and attentive, giving Brand the impression that he was the sole focus of the man's attention from the moment he'd walked into the room. It was a bit unnerving, to be honest.

"My name is Brand Chamberlain," Brand said, holding up the wallet containing his badge and I.D. briefly. "I'm an officer with the Aechestanian Metropolitan Police."

Marque looked intrigued. "Is there some kind of problem?"

"No, no problem." At least not the way Marque was insinuating. "I just recently transferred in from Maru Sands, and I'm trying to get a feel for the area. I've been visiting each of the local businesses to introduce myself." Which wasn't precisely true, but it was reason enough to explain his presence here.

Brand had been on the police force for just over a year now, and while his superiors often chastised him for being too earnest about fulfilling his duties, he wasn't the type of person who could let a perceived injustice slide. Unlike many of his peers, he took it on himself to actively find criminal incidents to address, instead of just going through the motions of law enforcement.

Maru Sands was a relatively small town in which not much happened on a day to day basis, but Aechestan was turning out to have all of the intrigue and excitement he could desire. One of the city's most prominent features was its proximity to the notorious House of Silence. Brand had heard about the brothel in the past, of course, but never paid the thought of it any particular mind. Now that he was working so close, he couldn't resist the urge to do a little digging and find out what he could about it. In his experience, even small-time brothels generally tended to be nothing but trouble for law enforcement.

The problem was, he couldn't find any evidence that Charon Marque had existed more than thirteen years ago. The man had appeared virtually out of nowhere with the deeds to this property in hand, where he immediately set about starting his extremely lucrative business. And that was another thing Brand couldn't fathom; either Marque was a businessman of unheard of acuity, or else someone had paved the way for him. Because no one went from complete obscurity to being arguably one of the most powerful men in the country in as short a time as he had without some kind of guardian angel sitting on his shoulder.

If Marque was at all uncomfortable with the thought of having a police officer inside his establishment, it didn't show. "That's very diligent of you, Officer," he said, leaning back in his chair to fix Brand with an inquisitive look. "I commend your devotion to your duty. However, I'm sure you realize we're in the jurisdiction of the provincial government here, and not the municipal police department."

"Yes, I'm aware of that." Intriguing that Marque would point that out so boldly. "However, the border of Aechestan is only a handful of miles from here. It's entirely possible that officers from the city will be the ones to respond if you're ever in a situation where you need assistance."

Marque's eyes crinkled slightly at the edges. "I thank you for the thought, but I can't imagine any circumstance in which I would need to call for police assistance. I employ my own security force here, which has always been sufficient for our needs."

Yes, Brand had come across that bit of information during his research before coming here. He didn't understand why it didn't make more people nervous to know that Marque was sitting out here on the country's border with what basically amounted to his own private army. Yet another mystery surrounding the enigmatic House of Silence.

"I'm going to be honest with you, Mr. Marque. I've never heard of a brothel that wasn't a front for some kind of illegal operation. Drugs. Smuggling. Robbery. You get the idea."

Marque didn't look offended by the insinuation. "I assure you, Officer Chamberlain, we have no need to stoop so low as to rob our guests. And I do not allow any of my employees to use illegal drugs of any kind. It may not seem like it to an outside observer, but this is a very demanding business in which one must always be attentive to the given moment, picking up on subtle cues and adjusting oneself accordingly as the needs of the guest dictate. Any kind of, ah, recreational pharmaceutical would greatly hamper the successful completion of those duties, and that I would not abide."

Brand had never thought there was much of a job description for prostitutes aside from the obvious. His eyes narrowed. "You have a very high opinion of the workers here."

"My boys are professionals, whether you approve of their chosen vocation or not. I don't hire just any riffraff off the street; every single employee in this estate has been hand-picked by me personally."

Interesting. "I never said I didn't approve of what they do here."

"You didn't need to." This time, Marque's smile had a bit of an edge to it. "You're a very moral man, Officer Chamberlain, with a strong sense of ethics. I can see that in you right away. It doesn't sit right with you that these boys are using their bodies to curry favor. That seems dishonest to you."

Brand frowned, disconcerted by the directness of the observation.

"Don't get me wrong." Marque leaned forward, folding his hands on the desk in front of him. "I admire you for your zeal. Such ethical fortitude is sadly lacking in many of the young officers today. However, take care that it does not lead you to see transgressions where there are none. I run a legitimate business. I take care of the boys who work here, and I offer better than fair wages for the services they provide."

"And none of them are underage, I would guess?"

"Hiring underage boys to engage in sexual acts for money would be illegal. I assure you, I have no interest in exploiting minors for profit, or in violating innocence of any kind."

None of which actually answered the question, Brand noted.

"I'll tell you what," Marque said, looking as if he'd come to a decision. "Why don't you feel free to spend the day here in the House? Walk around, talk to whomever you'd like, provided they agree to speak to you. Do whatever it takes to convince yourself that we are not engaged in any kind of illegal activity here." He paused, considering. "That is not, under any circumstances, an invitation to help yourself to any of my boys." He smiled slightly.

Brand's face heated. "You don't have to worry about that, Mr. Marque. I have no interest in engaging in business with you."

"Hmm. You should find this place free of temptation, then." For some reason, he seemed to find the thought amusing. A moment later, he sobered. "Just keep in mind that I do take the welfare of my boys very seriously. If any of them choose not to discuss their pasts with you, I would ask that you respect that."

"Of course. I'm not here to dig up any kind of scandal."

"Good." He looked pleased. "I'm sure we'll all get along fine, then. Would you like me to arrange for a guide to show you around?"

"No, thank you. I'd rather look around on my own, if you don't mind."

"Wonderful. If you need anything, I trust you won't hesitate to let me or a member of my staff know."

Which apparently marked the end of the interview. Brand turned to go, feeling a bit unsettled. Marque was certainly blasÃ© about the fact that his business was under investigation, unofficial or otherwise. Did he really feel he had nothing to hide? Or was he that sure that whatever secrets he was hiding couldn't be uncovered?

Brand hadn't been a police officer for very long, but he thought he had pretty good instincts. And right now, his instincts were telling him that Charon Marque, for all his outward polish and inner poise, was as dirty as they came. He just wasn't sure what exactly the man was involved in. Tensions had been rising lately among the various mercantile cabals that laid claim to this area, but he couldn't see Marque getting involved in anything as sordid as a territorial dispute. And despite what he'd said earlier, Brand couldn't see him indulging in petty theft from his customers, either. Drugs, then? But the primary motivation for engaging in the illegal drug trade was money, and Marque clearly already had all of the money he would ever need.

It was a puzzle, that was for sure. Emerging into the lobby once again, he stopped to look around and get his bearings. It surprised him that he had more or less been given the run of the place, although he was under no illusion that he wasn't under some kind of tacit surveillance. He wondered briefly if he should be nervous about Marque's private security force. But there would be no benefit in accosting a police officer who had nothing but suspicions to go on; the moment he actually found something concrete, then he could start to worry.

The sound of music, faint yet surprisingly beautiful, drew his attention upstairs. A cello, maybe, or a viola? Not having a better destination in mind, he moved toward it.

He found a young man seated in what looked like a fully furnished music room toward the back of the second floor. The extent of the furnishings in the room surprised him; there was a full-sized piano, a harpsichord, various stringed instruments, a six-foot-tall harp inlaid with what might be real pearls, a woodwind collection that would put the concert hall at Stockton to shame, an authentic-looking set of Towanian drums. He wasn't sure why it should surprise him to find such a collection here, but it did.

The man looked up when Brand entered the room, the stringed instrument he held dropping down to his lap. There was no doubt in Brand's mind that this was one of the "boys" Marque had mentioned; he was absolutely beautiful, with long black hair and an exotic look that marked him as Vargessian. His left eye was covered by a black eyepatch, adding to his mysterious appeal.

The corners of the man's mouth turned down in a frown. "Who are you?" The words were curt, but still courteous, as if he didn't appreciate the interruption but weren't quite sure that Brand wasn't one of the House's customers.

So much for being welcomed with open arms by the inhabitants here. Smiling ruefully, he held up his badge and stepped into the room. "Officer Brand Chamberlain, Aechestanian Metropolitan Police. I have permission from the owner to be here today and ask a few questions. What's your name?"

"Vincent."

"And your last name?"

A pause. "Michaelis."

Definitely Vargessian. "How long have you worked here, Vincent?"

"I'm not sure. A couple of years, maybe."

The answer was terse, grudgingly given. Clearly, he did not like being asked personal questions. Brand decided to try a different tack.

Putting his badge away, he sat down in a chair in front of the window. "What kind of instrument is that?"

Vincent glanced down at the instrument in his hands, his fingers tightening around the long neck of it. "A viola."

"Really? You sounded amazing on it earlier. Have you known how to play it for very long?"

"Since I was very young. My sister taught me."

Something in this man's accent made Brand think of the gypsy tribes that wandered Vargess's eastern mountains. He wondered if Vincent was from one of those tribes, and if so, just what the hell he was doing here.

"Something like that takes real dedication, doesn't it?"

Vincent shrugged. "It makes the hours of the day go by."

Brand wondered suddenly what kind of customer this man had spent the previous night with. The thought made the skin of his face prickle. Vincent had to be one of the most purely beautiful men he had ever seen, without seeming feminine at all. That had to be appealing to some men.

He cleared his throat uncomfortably. "Have you known Charon Marque for long?"

"Ever since he hired me."

Just what kind of a job interview did prostitutes go through when they were applying for this kind of position? Brand scratched at the back of his head, turning his mind forcefully away from that line of supposition.

"I see. And would you say he treats you well here? Doesn't take advantage of you in any way?"

This time when Vincent frowned, there was a definite edge to it. "Are you investigating Charon?"

Charon. That told Brand everything he needed to know about Marque's relationship with his employees.

Before he could think of an adequate reply, a new voice intruded from the direction of the hallway. "Who's investigating Charon?"

Brand turned to see a young man with dark red hair saunter into the room, thumbs hooked over the belt of his tight leather pants. His features were comely, disarmingly young, but there was something in the flash of his eyes and the challenging jut of his hips that made Brand sit up a little straighter, unconsciously checking the weight of the handgun strapped at his ankle under his pantsleg.

Vincent sighed visibly. "Reiji. This is Officer Chamberlain. Charon's given him permission to ask us some questions."

"No shit?" Reiji gave Brand an openly curious stare, grabbing the back of a nearby chair and swinging it around so it faced backwards. He folded his arms over the back of it as he sat down. "You're a real cop?"

"I'm a real cop," he confirmed. "Your name's Reiji? What's your last name?"

"What the fuck does it matter to you?"

Brand smiled slightly. "I'm not here to cause trouble for anyone, Reiji. I'm just trying to get some information about how things work here."

"Why? Seems pretty straightforward to me. You pay money, you get to fuck a whore for a night. Isn't that right, Vin?"

Vincent had lifted the viola to his shoulder again and was absently fingering notes. He didn't respond.

"Of course, I don't think you'd be able to afford either one of us on a cop's salary. Unless you were dirty and taking bribes on the side. *Are* you a dirty cop?"

Brand guessed that Reiji had had run-ins with police officers in the past, and wasn't particularly fond of them. "No, I'm afraid not."

"Pity. I would have done you if you were." Sharp flash of a smile.

This, Brand thought, was going to be a challenge he could sink his teeth into.

Chapter 14
A Simple Business Proposition

Brand leaned back and considered the situation. "Have you worked here long, Reiji?"

"Longer than almost anyone else here. Boys tend to not last very long in this kind of business."

"And why is that?"

"Because it's miserable fucking work, that's why. *You* try taking it up the ass every night for six years and see if you don't start feeling a little psychotic from time to time."

Six *years*? Gods, no wonder the kid had such an attitude problem. "You look a little young to have been in this kind of business for that length of time."

"Well, *you* look a little young to be a cop. Vincent, did you check out this guy's credentials? He could be some kind of damned pervert trying to get one in for free."

Brand sighed and took out his badge again. "It's real, I promise you. You're welcome to call the department to verify it."

Reiji leaned forward to peer at the badge. "Nah, I was just fucking with you. I know you're the real thing."

"Really?" He was intrigued. "How can you be so sure?"

"'Cause you never would have made it upstairs otherwise. If you're here, it's because Charon wants you to be." He chuckled dryly. "You look like a dork in your I.D. picture, you know that?"

A chill ran down the back of Brand's neck. *'Cause you never would have made it upstairs otherwise.* He remembered his earlier impression of invisible eyes watching him, tracking his every move.

"Charon runs a pretty tight ship here, doesn't he?" he said.

"You even have to ask that question, you're a lot stupider than you look."

It didn't escape Brand's notice how deftly the conversation had been turned away from the question of whether Reiji had been under-age when he'd started working here. He decided to let it go for now.

"So how many boys are there who work here?"

"Enough to get the job done." Reiji's grin was full of juvenile innuendo.

Brand glanced at Vincent, who met his gaze with a sigh. "I don't know. Twenty, maybe thirty. It varies."

"Wow. That's a lot of mouths to feed. Plus the security guards he employs?"

"Bouncers," Reiji said, scowling slightly. "We call them bouncers."

The scowl drew Brand's notice immediately; he wondered what the history was *there*. "Bouncers, then. What can you tell me about them?"

"Not a lot. They patrol the place, keep an eye on things. Make sure the guests don't get too excited and start breaking the rooms, or the boys, or both."

Egads, what a line of work to be in. "You don't seem to like them very much."

"Is it that obvious?" The light in his eyes sharpened, giving him a feral look that made Brand distinctly nervous. "Bunch of useless bastards. The whole place would be better off without them."

The venom in his voice was different now than the playful mockery from before. Brand wondered just what kind of hell his previous customers had put him through, and why the bouncers hadn't been there to stop it.

"It has to be a difficult job, looking after the safety of thirty boys in a place like this," he said quietly.

Vincent's expression was solemn. "If you're trying to save the world, Officer Chamberlain, you've come to the wrong place."

That seemed an odd sort of comment for him to make. "Are you saying the boys here are beyond saving?"

He seemed to consider the question. "Personally, I don't feel that we're worth saving; but that may just be me. We are whores, after all,

117

as Reiji so delicately described us." He smiled slightly, although the expression seemed more sad than amused. "I suppose it would help if I had some idea what you were hoping to accomplish here."

Brand was beginning to wonder that himself. "I'm just trying to figure out who Charon Marque is, and what the hell he's up to out here."

Reiji snorted. "You figure it out, you let us know, all right? We're just the chess pieces."

And that, Brand realized with a sense of finality, was exactly the reason Marque hadn't had any problem letting him run around loose here today. Any door that could possibly lead him to the answers he sought would be locked, just as anyone with any real knowledge of the secrets Marque was hiding would be far beyond his reach. He could wander through this House forever asking his questions, and no one he was allowed to meet here would ever be able to answer them.

"I'm not going to give up," he said, surprised at the steel he heard in his voice. The look Vincent gave him was vaguely pitying.

Reiji looked thoughtful. "If you're a cop, you must have some kind of fighting experience, right? Hand-to-hand combat, that kind of thing?"

"I suppose so." His eyes drifted over the lean musculature of the other man's arms evaluatingly. Reiji had seen his fair share of hand-to-hand fighting, too, unless he missed his guess.

Honest interest sharpened Reiji's gaze for the first time since Brand had met him. "Wanna spar?" he asked hopefully.

Interesting idea. However.... "Sorry," Brand said, shaking his head. "I get the feeling I'd have my hands forcibly removed if I tried touching any of Charon's property without his permission."

"Coward," Reiji accused. He did not, however, contradict the assertion.

Vincent snorted in amusement. "I have to go," he said, returning his viola carefully to its case. "You two feel free to continue without me."

Brand watched him leave, again feeling struck by the unassuming beauty of him, the unconscious gracefulness of his movements. Beside him, he heard Reiji chuckle.

"He's something else, isn't he?"

Brand glanced at him. "What do you mean?"

Reiji laughed out loud at that. "Come on, I saw you undressing him with your eyes. You want to fuck him."

Heat crawled up Brand's face to hover around his hairline. "I most certainly do n—"

"Well, I'm telling you as a friend to forget it. You could never afford him." The grin he gave was positively wicked. "I, on the other hand...."

Brand was amused despite himself. "You're more within my price range, I take it?"

He sniffed disdainfully. "Hardly. But I, however, am willing to do it as a bribe."

With a smoothness of motion that seemed almost inhuman, he slid off of his chair and onto his knees in front of Brand. He settled one hand on Brand's knee, looking up at him from beneath lashes that seemed ridiculously long for a man his age.

Brand sat up straight so quickly his spine popped. "Reiji," he said warningly.

"Hush." A hand settled over his groin, squeezing tightly. "Everyone does it, you know."

His fingers closed hard around Reiji's wrist, pulling the offending limb away from his body. "*Reiji*. Stop it."

The look in Reiji's eyes was coy. "What's the matter, Officer?" The way he said it, the title felt more like a slap than a courtesy. "You think this'll be the first cop I've gone down on my knees in front of? I know you puffed-up macho types are all alike. You want a little something in trade before you'll let us carry on with business."

Brand felt nauseous at the thought of officers on the street confronting kids with these kinds of 'business transactions'. "Reiji, no. I don't know what kinds of cops you've dealt with in the past, but I'm not like them."

Reiji's eyes narrowed to slits. "Bullshit. You were hard when I touched you."

Brand swallowed forcefully. "I don't—"

"Or is giving you head not good enough? You want I should bend over for you? That's a little extreme for just a bribe, but I guess I can do it since Charon sent you up here. Or do you want more? You want to hit me?" Cruel glee shone in his eyes, making Brand feel ill. "Is that what turns you on? You've certainly got a tight enough grip on my arm."

Brand released his hold on Reiji's wrist as if it had burned him. He was disgusted to see finger-shaped red marks on the pale skin there. "*Gods*, no. Will you fucking *stop* it already?" The words were more pleading than angry.

"Or maybe you're the type who likes to watch?" Reiji wet his lips and dropped a hand to his lap, tracing a line up the inside of his thigh to his groin. He rubbed his palm against the tautly stretched leather there briefly before shifting position and dipping his fingers underneath the waistband of his pants. "I can do that, too, you know. Jerk myself off while you watch, and you won't ever have to dirty yourself by touching me."

A dull roaring started up in Brand's ears, making it difficult to breathe, to think. In front of him, Reiji's body language had shifted from aggressive and confrontational to seductively lascivious, all in a matter of moments. It occurred to him rather suddenly that he was facing a man who made quite a comfortable living doing exactly this kind of thing—preying on men's weakness and offering his body as compensation for whatever gifts of money or services he was being offered in return. A whore, to use Reiji's vernacular, and quite a talented one at that.

"This isn't going to work," Brand said, trying to inject a note of authority into his voice. His heart was pounding. "So you might as well stop trying."

Reiji ignored him and rose smoothly to his feet, shoving his fingers further down the front of his pants. His knuckles strained the fabric there as he took himself in hand. "Mmm," he said, leaning his weight back onto one leg so that his hips jutted forward. The tip of his tongue darted out to moisten his lower lip. "There's nothing like a good hand job first thing in the morning, is there?"

Brand's eyes rose to follow him involuntarily, his hands closing into fists on top of his thighs. He met the other man's challenging gaze with a glare of his own, a dull heat creeping up the sides of his face. Obviously, Marque had put Reiji up to this. Either that, or he was working alone to protect his own interests. Who knew what secrets lurked inside this place, and what the people here would be willing to do to protect them? Not that it was going to work. Did Reiji honestly believe he was going to turn tail and run away if he was confronted by the more tawdry tricks in his arsenal?

Reiji's eyes fell half-closed as his wrist began to move, his entire body oozing sensuality as it rocked in time with the motions. Brand thought with a degree of desperation that he should do something to stop him, but that would entail actually *touching* the man, and that he most definitely did not want to do. Not right now, not while Reiji was touching himself like that.

He could see the head of Reiji's cock peeking above the waistband of his pants on each downstroke, the fleshy curve of it flushed and glistening. The sight of it made Brand's mouth go dry, his chest tightening.

Reiji made a pleased little murmur. "I wish you could see your face right now." He took a languid step forward and sank down to straddle Brand's lap, all without letting up on the rhythmic stroking inside his pants. Brand stiffened and jerked backward, but some stubborn inner core of pride he hadn't been aware he possessed until now refused to let him react any more than that. He'd be damned if he'd let this punk get a rise out of him in the way he was so blatantly trying to do.

"I could arrest you," he said, feeling proud that his voice didn't waver at all when he said it. He didn't look away from Reiji's eyes when he spoke. "Right here, right now. Attempting to bribe a sworn officer of the law, interfering with a criminal investigation, withholding information, public indecency, unsolicited licentious propositioning...."

Reiji's hand fell on Brand's shoulder, tightening painfully. His lips curled up in a small grin. "I don't know who you think you're fooling." His voice was uneven, his breaths deepening. The amusement in the words took on a darker edge. "I can see right through you, you know. You're trying so hard to pretend you don't want this, but deep down you just want to throw me down over this chair and fuck like bunnies. Isn't that right?"

It angered Brand that Reiji was assuming he was just as corrupt and opportunistic as the other police officers he'd dealt with in the past. Brand's sense of personal integrity insisted he do something to change that opinion, but he wasn't sure *how* other than to keep resisting the brazen display he was being subjected to. He refused to let himself flinch, refused to so much as let his breathing change to show how much he was being affected by all of this. It was a battle of wills at this point; the steady, unwavering morality of his purpose here versus the sheer sensuality and audacity of the man trying to seduce him into forgetting his mission. It was nothing like any sparring match he'd undergone during training at the academy, but something told him in the long run it was going to end up being just as significant.

"Almost there...." Reiji's eyes were bright, drinking up Brand's suffering like it was wine. He was attentive for the slightest sign that Brand really wanted him, final proof that Brand truly was as dishonest as he was assuming him to be. Brand held his gaze steadily and refused to give it to him.

The man smelled like sex and sweat and *hells*, it had been far too long since Brand had gotten laid. He couldn't believe he was finding any part of this shameful performance erotic, but the sight of Reiji jerking himself off like this was making his balls ache. He was so damned hard, and that did *not* have anything to do with the whore currently writhing over his lap.

It *didn't*.

Reiji cocked his head to one side, considering him. His free hand moved to the inside of Brand's thigh and squeezed in unmistakable invitation. "If you're worried about Charon, don't be. So long as you go away and leave us alone afterward, he can write this off as a business expense."

The outrageousness of that statement made Brand's throat seize. He wasn't sure what he was more incensed over—the suggestion that he would actually willingly employ the services of a prostitute, or that he was the type of officer who would stoop so low as to accept a bribe.

His brain was still struggling to come up with a response when Reiji gave a broken-sounding gasp and stiffened on top of him. He pressed his forehead firmly against the side of Brand's neck as his hips jerked forward a final time, and the air was suddenly filled with the aroma of ejaculate.

Dear gods, what the *hell* was he doing here? Fury exploded in Brand's chest, driving him to his feet. Reiji slid backwards off his lap to land unceremoniously on his ass in front of the chair, glaring up at him resentfully.

"*Enough*," Brand said, pressing his shaking hands against the sides of his thighs. He wondered again if Charon had been the one to send Reiji up here, or if the brat were working on his own. "You're *not* going to chase me away like this. So give it up, already."

For a moment he seriously thought Reiji was going to hit him, and he tensed reflexively before he even realized what he was reacting to. Then Reiji's gaze dropped to the floor.

"I'm sorry," he said. His voice was rough.

Brand stared at him. "What?"

"You heard me." He looked up at Brand with a kind of bitter misery in his eyes. "Hate me as much as you want. I don't give a damn, seriously. But leave Charon alone, okay?"

Brand revised his earlier opinion that Marque might have been the one to put him up to this. He felt cold inside. "You'd really do anything for him, wouldn't you?"

Reiji didn't answer, but then he didn't need to. Brand was a fair judge of personality himself, and right now the look in Reiji's eyes didn't need any interpretation. This was a man who would absorb blows against himself without much thought, but the moment a hand was raised against someone he cared about, it hit him deeper than anyone would have thought possible. Brand couldn't help wondering what Marque had done to earn that kind of loyalty.

"Look," he said, gentling his tone. "So long as he isn't doing anything wrong, he doesn't have anything to worry about."

"Wrong," Reiji said with a small curl of his lips. "That's such a subjective word."

No, it wasn't. Not in Brand's opinion. Some things were right, and other things were wrong, and taking bribes from whores who gave every indication of having been abused horribly by police officers in the past was definitely at the top of the "wrong" category.

And if what Marque was doing in this place—whatever it was— was wrong, then Brand would see that he was brought to justice for it. That was his job, the reason he'd chosen to become a police officer in the first place.

The glitter in Reiji's eyes was darkly amused. "He is going to chew you up and spit you out."

Highly possible. But that didn't mean Brand wasn't going to try to find the answers he was looking for.

"We'll see," he said, and turned to leave.

He had a feeling his assignment in Aechestan was going to be more interesting than he'd originally assumed.

Chapter 15
Charon

Charon Marque was a man of many moods.

Right now, that mood was frustrated. He looked up from the paperwork he'd been working on and schooled his features into a bland expression, keeping the irritation he felt locked firmly behind his eyes. His mouth curled in a polite smile.

"Lord Montgomery. What can I do for you this morning?"

Montgomery wandered over to a bust displayed on a surface next to one of the bookshelves and peered at it with a vaguely disapproving air. "You're still employing the Kendo boy?" While the question was casually asked, there was an unmistakable edge to it. "I'm surprised he's lasted this long."

There were those who had questioned Charon's decision to bring Reiji Kendo into the fold, but Charon had been quick to recognize the unparalleled potential in the boy. Reiji had a kind of rough charm, a feral quality, a touch of wildness that suggested that—maybe—he could be tamed for a night. That kind of challenge was very attractive to the right kind of customer.

Darwin Montgomery was not the right kind of customer.

He was a tall, thin man with quick, precise movements like a bird's. His hair was platinum blond and very fine, with eyes the palest shade of blue Charon had ever seen. There was a kind of refined elegance to him that suggested he might be older than he looked, although if his hair had begun to whiten with age, it wasn't readily apparent with his coloring. His trim form was dressed in an exorbitantly expensive suit of grey Merino wool.

During one of the man's infrequent visits, he'd taken notice of

125

Reiji and asked in his politely insistent way to spend an evening with him before he left. Charon prided himself on his ability to pair up the right employee with the right guest; a good match made the employee happier, made the guest happier, and was generally a good influence on business all around. He'd known from the start that Reiji had been the exact wrong kind of boy for Montgomery, but the man had been persistent. In the interest of preserving the peace, Charon had eventually agreed. Reiji, he believed, could take care of himself, and he'd completely underestimated the degree of brutality that this particular guest was capable of.

Montgomery had not appreciated Reiji's unique brand of rough youth attitude, and things had gotten very bad very quickly. It was still one of Charon's biggest regrets since he'd gotten involved in this business. The boys in his care trusted him to look out for their welfare; it was a responsibility he took very seriously, and the fact that he'd failed one of them, however briefly, did not sit well with him.

"Yes. He's quite popular among the clientele, and has his own list of dedicated customers. I'm very pleased with his work here."

A small smile curled Montgomery's lips. "Not surprising; you always have been a businessman of exceptional aptitude. Quite impressive, as always."

Charon resisted the urge to sigh. "Is there something I can help you with?"

"As a matter of fact, there is." Montgomery curled a hand over the top of his long cane as he turned away from the bookshelf. The cane was made of black wood and highly polished, with a knob of azure-tinted crystal affixed to the end of it. "There's a young businessman by the name of Albertine Pierpont I wanted to bring to your attention. I thought he might be deserving of an invitation to your charming little home."

"Associated with one of the cabals?"

"Of course. He's the illegitimate son of Ferdinand Rocha, and he's making quite a name for himself in the central provinces. A very high-spirited young man, very forward-thinking. There are those who think he might be leading the North Atrianic Cabal five years from now."

"Impressive."

"I thought so. He's already established his own supply lines throughout Atria and part of Mongless. A very bright young man, no matter how you look at it."

This time Charon did sigh, just slightly. "I'll send out an invitation this afternoon."

Montgomery gave a quick, terse smile that completely failed to reach his eyes. "I knew I could count on you."

Charon considered the fact that he seriously disliked this man. If not for certain overriding circumstances, he would never have allowed him inside his House.

"Is there anything else I can do for you?"

The smooth courtesy in his tone made Montgomery's smile deepen. "No, that should be it for today. Of course I'll let you know if we have any further need of your services."

"Of course."

"Well. I suppose I'll be off, then." He glanced at the closed door leading out to the hallway. "Perhaps I'll help myself to one of your boys before I leave."

Charon's eyes narrowed slightly. He believed firmly that Montgomery had known precisely how that evening with Reiji was going to unfold, and that that had been the reason he'd chosen Reiji in the first place. Despite his unassuming nature and highly bred courtesy, the man was a sadist of incomparable cruelty.

Before he could come up with an adequate reply, Montgomery gave him a sharp grin. "Just kidding. I'm late already for my next engagement."

"Perhaps another time," Charon said stiffly. He wondered if Montgomery was serious about wanting to partake of the House's entertainments, or if this was really all just a game to him.

Wondered what he would do if the man did, indeed, insist.

"Good day to you. I'll be seeing you again." With a slight nod, Montgomery left.

Charon sat staring at the door he'd disappeared through for a long minute, dark thoughts churning around in his head.

"You want I should throw him out on his ass the next time he shows up here?" a voice spoke at his elbow.

He smiled, some of the tension draining out of him. "Tempting," he said. "Very tempting."

The woman standing beside his desk was tall and athletically proportioned, her slim form dressed in a sharp black pinstriped business suit. Her skirt was short and showed off a fair amount of leg, giving her a femme fatale kind of appearance that never ceased to amuse him. Her hair was dark and curled severely around the sides of her face, which was slightly too long to be actively pretty but still appealing to look at.

Her habit of appearing out of thin air when he least expected it had long ago ceased to surprise him. This House was riddled with nooks and various passages that those with knowledge of them could make use of. Phoebe Grayson, for all her uncouth speech and obvious feminine charms, was as skilled in their use as anyone.

"I don't like the way he walks in here like he owns the place." She glanced down at the red-painted nails of one hand, a scowl tightening the skin between her eyes.

Neither did Charon, to be honest. But there were some things in life that had to be endured for the greater good, even if it did leave him feeling used and impotently dangerous for days afterward.

"You heard what he said, I take it?"

"Of course." She seemed offended that he would have thought otherwise. While she hadn't been in the room while Montgomery had been here, he knew she would have been listening closely to the conversation over the concealed video feed that was transmitted to her office next door. The security forces in this House took their jobs as seriously as he took his, and even his office — no, *especially* his office — was under near-constant observation.

"Good. I want you to find out everything you can about Mr. Albertine Pierpont. Do you think you can have a packet on my desk by this afternoon?"

"Sure thing. I'll get Ruben on it right away."

Dependable allies were of inestimable value to a man in his position. "Excellent." He stood up and crossed to where his coat hung on a rack by the door. "When you're done, would you bring the car around to the front? We're going out."

"Yes, sir." There was a wry note in her voice that made him smile.

He looked up as he shrugged into the heavy folds of his coat. "Bring your winter boots. It's cold outside."

"Any particular destination in mind?"

He thought for a moment. "No, just drive around for now. I need some time to think."

The crunch of the tires on pavement was vaguely soothing as she pulled the limo out of the driveway. Wearing a long dark coat and white gloves, Phoebe looked every inch the polished chauffeur where she sat in front of him in the front seat. The chauffeur's cap on her head was struck at a jaunty angle.

Charon considered asking her to take him into town, but quickly discarded the idea. If he went there, he would be tempted to visit Angelo's no matter how bone-tired exhausted he was feeling at the moment, and that just wouldn't be good for him.

Marcus Angelo had been his friend for going on eight years now, insofar as men of their social standing could be said to have "friends". Angelo was one of the more well-known eccentrics in Aechestan, resourceful enough to be creatively bizarre and rich enough to get away with it. He lived in an expansive mansion at the end of the city with his horses, his dogs, and his personal harem.

It was this last point that drew Charon to visit with him on rare occasions. Angelo was intrigued by him, and as luck would have it, he wasn't above sharing his possessions with people he found interesting. That list was gratifyingly small, but Charon consistently seemed to find himself at the top of it. Not once in all the years he'd known the man had Angelo ever turned him away.

One of the things Angelo found intriguing about him was the fact that he refused to touch his own whores. Sure, he had sex with them once when he first hired them to get a feel for what kind of customers they should be placed with, but that was just business. When it came to satisfying his own yearnings and physical desires, he found it best to look elsewhere.

It was important to him never to take advantage of his position as the boys' employer. The success of the entire business hinged on their respect for him and their willingness to do what he asked without coercion. For that reason, he encouraged them to come to him with any problems they might have, and he liked to think he had a fairly close relationship with each of them because of it.

But that relationship was by necessity hands off. He'd heard of the owners of less affluent brothels who considered their employees their own personal playthings to use however they pleased. Such an attitude was repugnant to him. This was not an easy line of work to be in; he knew that each of his boys had come to him from a variety of very difficult and oftentimes traumatic circumstances, and it was important that they be compensated for each and every time they debased themselves for a client. Requiring them to make themselves available at the whim of the person who "owned" them.... Well, that would provide him with a class of employees he had no interest in engaging in business with. "Take us to see the Weasel," he said, making his decision abruptly.

He could imagine her hands tightening around the steering wheel. "Yes, sir," she said after a moment's hesitation. The words were clipped.

Her obvious reluctance made him smile to himself. The Weasel was a small-time information monger who lived on the outskirts of the city. Reputation had it that he could find out anything about anyone, anywhere at any time. In Charon's opinion that reputation was a bit overblown, but still, he'd found the man's information to be useful from time to time.

The Weasel's lair was a ramshackle pub toward one of the seedier ends of town, but not so much off the beaten path that its more high-class customers would stand out unduly. Phoebe made a face as she pulled the limo up alongside the wall of the building, in full view of the windows where she'd be able to keep an eye on it from inside.

"Cheer up, Ms. Grayson," Charon said as he climbed out of the car and closed the door behind him. "We shouldn't be here for very long."

The look she gave him was eloquent in its assessment of that opinion.

A small bell chimed over the door as they stepped inside. The interior of the bar was a lot cleaner than its crumbling exterior would indicate, with polished wood tabletops and blown green glass lamps that provided a subtle, intimate lighting. There were no customers that Charon could see, but that wasn't too surprising at this hour of the morning.

"Well, if it isn't the infamous Charon Marque." The voice came from the direction of the kitchen, where a man in loose jeans and a white T-shirt pushed open the swinging door and stepped out to greet them.

His real name was Lenny Troy, or something equally forgettable. To Charon's knowledge, no one ever called him that. He was just the Weasel, who found information. At below average height, he was skinny enough that his bones seemed to jut from the skin, with a kind of frantic energy that suggested the missing flesh had been burned away in pure manic glee. His hair was bright yellow and cut short against his skull, his slightly protuberant eyes pale and colorless in a way that reminded Charon of a fish.

The Weasel's eyes glittered as he greeted them, giving a sketchy kind of half-bow. "And the exquisite Ms. Grayson. Welcome, welcome to my humble abode." The expression on his face was openly leering.

Her eyes narrowed alarmingly, giving the impression that he was something she was considering scraping off the bottom of her shoe.

The Weasel turned his attention quickly to Charon. "We can go into the back if you'd like," he said, his hands twitching with nervous energy, "or we can sit out here. There's no one but us here at the moment...."

"No, this is fine." Charon sat down on one of the bar stools, smiling inwardly when Phoebe took her accustomed place behind his left shoulder. Disapproval rolled off of her like a black cloud, but there wasn't anything he would discuss with this man that he'd be pained to have overheard in any case.

Not that the Weasel was likely to share information about his clients, unless the pay was very, very good. He might be outwardly reckless and dimwitted, but there was a cunning mind locked inside his head. For all his physical and social shortcomings, he was exceptionally good at what he did. And that included keeping a degree of confidentiality among his various clients to ensure their return business.

Not that that was something Charon had ever felt tempted to test. He had very little liking for people who could be influenced by money, and even less trust for them.

Still, they had their uses. "You don't seem surprised to see me."

"Well, you know." He shrugged, more or less falling into a seat a couple of stools down. His fingers drummed absently against the bar top. "Word tends to get around. I hear you had an officer from the city out sniffing around your place last week."

"Yes." Of course that bit of news would have made the rounds in the circles this man moved in. "One of my employees took it on himself to try bribing the man." He smiled slightly, remembering.

The Weasel gave him a crooked grin. "And that doesn't sit well with your conscience?"

"Maybe it wouldn't have, if it had worked. But the officer remained unbribable till the end."

"Ah. There is nothing so troublesome as a moral man."

Charon tended to agree with him. "This man won't be any trouble. Besides, the problem with bought men is that they seldom stay bought. I prefer my obstacles out in the open where I can see them."

"Spoken like a true entrepreneur, my dear Mr. Marque." His grin took on a slightly demented cast. "We wouldn't want anyone to start wondering who's been paying the bills, now would we?"

Behind Charon's shoulder, Phoebe shifted slightly. He narrowed his eyes and said, "I'm not sure what you mean. It's common knowledge that my client list is a proprietary secret known only to myself and the financial experts on my staff."

"Clients, yes. Of course." He dropped his gaze, but whatever look of contrition he was aiming for was ruined by the grin that steadfastly refused to fade. "The cream of the crop of Khatar, the country's finest, most morally bankrupt few."

The problem with engaging in business with madmen, Charon mused, was that it became difficult to sort out the truth from amongst the inane prattle. What exactly did the Weasel know, or think he knew? While Charon strongly doubted he had any knowledge that would be damaging to him, even an educated guess could prove troublesome. And the Weasel, more than anyone else, might not be constrained by logic or commonly held suppositions when reaching his conclusions.

Charon shared a brief glance with Phoebe before continuing. "In any case, I'm still in need of your assistance." He reached into his coat pocket and pulled out a folded fistful of fifty-dollar bills. Without looking away from the Weasel's eyes, he set the sizeable stack of bills down on the table between them. "What can you tell me about Marcel Delafonte?"

"Hmm." He tapped his lip with one finger, eyeing the mound of money thoughtfully. "I might be willing to help you out with that, in exchange for a night with one of your boys."

As if he'd ever allow this man onto the House of Silence's grounds. His hand hovered over the stack of money, ready to take it back if necessary. "Are you sure? This is an awful lot of money to throw away for a man in your position."

The Weasel's eyes never left the money. "Well, maybe I'll be able to help you out just this once. Out of the goodness of my heart."

"You're a very altruistic man." He shoved the money across the table toward him.

The money vanished almost as soon as the Weasel touched it. "So. You had a question?"

"Marcel Delafonte," Charon prompted. "What can you tell me about him?"

The Weasel considered the question. "Not a lot, unfortunately. At least not much that isn't public knowledge. He's a member of the senate out in Vargess. Very big, very influential. He's been on the cabinet for, ah, I'd say six years now. He's got less than a year to go till he's up for reelection."

"What can you tell me that isn't public knowledge?"

"He's one of the most racially prejudiced sons of bitches you'll ever have the misfortune to meet. His adoring public doesn't know that about him, or at least they don't let on that they do. I've heard stories that will curl your hair, my dear Mr. Marque." His grin looked big enough to split his skull in two when he said it.

Charon chewed at his lower lip thoughtfully. "I'll want to hear those stories. All of them."

The Weasel's eyebrows shot up to his hairline. "I hope you've got a lot of time on your hands this morning."

"I do," Charon said grimly, ignoring Phoebe's almost tangible annoyance behind him.

Leaning back on the stool, he settled in to listen.

Chapter 16

Staying the Course

"Who the hell is Marcel Delafonte?" Phoebe's voice was glacially calm as she pulled out of the pub's parking lot and back onto the street. She refused to look at him, even in the rearview mirror.

Charon smiled. "Just a name that came up during some unrelated research last month."

She fumed silently for a moment. "And it was important enough to drag us all the way out here? I always feel like I need to update my vaccinations when I leave that place."

"Hmm, I'm not sure. Time will tell whether it turns out to be anything useful or not."

He knew her real reasons for disliking making the journey to the Weasel's lair were a lot more complex. She took her job as his bodyguard very seriously, and she considered that place to be an unacceptable risk when it came to maintaining his personal safety. She would have far preferred to have a team of bodyguards around him when he went there, but Charon had never felt comfortable traveling around with an entourage. Partly it was ego, but partly it was calculated strategy; he believed in making himself seem approachable so as to encourage the people he dealt with to open up to him in turn.

This time her eyes met his in the mirror. "Are you planning to tell me what this is all about?"

"Maybe. If it turns out to mean anything."

Her mouth pressed together in a thin-lipped frown, her eyes flicking forward again sharply. After a moment, she said, "This has something to do with one of those boys you hired, doesn't it?"

Charon turned to look out the window, not saying anything.

134

Outside, the city streets rolled by in all of their squalid, disreputable grandeur. Not even the omnipresent blanket of snow that covered everything could hide the seedy nature of the place. But that was what made this part of the city of Aechestan so intriguing; all of these people, living together, each of them coming from different backgrounds, with different views and different beliefs. Some were rich, some were poor, some were earnest or lazy or altruistic or malicious. But all of them, no matter who they were or where they'd come from, had to find a way to coexist. And they were successful, for the most part.

"How much do you think the Weasel knows about you?" Phoebe asked.

He thought about the question. "It's hard to say. He is in the business of collecting information, isn't he?"

Her reflection in the rearview mirror was grim-faced. "I'll assign someone to keep an eye on him. Make sure he doesn't start spreading uncomfortable rumors."

"Hmm. And if he does?"

Her eyes flicked toward his again, then away. "We'll handle it."

He had no doubt about that. He wasn't in the habit of hiring incompetent people, after all.

The city street slid by, restaurants and houses and offices and stores. And people, uncounted numbers of them, everywhere he looked.

"It's an interesting world we live in," he said.

He could feel her eyes on him without having to turn and look. "Yes, sir. That it is."

He pulled his coat tighter around himself, feeling suddenly chilled. There was a mound of paperwork waiting for him back at his office, and Montgomery's little task, and he still hadn't slept in nearly two days. Yet....

"Take the next right, would you? I think we'll be going to Angelo's after all."

She didn't say anything in reply, but her hands moved smoothly to turn the car in the direction he'd indicated. If there was any disapproval in her over this latest turn of events, she kept it carefully hidden from him.

Closing his eyes, Charon leaned his head against the back of the seat and let the low hum of the car's engine carry him forward.

Charon arched his head back with a sigh as a talented mouth traced patterns of liquid heat across his bare chest, a wicked little tongue sliding down to lap at the curve of his rib. Another mouth trailed hot kisses over the side of his face, while yet another suckled reverently at the inside of his thigh. Warm arms wrapped around him from every direction—caressing his hips, his legs, his shoulders, his neck, one particularly devilish hand slowly massaging the sensitive skin behind his balls—until he felt like his entire existence had been reduced to his body and the sensations that were being wrung out of it.

Angelo's boys were undeniably good at what they did for a living.

The feel of warm breath ghosting over his cock made his throat tighten. He glanced down to see a chestnut-brown head moving over his groin, cheeks hollowing out as it moved over the girth of him, taking him inside. Oh, that was a pretty sight. Angelo definitely made it a point to choose his whores for their aesthetic value in addition to their professional skills.

Charon closed his eyes briefly at the feel of the wet mouth sucking him in, sending little slivers of pleasure vibrating under his skin. The heady heat of it pulled at him for a minute or so before pulling away, giving the side of his cock a fluttering kiss as it withdrew.

"You look preoccupied today, Mr. Marque." Cyril's liquid brown eyes gazed up at him from where the boy lay with his chin propped on Charon's thigh, one fist curled underneath his chin. His hair half-covered his eyes in a feathery tangle, framing the delicately pretty lines of his face. A single large emerald sparkled at one ear.

"Mmm. Maybe a little." Charon ran his fingers through the boy's hair, smiling when Cyril's head rubbed up against his palm in response.

"Well, you've come to the right place, then." That was Nero's voice, the mischievous blond-haired scamp whom Charon tended to prefer when he was feeling particularly edgy. The boy knelt behind Charon's shoulders, massaging heavily at his chest with both hands.

At the other end of the bed, a third boy with sable brown hair rubbed at the bare soles of Charon's feet, expertly easing the last of the tension out of him.

Charon sighed heavily under the delicious warmth of the sensations and glanced toward the window. Outside, he could see Angelo's tall form moving across the large back yard toward the pens where his dogs were quartered, shadowed by the slim, dark-haired shape of yet another of his boys. There were four of them in total; professional and highly qualified members of his personal harem, each of them with unique specialties and areas of expertise that made them an overwhelming and impossible to resist erotic team.

Without warning, he grabbed one of the bodies above him and pushed it down to the bed, leaning down to drape himself over it. A glimpse of pale blond hair told him it was Nero; with an inward smile, he grabbed hold of the boy's wrists in one hand and held them down against the pillow over his head, bending down to nip at the side of the boy's neck.

Nero lifted his chin in open invitation, his breath hitching. The sounds he made when Charon's teeth pinched down, drawing livid bruises to the surface of his pale skin, were anything but disapproving. Such a ribald little imp this one was, so full of erotic mischief and audacious fantasies. He liked it when Charon got a little rough with him, liked just a small bit of pain interspersed with his pleasure. He liked to push, just a little, and even more he liked to be pushed against.

Which was fortunate, because Charon was in the mood to do some pushing today. He rolled Nero's body over perfunctorily and lay down to cover him, nestling his erection in the crevice between the boy's thighs. Nero's back arched under him; Charon tightened his grip around the boy's wrists and slid his body more heavily against him, enjoying the smooth slide of skin on skin.

"Mr. Marque," Nero said, sounding breathless. He glanced back at Charon from under a tangle of silken blond hair and gave him a sultry-looking smile, stretching his body like a cat's. His fingers curled against the pillow where Charon held his hands down.

"Slut," Charon answered, smiling against the back of his neck. It wasn't an insult.

A small shift of his hips, and then he was sliding into the boy's eagerly waiting body. Nero was practiced enough at this kind of service that no preparation was necessary; his passage was already oiled in anticipation of exactly this kind of activity, as it was every time Charon visited. Charon closed his eyes in satisfaction at the feel of warm flesh squeezing around his cock, pulling him inside. Yes, this was just what he needed after the day he'd had. Physical indulgence without any strings attached; pleasure demanded and then expertly given, as clear and straightforward as any business transaction.

Heat coiled at the base of his spine, urging his hips to move faster. Nero met his thrusts without flinching, making softly encouraging noises as Charon's desire peaked into inescapable urgency. The others were clustered around them now, touching him, arousing him, and there was no way he could last against that kind of provocation. He thrust a final time into Nero's body and came with a low groan, giving a bone-deep shudder and then just *melting* into it, pleasure throbbing with a high, wild abandon throughout every part of him.

There were days when Charon toyed with the idea of hiring a harem of his own. The contract these boys worked under wasn't markedly different from the ones he used to detail his own boys' employment, albeit for a much longer term. But the idea of long-term relationships of any kind made Charon uneasy, especially if it involved the exchange of money. Bound by contract as they were, if ever the boys in Angelo's harem decided they no longer wished to be employed by the man while they were still under the terms of their indenture and chose to leave, Angelo would be able to go after them and force their return through perfectly legal means. Such means of keeping a lover — or even a whore, no matter how skilled he was at his craft — by one's side was abhorrent to Charon.

Of course, if a member of a harem felt he was being mistreated, there were legal avenues he could follow to have the contract annulled. Charon had heard of that happening on occasion, and it always made headlines when it did. The public loved hearing about sexual scandals, apparently, particularly in regards to harems (which were generally the exclusive realm of the insanely rich). Angelo's boys, however, showed no sign of wanting to annul any part of their service. They clearly adored Angelo — or at least were well practiced at pretending they did. Charon knew full well that Angelo was extremely generous when it came to compensating his employees, indentured or otherwise.

With a sigh, he flopped onto his back on the bed, laying one forearm across his eyes. His heart pounded as he came down from the high of the orgasm, barely noticing when the other two moved in around him, petting him soothingly and cradling his body against them.

Charon thought of his own boys suddenly, back at the House of Silence. Each of them was indispensable to him, with unique strengths and weaknesses that made them an inimitable part of his House. They were more like a family to him than anyone else he had known in a good many years, giving his life a much-needed focal point. It made the job he'd taken on as their master and guardian even more important, both for their sake and for his own. Perhaps it was that reason more than any other that wouldn't allow him to treat them as objects and put them to the use that Angelo's harem was all too willing to be used for.

Pushing the troublesome thoughts aside, he reached for the body nearest to him and pulled it down beside him, rolling to half-cover it as he bent to meet an open and delightfully eager mouth in a heavy kiss. It didn't really matter which of Angelo's boys it was this time; all Charon cared about was that there was a willing body pressed warm and sinuous against him, slender thighs wrapping around his hips to draw him further in. Sex, the purely physical necessity of it, sang in the air between them, strident in its demands despite the fact that he'd already come once this morning.

It was, perhaps, the best that a man in Charon's position could expect.

It was good that Angelo had given him three of them today. He had a feeling they would each be getting a work-out before he went home.

Chapter 17
Entering the Maze

Tam leaned back against the edge of the counter and closed his eyes, thinking.

"Hmm," he said. "I taste red peppers, garlic, and...."

"A touch of coriander," Danny said, looking anxious. He stood in front of the stove with a wooden spoon in hand, waiting to hear Tam's verdict on the soup he'd just finished cooking. "It was my mom's recipe."

"It's really good." Tam smiled at the relieved look on the younger man's face. "Your mom sure knew how to cook."

"Yeah." Grinning to himself, Danny turned to stir the soup again, lowering the heat of the burner. "She sure did."

Tam considered the fact that while Danny was an undeniably strong individual—as all of them had to be in order to work here—there were some things about which he was endearingly fragile. His self-esteem seemed to wax and wane like the moon, a phenomenon that was oddly commonplace among the boys who chose to make their home here. But whenever he talked about his mother—not the stepmother he'd mentioned on one or two occasions, but his real mother—he always seemed to be at his happiest. Tam thought it best to encourage that in him whenever possible.

"You two are going to get your asses kicked as soon as Madam Mirian finds out you've been mucking around in her kitchen."

Tam glanced over his shoulder at the kitchen doorway. "Good evening, Reiji."

Reiji ambled over to the stove with his hands in his pockets and leaned over the pot to sniff at it, his brow furrowing. "You guys are so dead when she sees this."

Danny ladled some of the soup into a bowl and held it out to him. "We have permission to be here, so relax."

Reiji's expression said he was highly skeptical of that. But whatever fear he had of the wrath of Madam Mirian clearly wasn't enough to stop him from the offer of food. Snatching the bowl out of Danny's hand, he went to the table and sat down with one knee pulled up against his chest, looking irritable.

"Not bad," he said grudgingly after the first spoonful.

Receiving praise from such a reluctant source was a hundred times more meaningful than any compliments Tam could give him. Grinning, Tam peeled himself away from the counter and said, "Thanks for cooking dinner, Danny. If there's any left over, I'll grab some after work tonight."

"No problem. Thanks for taste-testing for me." Danny cast him a last distracted smile as he turned back to the pot.

Tam was feeling pretty good about life in general as he made his way upstairs. He ran into Charon just outside the lobby.

"Ah, Tam." Charon looked pleased to see him. "We have a client coming in this evening that I'd like you to take care of."

"Sure thing." Tam leaned one elbow against the stair railing. "Anything special I should know about him?"

"Just that he requires a delicate touch," Charon said with a smile.

"I'll take good care of him," Tam promised, although inwardly that smile worried him. Charon's sense of humor was sometimes a bit unpredictable.

"Good. I'll leave him in your capable hands, then. I'll send him up to the Green Room to meet you."

"Sounds good. I'll be waiting."

Tam thought longingly of the dinner Danny was cooking downstairs, then let it go with a sigh and started climbing up to the second floor. Despite its name, the Green Room was actually decorated in soft creams and beige, with mint accents that gave it a kind of open, airy feeling. It was one of Tam's favorite suites in the entire estate.

He lay back on the bed once he got there, kicking off his shoes against the wall and stretching his arms out luxuriously over his head. He didn't have to wait long before there was a timid knock on the door. The knock made him raise his eyebrow; most of the House's clients tended to strut about like they owned the place, instead of acting the part of the guests they were.

"Come in," he called, sitting up and looking toward the door curiously.

The door opened to reveal a tall, thin man in a voluminous grey cloak and fur-lined boots. His face was narrow and deeply lined, with a mouth that didn't look as if it were especially used to smiling. His hands were long with tapered fingers, which were decorated with a number of colorful rings. His hair was the most beautiful thing about him, long and chestnut-brown, falling well below his shoulders. There was a fair amount of grey in it, but that only added to the quietly regal aura he projected.

Judging by his clothing alone, he was definitely one of the higher-ranking lords. His bearing seemed to support that assumption in a way that wasn't readily definable; Tam had always had a knack for picking out the truly high-bred among the multitude of pretenders who had visited the House as guests over the years.

"Hello," the man said, sounding unsure. "I'm Ander. Mr. Marque told me to come upstairs to this room...."

So this was the infamous Lord Ander Delacroix. Tam had heard Danny mention him on a few occasions.

Tam rolled to his feet and sketched a short half-bow. "It's nice to meet you. I'm Tam." He smiled in what he hoped was a welcoming manner, wanting to put the other man at ease. "Have you been to the House of Silence before, sir?" There was no point in letting him know the boys of the House had been talking about him.

Ander still looked uncertain. "Er... yes. I've been here a couple of times before. A few times." A few times was a far more accurate description, judging by what Danny had said. In recent weeks, he'd become a fairly regular visitor. "I usually meet with a young man named Danny...?"

"It's Danny's night off. We get one of those each week."

"Oh," Ander said, looking surprised. Then he looked guilty about looking surprised, as if it hadn't occurred to him that whores could get time off just like normal people.

Tam smiled inwardly. "I promise you, you'll get every bit the attention from me that you get from him."

"Hmm, yes." Ander pulled the scarf from around his neck, glancing around the room. "I suppose I should tell you that I'm not particularly used to visiting these kinds of establishments."

As if that hadn't been perfectly obvious from before he'd stepped into the room. "That's not unusual," Tam said, keeping his voice mild. He walked forward and reached for Ander's hand, curling a reassuring grip around the long fingers.

Ander's eyes snapped up to meet his at that. Uncertain as he might be about being here, there was no meekness in that gaze. This was not a man who was used to being touched.

Tam decided it would be best to tread very carefully with this one. "Will you give me a chance, Ander?" he said quietly. "I'd like to try to make you feel good tonight, if you'll let me."

He could see the struggle in Ander's eyes. What had brought the man here tonight, he wondered? A lord of his age would normally be happily—or not so happily—wed. Had he left a young bride at home to come here and drench himself in debauchery for an evening? He didn't really seem the type at all. There was an almost tangible aura of sorrow around him, so pronounced it made Tam want to pull him close and pet that beautiful, long hair of his until the poignancy of whatever had saddened him faded. Maybe later Ander would let him.

But for now, there were other, more urgent needs to be met. Holding Ander's gaze, Tam settled a hand onto his arm, then his shoulder, keeping the boundary of the clothing between them. Then, when there was no obvious protestation, he slid his hand up to touch the skin at the side of the other man's neck.

He felt so very warm.... Ander's eyelids fluttered briefly before he dipped his head, and Tam leaned in to kiss him.

Kissing was not something that most of Tam's customers were particularly interested in, but he'd always been rather partial to it himself. Ander soaked up the intimacy of it, leaning forward with a sigh that seemed to come from his toes. Hands closed over Tam's hips, holding him firmly as Ander's mouth opened to his, tongue sliding against Tam's with a kind of silent hunger that left Tam feeling somewhat shaken. Whatever reservations Ander had about being touched, this was a man who was starving for physical contact.

Without breaking the kiss, Tam reached for the broach that held the cloak closed at Ander's throat and unhooked it, pushing the heavy material off of his shoulders. Looking away briefly, he tossed the cloak onto a nearby chair and then leaned in for another kiss, his fingers already moving toward the buttons of Ander's vest.

It was a laborious process, this kind of painstaking seduction, but it was one that Tam was particularly skilled at. A brief touch here, a caress there, gradual removal of the clothing one slow piece at a time. Then there was a surprisingly toned chest bared beneath his questing hands, pale skin covered in a dusting of chestnut-colored hair. Ander let out a soft gasp when Tam's fingers brushed across one of his nipples; the sound made Tam's heartbeat spike briefly before settling down into a slightly faster rhythm.

"What can I do for you?" Tam asked in a low voice, holding Ander close with one hand cupped around the back of his neck. He lapped lightly at the skin behind his ear.

Ander shuddered. "Make me feel," he whispered, clutching Tam's waist tightly. His cheek pressed hard against Tam's as his head dipped forward; Tam felt thin lips brush across his exposed collar bone, dry breath wafting across his skin.

Make him feel, huh? Well, Tam could certainly do that. He guided the two of them back toward the bed, reaching for the button of Ander's trousers as he went. He could feel that the other man was already half-hard underneath the stiff fabric.

Tam was in a similar state himself. He ignored his own arousal, though, and cupped a hand over Ander's groin, molding the growing hardness there under his palm. Ander gave another of those delightful little gasps and tipped his head back, catching his lower lip briefly between his teeth.

"It's okay if it feels good," Tam said, because Ander's expression didn't seem to be showing any enjoyment of what they were doing at all. The small line between his brows had appeared when Tam first kissed him, and it hadn't faded since. His body seemed to be working on an entirely different wavelength, however; his hands pulled Tam's body close whenever Tam moved even the slightest distance away, his mouth trailing kisses over the slope of Tam's shoulder and up the side of his neck.

Tam felt a bit breathless as he eased the zipper of the other man's trousers slowly down. "It's okay," he said again, wanting to reassure. He didn't know what authority he had to promise any such thing, but it seemed to do the trick, causing Ander to relax slightly against him. "Tell me what you want. Just let me know, and I'll do it."

"I don't *know* what I want," Ander said, sounding as if the admission were physically painful. His arms tightened around Tam's waist, his face pressing down against the crook of his shoulder.

Tam wondered again why Ander had come here. He wanted to feel, he'd said. He wanted to experience something intensely physical, something that would break him free of whatever prison of sorrow he existed inside of. That much was obvious. Whatever he'd experienced in the past, it had left him mistrustful of feeling of any kind. Perhaps the only thing he knew how to feel on his own anymore was that pervasive sorrow. But Danny had begun to teach him that not all feeling had to be bad; that it was okay to trust, to reach out, even if it was just a little. That was something Tam wanted desperately to reinforce here; there was something about this man that pushed his protective instincts into high gear.

To the bed, bare chest to bare chest, and Ander seemed to be entirely on track with what they were doing. Tam slid a hand down the side of the other man's ribs, feeling the smoothness of the skin there, before wriggling out of his own trousers and pulling Ander's down over his hips. It was a delicate dance, keeping up the physical contact between them without allowing it to become overwhelming. Ander was a bit hard to read at times, but Tam decided to trust his instincts and keep going.

For the first time, Tam wondered why Charon had paired the two of them together this evening. It would have been a simple matter to inform him that Danny was unavailable tonight; judging by Ander's earlier preoccupation with the younger man, he would likely have agreed to come back at a later time. But instead, Charon had sent him up here and told Tam to wait for him. Clearly, there was something he believed Tam could provide for this particular customer that Danny could not.

Horizontal on the bed now, Tam hooked a leg around Ander's

thigh and pulled him close, grinding their hips slowly together as they kissed. He wasn't used to this much kissing; it was heady, addictive, making him feel a bit dizzy. His hands moved of their own accord to touch the places Ander reacted to the most, trusting the other man's body to tell him how to proceed.

Without thinking much about it, he rolled until Ander was beneath him. Ander gave another of those long sighs at that, his eyes fluttering closed. Tam looked down at him for a moment, sliding his fingers through the hair at Ander's temple.

It occurred to him that maybe what Ander needed right now wasn't a body to embrace; maybe what he needed was to be embraced himself. It really wasn't that unheard of. The vast majority of Tam's customers wanted to top (and were often very emphatic about it), but there were the occasional few who needed to give up control, just for a little while. He'd had one client about a year ago who wanted to be tied up and whipped like a slave; *that* had been an interesting assignment, and no mistake.

But Ander's needs were a bit more simple, in Tam's opinion. Whatever motivations had led him here, he felt guilty about accepting pleasure, about being on the receiving end of any kind of physical gratification. For that reason, it was difficult for him to take the lead. He would do it, as evidenced by his history with Danny, but it wasn't easy for him. And, at the heart of things, it wasn't what he really needed.

Experimentally, Tam trailed his hand down Ander's side to the area just beneath his tailbone, sliding his fingers over the other man's ass to lightly brush across the skin there. Ander twitched at that, his head lifting where it pressed against the side of Tam's neck. His fingers tightened where they gripped Tam's hips.

"Okay?" Tam whispered, kissing him soothingly on the side of the face. He slid his fingertip down to brush the opening of Ander's ass once, then again, barely touching the skin.

Ander seemed to freeze for a moment. No doubt his mind was racing, presenting him with all kinds of excuses for why this was an incredibly bad idea, but his body had its own desires about what they were doing here tonight. He breathed out hard against Tam's shoulder.

"Yes," he said hoarsely. He shuddered once and then dropped his head back to the pillow, closing his eyes.

Like a sacrificial lamb offering himself up to the slaughter.

Tam grinned once before schooling his features into a more appropriate expression. Ander was so darned cute; Tam was looking forward to teaching him that there could be pleasure in submission, just as there was pleasure in topping a willing partner. The human body was infinitely variable in its ability to accept and experience different kinds of physical pleasure.

"Just relax. I'm not going to do anything that will hurt you." He had to move *very* carefully if Ander was really the virgin Tam thought he was. Being on the receiving end of this kind of activity was an entirely different thing than being on the giving end, as he knew from his own experience.

He could still remember *his* first time; he'd been a teenager at the time, headstrong and eager for new experiences. It had been a sweaty, frantic groping in the loft of his father's barn with one of the stable hands, surrounded by the smell of hay and the dizzying warmth of the summer sun. It had been awkward and strange and kind of painful, but he still remembered the experience with a great deal of fondness.

He wanted to give Ander that kind of memory, only with a little more finesse, hopefully, than *his* first partner had shown. He reached into the drawer of the bedside table and pulled out the tube of lubricant he found there, setting it down on the mattress nearby.

"Are you ready?" he asked, leaning down to kiss Ander lightly on the forehead.

Ander stared up at him for a moment, looking torn.

Then he nodded.

Chapter 18

A Matter of Trust

Ander's eyes were very round. Tam smiled at him. "Second thoughts?" he asked, brushing the hair back away from Ander's face.

"No." The immediacy of the response was somewhat startling. Despite the apprehension in his eyes, Ander didn't shift his gaze away. "I trust that you aren't going to do anything to hurt me."

Interesting. "You don't really strike me as the trusting sort."

That earned him a small smile. "I'm not. But there's something in you that reminds me of Danny. I don't think either one of you is the type to willingly harm another."

This man was either exceptionally naive, or else an exceptionally good judge of character. Tam considered him thoughtfully. "It might hurt a little your first time, no matter how careful I am."

Ander didn't look surprised. "I know," he said seriously.

Hmm. It was possible Ander was just looking for new experiences and would change his mind the second his body was penetrated, but further delay wasn't going to be good for either of them.

"I'll go slow," Tam promised. "You have to let me know if you don't like anything I do. Okay?"

Ander nodded. His eyes followed Tam's movement with a tight-lipped expression as Tam reached for the lube, a muscle in his jaw twitching.

"Easy," Tam soothed, leaning down to kiss him again. "This is supposed to be fun, remember?"

For a while it was nothing but slow, easy kissing, and skin sliding against skin underneath the sheet. Tam could feel that Ander was still hard, which he took to be a very good sign.

Easing Ander onto his side facing him, Tam popped the top off the lube and squeezed a small amount onto his fingers. Reaching down behind Ander's body, he slid his middle finger slowly into the crack of the other man's ass and touched the opening there.

Ander stiffened immediately in his arms. "Shh," Tam said, nuzzling into the hair above his ear. "It's okay."

He moved his fingertip around a bit without penetrating, getting the small opening nice and slippery. After a few moments he moved to kiss Ander again, stroking deep with his tongue just as his fingertip slipped inside.

"Okay?" he whispered, brushing his lips over Ander's ear. Ander nodded jerkily against his shoulder.

Eager for new experiences or no, that had to be feeling pretty damn weird. Tam distracted him by reaching down to palm his erection, stroking the stiff flesh to encourage it to harden even more in his hand.

"Ah," Ander said, and relaxed with a quiet sigh.

Good gods, the man was a natural. Tam slid his finger further inside, watching closely for any adverse reaction. This was his first experience topping a lord of this caliber, although he knew full well that social standing had nothing to do with sexual orientation of any kind. Some people liked to top, some liked to be topped. That was just the natural order of things, in Tam's opinion.

Besides, Ander wasn't a lord here. He was just Ander, a guest in the House of Silence and Tam's client for the evening. Maybe that was the real appeal of coming here for him; it gave him the chance to step out of the role he was forced to inhabit on a day-to-day basis and be someone else for a change. That was the motivation the majority of the House's clients had, to some extent. And that was the purpose the working boys here served; to help their clients break away from reality for a short while, or to intensify it, depending on the customer's individual needs. The way Tam understood it, that was the reason Charon had founded the House in the first place.

Two fingers now, and that was a bit of a stretch for him but Ander muscled through it, his hands tightening around Tam's arms. Tam soothed him as best he could, keeping up the slow stroking on his erection. "Okay?" he asked again, wanting more feedback than the restrained sighs he was getting.

Ander swallowed audibly. "To be honest," he said, "I'm not sure."

Tam chuckled. Dipping his head in concentration, he adjusted the angle of his wrist until he found the hard gland inside Ander's body and prodded it gently, smiling at the low gasp the action caused.

"That," he explained, "is your prostate. Imagine how good that's going to feel once I'm really inside you."

Ander was breathing too heavily now to make a coherent response. His fingers hooked like claws around Tam's upper arms, not pushing him away but holding on as if he were drowning. Tam could only hope that that meant he was enjoying it.

Carefully, he added a third finger. For a virgin like this, he wanted to be *really* sure that his body had been prepared before Tam attempted to mount him. To his surprise, the finger went in fairly easily. Ander breathed a soft sigh against his ear, his grip on Tam's arms lessening. Whatever demons were dancing around inside his head, his body was definitely interpreting the sensations it was receiving as pleasure.

Which made it easier for Tam to give in to the promptings of his libido and move into the unaccustomed role he was being asked to perform. Excitement thrummed through him as he gently removed his fingers from Ander's body and wiped them clean on the edge of the sheet. He was going to be *really* disappointed if Ander decided to freak out at some point over the next several minutes and declare that he wasn't about to let himself be on the receiving end of this kind of joining.

Not that that was looking to be a very valid concern. Ander's eyes were closed, but there was anticipation in the line of his jaw and the faint flutter of his eyelashes. His breathing was harsh and shallow, edged with a subtle breath of expectation.

Normally, Tam would choose to put a virgin on his hands and knees and take him from behind, since that was the most comfortable position for someone unused to these activities to be mounted in. But for someone with Ander's desire for intimacy, Tam thought it best to approach the joining between them face-to-face.

"Relax," Tam urged, looping his arms underneath Ander's knees and scooting forward until he was framed in between the other man's thighs. Ander stared up at him with a worried expression, looking vaguely shell-shocked. That wasn't surprising to Tam at this point in their adventure together; so long as Ander had time to stop and *think* about what he was doing, worried seemed to pretty much be his usual frame of mind. But as soon as his body was given the reins and started making its desires known to him, he forgot all about being self-conscious or anxious or scared.

"This part might be a little uncomfortable, just at first," Tam warned. Full disclosure was the best way to go; he didn't want there to be any surprises. Ander gave a slight nod and closed his eyes again, swallowing forcefully.

Tam breathed out heavily as he eased into Ander's body. For a moment, the unaccustomed sensation of hot, slippery warmth enclosing his cock made his breath catch in his throat, his arms locking where they held up his weight to either side of Ander's head. He forced himself to calm down, his heartbeat thudding inside his chest.

Go slow, Tam, he reminded himself. With an effort, he relaxed and slid an arm underneath Ander's shoulders, holding the other man close. It felt more like making love than fucking this way, which was a nice change of pace. Ander seemed to appreciate the difference, too, because he relaxed into Tam's arms with a sigh.

Carefully, Tam eased his way inside bit by bit, moving in small in-and-out motions that threatened to drive him insane. But he was rewarded for his patience when Ander's body opened up for him, thighs tightening briefly around his hips to welcome him inside.

Hells, yeah, Ander was born for this. His body responded beautifully as Tam touched him, held him, the slight stutter in his breathing making Tam's libido soar. He'd make a damn fine whore if only he weren't such a high-ranking lord; then again, Tam himself was proof positive that high-ranking lords could become whores if they really wanted to.

The thought made him grin as he slid the rest of the way inside. And oh, yeah, that was exactly what his body had been missing—all that tight, slick warmth wrapped around him like a glove, urging him to move. He held himself still with an effort, waiting for Ander to adjust. Sweat gathered between his shoulder blades, making him itch.

"Good?" he asked, a bit breathlessly.

"Not particularly." There was a definite strain in Ander's voice. The line between his brows was back again.

Tam knew it had to be hurting him. For a first-timer, that initial experience of being filled was rarely a pleasant one, although it could get better with a patient partner and an inherent spirit of adventure.

It was Tam's goal to provide the patient partner end of the equation. Forcing his breathing into an even rhythm, he held still and waited while Ander's body relaxed in increments beneath him. Such a lean, hard body this man had; he certainly didn't practice a sedentary lifestyle. Lots of exercise, lots of exposure to the open air — hiking, maybe, or horseback riding. Some kind of physical activity that was common to the idle rich.

Finally he felt a telltale twitch of Ander's hips that indicated he was ready to start receiving more stimulation. Biting back a sigh of relief, Tam shifted and leaned his weight forward, pulling his hips back just slightly before easing back inside.

And *oh....* Ander's eyes grew so very round at that. Tam's own ass ached at the memory of his first exposure to the joy of having that amazing sense of fullness inside him for the first time. Ander's head tipped back against the pillow, exposing his throat, and Tam couldn't resist the urge to bend down and kiss him there, biting down just a little bit.

"That's it," he murmured, trailing the tip of his tongue up the side of Ander's neck to his ear. "Just lie back and feel it."

He'd used a *lot* of lube, so it was very slippery inside there, and hot, and it took every ounce of willpower he possessed to keep his movements slow and cautious as he took Ander's virginity away. He felt Ander's hand close around the back of his neck, sliding once down his back before moving back to his hair and holding him close. Tam hugged him tightly, using the leverage to get as deep as he could.

"Ah," Ander gasped against his ear, sounding pained.

"Good?" Tam whispered.

"Mmm... yeah. Yes." And then, after a deep, shuddering breath, "More."

Well, well, well. Bracing himself on one arm, Tam allowed himself to move faster, angling his hips toward that spot that made Ander moan the loudest. Ander's entire body jerked at that, but it didn't seem to be in pain at all anymore.

So good.... Tam lost himself a bit toward the end of it all, but he retained enough self-awareness to remember to grab hold of Ander's cock and urge him on to the climax they both wanted. A few quick strokes and Ander's body thrummed beneath him, his hips thrusting upwards once before his seed spilled with satisfying warmth over Tam's hand.

Ander cradled Tam's head against his shoulder as Tam finished the race to his own completion. Tam bit down onto the curve of Ander's neck as he came, pleasure arcing through his overtaxed nervous system with the clattering dissonance of an out-of-tune orchestra, strident and shattering. His hips snapped forward completely without his conscious volition, making him worry that he was being too rough despite his best efforts to take it easy on his extremely inexperienced partner. But then even that thought burned up in the force of his climax, and there was nothing but the pleasure.

He collapsed down onto his elbows when he was done, shuddering. It took him a moment to realize that Ander was holding him, one hand stroking at his hair. The idea of being comforted by this man made him feel at once intensely amused and intensely touched.

Very carefully, he eased himself out of Ander's body. He could tell from Ander's expression that that wasn't especially comfortable for him, but he made no complaint as Tam settled down at his side.

"Well?" Tam prompted, brushing the hair away from Ander's face with the fingers of one hand and leaning in to kiss him on the tip of the nose. "Was it what you were expecting?"

Ander didn't answer for a long moment. "Yes," he said at last, "and no."

Tam chuckled lightly. "Well, good. I guess."

The smile Ander turned up at him was wry. "I expected it to hurt a bit in the beginning. That part didn't surprise me. But I didn't expect...." His face colored slightly. "I didn't expect to enjoy it as much as I did."

Definitely a natural bottom. "There are all different ways to experience pleasure," Tam told him. "There is no right or wrong way to go about it. Whatever works for you, whatever you need to make yourself feel good...." He shrugged. "It's all good."

Ander looked amazed at that. "I think you're a much braver person than I am."

If only you knew. Tam thought about the home he'd abandoned, the family he'd run away from, the father that even now haunted his dreams and refused to let him get on with his life the way he should. Determinedly, he shook the depressing thoughts away.

He shifted into a comfortable position and lay down, cradling Ander's head against the crook of his shoulder. Ander relaxed against him with a sigh, sounding at ease and delightfully satiated. They would rest here for a bit, then they'd head into the adjoining bathroom to take a bath together. Once there, they'd scrub each other clean, and maybe Ander would let him wash that beautiful, long hair of his. And then, after they were all warm and scrubbed pink and smelling of soap, they'd return here to the bed to make love together again. Ander would probably be too sore for another round like they'd just done, but there were—as Tam had said—all different ways to experience pleasure. Even lying here in the warm darkness and touching each other beneath the sheets would be blissfully erotic once they were a bit sleepy and high on the humid heat of the bath.

And maybe—just maybe—if Tam continued to talk to him and encourage him, Ander would choose to be open with him in turn. Maybe he'd tell Tam a little about that sorrow that still clung like a fog around him. In these situations, Tam considered the things his clients told him as sacrosanct as confessions told to a priest; in many situations, what the client really wanted wasn't sex at all, but a willing ear to listen so they could unload some of their woes. It was a part of the job that Tam was eminently good at, and he was experienced at drawing out the secrets they most desperately wanted to tell. Maybe, when it came down to it, that was what Ander really wanted.

Tam hoped so; he wanted to do something to help this man if he could.

"Just relax," he said, kissing Ander's bent head fondly. "Get some sleep if you want to. We have the whole night to spend together."

"Yes," Ander said, curling forward against his chest. Tam wasn't sure, but he thought he felt the moisture of tears dampening the skin there.

"It's all right," Tam said, because it was the only thing he could do. He tightened his arm around Ander's shoulders, holding him close. "I'm here with you."

Ander's body was lax against him, without any of the rigidity it had had at the start of the evening. Ander had learned something important about himself tonight, and that was always a frightening thing. But Tam didn't get the impression he regretted the newfound knowledge; on the contrary, the discovery seemed to thrill him, as if the intensity of the sensations Tam had made him feel were cause for celebration.

Whatever had brought Ander to seek out what the House of Silence had to offer, he was no longer a stranger here. He had entered into something larger than he was; he'd become an integral part of the life and breath of the House, just like the boys who worked here, just like Charon himself was. The best of the customers — the ones who really understood the House and what it stood for and what it was trying to accomplish — usually came to that realization sooner or later.

Tam had a feeling that Ander wouldn't be asking for Danny the next time he visited.

Chapter 19
Dreaming

There were, Vincent thought, far worse things than dying.

The thought passed through his head in a kind of haze as he looked up, gagging a bit on the taste of his own blood. He was on his knees, with hard hands holding his arms up behind his back so high he thought they were likely to break at the slightest movement. He fought against the grip regardless, fury and anguish driving him into a state not entirely unlike madness.

His sister's face swam in front of him, blurred by smoke and the shimmering distortion of heat from the flames. The sound of the fire was like a wounded animal's roar, accompanied by the creaking of falling timbers and the screaming stampede of horses as they fled the chaos that had been their home. The horses had been his family's pride, their livelihood, but they were gone now, scattered to the winds if they even managed to survive at all. And his sister....

Horror rose in his throat more pungent than the blood, making him feel faint. Her face was streaked with blood, her eyes wide and staring, her red mouth forming an O of perfect terror. She'd been so beautiful, his sister, with her long, black hair and dark eyes, so deep and soulful, the envy of their entire clan. There was little about her of beauty now as the men surrounded her, pushing her down, laughing coarsely amongst themselves as they moved in to hurt her.

"No, no, no," she said, thwacking him hard across the shoulder with her bow. He flinched, rubbing at the stinging skin of his arm.

"I'm trying," he said petulantly, shifting his grip on his viola. It had been a gift from their father; music was a gift handed down through the generations in the Michaelis family line.

"Try harder," she said firmly, and lifted her own viola to her shoulder. Brows furrowing in concentration, she started playing the piece of music they were practicing again, her body swaying slightly in time to the complex melody.

There were those who called his sister lovely, headstrong, the flowering beauty of the families that made up their clan. To Vincent she seemed fierce and hot-blooded, intimidating in a way that seemed laughable because of the slightness of her frame. But their father was fond of saying that you couldn't judge the size of a person's spirit by the size of the body it inhabited.

Like the men hurting her now. The sound of viola music faded to be replaced by the crackling scream of the fire. The men were huge, tall and muscular and impossible to fight against, but their spirits were almost nonexistent. They were cowards, every one of them; they were *nothing*. And he hated them all.

The sound of their laughter grated in his ears. His sister was sobbing now, cursing at them in a voice gone raw from screaming. The sound of it broke his heart. Blind rage gave him the strength to wrench away from the hands that held him, breaking free of their grip long enough to scuttle forward across the blood-soaked ground and grab hold of a jagged piece of fallen timber. Grimacing, he swung it hard, around and upward, catching one of their attackers alongside the head. The man went down without a sound, but there were others on him now, kicking him, hitting him, pulling at his hair as they dragged him forward away from the burning wagons.

"Fucking vagabond," they called him, and other names that were much, much worse. He didn't care. The sound of his sister's screams filled the entirety of his mind, making it impossible to think of anything beyond the fact that she was hurting and he couldn't do anything to help her.

"Little gypsy wants to play," one of them said, his voice sickeningly cold. His eyes were the most vivid shade of blue Vincent had ever seen. Fingers knotted in the back of Vincent's hair, yanking his head back. The stones of the ground cut into his knees where he knelt, darkening the front of his pantslegs with blood.

He stared upward in terror, his heart pounding, as the one who'd spoken stepped in front of him. There was a knife in the man's hand.

157

Light from the flames danced along the blade, giving it a demonic appearance that seemed entirely too real to Vincent's grief-numbed mind.

"He's kind of pretty for a boy," the man said, with an edge of sick amusement that made Vincent's skin crawl. "Maybe we'll have some fun with this one, too, after we're done with the girl."

Rough laughter greeted that statement, making Vincent's scalp prickle with trepidation. The hands restraining his body turned suddenly groping, sliding down to fondle him in places he had no desire to be touched. One of them dipped inside the front of his pants, gripping his genitals roughly. He bucked his body reflexively to get away from them, but all he accomplished was to push himself further into their grasp as their hold on him tightened.

The man with the knife grinned down at him. "The kid's practically begging for it, isn't he? Hell, he's probably used to it. All gypsies are just beggars and whores anyway." He reached down to touch Vincent's face, rubbing the pad of a thumb over his left eye. "But first he needs to be taught a lesson. I think you killed Gerald, you little shit."

Fury twisted Vincent's features as he lurched forward to spit at him, crying out loud as he was yanked backward again by his hair. There were at least three of them holding him now, maybe four. Far too many to fight against, but that didn't mean he wasn't going to try. The man with the knife stepped closer, the hand gripping Vincent's skull holding his eyelid open as in the background, his sister screamed and screamed and screamed....

With a start, Vincent jerked awake. He was breathing so hard he was dizzy, sweat soaking his body and causing the sheets of his bed to cling to his skin. Feeling nauseous, he kicked them off in a frenzy and sat up, swinging his legs over the side of the bed to settle his feet on the floor.

"Angeline," he whispered, sliding his hands back through his hair.

It took a few minutes for his heartbeat to settle, for the horror of the dream to fade enough where he mostly stopped shaking. Slowly, the walls of his bedroom in the House of Silence seemed to solidify around him, reminding him of where he was and what his purpose was, and just how far away he was from the past that had brought him here.

Fucking hells, he wished he could stop having that dream. It served no purpose other than to shake him up, and show him how weak he was. Angrily, he pushed himself to his feet and padded into his bathroom to take a shower. It was still early, but he wasn't going to be getting any more sleep today.

The feel of hot water running down over his body felt surprisingly good, soothing the shakes out of him until he was almost calm again. He touched the scar at his left eye briefly, trying not to think about the way in which he'd received the injury.

He still didn't know who the men had been, or why they'd attacked them. There had been such hatred in them, it seemed to consume everything in its path. Vincent's family had been a part of a clan of gypsies who lived on the eastern face of the Bartolia Mountains in Vargess, a country to the north of Khatar. They kept mainly to themselves, visiting the major cities only occasionally in order to obtain supplies or conduct other forms of business. They generally participated in street fairs and festivals where they sold their horses and played their music, and offered up the other varied skills that their families had to offer in order to make their living.

To his knowledge, they'd never hurt anyone. Their lives had been simple, uncluttered by possessions or roots to any particular geographic location. The territory they considered their home spanned several provinces, with a route they would habitually follow throughout the course of the year to hit up each of the seasonal festivals in the towns they passed through. It had been a good life, and he'd never had cause to regret being a part of it.

The adults of the clan were killed outright when the attack came, a surprising wash of violence that cleaved their entire community in two. Vincent could still remember the sight of his father running forward to defend their home when the men came to burn it, his strong features etched with anger even as they cut him down. Vincent's mother had lived longer; she was beautiful like her daughter, but with a physical strength that made her a match for any of the men in the clan. She had been the one who organized several of the clan members into striking back against the invaders, an effort which was undeniably brave but ultimately ineffectual.

At least they had killed her quickly. Vincent and his sister hadn't been so lucky. Their mother concealed them in the back of one of the wagons and extracted a promise from them to keep themselves hidden before she ran off to free the horses, but the men had found them there anyway.

Vincent had been seventeen at the time, Angeline a couple of years older. Not children, but not fully adults, either. They'd been sheltered growing up in the clan; they'd never had exposure to violence or cruelty or hatred of any kind, aside from the prejudice they sometimes ran into inside the villages. This level of concentrated brutality was something completely beyond their understanding.

It was ancient history, in any case. Shivering, he turned off the water and stepped out of the shower to towel himself dry.

He didn't see any point in dwelling on the past. He didn't like when it grabbed ahold of him like this; he blamed it on that damned dream, which was taking an annoyingly long time to fade. Hopefully Charon would have a good client for him tonight, someone who would be able to knock him free of the prison of his thoughts and turn his focus to more visceral matters.

Pulling a brush through his hair, he went to get dressed for the evening.

"You seem preoccupied today."

Vincent turned his head on the pillow, looking up at Aburon where he lay beside him. They were both breathing heavily, still riding the edge of the sexual high that had sustained them throughout most of the night. Vincent's body was sated, his limbs seeming to melt into the mattress of the bed as the smooth comfort of the sheets cooled the fire raging in his body. Pain seemed to flow in waves over his back and ass, crawling down the backs of his thighs. Aburon had been refreshingly thorough this evening.

"I'm not," he lied, and immediately felt guilty for saying it.

Aburon didn't look irritated at him for not being more open with him. "Hmm." He trailed a hand down the slope of Vincent's spine, brushing lightly at some of the more prominent welts along the way, then slid a thumb into the crook of his ass to probe at the opening there.

Vincent closed his uncovered eye. It hurt a bit when Aburon's thumb pushed inside of him; his ass was slick with lube and with Aburon's come, but that part of his body had been too heavily used tonight for any kind of contact there to be entirely comfortable. The sensation crackled along his already overtaxed nerve endings, distracting him from the darker thoughts that stirred at the back of his mind.

He couldn't help moaning a bit when Aburon reached for a dildo lying on the nightstand and eased it into his slippery passage. The dildo was large and oddly shaped, making him excruciatingly aware of every inch that slid inside of him. That was one of the things he appreciated most about this particular client; he was fond of toys and exceedingly skilled in the timing and manner of their use. There had never been an occasion where Vincent had grown bored during their time together.

Vincent's hands were shaking. He clutched fistfuls of the pillow under his face to stop it, forcing his breathing to stay even as his hips flexed to accommodate the uncomfortable sensation filling him.

"Is it good?" Aburon asked, brushing Vincent's hair back away from his face with one hand.

Vincent breathed out heavily. "Yes."

And it was. His hips were moving now of their own accord, rubbing his sensitized cock against the sheets underneath him until Aburon's hand on his hip urged him to still. Then there was no choice but to lie there and feel it, letting the almost-but-not-quite pain of it flow through him.

"You're so good at this," Aburon said, his voice roughening around the edges. He tapped a nail against the end of the dildo, making Vincent bite back a whimper. His hand molded around Vincent's ass, feeling the skin there. "Your body is so sensitive. You respond to everything."

Which could be both a blessing and a curse, depending on the client. Vincent buried his face in his arms and concentrated on breathing.

"I think I want you to keep this inside of you for the rest of the night, until I'm ready to take you again."

Hells, that would make sure he stayed in the over-sensitive state he was in, without giving him any reprieve. His ass twitched at the thought of it.

"You're beautiful." He could hear the smile in Aburon's voice. A heavy hand stroked through his hair, calming him.

He rolled onto his side when Aburon urged him to do so, tilting his chin up so the other man could lean down to kiss him. He didn't particularly care for kissing, but considered it a necessary part of the job. It always seemed too intimate to him, more so than allowing relative strangers to shove a variety of different objects up his ass. Physical intimacy was something he considered insignificant, forgettable even, but emotional intimacy — which kissing was skating perilously close to the edge of — was something else entirely. There were parts of himself that Vincent didn't plan to share with anyone, no matter how much they paid him.

After a few moments Aburon applied gentle pressure to his shoulder, urging him to lie flat on his back. Vincent bit hard into his lower lip when he did so, feeling the pain of the whipping he'd gotten flare up anew as his flayed back pressed against the sheets.

"That's it." There was a low purr in Aburon's voice now. Vincent turned his face away at the sound of it, not wanting to admit how much it meant to him. The knowledge that he'd managed to please this man was heady, addictive, filling him with emotions he didn't want to examine too closely.

With a last lingering caress over Vincent's thigh, Aburon got up from the bed and padded barefoot over to the tall wardrobe against the wall. The sight of his bare back, broad and muscled, consumed Vincent's vision. There was something undeniably appealing about this man, despite the fact that there was nothing traditionally beautiful in his appearance. There was power in him, and strength, and a purity of focus that only someone with Vincent's particular needs could perhaps truly appreciate.

Aburon rummaged around inside the wardrobe for several moments before returning to the bed. Vincent's heart began to beat a little faster when he saw what he held in his hands; it was a coil of sleekly shimmering silk rope, dyed ebony black. He glanced upward and saw

Aburon gazing down at him with his customary intensity, gauging his reaction.

"It's been a while since we've done this." The smile in the words told Vincent that his sudden sharpening of interest had been noted. Aburon smoothed his palm over Vincent's forehead, pushing the hair back from his face.

Vincent's heart was pounding. He couldn't help shivering when Aburon trailed one of the ends of the rope over his chest, drawing a tantalizing circle around his nipple. Without thinking about it, he raised his wrists and pressed them together, holding out his hands in silent offering. He didn't look away from Aburon's eyes.

Aburon's low chuckle warmed him. Carefully, the older man began to uncoil the rope until he had a reasonable length to work with. Then he began to painstakingly wind it around Vincent's forearms, starting at his hands and working his way down toward his elbows in a rhythmic crisscrossing pattern.

"I don't know what thoughts are racing around in your head today," Aburon said. His head was bent in concentration as he worked. "But I want you to focus on me tonight. Can you do that for me, Vincent?"

As if he could do anything else when he was with this man. Vincent bit back a whimper when Aburon tugged gently on his hands, urging him to stand. Stiffly, he rolled toward the edge of the bed and obeyed, rising up to his feet on shaky legs. Aburon's hand on his elbow steadied him.

"That's good." Aburon stood and looked at him in silent contemplation for what seemed a very long while, his gaze moving over Vincent's naked form as he visualized how he was going to proceed. Vincent stood straight-backed under the scrutiny, waiting with a kind of distant anticipation fluttering in the pit of his stomach. His muscles clenched hard around the dildo in his ass, betraying his nervousness.

With a small smile, Aburon began. Vincent's eye fell closed as the long ropes wound around his body, occasionally loosening or pulling taut as Aburon worked new knots into their length. It was extremely difficult for him to stand without moving like this for extended periods of time, which was a weakness Aburon was well aware of and obviously not hesitant about exploiting. Even more annoying, the dildo in his ass felt even larger and more uncomfortable when he was in an upright position, making his thighs tremble despite his determination to remain motionless.

"This is one of the hardest things for you, isn't it?" Aburon mused as he bent to tie a particularly intricate pattern across Vincent's thighs. His breath was warm and moist on Vincent's hip, his fingers sure as they pulled a length of rope out through the knot he was forming. "Being still and quiet like this." He glanced up at Vincent's face briefly, smiling. "But it's necessary. You understand why that is, don't you?"

Yes, Vincent did understand. Forcing him to stand still and submit to this, regardless of the difficulty he had with it. His heart was racing inside his chest despite the simplicity of the task Aburon was asking of him. Glancing down, he saw the black rope stretched in a dizzying array of geometric shapes across his chest, his stomach, working their way down his legs as Aburon continued to bind him. Aburon really was extremely skilled at this kind of bondage. The contrast of the ebony silk against his skin was oddly beautiful, filling him with a distant sense of pride that he couldn't adequately explain.

"You're doing great." Aburon's mouth brushed across the side of his knee, making his thighs tremble. Vincent closed his eye again and concentrated on breathing deeply, forcing himself to remain still. This kind of bondage always felt so much *more* than wrist or ankle cuffs. It was full-body constriction, like being wrapped in a cocoon, warm and tight. By the time Aburon was done with him, he wouldn't be able to wiggle so much as a finger; he'd be unable to move even the smallest part of his body, leaving him subject entirely to Aburon's will.

The thought was intoxicating.

"That's it," Aburon breathed, trailing one hand up the back of his calf. Vincent shivered under the caress, biting into his lower lip briefly. As sensitive as he was right now, even an accidental brush of skin would be stimulating for him.

His eye fell half-lidded and his breathing slowed, his respect for Aburon's mastery deepening as a hand slid heavily across his cock, keeping his body expertly aroused. Every brush of rope against his skin felt excruciatingly erotic, particularly where it chafed against the scores on his back. He felt on edge, stretched thin and trembling, but soon his agitation began to fade as he slowly entered into the headspace that was the inevitable result of these kinds of activities, where he existed purely as a creature of sensation without the burden of complex thought.

Aburon chuckled as he rose up to his feet again. Vincent's breath hitched when he felt fingers on his cock, sliding slowly up the hardened length of it to caress teasingly across the tip, smearing the pre-come that had gathered there. Gods, he was so damn hard over this. Being bound, having Aburon touch him like this.... Even the uncertainty and distant anxiety of not knowing what was going to happen to him next was arousing in its way, making his skin tingle.

A strong hand closed around his balls, lifting them away from his body for a moment before pressing them hard against his erection. He grunted softly under the feel of it, his brows pulling together. It wasn't pain, exactly, but the threat of it was definitely there.

When he looked up again, Aburon was smiling. There was an unmistakable glint of amusement in his eyes, but there was honest appreciation there as well, and hunger. "You really are beautiful like this," he said, trailing the backs of his knuckles over Vincent's cock. He leaned down to kiss him with an intensity that seemed somehow possessive and tender at the same time.

Vincent couldn't help shuddering when he felt a leather thong wrap tightly around the base of his cock, trailing down to wind around his balls, separating them and lifting them away from his body. The constriction was so tight it left him panting, the feel of Aburon's fingers moving over him an agony of its own as his body ached for more — pain or pleasure, he wasn't sure which. It was all sensation, and it was all as necessary to him as breathing right now.

More, his mind whispered. *Give me more....*

Chapter 20
Reflection

"Such a passionate little animal." Aburon's voice had a twist of wryness to it. The words made Vincent's face heat, even as they warmed something deep inside of him. It occurred to him that submission—real submission—had nothing to do with letting an endless parade of strangers have access to his body. True submission wasn't a part of his physical body at all; it existed in the mind, in the heart, and perhaps in places deeper still.

This time when Aburon kissed him, there was no resistance in him at all. Aburon groaned low against his mouth and pressed forward against him, letting the ropes that bound Vincent's body rub against his skin.

"Gods, yes," Aburon sighed, mouthing at the side of Vincent's face. He pressed his palm flat over Vincent's trussed cock, grinding downward firmly with the heel of his hand. His other hand reached around to press on the dildo in Vincent's ass, moving it inside of him.

Vincent couldn't help making a small cry at that, his hips twitching forward needily. "Please," he whispered, so softly he wasn't sure Aburon even heard him. He pressed a beseeching kiss to the curve of the shoulder in front of his face.

He whimpered when Aburon curled strong fingers in the ropes at his chest and turned him around roughly, shoving him down onto the bed. The sudden pressure of the knots pushing into the tender skin of his whipped back dragged a hissed curse out of him, his jaw clenching.

"Good?" Aburon asked with a knowing smile, bending over

him.

Vincent stared up at him, panting. "Yeah." Bound tight as he was, he couldn't squirm into a more comfortable position, or even pull his ass fully up onto the bed. The defenselessness of his situation enflamed him, driving home just how helplessly constricted his body was.

Aburon slid an arm under his waist and dragged him toward the center of the mattress, arranging his body in the position that was required of it. Vincent closed his eye and breathed out heavily, feeling like a rag doll being played with by an especially amorous child.

A hard slap to his cheek brought his attention back to his current predicament forcefully. He stared guardedly up into Aburon's face, unable to hold back a shiver of uneasiness at the expression he saw there.

"Focus," Aburon reminded him gently. His knuckles trailed over the side of Vincent's face, lingering at the edge of the eyepatch.

Vincent turned his head away at that, his mouth tightening, but a hard grip to his chin wrenched his face back forcefully.

"One of these days," Aburon said, "you are going to let me sit back and admire you without fighting against it." He sounded more rueful than upset.

Vincent held Aburon's gaze evenly when the other man's hand moved down to his trussed cock, pinching the tip of it between his thumb and forefinger. The corners of Aburon's eyes crinkled as he lifted his fingers and slid them into Vincent's mouth so he could taste himself, massaging his tongue firmly.

"Mmm, that's it." The purr was back in his voice again. Vincent stared up into the other man's eyes as he sucked on the fingers in his mouth obediently, feeling a dull buzz start up in the back of his head. One by one, all of the troubled thoughts that had consumed him at the start of the evening were starting to fall away from him, leaving him with only a low susurration of *yes, yes, yes* whispering through his mind.

"Such a good boy." Aburon's voice was deepening now. He fucked Vincent's mouth with his fingers for a couple of minutes, bending to trail a kiss over the side of his neck, his jaw, the flat plane of his chest. His teeth found Vincent's nipple and bit down sharply.

Vincent cried out around the hand in his mouth, his back arch-

167

ing. The pain of the bite seemed to shoot down through his entire body, centering in his groin. He was suddenly desperate for the taste of Aburon's cock, for the feel of the hard length of it filling his throat, fucking him until he didn't think he could take it any longer.

As if he could read Vincent's mind, Aburon removed his fingers and shifted to straddle the younger man's shoulders, using one hand to angle his erection into Vincent's mouth while the other braced his weight against the headboard of the bed. Vincent sucked him in eagerly, his cheeks hollowing as he did his best to give pleasure to the man above him.

Aburon groaned low in his chest and cupped a hand under Vincent's neck, angling his head upward so he could achieve the greatest possible depth. Vincent gagged as the hard flesh thrust into him, tears dampening his face, but Aburon refused to give him any quarter. He fucked Vincent's mouth with a kind of uncompromising determination, moving hard and fast as he found his rhythm.

"Fuck, yes," Aburon whispered, trailing his thumb over Vincent's cheek. Vincent arched into the caress, almost purring himself.

His throat felt flayed raw by the time Aburon came, flooding his mouth with a burst of bitter semen that filled his senses. He did his best to swallow it all, lapping at the cock above him and mouthing earnestly at the side of it as it withdrew.

Aburon sighed in appreciation, sliding down to lie beside him. He wrapped his arms around Vincent's shoulders and pulled him close, nuzzling down against his hair. Vincent made a small sound in the back of his throat and pressed forward against him, his hips moving in slow jerks as he fought the urge to rub his aching cock against the body in front of him. Aburon's hand slid over his back, soothing him.

"You want to come." It wasn't a question, and Vincent didn't bother treating it as one. Aburon smiled against the side of his head. "Not for a while yet, I think."

Vincent lowered his gaze and concentrated on breathing, curling in against the other man's chest. The feel of Aburon's hand stroking over his hair was as far from comforting as this man's touch had ever been.

He didn't end up getting any sleep that night, not even for the brief hour in which Aburon dozed beside him on the bed. He lay awake in the darkness during the unaccustomed break, feeling the throb of the dildo in his ass and the muted white noise of the pain still crackling for attention on his back, his thoughts racing. He did his best to keep his mind blank, not thinking of anything at all, but it was difficult today for some reason.

In the morning, after they'd washed up one last time and sorted out their respective clothes to get dressed, Aburon stopped him by the door of the room. He paused in the act of tying his tie and settled a hand on Vincent's head, a curiously affectionate gesture that made Vincent stop and look up at him.

"I won't be getting time off again for a while," Aburon said, looking into his face with a serious expression. "But I'll try to make it here again by the beginning of next month."

"I'd like that," Vincent said, and surprised himself by meaning it. He didn't suppose it would be an exaggeration to say that Aburon was one of his favorite customers.

That made Aburon smile slightly. He ruffled the hair on Vincent's head and turned to go, picking up his sport coat from where it lay on the back of a chair by the door.

Vincent followed him downstairs and said a final good-bye to him before they parted ways in the lobby. He paused for a moment, trying to decide if he was tired enough to need sleep immediately, or if he might want to go to the common room to watch some TV. After a few seconds' contemplation, he headed in the direction of the kitchen.

Tam was standing at the head of the hallway, one elbow leaning nonchalantly against the banister of the stairs. He cocked his head to one side and favored Vincent with a crooked smile as he approached.

"You and Aburon seem awfully chummy," he commented, falling into step beside him.

Vincent knew that Tam had entertained Aburon one evening while he'd been with another guest; gossip had a way of traveling faster than light through this House. He shrugged. "Maybe. He's a good client."

"Mmm-hmm." Tam nodded seriously. "Always pays his bills on time, never breaks the furniture. That kind of thing?"

Vincent gave him a sideways glance and refrained from commenting.

Tam's grin softened slightly as they made their way downstairs toward the lower level. "It's just curious, that's all. I mean, we don't know anything about him."

It occurred to Vincent that he would ordinarily brush off Tam's attempts at drawing him into a conversation, but he really didn't feel like being alone at the moment. He wondered if Tam could sense that somehow, and if this was his attempt at being helpful.

"What's to know?" Madam Mirian was not in residence this morning. Vincent opened the refrigerator and pulled out the leftover soup Danny had made the previous day, turning on the front stove burner to heat it up. "He's a businessman, and he works an erratic schedule. Not that different from a lot of our other customers."

"Hmm." The noncommittal sounds Tam was making were really starting to get on Vincent's nerves. "Is that what he told you?"

Vincent turned to stare at him. "If you have something to say, say it already."

Tam's mouth quirked. "It's nothing, really. I've just thought for a while now that he looks kind of familiar."

"If you used to move in the same circles he does before you came here, that's not too surprising." Having transferred the soup into a pan and gotten it situated on the burner, he opened the cupboard and pulled down two bowls.

"Maybe." Tam leaned back against the counter and looked out across the room, chewing thoughtfully on his lower lip. "The thing is, I don't think his name was Francois Aburon when I met him the first time. Why do you think he'd use a fake name while he's here?"

That made Vincent glance at him out of the corner of his eye. "Did he recognize you when he met you here?"

"No, I don't think so. I don't think we were ever formally introduced before."

It didn't seem like a particularly interesting puzzle to Vincent. "Well, maybe he just enjoys his privacy. Some people do," he added pointedly.

Tam grinned at him. "I suppose so."

When the soup was warm, they settled down to eat together in a surprisingly companionable silence. A couple of boys came into the room after a few minutes, shoving each other playfully and laughing, and moved straight for the snack cupboard. Vincent met Tam's gaze at that and stifled a smile, knowing that Madam Mirian would have something to say to them about skipping breakfast in favor of junk food.

"Newbies," Tam scoffed once they were gone, and Vincent chuckled.

After they finished eating, Vincent considered heading upstairs to bed. He was bone-tired and his body still ached terribly from the whipping it had gotten, but again, the idea of retreating into solitude with nothing but his own thoughts to keep him company was far from appealing.

Tam regarded him thoughtfully for a moment. "Want to go for a walk?" he asked.

Which was what led to him being bundled up in a heavy coat, boots, and scarf, and heading out with Tam Temetria in the direction of the woods behind the estate. It had snowed sometime during the night, so the hills were covered in an unbroken blanket of white that was almost blinding under the light of the newly risen sun. The air was crisp and smelled vaguely of woodsmoke and rich green conifers, with an underlying spice from the copse of cedar at the side of the main building.

"Beautiful, isn't it?" Tam said, turning around to take in the view on all sides. Vincent couldn't disagree with him. Even in the winter, the grounds here were a work of art—not in an artificially kept stasis like he'd seen in some of the richer folks' gardens in the cities he'd visited in Vargess, but with a kind of wild beauty that called to his adventuring soul. He was struck with the sudden desire to lose himself in the woods and see where his feet led him, leaving all other ties behind. It was a passing fancy, however; the House of Silence was his home now and probably would be for a very long time.

Aburon had removed the dildo finally, but he could still feel the shape of it inside him. The ache of it felt surprisingly good in a way that reminded him again of why Aburon was one of his favorite customers. He smiled slightly, tilting his face up into the breeze and enjoying the sting of the cold air against his cheeks.

He could feel Tam looking at him. "Gets a little claustrophobic in there sometimes, doesn't it?" Tam said after a few minutes.

Vincent didn't reply. They'd advanced far enough up the hill to be in the shadow of the forest now. It was colder here, even though they were out of the wind. He wrapped his arms around himself and shivered, wincing as the movement upset the wounds on his back.

"Here, sit down." Tam indicated a mossy boulder, sweeping the snow off of it with one gloved hand. "You know, there's nothing wrong with getting medical attention when you need it. I mean, *if* you need it. Some of our clients get a little enthusiastic sometimes."

"Yeah, I suppose so." Vincent sat down carefully, refusing to show how grateful he was for the place to rest. A hot shower and a few hours' sleep would put him to rights again, but right now he was running pretty much on empty after the night's efforts.

Tam leaned against the tree beside him. Above them, the tree's branches were thick and dark, hanging heavy with snow. "I have to wonder what makes them like doing that to us so much. Is it a power thing?"

"Maybe for some of them." Vincent looked down over the grounds, his gaze moving over the rear windows of the House beneath them. Sunlight caught on the edges of them, giving them a golden sheen. "For Aburon, I think it's less about dominating than about having someone submit to him."

"Yeah, I got that impression, too. He's all about submission." He grinned slightly. "Drives him crazy when you challenge him, even just a little."

Vincent glanced up at him. "Tell me you didn't bait him the night you were with him."

Tam's grin took on a wicked cast. "Maybe just a little."

Vincent could just imagine how Aburon would have reacted to *that*. And Tam wasn't one who seemed naturally inclined to masochism.

He shook his head. "You like making things difficult for yourself, don't you?"

"Sometimes. It sure keeps things interesting, doesn't it?"

It occurred to Vincent that each of them who worked here might be just a little mad. The thought was oddly comforting.

"So, have you remembered where you've seen him before yet?"

"No, and it's bugging the hell out of me. I'll let you know as soon as I figure it out."

Vincent thought about it for a moment. "You know who I bet *does* know? Charon."

Tam leaned forward, looking interested. "Yeah, I bet you're right."

It wasn't so much that they believed their employer knew everything about everyone who stepped foot inside the House of Silence— which was more or less true, as far as Vincent had seen—but that he researched all of the guests so painstakingly before allowing them to sign a contract. Part of it was covering his investment and making sure the guests were financially capable of maintaining their end of the agreement, but part of it was that Vincent believed he truly did care about the boys, in his own way, and was looking out for them.

"This could be interesting," Tam said. There was an edge of excitement in his voice that immediately made Vincent wary.

"What? It's not like he'd ever tell you if you asked him. He doesn't share personal information about anyone, employees *or* guests."

Tam scoffed. "Of course he wouldn't *tell* us. But he has to have records somewhere, right?"

Vincent stared at him. "You are insane. You are undeniably, certifiably—"

"Come *on*, Vin. He can't be in his office all the time, can he? There has to be some kind of file somewhere. A client list, or something along those lines."

"I am *not* going to be a part of this."

"You're already a part of it." He looked entirely too cheerful about the whole thing. "If Charon finds out afterward that you knew what I was planning, and didn't do anything about it, then you'll be just as guilty as I am."

"I should go tell him right now."

"Are you?"

Vincent glared at him. Tam's gaze was guileless, innocently curious, as if it weren't his hide on the line if Charon found out what he was up to.

"This isn't just a prank, Tam. This is one of Charon's rules; we *never* ask about people's pasts here."

"Well, it's a good thing we're not asking anyone, then, isn't it?"

"We don't pry into their pasts, either."

"I don't remember that ever being explicitly stated."

Vincent surprised himself by choking back a highly inappropriate surge of laughter. He doubled the intensity of his glare to make up for it. "You *are* insane. And you are trying to drag me down with you."

"Lighten up. It'll be fun."

"*Fun*?" The absurdity of the notion left him incapable of coming up with a more eloquent response.

"Yeah, fun. You've heard of it, maybe?" He poked lightly at Vincent's shoulder with one finger, being careful to avoid any places that might have been injured during the night's assignment. "It's what people tend to do when they've been locked up indoors for too long, doing the same thing night after night until they almost go out of their heads with boredom. Fun."

Vincent stiffened. "I prefer to have my 'fun' without fear of serious repercussions."

"Oh, but *Vin*." The smile Tam gave him was dazzling. "That's the best kind."

Vincent crawled into bed later that morning with a feeling of profound relief. Exhaustion rolled through him in waves, eclipsing the pain that still buzzed along the nerves of his back and thighs. Despite the turmoil in his thoughts, his mind was still filled with the peace of the snowy walk he'd taken with Tam through the base of the woods.

Tam really was crazy to even think of trying to break into Charon's office. But Vincent knew he wasn't going to say anything about it, to Charon or to anyone else. He wasn't the type to rat out a coworker for any reason, which was something Tam seemed to be fully aware of.

As for actually taking part and helping him, well... that was a fool's game. If they were caught, they'd be disciplined, fired, or worse. Just the thought of being cast out of the House of Silence and not allowed to return was enough to make him break out in a cold sweat.

But—the more he thought about it—he couldn't really imagine Charon responding that way. They were more than just employees here; they were family, and Charon had always treated them as such.

After all, what could it possibly hurt to sneak a peek at one little record? If he was being honest, Vincent had to admit that he was curious now about Aburon's true identity. If he wasn't a businessman, what did he do for a living? Why would he lie about it?

With a groan, he buried his head underneath his pillow and forced the uneasy thoughts out of his head. He had to get some sleep if he was going to be any use to the client this evening. Forcing his breathing into an even rhythm, he relaxed when he noticed his thoughts begin to drift, breaking apart as fatigue finally started to catch up to him.

It didn't escape his notice that while he was just as preoccupied as he'd been that morning, at least this time it wasn't a fixation on the past.

Chapter 21

Into the Fire

"Oh, gods," Danny said, hugging himself tightly outside the closed doorway of the room.

He felt more than heard Reiji step up behind him. "What's *your* problem?"

Danny glanced back at him. "I've never worked the Den before."

Reiji smirked. "No kidding. Why do you think Charon sent me along to keep an eye on you?"

"I don't need a babysitter." Danny's pride still stung at that. "There was no reason for him to send you with me."

"Oh, well, if you're such an expert then I'll just leave." He glared at him. "Idiot. Charon told me to go with you, so I'm going. End of story."

Danny refused to admit how relieved he was to hear that. He turned to look forward at the door again. "I really don't like servicing more than one client at the same time."

Reiji gave an exasperated sigh. "Look, if you really can't do it, you have to let Charon know that."

Danny felt something twinge inside of him at the comment. "It's not that I *can't* do it," he protested.

"Well, what are you bitching about, then?" The look Reiji gave him was annoyed. He reached past Danny's arm for the doorknob and pulled the door open. "Let's get going, shall we?"

It took a moment for Danny to unlock his legs and step forward. The low throb of music, almost inaudible when the door was closed, washed over him, making his heartbeat quicken. There was a subtle hum of conversation inside the room, a strident clinking of glasses, a low, formless shuffling from the dance floor off to the right. The lighting was low, with various niches around the walls cast in more or less shadow depending on the placement of the overhead lamps. The overall feel of the room was of dreamy, glittery decadence, a place where rich men could come to partake of carnal luxury for an evening.

"Breathe," Reiji said, sounding amused. "I'll be close by, so don't panic, all right?"

"Yeah." Danny nodded jerkily, trying not to look as anxious as he felt. A moment later, he shoved the uncertain thoughts away. Was he a House of Silence whore or wasn't he? It might not be a glamorous job, but it was the job he had, and he was rather proud of it. There was plenty of security to keep things from getting out of hand, and Reiji had said he'd be staying nearby. So what the hell was he so afraid of?

Clenching his jaw to steel himself, he moved forward into the room. Instantly, he felt the gazes latch onto him. He was an unfamiliar face, and young as well, which was chum in the water to the types who tended to frequent this place. The thought made him uneasy, but it was too late to back out now.

A tall man in a brocaded vest with a loose-sleeved shirt stepped in front of him.

"Why, hello," the man said, with a smarmy kind of smile. There was a half-finished glass of champagne in his hand; judging by the way his words flowed together, it was not his first glass of the evening. "Are you new here?"

"Um, yes." He glanced around uncertainly. "It's my first time here in the Den."

"*Really?*" Long fingers closed around Danny's arm, latching on with the force of a bird catching hold of its prey. He looked over his shoulder. "Shalon! You have got to see this. We have a new Companion here with us to play this evening."

A short black man with a tidy, buttoned-down appearance appeared at Danny's elbow, giving him a look of critical appraisal. "Well, well. Isn't he a pretty little thing, Marcus?"

"Isn't he just *darling*? Definitely one of the House's better offerings, if I do say so myself."

177

Danny was uncomfortable with the way they were talking about him as if he weren't even there, but that was really nothing new to him. Clients did it all the time, even when he was the only one in the room with them.

"Well, come on... um, what did you say your name was?" Marcus pulled on his arm, herding him in the direction of a table at the side of the room.

"Danny." He swallowed hard and tried to pretend there weren't dozens of pairs of eyes following him, trailing after Marcus with varying degrees of curiosity and envy.

"Danny. What a nice name." He pushed Danny gently back against the edge of the table, looking down into his face. "Do you have any particular talents, Danny? Anything you're especially good at that you'd like to share with us?"

His face went hot at the question. "Uh, no. Not really."

"Oh, my," Shalon said, peering at him from around Marcus's shoulder.

Marcus's expression was still mildly inquisitive, but there was a sharpness in his eyes now that reminded Danny of a predator focusing in on its prey. "He *is* an innocent one, isn't he?" he breathed.

Danny shivered at the feel of a hand tracing down the front of his throat. He didn't look away from Marcus's eyes as long fingers moved to unclasp the buttons at the top of his shirt.

He held himself very still as those hands finished unbuttoning him and skinned the shirt back off of his shoulders, leaving him barechested. While the air in the room was warm, he couldn't help shivering.

"It's almost like he's never been touched before," Marcus said, flicking a nail over Danny's nipple in passing. Danny gasped at the feel of it, which made the hard edge in Marcus's eyes deepen.

It wasn't that he'd never been touched before. It was that being *watched* while he was being touched always made everything *feel* so much more. He couldn't help being embarrassed at the gazes he could feel raking over him, drinking in his vulnerability and his nakedness as if it were wine.

Marcus had his pants open now, one hand reaching in to stroke at the flesh inside. Danny closed his eyes as he felt himself start to grow hard, knowing full well that everyone in the room around them would be able to see.

"Beautiful," Shalon said, reaching past Marcus to grope at Danny's ass. Danny shuddered when he felt a finger press into his crack, probing his body's entrance.

There was a tinkling of fine china as the plates on the table were slid aside, and he was urged to lie back onto the table's surface. The polished wood felt smooth underneath his back, cooling the sweat that had gathered there.

They had his pants and shoes off now, leaving him entirely naked. He knew there were other boys around the room, many of them as naked as he was and engaged in far more embarrassing acts than this, but that didn't lessen his own self-consciousness any. His face felt like it was on fire, throbbing with a dull heat that covered him from his hairline all the way down his throat.

"Look at how he reacts when you touch him like this," Shalon said, pressing the tip of a finger inside of him. The clinical detachment in the words was insulting, as if he thought Danny were nothing more than an object to be played with.

"Oh, *very* nice." Marcus's nails trailed down Danny's chest, striking a nipple none-too-gently in passing. He reached Danny's cock again and gave it a hard squeeze, encouraging it to swell even larger. "Look how much he's enjoying it. They have the boys here trained so very well."

I'm not enjoying it! he wanted to scream, but the iron discipline that had driven him into the room kept him silent. His entire body felt sensitized, overwhelming him with the sensations these two men were forcing it to feel. The knowledge of other eyes watching him, of dark, anonymous figures moving around the table to observe what was happening, was excruciating.

"I think he wants more, Marcus."

"Do you really think so? Well, we wouldn't want to disappoint him, now would we?"

Danny cracked one eye open, unable to resist looking as Marcus leaned across him toward the plates pushed toward the back of the table. He just about jumped out of his skin when Marcus glanced down at him, giving a smile that was probably supposed to be encouraging but instead made him want to leap off the table and run from the room.

"My dear boy, you look good enough to eat." Marcus ran a hand over the side of Danny's face, tilting his head up, and *now* Danny could see what he had in his hand. It was a wedge of sliced carrot with one end dipped in some kind of white vegetable sauce.

Oh, gods.... Danny clenched his teeth, raising his arms to cover his eyes. He could feel Shalon's hands pushing his knees up toward his chest, exposing his genitals to the entire room.

"Oh, come on, honey. It's no fun if we can't see your face." Marcus tugged on one of his arms, urging his hands down toward his sides.

Danny sucked in a long breath and stared up at the ceiling as the carrot pressed against his entrance and then slid inside of him. It wasn't particularly large, but it had edges that weren't very comfortable. He could feel Marcus's knuckles bump against his ass as the small phallic object was pulled out slightly and then pushed in again, mimicking the sexual act.

He was breathing so hard now he thought he was in serious danger of passing out. His chest ached from the force of his heart pounding away inside it. Danny was just considering the possibility that he'd significantly overestimated his ability to deal with this kind of shit when Reiji appeared at the table beside him, looking down at him with an insouciant grin.

"Well, aren't you jumping right into the thick of things," he said, bumping a hand against Danny's shoulder in a friendly sort of way.

Danny resisted the urge to tell him to get him the hell out of here. "Reiji...."

"Hey, no worries. Charon knew they'd love you." He reached for a carrot on the plate at Danny's head and popped it into his mouth, chewing noisily.

Danny glared up at him. "You are *not* helping."

"Hey, it's not my job to be helpful. To be honest, this is the sexiest damn thing a lot of these people have seen in a long time. Myself included." He waggled his eyebrows suggestively.

The comment made Danny bite back a surge of laughter. The idea of Reiji being sexually interested in him was beyond ludicrous.

Reiji looked relieved that he seemed to be relaxing, even just a little. "Hang in there, all right? It's no different than servicing a client in a private room, if you think about it. How much longer do you think it can last?"

Danny let his head fall back against the table, clenching his fists at his sides. Marcus and Shalon were murmuring to each other excitedly at the end of the table, heads bent together as they focused on his body's reactions. They'd abandoned the carrot in favor of a wedge of cucumber, which was thicker around and longer, giving them more interesting reactions to enjoy as they shoved it deeper inside him.

Lying there, Danny considered the fact that he apparently had no pride left at all. How else could he let people do these kinds of things to him? But that evaluation of the situation didn't seem right at all; he'd worked hard to earn Charon's trust over the past few months, and he was intensely proud of his position here. Most days, he enjoyed his work; servicing customers in the way they needed to be served made them happy, and that was fulfilling on any number of levels. Then there were nights like tonight, when he stepped outside his comfort zone and was forced to stretch himself, putting up with things that were uncomfortable if not downright painful. Charon seemed to enjoy springing these little surprises on him, which Danny sometimes found irritating.

But it was proof of the trust Charon had in him. He might be new to the House, but a real "newbie" would never be asked to serve customers in the Den. This was definitely an advanced kind of work, maybe not on the level that Reiji or Tam were used to, but it wasn't entry-level stuff, either. That knowledge settled down in his chest and warmed him even as Marcus tossed aside the cucumber wedge and reached for an unsliced avocado.

He glanced up at Reiji to see that a customer had stepped up behind him and wrapped an arm around his waist, groping at the front of his leather pants while dry-humping him from behind. Reiji's eyes were closed, his body moving fluidly in rhythm with the motion, his hands clenched hard around the edge of the table to steady himself.

There was a definite air of eroticism in this corner of the room now. There were at least a dozen people clustered around the table, watching intently to see what Marcus and Shalon would do to him next. Hands from multiple directions trailed over Danny's arms, his legs, brushing over the hair at his groin. He sucked in a breath as someone mouthed wetly at the underside of his arm, teeth pressing briefly into the skin there.

His back arched as the end of the avocado was pushed into him. Marcus made a sympathetic noise and pushed it in deeper, bracing him with one hand clenched tight around his thigh. Danny's mouth hung open now, panting as long fingers closed around his neglected cock, stroking him back to hardness.

Reiji's customer had opened the front of his pants now and pushed them down over his hips, groping him lustily as he leaned in from behind. Danny couldn't be sure from this angle, but it looked like the guy was actually fucking him there against the side of the table. Reiji's back was stiff, a thin line between his brows suggesting that the current client had foregone the use of any kind of lube. His arms were locked where he leaned against the table, his body rocking with the thrusts the client made behind him.

Danny's mouth was dry. He'd never seen Reiji have sex before; it had never even occurred to him that he would. He felt embarrassed for the other man at first, but the complete lack of self-consciousness on Reiji's face made that emotion fade away after a few seconds. Eyes closed, Reiji's concentration was entirely on what was being done to him, and what he needed to do to make the customer as pleased with him as possible. That was the job they did, but there was an elegance to the way Reiji accepted his role in it that seemed to transcend the paltry lust and baseness of the room around them.

Looking up at him, Danny found himself growing hot in a way that had nothing to do with self-consciousness. He felt Marcus's fingers tighten around his thigh.

"Yeah, that's it, baby," Marcus said, sounding breathless. He slid his hand down to pinch Danny's ass, making him jump. "Feels good, doesn't it? Damn, you're such a hungry little whore."

Danny wondered if that was supposed to be interpreted as a compliment. He gasped when the avocado was pulled unceremoniously out of his ass, his hips lifting from the table briefly at the shock of it.

"I don't think I'm going to last much longer, Marcus," Shalon said, leaning in around Marcus's side and staring down at Danny with greedy eyes.

"Yeah," Marcus said, his repertoire of clever patter apparently exhausted. He pushed Danny's knees further back against his chest and, after unbuckling his belt one-handed, moved in to claim him.

Chapter 22

Dissension

Marcus's cock was a lot harder to take than the entire arsenal of vegetables had been, despite the fact that the avocado had had more girth to it. Danny supposed that was because it was more personal to be fucked like this, more degrading, giving him yet another shame to hold up on pubic display. He deliberately avoided looking at the crowd that had gathered around them, turning his attention instead to Reiji's face. Reiji really was pretty in a rough kind of way, and the sight of him in the midst of sex was breathtaking. Somehow, having him here made the entire spectacle seem less overwhelming.

Reiji opened his eyes at one point, still moving rhythmically in time with the body thrusting behind him, and winked down at him, grinning. Danny couldn't help grinning at him in return. It seemed that even shame had its limits, and there came a point when he couldn't feel any more horrified or debased than he already did. At that stage, there didn't seem to be anything else to do but find humor in the situation, however bleak.

Marcus finished with a low moan, hips slamming forward against Danny's ass as he emptied his seed inside of him. Then Shalon moved to take his place, his small hands clasping Danny's hips as he slid inside without waiting for him to catch his breath.

The endless, repetitive rocking motion was making Danny feel vaguely nauseous. There was something cold and sticky sliding down the inside of his thigh; probably some kind of condiment, judging by the obsession these two had had with him. His thighs ached, and his back hurt from being pressed against the hard wooden table for so long. All in all, he figured he had entirely earned his pay for the evening.

Shalon was done with him rather quickly, which surprised Danny not at all. The two of them had worked themselves up into such a frenzy that they seemed likely to go off at the slightest touch. He breathed out heavily when Shalon pulled out of him, and carefully lowered his legs.

"You were beautiful, darling," Marcus murmured, bending low over his ear. Danny shivered, making a small sound in the back of his throat when Marcus's hand closed around his cock. "We can't just leave you hanging now, though, can we? Not when you've been so good to us this evening."

Danny bit back a moan and arched his back, hissing through his teeth as Marcus's hand moved faster and faster over his sensitized flesh. His ass still felt loose and full of the things that had filled it over the past hour or so, which, coupled with the friction on his rapidly firming erection, brought him quickly to the edge. He tried to fight it for a moment, not wanting to give in to this final humiliation, but then he surrendered with a groan, knowing that they would have this from him whether he wanted to give it up or not.

He made a wounded-sounding cry when he came, curling forward to try to hide himself as much as possible. Marcus's fingers closed around his wrist, forcing his hand down and refusing to let him cover his face.

A collective sigh seemed to move through the room. Marcus's hand, wet with semen, smeared over his belly in a final farewell. "Maybe we'll see you here again, sweetheart."

Danny was shaking when he sat up, wincing at the soreness in his nether regions. More than anything, he wanted desperately to take a shower.

A hand on his arm steadied him. Snapping a glance at the offender, he froze in the act of pulling his arm away when he saw that it was Reiji.

There were other men around him now, fixing him with hungry stares as they moved in toward him. Danny's heart caught in his throat before Reiji held up a hand to stall them.

"That's enough for now," Reiji said in a voice that snapped with authority. "Go find someone else to play with."

Danny's shoulders slumped in relief. Groping for his clothes, he leaned gratefully against Reiji's shoulder while he got himself dressed again. "Thanks, Reiji. I mean, really. *Thanks.*"

Reiji's smirk was ironic. "I figured you'd had enough for one evening. Maybe later tonight you get down on your knees and blow a few customers to make Charon happy, but I think you've been through enough for now." One eyebrow raised in mock innocence. "Unless I was wrong? I can call those guys back here if you want."

Danny punched him on the arm, grinning. He felt much better once he had the armor of his clothes on. He rubbed at the back of his pants with a grimace. "Yuck. How do you stand doing this every night?"

"Usually the guests aren't so obsessed with... culinary experimentation." He was clearly fighting the urge not to laugh. "I can't believe you ran into a couple of nutjobs like those on your first night here."

"Yeah, just my luck, huh?" He raked a hand back through his hair, already feeling his equilibrium returning. "So long as it's not going to be like that every time."

The look Reiji gave him was evaluating. "You actually did all right, you know? You freaked out a little there in the middle, but you kept your head, and you kept your mind on the task at hand. I know a couple of boys here who would've hauled off and punched the bastards."

The praise made him feel warm inside. He considered the fact that while Reiji liked to come across as confrontational and bad-tempered, at the heart of things he was as protective of the boys in this House as Tam was. All of the senior boys seemed to share that quality to some degree or other, but in those two it was even more pronounced.

"Well, it's our job, isn't it?" He smiled wryly.

Reiji's eyes glinted with humor. "Yeah. Now why don't you go take a break and get yourself something to e —"

He broke off in mid-syllable, making Danny look at him questioningly. Reiji's eyes were focused at some point across the room, his entire body rigid.

Danny followed his gaze and saw a man with hair so blond it looked silvery-white watching them from across the room. He glanced back at Reiji in confusion, but Reiji was already moving. Startled,

Danny ran to catch up to him.

The man didn't look surprised when Reiji walked up to him. "I don't believe you have permission to be here," Reiji said, glaring.

Danny had never heard that particular tone in his voice before. It raised the hairs along the back of his neck.

"Mr. Kendo," the man said with a smile that didn't reach his eyes. "You might be surprised at what I have permission to do." The smile deepened into a smirk. "It's good to see you again."

For a moment Danny seriously thought Reiji was going to physically attack the man. His hands were curled into fists at his sides, his body thrumming with whatever pent-up emotions he was holding back.

A hand fell onto Reiji's shoulder, stilling him. Danny looked up in alarm, seeing one of the bouncers.

"It's okay," the bouncer said, obviously trying to calm him. "We'll handle this."

Reiji shook the hand off his shoulder with such force that it made the bouncer stagger. "It doesn't look to me like you're handling anything."

The bouncer's face remained composed. He bowed slightly in Montgomery's direction, looking apologetic. "If you'll come with me, sir?"

The blond-haired man gave Reiji a last mocking smile before turning to leave. "As you wish," he said with a bored expression, tightening his grip on the cane in his hand.

Danny watched the two of them go, his heart pounding. He was afraid to look at Reiji where he stood beside him.

"Who was that?" he asked.

Reiji didn't answer right away. Danny was surprised to see that he was actually shaking. Nothing ever seemed to faze him, but something about this man had completely unhinged him.

"Stay away from that man," Reiji said at last. His voice was unsteady. "Promise me, Danny. Don't ever go near him."

"Yeah, okay. I promise." Danny had no problem with making *that* vow. If this was someone *Reiji* was afraid of, it certainly wasn't anyone he wanted to meet.

"Okay," Reiji echoed with a sigh. He unclenched his fists, shaking out his arms in a visible effort to relax, although his gaze never left the doorway that the bouncer and the blond man had disappeared through.

Who the hell *was* that? And what the hell had he done to unsettle Reiji so badly?

Danny wasn't entirely sure he wanted to know.

Charon looked up when a shadow fell across the doorway of his office, his eyes narrowing. Montgomery stepped into the office as if he owned it, completely ignoring the bouncer looming behind him.

"Thank you, Jacob," Charon said, keeping his voice even. "That will be all."

Jacob bowed his head and turned to leave the room, closing the door behind himself on the way out.

Pushing back from the desk, Charon stood up and walked slowly around it. He always preferred to face Montgomery on an even footing. "I hear that you've been bothering some of my boys."

If Montgomery was surprised that the news had gotten to Charon so quickly, he didn't show it. "I was only helping myself to some food and drink in your lounge area. You really should train your whores not to be so confrontational."

Charon knew what kind of exhibition Danny had been a part of in the Den that evening, and knew that that was doubtlessly what had drawn Montgomery there. The man was irresistibly drawn to suffering of any kind, no matter how subtle. He held his tongue, however, not wanting to push the matter.

"What is it I can do for you this evening, Lord Montgomery?"

Montgomery smiled at him, as if he knew full well how difficult it had been for him to let the matter drop. "I hear you have a young Vargessian man working here."

The comment surprised him, although he was careful not to show it. "Why would that interest you?" he asked cautiously.

Montgomery's hand flexed over the crystal knob of his cane. "I've come across a buyer who's interested in purchasing the lad," he said casually, as if it were a matter of no great consequence.

Charon was instantly suspicious. "My boys are not for 'sale', Lord Montgomery. They are employees who work here of their own volition."

Montgomery didn't look as if that argument held much meaning for him. "The buyer is a man of some influence, who will not take kindly to being refused." Seeing the continued suspicion in Charon's eyes, he added, "At least let me approach the Vargessian boy with the buyer's offer. You never know," he said with a smile, "he might find himself swayed by it."

Charon leaned back against the edge of his desk, his mind racing. "Who is the buyer, if I may ask?"

"Marcel Delafonte," Montgomery said, "a man of some authority in the neighboring country of Vargess." As if he thought Charon had never heard of the place before. "He's looking to purchase a boy that he can bring into his home and take care of, who would be willing to offer sexual services in return. Certainly it's nothing the boy hasn't been exposed to during his employment in the House of Silence, wouldn't you say?" His smile was ingratiating. "Plus it would have the added benefit of requiring him to please only a single master instead of the droves he's obliged to serve here. The boy—Vincent, did you say his name was?—would live in unspeakable luxury, finer even than you could provide for him, with servants to wait on him and a small fortune in allowance for him to spend as he pleases."

No, Charon hadn't said. Which raised all kinds of questions that he wanted the answers to as soon as humanly possible.

"I've met with Delafonte and have judged him a good man," Montgomery continued with the air of a man sealing a deal, "strong-willed but fair. Doubtlessly Vincent will find him a pleasant master to serve."

A chill ran down the back of Charon's neck. "Did Delafonte also tell you that he's prejudiced against the gypsies of the East Vargessian mountains, of which Vincent was a clan member before he fled the country six years ago? He likes to have them arrested under false pretenses and beaten, raped, chasing them out of his cities with fear and spreading terror among their population. It's not just a hobby for him; it's more like a religious calling. He's not looking for a whore to fuck, Lord Montgomery. He's looking for a slave to torture and keep handily out of view of the public eye."

The expression on Montgomery's face was mild, suggesting that this news did not come as a surprise to him. "In any case, it is the decision of people much higher than you or I that this man be appeased. I ask that you let me talk to the boy and see what he has to say about this."

"I refuse. Unequivocally." The safety of his boys was paramount to him, and he was not about to give Montgomery the chance to spin some appealing lie to draw Vincent into the trap that was waiting for him.

Montgomery looked angry at that. "Please reconsider this course of action very carefully, Mr. Marque. Is it really worth throwing everything you've worked so hard for away, all for the sake of a whore? The buyer is of political interest in very high places, and it's going to come down hard on you if the man is," – the pause was filled with possibilities – "*distressed* over this incident."

Charon straightened, which gave him the satisfaction of seeing Montgomery shrink away from him slightly. "I gave you my decision. The boys here are not for sale, and I will not allow you to lure them in to be tortured and killed so you can line your pockets with money or political influence or whatever else it is this man promised you. Go find someone else to give him."

Montgomery's expression twisted. "You know as well as I do that the Vargessian gypsies are in hiding these days. Those few that frequent the cities are known there, and a man of Delafonte's stature cannot risk getting involved with them without tarnishing his reputation."

"But Vincent isn't known in Vargess anymore, so he's fair game. Is that it?"

"You know full well that Delafonte can't risk any scandal with the public elections coming up next year. Vargess is still a democracy, and his position is dependent entirely on the public's opinion of him. Right now they see him as a fair and benevolent leader, a man of progressive vision who is leading them forward into a new decade of peace between our two countries. It would be a shame to hinder that image of him, wouldn't you say?"

"Oh, yes. It would be a shame if the Vargessian people saw him as the violent, bigoted, sadistic dictator he really is."

Montgomery's eyes narrowed. "It is not our place to question the commands of *our* government, Mr. Marque. You of all people should understand that. You *will* hand the boy over to me."

Charon glanced down, the corner of his mouth lifting slightly. "I'm sorry, Lord Montgomery, but I will not. I told you, these boys are not for sale."

Montgomery stared at him for a long moment. "You will come to regret this decision."

"Entirely possible. It changes nothing, however."

Montgomery fumed for a few seconds longer before turning and leaving the room. He slammed the door behind himself when he left.

"Make sure he leaves the grounds," Charon said quietly.

"On it, boss." Phoebe appeared from a corner of the room and stepped up to stand beside him. "Jeremy's trailing after the worm as we speak."

Charon smiled slightly at that, although the expression soon faded. It occurred to him that he'd never once disobeyed any of the orders Montgomery had passed on to him, not since the very beginning when he'd made the bargain that gave him ownership of the House of Silence. He was a little unnerved by the prospect of what this kind of defiance might result in, but he was determined not to give in. There were some things that were more important to him than any promises he'd made, and this was one of them.

"You do realize this might mean trouble?" Phoebe said, looking at him seriously.

He sighed. "Yes." Not for the first time, he wondered just what she knew about Montgomery, and who the man worked for. "But we don't really have any choice in the matter, now do we?"

She didn't look convinced. "If you say so."

That made him chuckle. "I do say so. I want you to heighten security around the House until further notice. No one goes in or out without being personally okayed by me. And have someone keep an eye on Vincent at all times. I want to make sure Montgomery doesn't try to get to him behind my back."

"Done, done, and done." She buffed her vividly painted nails against the front of her suit jacket, looking bored. "I was looking for a challenge, anyway. This should liven things up a bit."

Charon had a feeling she was going to have all the excitement she could want before too much longer. He figured it was extremely unlikely that Montgomery would just return home with his tail between his legs and accept defeat gracefully.

"While we're waiting for Montgomery to make his next move, I want to find out everything I can about Delafonte, his office, his campaign, his personal life, his 'extracurricular activities', everything you can dig up information on. I want to know him better than I know myself by the end of the week. Do you think you can handle that?"

The look she gave him was affronted. "I'll take care of it personally."

"Good." He moved around behind his desk again and sat down, leaning his head back with a sigh. He'd known it would come down to this, sooner or later.

He could beat Montgomery at any game the man wanted to play with him, no matter what resources the other man had at his disposal. So long as they kept their heads, and stuck together, anything was possible. He believed that from the bottom of his soul.

They were going to be just fine. They would.

Chapter 23

Incursion

"This," Vincent said, "is by far the stupidest idea I have ever heard."

"Yeah, but you're here, aren't you?" Tam grinned at him, the expression barely visible in the darkness.

The sides of the tunnel pressed in around them, giving Vincent a sense of claustrophobia that tickled pervasively at the back of his mind, making his palms sweat. He had never particularly liked enclosed spaces, even when his reasons for being inside them met with his full approval.

He'd known there were secret passages in the House of Silence for a long time now; news like that tended to spread in a place like this. Most of the boys didn't know where they were or how to access them, though, which was probably the best thing for all concerned. However, there were apparently those like Tam whose exploration of the House over the years had led them into areas where they should never really have gone.

Like stumbling onto the passage that led directly into Charon's private office. Just the thought of it was enough to make Vincent break out into a cold sweat, although he had to admit there was a sense of power to using it that appealed to him. He liked feeling in control of his surroundings—odd for such a confirmed masochist as himself, maybe, but there it was—and this added bit of information made him feel that much more secure inside his home.

He bumped into Tam when the other man stopped walking abruptly. He took a half-step backwards, stifling a curse. "What is it?" he hissed.

"Shh," Tam said. There was something taut about the way he said it that made Vincent fall immediately silent. After a moment, Tam said, "I can see the entire office from here. I don't think there's anyone in there right now."

He didn't *think* there was anyone there? Vincent was reminded yet again of why he seriously disliked Tam Temetria. "Maybe we should come back another time," he whispered.

The look Tam cast over his shoulder at him was incredulous. "Are you kidding?" he said, keeping his voice as low as Vincent's had been. "We know Charon's downstairs eating breakfast. We're not going to get a better shot at this."

All of which Vincent already knew. None of it made what they were doing any easier.

There was an almost-inaudible click as Tam swung the end of the passageway slowly open. Heart pounding, Vincent followed him out into the room. As Tam had surmised, they appeared to be the only ones there.

The passage came out through a cunningly hidden doorway in a rear corner of the room, concealed in the shadow of one of the book-shelves. Whoever had designed it certainly knew what they were doing; in all the times Vincent had been in this office, he'd never once suspected its existence.

"Well, then." Tam rubbed his hands together eagerly. "Let's see what we can see, shall we?"

"Remember, we're just here to look up Aburon's paperwork," Vincent said, casting an anxious glance at the closed office door. How long would it take Charon to eat breakfast? Everyone knew that he practically lived in this office.

"Yeah, yeah." Tam moved toward a tall filing cabinet to one side of the door and ran his fingers over it, testing one of the drawers. It was, not unexpectedly, securely locked. "I don't see a safe. So the files have to be in here, wouldn't you say?"

"Of course he doesn't have a safe. Safes would draw the attention of unscrupulous types like us."

"We're not unscrupulous." Tam looked offended at the sugges-tion. "We're just... curious."

Vincent refrained from commenting further. He walked around the large desk to join Tam by the door, giving the large piece of furniture a wide berth. For all he knew, Charon had the thing booby-trapped if anyone besides him touched it. His eyes flickered around the room, looking for hidden surveillance cameras; he didn't see any, but that didn't mean there weren't any there.

"I don't know what you think you're going to get out of those drawers," he said, frowning. "He's going to have all of them locked."

"Yeah, maybe." Tam's brow furrowed in concentration. He tilted his head to get a better view of the drawer in front of him, his fingers dancing lightly over the lock. A moment later, the drawer pulled open with a soft click.

Vincent stared at him. "How the hell did you do that?"

Tam grinned at him. "I wasn't always a Companion, you know."

No kidding. Lock-picking was not generally a skill required in the boys Charon hired here. His heart seemed to beat a little faster as he realized they might actually be able to find the information they were looking for.

"So," Tam said. "Top drawer would have the A's, don't you think? Or maybe it's filed under his real name? If that's the case, it could be anywhere...."

"Wherever it is, just *find* it already." Vincent glanced toward the door again, feeling restless. He usually had pretty good self-preservation instincts in recent years, and something was telling him to hurry up and get the hell out of there. Which was crazy when he thought about it; what was the worst that could happen if Charon were to walk in that door right now? He and Tam would be scolded, certainly, and probably disciplined. Maybe for him it would mean a *lack* of sadistic customers for a while as punishment. Certainly nothing to work him into the frenzy he was working toward.

Tam hummed softly under his breath as he flipped through folders, looking inordinately cheerful as he perused their boss's private files. Whatever subliminal signal Vincent was reacting to, he definitely wasn't picking up on it.

"Hurry," Vincent said, turning his gaze toward the door again.

Charon enjoyed eating breakfast in the kitchen of his House. By all rights, he could retreat to his private tower and order that his meals be brought to him there, or have them catered in his office so he could keep working while he ate, but he far preferred spending time with his boys while he was eating. Breakfast was the one meal of the day where he could be sure to find at least a few of them there. They generally seemed more open to talking to him at that time of the day, particularly as they'd usually just gotten off of their shifts from the previous night and had all kinds of complaints or acclamations or funny stories to share with him.

This morning, there were only two of them present. Danny sat with his heels propped up on the edge of an empty chair beside him, showing a youthful disregard for the furniture that he would never have dared if Madam Mirian had been in the room. The thought made Charon smile inside. He could still remember Danny as he'd been when he'd first come to work at the House of Silence; he'd been disturbingly timid, beaten and worn-down, half-starved and anxious with a flagging sense of self-worth that was due in large part to the way his stepmother had treated him. It had taken a long time to build up his self-confidence by giving him progressively more difficult assignments, but the strategy seemed to be paying off beautifully. The boy had blossomed in recent months, turning from a shy, self-effacing urchin into the cheerful and confident young man he was today.

"Oh gods, you had to deal with him, too?" Danny said, nibbling on the side of a cold chicken leg he'd pulled from the refrigerator. Mirian had opted for a picnic-type dinner the previous evening, and the leftovers this morning showed it.

Meron—the boy sitting across the table from him—nodded, his eyes scrunching with amusement. There was an anxious air about him as he glanced at Charon; he was one of the newer boys, and it showed. Short and slight of frame, he wore a denim vest over a sleeveless black shirt with a colorful rope bracelet around one wrist. He had a pixie-like face and an expensively messy haircut that made him look like some kind of rich lord's son who'd decided to go slumming for an evening. He was still trying to cultivate the "look" he wanted to use while he was on duty, but so far it was working for him.

"Twice," Meron said, grinning down into his bowl of cereal. "He's a riot, isn't he?"

Listening to the boys discuss a mutual customer with such good cheer made Charon feel happy inside. He liked it when his boys enjoyed their work; it made things so much easier when there was satisfaction on all sides of the equation.

"So tell me," he said, fishing gently for more information, "are there any customers you *wouldn't* want to see come back here?"

Danny leaned back in his chair, crossing his arms behind his head. "Where to start?" he said with a grimace. "But it's all a part of the job, isn't it?"

The answer pleased Charon. He knew Danny had had a particularly difficult time of it this past week with his debut in the Den, but as he'd done with all of his previous assignments, the boy had taken it in stride. In time, Charon believed Danny might become one of his most versatile employees.

Meron was still trying to come to grips with the reality of being asked a direct question by his boss when a figure appeared in the doorway of the room, gesturing for Charon's attention.

Charon was on his feet immediately. "What happened?"

Arber was a member of Charon's personal security force, or "bouncers" as the boys liked to call them. He was dressed in the usual uniform, a dark pinstripe suit with glossy black shoes. Trim and professional-looking, they looked more like businessmen than the lethally competent specialists they were. Which was, of course, the entire idea.

Arber's expression was not comforting. "I think you should come with me, sir. There's something that requires your attention."

Which meant it was something he didn't feel comfortable talking about in front of the boys. Charon dropped his cloth napkin onto the table, glancing at Danny and Meron. "Sorry I have to cut this conversation short, but there's apparently something I need to attend to."

"Sure, okay." Danny's eyes were very round; apparently he'd picked up on the fact that there was something big going on. Charon wished he could reassure him, but until he had more information, he couldn't do so without turning it into a lie.

Charon followed Arber out of the room, climbing the stairs toward the ground floor hurriedly. "Tell me," he ordered.

Arber's mouth pressed into a grim line. "The police are here."

That was the last thing Charon had expected him to say, although in retrospect maybe it shouldn't have been. Montgomery sure worked fast.

"Stall them," he said, mind already racing to try to think where Vincent might be. "Find out who's been tailing Vincent this morning and have them make sure he stays out of sight upstairs for the time being."

Arber glanced at him. "Do you think that will stop them?"

Charon smiled grimly. "Absolutely not. But we need time to think about how we're going to deal with this."

They were on the first floor now, and he could already hear unfamiliar voices clamoring from the direction of the lobby. Steeling himself, he quickened his stride to move past Arber toward the end of the hallway.

"Marque." Their gazes shifted to latch onto him immediately; there had to be at least a dozen of them, with more milling about on the portico outside. The speaker was a tall, burly man in full riot gear bearing the crest of the provincial police force. The insignia of a sergeant was sewn into his collar.

Standing in front of them was Branwyn, a petite, redheaded security guard whose slight stature and quiet nature masked a silently patent ability to do harm. She appeared almost comically overshadowed by the armored and visibly armed men in front of her, a misapprehension which Charon knew she would not hesitate to use to her full advantage if the situation were to escalate. She glanced at Charon as he approached, raising one eyebrow questioningly.

He shook his head almost imperceptibly at her and stepped forward to meet the officer who'd spoken, forcing a welcoming smile. "What a surprise to have you visit us this morning, Sergeant...?"

"Krantz," the officer said, giving him a look that suggested he was something the man had found lying at the side of the road covered in filth. It was not an expression Charon was used to seeing on the faces of authority figures who spoke to him, which meant that something vital had changed in the way the provincial government viewed his presence here. "We have a warrant to search the premises."

Indeed. "For what, may I ask?"

"Officer Gestault will fill you in on the details while we get started." Krantz gestured for an officer standing behind him to come forward, then turned away as if Charon weren't worth another second of his time.

Charon's eyes narrowed slightly at that, but he kept his expression mild as he turned to face the new officer. "Officer Gestault, then. What is it my House can do for you today?"

His attention was snagged by a familiar face toward the rear of the group of officers. Dressed only in his uniform without the riot gear many of the other officers sported was Brand Chamberlain, the Aechestanian police officer who had visited the House on one other occasion. As soon as he noticed Charon looking at him, he pushed his way forward to stand in front of him.

"Mr. Marque," he said politely. His expression was unreadable, even for someone of Charon's empathetic talents.

"Officer Chamberlain." He didn't have to feign the confusion in his voice. "Forgive me, but I'm a little unclear as to why an officer from Aechestan is here serving a warrant."

Brand looked uncomfortable at that. "We're not the ones serving the warrant. The provincial police force approached us and asked for assistance, so we're here primarily as back-up. That's all."

Which meant that the provincial police were well aware of the private security he had at his disposal, and were uncertain about their ability to defeat it alone if the House were to front an organized resistance. The thought that they had such poor faith in their own capability was comforting; the presence of so many additional officers was not. Not that any of them would be leaving this House if Charon gave the word; but that wouldn't solve any of their problems in the long run, now would it?

He forced himself to smile. "I wish I could say welcome back to the House of Silence, but under the circumstances...."

Brand's expression did not change; he must have aced his Impersonal Interactions With the Public class, unlike the esteemed Sergeant Krantz. "I apologize for the inconvenience, but you have to admit it had to happen sooner or later."

Curious. "And what exactly are the officers looking for?"

Officer Gestault gave Brand a dark look. "Financial records. We have reason to believe that you haven't been paying taxes on the income you've been making here."

Which was the most bullshit charge Charon had ever heard in his life. Montgomery was sure lacking in imagination.

"That's a bit of a dicey proposition," he said, watching closely for Gestault's reaction. "I do believe a number of those records are protected as confidential documents by law. Perhaps in a formal court proceeding...."

"The warrant was signed by the provincial governor himself." Gestault seemed to take an inordinate amount of pleasure in informing him of that.

Well. That did put a bit of a different spin on things, now didn't it? Legal or not, they had all the political backing they needed to do whatever the hell they wanted here.

"That seems a little excessive for a tax evasion investigation, wouldn't you say?"

Gestault didn't look impressed by the observation, but Brand's impassive expression cracked slightly to show a shadow of doubt lurking in the backs of his eyes.

"Chamberlain!" Krantz barked from across the room. "You've been here before on an investigation, haven't you? Make yourself useful and show Norwich where they can find this guy's office."

Brand looked over his shoulder and nodded. Giving Charon one last unfathomable glance, he gestured for the team to follow him.

Charon watched him go, wondering if he should be worried about the man. If they were here searching for Vincent and not financial documents as they'd claimed, Brand was the only one of them to have met Vincent in person in the past. He'd seemed harmless enough before, but that had been before the entire multi-jurisdictional police force had risen up against the House. Charon had judged him to be a man of good character, but pressure—political or otherwise—did strange things to people.

Giving Branwyn a long glance that he knew would easily be interpreted, he turned back toward Gestault with a smile. "So," he said, "tell me more about this warrant of yours."

Branwyn nodded at him and slipped unnoticed out of the lobby down a side hallway to carry the message to the other members of the security force. Charon had no doubt that the order would spread to every security guard in the House within a matter of minutes. *Tighten the perimeter, secure the upper floors, and above all else, protect the boys.*

The House of Silence was at war.

Chapter 24

Defensive Maneuvers

Vincent realized suddenly what it was he'd been reacting to. The fact was, he knew full well that Charon had private security and that his office was likely to be under constant surveillance. He honestly hadn't expected him and Tam to get as far as they had, and the fact that they had suggested those security forces might currently be engaged in more important things than monitoring an empty office.

The thought seemed somehow ominous.

"Tam," he said. "I really think we should leave now."

Tam glanced up at him with an annoyed expression just as the door to the office opened. They both jumped, turning toward the door guiltily as a single figure stepped inside, closing the door firmly behind herself.

The woman was dark-haired and intimidating, dressed in the dark business suit of a bouncer with a short skirt. Her expression was fierce as she glared at them. "You two have got to have the worst timing in the history of the planet."

Vincent blinked at her. Whatever kind of chastisement he was expecting for being caught here, that wasn't it. "I beg your pardon?"

She frowned stonily as she moved to the intercom on the wall, touching a button there briefly in what had to be some kind of prearranged signal. "You need to get your asses back in that tunnel right fucking now, and don't look back."

The fact that she knew not only that they were here, but how they'd gotten into the room, suggested they'd been under observation for quite some time. Vincent swallowed uncomfortably.

Tam frowned at her with a narrow-eyed expression; obviously

he'd picked up on the oddity of her reaction as well. "Look, if this is about the files—"

"I don't care what kind of juvenile intrigue you two are trying to engage in." The sneer in her voice made Vincent's face heat. "Seriously, you're both adults. If you want to piss Charon off, that's your own business. I'm not your fucking babysitter." Her expression soured slightly. "Well, maybe I am for the time-being. Which means you need to *move* before I start moving you."

Vincent shared a long glance with Tam before starting toward the entrance to the secret passage. Whatever the hell was going on, they'd probably be better off talking about it upstairs.

He'd only had time to take a couple of steps before he heard the doorknob to the office jiggle. Apparently the woman had locked it behind herself when she entered. Before the thought finished crossing his mind, he felt a hard hand between his shoulder blades, shoving him in the direction of the bookshelf.

He stumbled forward just as the door burst open. He turned around in surprise, shocked that anyone would dare force the door of Charon's office. His throat seized when he saw a number of uniformed police officers spill into the room.

"What are you doing here?" the officer at the front of the group said, hand moving warily toward the handgun belted at his waist.

The woman stepped smoothly in front of Vincent, half-shielding him from view. Her hand gestured sharply behind her back for the two of them to keep silent. "These two screw-ups are waiting to talk to the boss about a stunt they pulled with a client last night. I'm keeping an eye on them to make sure they don't slip out before he gets here."

"And who the fuck are *you*?"

"Phoebe Grayson, head of House security."

That made Vincent glance at her in surprise. It occurred to him how very little he knew about the bouncers or their organizational structure. They tended to fade into the background until they were needed, which made them all seem more or less forgettable most of the time. But he had to admit that having the head of Charon's security here with them was making him feel a little bit better about this whole crazy situation.

"Well, Phoebe Grayson, 'head of House security', this place is under lockdown until further notice. We're looking for some very sensitive documents and you're only going to get in the way. We have a warrant," he added pointedly.

"Damn," one of the other officers said, sotto voice. "It's no wonder this place is falling apart with a woman leading the security staff." A low chuckle moved through some of the other officers around him.

A muscle in the side of Phoebe's jaw twitched; Vincent could only guess at the effort of will it took not to react to that. "We'll get out of your hair, then," she said stiffly. She gestured for him and Tam to head toward the door.

"Wait," someone said sharply, making Vincent freeze. He was uncomfortable to see that the man was staring straight at him. "Didn't Krantz say the guy we're supposed to be keeping an eye out for has an eyepatch?"

The officer at the head of the group turned toward Vincent, his gaze focusing in on him with uncomfortable intensity. "Yeah, I think you're right."

Vincent looked at Phoebe, alarmed at this newest development. Her expression frightened him; more than anything, he was bothered by the fact that she didn't look surprised at the officer's observation. Just what the hell was going on here?

Before anyone on either side could react, an officer from the rear of the group pushed his way forward. Vincent was surprised to see that it was Officer Chamberlain. Brand, he'd said his name was; he'd been to the House of Silence once before, and Vincent had spoken to him briefly.

Brand's gaze swept over the three of them, his mouth tightening in a thin-lipped frown. "I'll take the three of them to Krantz," he offered. "Just in case he's the one you're looking for."

The officer at the head of the group looked uncertain for a moment, then gave in. "Make sure they go directly to Krantz."

Brand nodded. "Come on," he said sharply, motioning for them to precede him out of the room.

Clearly, Phoebe didn't like the idea of leaving the officers alone in Charon's office, but considered it a higher duty to stay with the two of them. Vincent was very glad about that.

"Move," Brand said, giving Vincent a heavy glance as Vincent walked by him.

Briefly, Vincent was struck with a sensation of situational vertigo, as if his entire world had turned upside down in just a few seconds. Police officers in the House of Silence was unheard of; police officers ransacking Charon's office and insulting members of his staff was beyond the realm of comprehension. Something profound had changed in the way the House was viewed by the police department, and he didn't understand how or why it had happened. For now, however, his instincts were telling him to stay on guard and watch for any opportunity to react.

Sharing a long glance with Tam, he followed Phoebe out into the hall.

Brand fumed inwardly as he trailed behind his charges into the corridor, wincing at the sounds of drawers being forced and books being toppled from shelves in the office behind him. He didn't like being made a fool of, and he certainly didn't like being lied to. He'd been told that this was a simple warrant run, a search of the House of Silence on charges of tax evasion. He'd been pleased at first that the House was finally under some kind of legal scrutiny, instead of existing under the blanket of immunity it had seemed to inhabit for so very long.

He certainly hadn't been told anything about keeping an eye out for a man in an eyepatch, or the necessity of taking such man into custody if he were to be found. Apparently the provincial police had been given slightly different orders than the municipal officers sent to support them. The whole thing left him with a bad taste in his mouth; he felt like he was being used.

Once they had moved a reasonable distance away from the office, he turned on Vincent with a scowl. "Vincent, just what the hell is going on?"

He could see the surprise on the other man's face and realized with a sinking heart that Vincent was as much in the dark as he was. "I don't know," Vincent said, shaking his head. "You tell *us*."

"Wait a minute." The brown-haired man gave Brand a narrow

look. "You know each other? Who *are* you?"

"Brand Chamberlain," Brand said. "I'm an officer with the Aeches-tanian Police. We were sent here to look for documents, not people. I don't have a clue what they want with Vincent." He turned to look at Vincent again. "Did you do anything they might want to arrest you for?"

Vincent shook his head, looking honestly perplexed. "No! I don't have any idea what they want with me."

Brand's instincts were usually pretty good concerning people; he was inclined to believe him. "So where does that leave us, then?"

"That depends." Phoebe's voice was calm. "Are you really intending to bring the boys to your boss?"

The question was asked mildly enough, but there was a weight to it that made Brand's hand itch to reach for his gun. He regarded the woman closely for a moment, considering his answer carefully. Despite the casual misogyny the other officers had unthinkingly displayed toward her, Brand considered it a serious miscalculation to have sent this group out of the room with only a single officer guarding them. There was an air of quiet competence about this woman that made him extremely uneasy.

"What are you suggesting?" he said, throwing the ball back into her court.

She thought about it for a moment. "For now, we need to get off of this floor. There's too much of a chance he'll be seen here."

"Wait," Vincent said, sounding anxious. "You mean they *are* looking for me? *Why?*"

Phoebe didn't answer. Her eyes didn't leave Brand's face.

Brand hesitated, torn. He had a direct order to bring Vincent to the main force in the lobby. But he didn't understand why, and the thought of turning Vincent over into Krantz's custody made his stomach tighten uncomfortably. He couldn't see handing Vincent over to anyone until he had more information.

"You know why they're looking for him, don't you?" he said, watching her expression closely. She held his gaze coolly, not saying anything in reply.

Finally, he let his breath out in a ragged sigh. "Fine. We go upstairs for now until we can figure out what's going on. But the three of you are still in my custody, understand?"

She looked amused. "Let's go, then."

Fuming silently, he followed as she guided them down the hallway toward a narrow staircase that led upward. Damn, this place was a maze. How long did it take people to learn their way around when they came to live here?

He breathed a little easier once they were off the ground floor, although he knew the reprieve was only temporary. As soon as Norwich realized he hadn't brought Vincent to Krantz, there was going to be hell to pay. The thought of *that* conversation made him feel a bit ill; he'd never disobeyed an order before. But it didn't lessen his resolve to find out what was going on.

They climbed all the way to the third floor before Phoebe brought them to a suite toward the rear of the building, with tall windows that looked down over the hills behind the estate. Glancing around, Brand had to admit that the room would be easily defensible, with two outside walls and a small, windowless bathroom that could be locked from the inside, perfect for hiding civilians safely out of the line of fire if the situation did escalate to the point where there were bullets flying.

Which was crazy to even think about; there was no way Krantz would order the use of deadly force on a matter of tax evasion. But that argument was holding less and less weight with him; it was becoming more obvious with every second that passed that this didn't have anything to do with a warrant run, no matter what he'd been told. Even Marque had picked up on it, pointing out that this was a ridiculously large force to throw at a simple document crime. Whatever Krantz and his men were after, it had nothing to do with taxes.

"All right," he said, turning on Phoebe as soon as the door was closed and locked behind them. They had some breathing room, at least for the time being. "I want you to tell me everything you know about what's going on here. *Everything.*"

She gave him a narrow look, then glanced at Vincent. "Fine," she said with an irritable sigh. "Have a seat."

He watched while Vincent and the other man went to sit on a low sofa against one wall, looking nervous. For himself, he chose to forego the use of a chair and moved to stand beside the door where he could hear any movement in the hall outside.

"Okay." He turned around to face the room, blotting his damp palms on the front of his thighs. He couldn't help thinking that by refusing to turn Vincent in, a line had been irrevocably drawn. He needed to know more about just which side he was choosing here. "Start talking."

Chapter 25
Siege

Ander paused at the top of the stairs, shrinking back into the shadow of the hallway. His heart pounded fitfully; the sound of voices echoing up from the lobby — many of them quite angry-sounding — was not something he expected to hear when leaving the House in the morning.

Despite his initial resolve not to frequent the House of Silence more than the first time he'd visited, it was a temptation he'd been finding harder and harder to resist lately. Last night, neither Danny nor Tam had been available, and he'd indulged in the company of yet another Companion. He had to admit that, no matter what discomfort he still had over the idea, spending time in this place was becoming quite the addiction for him.

Peering around the edge of the railing, he caught a glimpse of at least a dozen uniformed police officers milling about the lobby floor. Sweet gods above, what had Marque *done*?

He moved quickly back down the hallway without really thinking about it, knowing only that he didn't want to be seen. Not that he felt he had anything to fear from the police, but facing any kind of official inquiry would shatter the veil of fragile anonymity he'd begun to enjoy here. The thought made him feel strangely violated; what right did the police have to barge into this kind of establishment, especially at a time when most of the guests would be leaving? Unless he missed his guess, some of the guests here were quite influential in their own ways. The police had to have some very compelling reason to draw them here against that kind of opposition.

Which surprised Ander, because Marque had not struck him as

an unscrupulous man. A bit shady perhaps, definitely with secrets of his own, but he didn't seem the type to do anything of a violent or blatantly illegal nature. At least not in a way that would be easily discovered.

Realizing that his endorsement of the man was waning a bit thin, Ander chewed on his lower lip worriedly and ducked into an empty room toward the end of the hall. Maybe it really would be best just to face the police openly and get the whole thing over with. They had no reason to detain him, and he could be on his way home within minutes.

But what if it didn't turn out to be that simple? He was still pondering his options, torn, when a voice behind him made him jump.

"Who the hell are you?"

He whirled around, heart in his throat. He relaxed when he saw a thin, casually dressed boy with dark red hair frowning at him. Unless his evaluation was totally off base, this was not one of the police officers.

"Ander," he said, breathing out heavily in relief. "Who are you?"

"Reiji." The young man's eyes narrowed at him. "Do you have any idea what the fuck's going on?"

Ander didn't particularly care for his language, but figured this wasn't the time to call him on it. "I have no idea. I was just heading downstairs when I saw the officers down there."

Reiji glanced anxiously over his shoulder at the hallway. "Well, they're starting to go room-to-room now, knocking on doors. They're confining everyone in their rooms, guests *and* boys."

"*What?*" Ander was outraged. "They have no right to do that."

The corner of Reiji's mouth lifted slightly. His eyes glittered. "I'll let you explain that to them when they get here."

Ander looked around, feeling bleak. "What are we going to do?"

Reiji looked annoyed at the question. "The hell should I know? One thing for sure is I'm *not* gonna sit around and wait for them to get here." His expression turned thoughtful. "There's a lot of them searching; they'll sweep through this floor before you know it. We have to go higher if we want to stay away from them."

Like rats fleeing a sinking ship. Ander sighed. "You'll never make it up the stairs without being seen."

"There's another staircase that goes up the back of the building. Customers don't usually use it, and I doubt they've had time to find it yet." He was already moving toward the door.

Ander's heart leapt into his throat at the thought of being left alone again. "Will you take me with you?" he asked, taking a lurching step after him. Reiji turned around to stare at him incredulously, so he hastily said, "If they do find us, I might have enough influence to make them treat us more kindly, or at least find out something about what's going on here."

Reiji swept an evaluating gaze over him, obviously taking in the richness of his clothing and the elegant style he was dressed in. Ander's face colored slightly under the scrutiny.

"Yeah, okay. You might be right." His eyes narrowed. "But if you slow me down any, I will leave your ass behind. Got it?"

Ander swallowed forcefully and nodded. "Got it."

He followed Reiji out into the hall, hunching his shoulders as if he seriously thought that would help keep him from being seen. He couldn't escape the sensation that there were eyes watching him from all sides, the weight of their silent observation pressing the breath out of him.

Reiji led them directly to a narrow staircase that led steeply upward into darkness. The stair was unadorned and dimly lit, clearly intended for private use by the House's residents only. Ander's fingers ached where he gripped the thin banister, shuffling his feet uncomfortably as he followed Reiji upwards. He just about jumped out of his skin when his boot touched on a creaky step that moaned like a sigh in the dimness.

The fierce look Reiji turned on him was profoundly annoying. "Watch it," he hissed.

Ander glared at him. "I'm trying," he whispered back.

His heart felt like it was ready to burst out of his chest by the time they reached the upper floor. On this level, there was no sign of the invasion force that had taken control of the House, for which he was very grateful. He'd never been to this floor before; he figured it had to hold the Companions' private rooms, and other personal facilities that were not generally open to use by the House's guests.

"Now what?" he said, glancing around uncertainly.

Reiji gave him an exasperated look. "You sure ask a lot of questions, you know that?"

Ander considered the fact that his erstwhile guide had no better idea of what to do next than he did. The thought was unsettling.

"Maybe we should just have turned ourselves in," he said worriedly.

Reiji was just opening his mouth to make what was sure to be a scathing response when a door a short ways down the hallway opened, and a tousled brown head peeked out at them. "Reiji? *Ander*?"

Ander blinked. "Tam." The relief he felt at seeing a familiar face was so profound it left his knees weak.

He followed Reiji quickly into the room and looked around as the door was closed behind them, noticing with surprise that they weren't the only refugees to have gathered here. There was a strikingly beautiful young man with a patch of some kind over one eye, a smartly dressed young woman, and—to his complete surprise—a uniformed police officer.

"It's all right," Tam said hastily, stepping in front of Reiji. "Brand's with us."

Reiji gave the officer—Brand?—a sullen stare. "Yeah. We've met."

Ander felt vaguely dizzy over the rapid change in circumstances. He listened with only half an ear as Tam made hasty introductions. "Do any of you know what's going on?"

Brand shook his head. "Ms. Grayson was just starting to tell us, but she hadn't gotten very far."

Reiji's gaze snapped to focus on the woman, his eyes narrowing suspiciously. "Are you saying the bouncers are a part of whatever's going down in here?"

Phoebe shook her head. "Don't blame me for this. I'm just trying to keep things from exploding out of control."

Reiji looked unconvinced. "What the hell do they want?"

To Ander's surprise, most of the gazes in the room moved toward Vincent. Vincent's face reddened slightly, but he looked just as perplexed as the rest of them.

Phoebe frowned at the boy, as if all of this were somehow *his* fault. "More importantly," she said, looking grim. "What do we do now?"

Reiji scowled at her. "Whatever it is, we'd better do it fast. All the boys are being placed under house arrest, sent to their rooms one by one. Any guests that are still here are being locked up with them."

Vincent turned toward Brand with a pained expression. "They have to know by now that you didn't turn us in the way you were supposed to. They're getting serious about looking for us now."

Tam looked incensed. "That's outrageous."

Reiji didn't seem impressed. "I didn't see Charon doing anything to stop it. He's down in the lobby arguing with their boss. They're probably going to arrest him before too much longer; they're demanding to see his client list now, but he's refusing to hand it over."

"As well he should," Brand said furiously. "They have no legal right to that list. The clients' identities here should remain confidential unless they're called in the course of a criminal trial."

Reiji snorted. "You're an idiot if you think this has anything to do with any kind of list."

"So what *does* it have to do with?" Ander asked quietly.

All eyes turned toward Phoebe. "Revenge," she said shortly. When that answer didn't seem to placate them, she crossed her arms over her chest in annoyance. "There's a buyer," she said, "who wants to purchase Vincent. Charon said no. End of story."

Brand looked taken aback. "You're saying there's someone who wants to sell Vincent into slavery, but Marque is protecting him? Someone who has enough influence to send the entire police force after him?"

"Yeah, that about sums it up." Phoebe sounded bored with the whole thing. "Except apparently the guy's some kind of bigot who really wants to torture and kill him."

Ander stared at her in horror, his chest tightening. "Dear gods, there's no way we can let them have this boy."

To his relief, there seemed to be general consensus in the room with that statement. After the infuriated chatter of conversation Phoebe's declaration sparked faded, Brand turned to her again.

"Is there anything you're not telling us about this?" he asked.

She held his gaze evenly. "Nothing relevant."

Even Ander, with his limited knowledge of these people, wasn't entirely certain he believed her. But pressing her for further details right now was not going to help their situation any.

"We have to get out of the House," Reiji said after a moment's contemplation. "They're not going to give up if they want Vin that badly. It's only a matter of time before they make it up to this floor."

The thought made Ander feel desperate. "You mean they're going to find us? There's no place we can hide?"

Tam glanced at Phoebe. "What about Charon's tower? Will they think to look there?"

Her expression turned pinched at the suggestion. "Uh-uh, forget it. I am *not* letting you into the boss's private rooms. Besides, do you honestly think that's not the first place they're going to look once they determine he's not in any of the other rooms?"

Reiji let out his breath in a frustrated sigh. "Like I said, we need to focus on getting out of the House." He glared at Brand challengingly. "What do you say, Mr. Police Officer? You gonna turn us in?"

Brand looked troubled. "I'm not sure I believe half of what's going on here. But," he glanced at Vincent, "I'm not turning Vincent in until I find out what they want with him."

Tam turned to look at Ander. "Ander?" he said, sounding hopeful.

Ander shrank back slightly under the gazes that turned to focus on him. It occurred to him that he was an outsider here, and that his cooperation was in no way ensured in their minds.

"I'm with you," he said firmly, wondering where the sudden resolve had come from. Despite the direness of their circumstances, it felt surprisingly good to have a goal to focus on, a cause to believe in. "I say we do everything in our power to protect this young man."

Brand nodded and turned to look at Phoebe again. "What's the quickest way out of the House?"

She looked contemplative. "There's a secret passageway leading outside from the kitchen," she said. "But you'll never get there."

"Bullshit," Reiji said. "The back stairs lead straight down there."

"But Mirian keeps the door locked at the ground level," Phoebe pointed out. "She doesn't let anyone but the senior members of her staff have the key. And no, before you ask, she doesn't let us 'bouncers' have it."

"Are you telling me you guys don't have any way to get down to the kitchen in an emergency?"

"Yeah," she shot back at him. "Usually we use the front stairs."

Before the argument could devolve into petty squabbling, Brand held up a hand to silence them. "We don't have time for this. Does *anyone* have an idea of how we can get down there without being seen?"

There was silence for several seconds, then Vincent's eyes moved toward Tam. He looked pale after hearing what Phoebe had told them, but otherwise he seemed to be holding up quite well.

"Tam?" he said quietly.

Tam looked surprised at being called to the floor so suddenly. A moment later, his expression cleared. "Yeah," he said, sounding thoughtful. "Maybe."

Brand looked confused. "What are you two talking about?"

Tam grinned at him, although the strained look in his eyes didn't fade. "I didn't always work here, you know. I wandered around a bit in the year or so after I left home before I found this place, and I hooked up with a kind of traveling circus outside of Dequoine. I worked as an acrobat for a few months before I decided that that wasn't near seedy enough a vocation to shame my father and went out to start looking for a new job."

"You were a circus acrobat?" Reiji said incredulously.

"And a damn fine one, if I do say so myself." Tam grinned.

This revelation came as a surprise to Ander, although he wasn't sure why it should. Tam had certainly had enormous flexibility during the time they'd spent together. The memory made his face heat slightly.

Vincent's expression was doubtful. "And that's where you learned how to pick locks?"

Pick locks? Ander was beginning to see where the conversation was headed, and how Tam's particular skills might be of use to them.

Tam looked surprised at the suggestion. "Hells, no. Well, not exactly. There was this guy in the strongman show that I kind of hung out with. Slept with, whatever." He shrugged. "He had kind of a business on the side where he let himself into people's homes and liberated them of their belongings. He took me along on a few jobs, and I learned a few things."

Brand's expression was highly disapproving. "You're saying you were a burglar."

"Only part-time." Tam looked affronted. "Besides, I bet you're damn glad about my shady past now, aren't you?" He smirked.

Phoebe stared at him. "Are you saying you can get us through the door down into the kitchen?"

"I don't know." At least he was honest. "I can try. But if it's anything like any of the other doors in this place, it can't be *that* much of a challenge."

Phoebe's eyes narrowed at that, leaving Ander with the impression that that statement was going to be examined in a lot greater detail once the immediate threat to their safety had passed.

It didn't take them long to come to an agreement that letting Tam try would be better than sitting around waiting for the police to find them. Brand was the one who opened the door and peered out into the hallway, declaring that it was safe to proceed.

Ander felt a lot less secure once he was out in the hallway again. He felt a little better once they reached the back staircase, although the claustrophobic confines of the small space made him jumpy as they descended.

Brand led the way downstairs, pausing for what seemed an extremely lengthy amount of time at the second floor landing before allowing them to proceed further. As he passed by the doorway that opened out onto the second floor, Ander heard a low murmur of voices from down the hall. The sound made the skin at the back of his neck tighten.

"Let *go* of me, you bastard." The words were indignant, drawing his attention toward the partially open doorway leading out into the hall. He peered out to see one of the uniformed officers standing with his back to them not twenty feet away, one hand clenched hard around the upper arm of one of the House's boys. The boy had his heels dug in and was struggling to free himself, his brows drawn together in a scowl that had more than a fair amount of fear in it.

"Shut *up* already." A sharp smack echoed down the hallway as the officer slapped him, drawing out a pained whimper from his captive. "Gods above, for whores who get paid to suck cock every day, you kids sure are averse to being touched."

A burst of coarse laughter echoed from further down the hall, proving that he wasn't the only one currently rounding up stray boys

216

from this floor. "Maybe that's the problem," a voice said from somewhere out of sight up ahead. "Maybe if you offer to pay the little shit, he'll start being more cooperative."

The kid's eyes narrowed, his lip curling. "Like you'd be able to afford me."

Ander tensed when the officer turned toward the boy with a scowl, raising his arm to hit him again. Seeing the kid get bullied like that made Ander's chest tighten in anger. Apparently he wasn't the only one; beside him, Reiji muttered a low curse and pushed past Ander's shoulder, doubtlessly intending to go out there and do something stupid that was going to give away their presence here.

"Reiji, *no*," Ander hissed, his throat seizing.

Phoebe appeared instantly beside them, her fingers closing hard around Reiji's arm to hold him in place. Reiji turned to glare at her, his entire body strung taut where it pressed against Ander's side. For a moment, Ander thought he was going to lose it entirely.

"Wait for it," Phoebe breathed, almost inaudibly.

Ander was at a loss as to what she meant at first, until a new voice intruded into the scene unfolding out in the hall. Turning to look, he saw one of the House's immaculately dressed security guards step into view.

"Excuse me, gentlemen," the man said, bowing his head politely. The smooth courtesy in his voice was at odds with the sharp attentiveness in his eyes as they raked over the officer, narrowing slightly. "Is there some kind of problem?"

The officer glared at him, looking irritated. "No. No problem." He gave the kid a hard shove, sending him stumbling forward down the hall. "Both of you, get your asses down to the lobby. No one's allowed to be wandering around up here."

Ander held his breath while the group of them turned away from the end of the corridor and disappeared in the direction of the main staircase, the sound of their voices fading as they went. His heart was knocking a staccato rhythm against the inside of his ribs.

Reiji yanked his arm out of Phoebe's grip with a disgusted-looking sneer. "Touch me again," he said, keeping his voice low, "and I will kick your ass."

She didn't look impressed. "Keep moving."

Ander didn't start breathing again until they passed by the landing and were descending safely toward the ground level. The House seemed to loom like some kind of living creature around him, a sprawling monstrosity of darkened corridors and perilous turns, with the possibility of discovery lurking around every corner. He'd never had a full appreciation for how *huge* this place was before. He was breathing hard by the time they came to the first floor landing, where their further progress was halted by a tall and very sturdy-looking oak door.

Tam pushed his way to the front of the group, resting one hand on the door's handle. Ander watched curiously as he felt around the knob in the dimness, running his fingers over the lock beneath it. Beside him, Phoebe reached for something inside the pocket of her suit jacket and shined the narrow beam of a palm-sized flashlight at his hands, giving him a better view of what he was dealing with.

"Thanks," Tam said, flashing her a quick grin.

Reiji gave Phoebe a dark look. "Are you telling me bouncers aren't trained to open locks?"

"Not without the proper tools," she said, sounding dangerous. Ander hoped they weren't going to start arguing again.

He looked around as they worked, thinking uncomfortably that if Tam *wasn't* able to open the door for some reason, they were pretty much trapped here at a dead end with a rather worrying bottleneck above them. He wasn't entirely convinced they'd be able to make it up to the third floor again undetected; those officers on the last floor had seemed awfully close to discovering the back staircase. He wondered fleetingly if the man who wanted Vincent was willing to kill to obtain his prize, or if the result of capture would just be shame and the disgrace of having his patronage here publically discovered.

In a surprisingly short amount of time, Tam made a triumphant noise and stepped back, shoving whatever twig of wire he'd been using back into his pocket. "Ta-da," he said, and pushed the door open.

Ander stared through the open doorway, his heart pounding. For the first time, he seriously considered the possibility that they were going to get out of here.

"Let's go," Brand said tensely, and led the way forward.

Chapter 26
A Hasty Departure

Coming around the corner into the kitchen, Brand ducked and jerked to the side just in time to avoid being brained with a heavy cast iron frying pan.

"No, no, wait!" Tam's voice was shrill behind him. "Danny, it's *us*!"

Brand looked up to see a kid who couldn't be more than seventeen standing over him with a frying pan in hand, looking startled. Scowling, Brand pushed himself to his feet.

"We're the good guys," he said, rubbing at his shoulder where it had bumped against the wall when he ducked.

Danny lowered the frying pan, eyeing him warily. "What's happening? There's all kinds of commotion upstairs. When I went up there to see what was going on, I saw a bunch of police officers leading a couple of the boys away." His mouth pinched into a hard line. "When one of the boys tried to get away, the bastard hit him. They didn't see me, though, so I ran back down here."

"Good call," Reiji said, stepping forward. He found a rack of steak knives on the counter and palmed one of them, sliding it into a pocket of his cargo pants.

A kid in a denim vest was huddling behind the table against the far wall, looking up at them with frightened eyes. Brand watched as Tam walked over and crouched in front of him, reaching out one hand.

"It's all right, Meron," Tam said. "We're going to get out of here, okay?"

Meron stared at him. "What do you mean, out of here? Who *are* those guys?" His eyes moved to Brand, his entire demeanor quailing. Brand felt ill at the thought that the sight of his uniform could inspire such fear in anyone.

Brand glanced at the stairs leading up toward the lobby. He thought briefly that he should probably go join his fellow officers once he was sure that Vincent was safely out of the House, but honestly, what kind of reception was he expecting to receive from them? At the very least, he was guilty of disobeying a direct order and helping a wanted fugitive escape, no matter what kind of trumped-up charges the department was using to detain him.

To be honest, he only had these people's word for what the police department wanted with Vincent. For all he knew, it was all an elaborate lie and there was a very good reason for wanting the man arrested. But he couldn't shake the sense of wrongness he had about this entire situation; there had been too many lies on his own people's end of things for him to trust them at all at this point, too many inexplicable contradictions.

What it all came down to was whether he trusted his instincts or not. And right now, his instincts were telling him that Vincent was someone who needed very much to be protected. He thought about the story Vincent had told him about being taught to play the viola by his sister, and the extreme sadness that had been in his voice when he'd mentioned her. Brand needed to find out more about the situation before he did anything as irrevocable as turning any of them in—including himself.

While they'd been talking, Phoebe had moved to a shadowed nook in the far corner of the room and somehow caused a line of wooden shelves to swing outward, revealing a shallow tunnel leading upward. Cold air wafted into the room from the opening.

"Let's go," Brand said shortly, his decision made. He glanced at them each in turn. "None of you has to come with us. Chances are, once they realize Vincent isn't here, they'll let the rest of you go."

"Don't be an ass," Reiji said. "Of course we're not staying here." Tam's face expressed a similar sentiment.

Danny's expression was grim. "I'm not going to hang around here with these bastards trying to take over the place."

Ander nodded, agreeing with him. Brand wasn't entirely sure

what would prompt such an obviously high-ranking lord to want to throw his lot in with them, other than the desire to protect his anonymity. Which was, now that Brand thought about it, a far more tangible motivation than the rest of them had.

He glanced at Phoebe. "What about you?"

She frowned at him. "The boss told us to keep an eye on Vincent, so that's what I'm going to do." The look she speared Vincent with suggested that if he tried to get away from her, she'd have no compunction about hog-tying him and carrying him around on her shoulder.

Brand smiled slightly and turned to look at Meron. He could tell from the look on the kid's face that he would not be coming with them.

"It's okay," Tam said, squeezing Meron's hand lightly. "You stay here and keep your head down. I'm sure all of this will blow over soon."

"Where are we headed?" Reiji asked, joining Phoebe at the mouth of the passageway.

"To the city, I think," she said after a moment's thought. Her fingers tapped against the front of her thigh impatiently. "We need to get lost in a crowd somewhere, at least for now."

Brand followed them into the tunnel, ducking his head so as not to bean himself on the low ceiling. Danny, Tam, Vincent, and Ander trailed behind him, pausing only briefly to swing the passage door shut again behind them. There was an unmistakable click as it locked firmly into place.

The passage was thankfully short, letting out behind a screen of bushes at a near-invisible crook at the House's rear wall. Brand's respect for whoever had designed the place went up another notch. After moving away from the opening for just a few steps, he wasn't sure that even he'd be able to find it again.

"Okay," Tam said, wrapping his arms around himself and shivering. "We're out of the House. Now what?"

Phoebe glanced toward a large, low-slung building off to one side of the House's rear grounds. "We need to get our hands on a car, unless you want to walk into town."

Brand considered their options. It was cold out and none of them were dressed for the outdoors, but the sun had climbed high enough in the sky that they weren't in immediate danger of suffering from hypothermia. Of course that meant the entire grounds were lit up, making them a very visible group of dark spots against a white backdrop, but what was life without a little challenge in it?

Phoebe's eyes narrowed in the direction of the front grounds. "I don't think they're looking back here yet. They won't expect anyone to have made it out of the House."

"I think you're right." Brand was already moving as he said it, urging the rest of them forward. Their only hope right now was to keep ahead of the wave that was following them, and hope that they could outrun it.

He didn't dare breathe as they trailed one by one across the grounds, keeping low as best they could while still moving as swiftly as possible. He kept one eye on the officers he could see milling about at the front of the House in the distance, tensed to react in case he saw any signs that they'd been spotted. The lights at the tops of the squad cars parked there painted lurid crimson and blue stains across the snow, bleeding in a shifting mosaic of light over the cobbled driveway. Fortunately, they were far enough away that none of the officers seemed to be looking in their direction.

The building Phoebe had indicated turned out to be a garage. Inside it was a fleet of very expensive and well-kept cars, including a limousine and a four-wheel drive rover.

She passed up both in favor of a dark sedan, probably because it was the most inconspicuous. "It might be a little tight," she said, sounding not at all apologetic, "but you're all going to have to make do."

Brand glanced around apprehensively as she pulled open the driver's side door and slipped inside. The sound carried easily throughout the large, hangar-like area, despite the fact that she was obviously attempting to be quiet about it. If there was any kind of surveillance outside of this place, there was no way the guards could have avoided hearing it.

He was just beginning to think their arrival had gone unnoticed when a small door at the side of the garage opened, spilling a curving splash of sunlight across the dimly lit floor. Brand glanced up to see a uniformed police officer step in through the doorway; the man glanced around the garage's interior with a wary expression, frowning.

Instantly, Brand shrank down behind one of the larger cars, dropping out of view. Looking around, he saw that not all of the others were as quick to react. The police officer at the doorway gave a muttered curse and drew his handgun as soon as he saw them, holding it steady in a classic two-handed grip as he advanced toward them.

"Don't move," he ordered. From where Brand was hidden, he could see that Danny was directly visible in the officer's line of sight, along with Ander and Tam. Vincent, thank the gods, had managed to slip behind one of the smaller sedans and was currently crouched safely out of view. "What the hell are you doing here?"

The man wasn't anyone Brand recognized; he wore the patch of the provincial police department on the arm of his uniform. The look he fixed their group with was suspicious but not particularly alarmed; obviously he didn't expect them to pose much in the way of a threat.

"Take it easy," Ander said, holding one hand out in a placating manner. His voice wobbled a bit, betraying his nervousness. "We don't want any trouble."

There was only the one guard, it looked like, despite the fact that the garage was the most obvious place for escapees from the House to converge on. Apparently Phoebe was right, and no one was anticipating any of them to have made it outside. That certainly seemed in line with the way a man of Krantz's arrogance would think things through. Brand's lip curled in disapproval. That kind of carelessness would never have been allowed under the direction of his own sergeant.

He was still trying to decide how the hell he should deal with this situation when a low rustling drew his attention. He looked up just in time to see Reiji move in on the officer from behind, reaching for the man's wrist.

Brand's heart plummeted to his toes. He lurched forward without thinking, certain that Reiji was going to get his fool self killed by acting so precipitously. To his surprise, Reiji grabbed hold of the officer's arm and neatly relieved him of his weapon with an economical movement reminiscent of the knife defense techniques Brand had practiced at the academy. He remembered his earlier impression that Reiji was a practitioner of martial arts; apparently that had been more than a vague supposition.

A low sweep of Reiji's foot sent the officer pitching to the floor, landing hard on his back with a soft grunt of pain. With a scowl tightening the skin between his brows, Reiji punched him once to keep him down and then shifted his grip on the confiscated handgun, turning it around in his hand.

"*No!*" Brand had no idea whether Reiji was in a murderous frame of mind, but he had no intention of waiting around to find out. He snatched the gun out of Reiji's hand and shoved him backwards, ejecting the ammunition cartridge from the weapon as he did so. The thought of such a dangerous weapon in this volatile man's hands made him dizzy.

Reiji stared at him incredulously. "What the hell do you think you're doing?"

"We are *not* going to shoot anyone." Brand's tone was unequivocal. He met Reiji's glare with a glare of his own, his heart racing. His palms were sweating. If Reiji took objection to being thwarted and decided to get physical about it, the resultant fight between them was going to be a pain in the ass.

"He's right," Phoebe said calmly from where she stood by the car. "The sound of the shot would tell everyone on the property exactly where we are."

That wasn't the point Brand had been trying to make at all, but he supposed it worked if it convinced Reiji to stand down. At the other side of the car, Danny was staring at them with wide eyes, looking terrified.

Reiji gave Brand a dark look before moving to join them. "I wasn't going to shoot him," he said sullenly, bumping his shoulder against Brand's none-too-gently in passing.

Brand sighed and crouched down to take the handcuffs from the half-conscious officer's belt, using them to bind the man's wrists securely behind his back. The man's friends would find him as soon as they came into the garage to investigate the missing car, but with luck this would keep him out of the way until they managed to escape.

He waited until they were all safely piled into the car Phoebe had chosen—Reiji and Danny in the front seat, the rest of them in the back—before squeezing in with them and shutting the door. Vincent was seated directly beside him, looking worried.

"It'll be okay," Brand said to him. He wondered which of them he was trying to reassure.

The look Vincent turned on him was somber. "I don't like the idea of you all putting yourselves at risk for me this way."

Apparently it had finally sunk in how serious a situation this was. The calmness of the expression on his face disturbed Brand, however. He was reminded of something Vincent had said to him the first time they'd met: *Personally, I don't feel that we're worth saving; but that may just be me.* Did Vincent believe that he wasn't worth saving? The thought was disturbing.

Brand was still trying to come up with a way to respond when Reiji looked back over his shoulder at them with a smirk. "Don't fool yourself into thinking we're doing this for *you.* Those whackjobs are trying to take on the House of Silence. They want to push us around, they'll have to deal with the consequences. We're just regrouping until we can find a way to fight back. Right?"

Vincent smiled at him, looking somewhat more at ease. "Right."

Brand looked forward, meeting Phoebe's eyes briefly in the rearview mirror. He could tell by her expression that she didn't think it was going to be as easy as that. He tended to agree with her.

"All right," he said, pulling his gun out of its holster and laying it on his lap. Just in case. "Let's go do some regrouping."

Chapter 27

Exodus

It had been less than a month since Tam had driven through Aechestan with his brother on the way to visit his former home, but the city seemed to have changed dramatically in the past few weeks. The streets they passed through seemed darker, closer, with far more suspicious gazes being turned toward them.

Of course, that probably had something to do with the fact that he was on the run from the police and potentially being pursued because of it. Shifting uncomfortably in the back seat of the sedan, he tried to ignore the way Ander's elbow was pressing into his ribs and wished fleetingly that Phoebe had opted for the limo.

"Can I drop you off somewhere?" Phoebe asked, looking at Ander in the rearview mirror.

Ander glanced down. "No," he said after a moment. "I'd like to stay with all of you for now, if you don't mind." He turned to meet Tam's gaze briefly before looking away again.

The comment didn't surprise Tam. It was true that he didn't know Ander very well at all, but he knew enough about the man's past to guess that their current situation was providing a welcome distraction for him from the grief he was still suffering over the death of his wife. While they'd been lying together in the warm, comfortingly anonymous darkness during the night they'd spent together, Ander had opened up to him about several things that Tam sincerely hoped the man didn't regret sharing with him.

"Where exactly are we going?" Danny asked from the front seat where he sat between Phoebe and Reiji.

Brand looked thoughtful. "What we need is information."

"I've heard of a man in town who makes a living selling information." Tam turned to look at him, wincing as the car went over a particularly large pothole. Phoebe wasn't in any danger of overusing the brakes. "They call him the Weasel."

Phoebe muttered something under her breath that he couldn't quite make out, but that sounded definitely unladylike.

Brand raised an eyebrow at her. "You disapprove?"

She glanced up at him in the rearview mirror, her expression darkening. After a moment, she said, "Don't worry about me. I'm just the driver."

Tam wondered what she had against the Weasel. Despite what she'd said—or hadn't said—it was obvious she disapproved of the idea of them going there.

But he really couldn't think of a better course of action for them to take. He had no idea what they had among them to trade for the information they needed, but the fact remained that they desperately needed to find out what was going on if they had any hope of fighting against it.

He was still reeling from the knowledge that the House of Silence had been targeted. No matter what, the House had always seemed inviolable, unchanging, sacrosanct. He couldn't believe how quickly things had fallen apart. From mischievous pranksters sneaking into Charon's office to fugitives on the run from the law in just a matter of hours; it seemed impossible that the situation could get any worse than it was.

Of course even thinking such a thing was like standing out on a hilltop waving his arms in the air and calling all gods fools. The only difference was, he didn't plan to stand still and wait for the lightning bolt to strike.

To his surprise, Phoebe brought them directly to the small pub that the Weasel called home. Tam had been here once before, just before he'd headed out to try his fortune at the House of Silence two years ago. He hadn't had much to trade then, either, but it had been enough to get him what he needed. He only hoped his luck would be similar this time around.

She parked the car close against the side of the building, scowling as she got out and headed into the bar. Tam watched her closely as he followed her inside, wondering just why she had chosen to come with them. He didn't know much about the bouncers, having preferred to pretty much forget they existed during the time he'd spent in the House. Phoebe wasn't at all what he would have expected Charon's head of security to be like, if he'd ever taken it on himself to wonder such a thing. Was it really loyalty to Charon that kept her here? Just how far could they trust her?

For that matter, how far would they be able to trust Brand? Both Vincent and Reiji seemed to know him, but neither had been particularly forthcoming about the circumstances in which they'd met. Tam was hesitant to trust any member of the police in their current situation, although he had to admit that the man had seemed to play straight with them so far. He definitely bore watching, though.

And how about Ander? Of all of them, he was the outsider Tam felt the most at ease with. Maybe it was just because they'd slept together, but there was something about the man that Tam found comfortable. He still seemed endearingly fragile to Tam, although there was a core of inner strength to him that shone through at odd moments.

The interior of the pub hadn't changed at all since the last time Tam was here, giving him the disturbing impression that he'd somehow stepped back through time. But the people around him were his current friends and temporary allies; he drew strength from their presence as he went inside and sat down at the bar.

The Weasel came out to greet them dressed in baggy jeans and a dark T-shirt with the logo of a popular local band printed on the front of it. His hair, bottle-brush short and vividly yellow, seemed designed to accent the prominent bones of his face.

"Wow, what a surprise," he said by way of greeting, his gaze sweeping over each of them in turn. His eyes glittered. "To what do I owe the pleasure of this motley assemblage?"

"You tell us," Brand said shortly, leaning one elbow on the bartop. "I hear you're a fount of information."

The Weasel grinned sharply. He leaned back against a shelf behind the counter, crossing his arms. "I might have heard a few things. Like how the House of Silence was being targeted in a raid this morning."

Danny made a small sound of dismay. "You mean you knew

about the raid and you couldn't *tell* us?"

The look the Weasel gave him was offended. "You didn't ask."

"And even if you had, the information wouldn't have come cheap." Tam smiled slightly, knowing full well how the game was played.

"A man has to make a living." The Weasel didn't sound at all ashamed over it.

Brand leaned back on his stool. "So what can you tell us about our current problem?"

"That depends. What do you want to know?"

"For starters, why are they after the House of Silence?"

The Weasel's eyes flickered toward Phoebe, looking surprised. "You mean you don't already know?"

Phoebe scowled at him. "Delafonte," she said, "is a senator in Vargess. He wants to get his hands on a gypsy slave, and certain members of our government want to keep him happy badly enough to turn on the House of Silence to get Vincent for him."

"Very good," the Weasel said sarcastically. "But do you know *why* he wants this young man in particular?"

That question left them all silent for several seconds.

"You're saying he targeted Vincent specifically," Tam said, thinking it through. "Why?" He glanced at Vincent. "Have you ever met Delafonte before?"

Vincent shook his head, looking bewildered. "Never. My family never got involved in politics."

The Weasel chuckled softly. "Maybe not directly."

Brand glared at him, leaning forward across the table. "If you know something, just tell us, already."

When several seconds passed without any further explanation forthcoming, Ander sighed and pulled off one of his jeweled rings, sliding it across the bar top. "How much information will this buy us?" he asked.

The Weasel scooped the ring up in his hand smoothly and gave it a cursory examination, turning it over in his fingers. "I'm assuming it's real?" he said with definite interest.

"Of course."

After another second, the Weasel slid the ring into his pocket.

"Senators in Vargess run a seven-year term. He's up for reelection next year. Does that mean anything to you?" He asked that last question of Vincent directly.

Vincent's face went pale. Tam glanced at him in alarm. "What is it?"

When Vincent spoke, his voice sounded hollow. "Six years ago," he said, "a group of men attacked my clan. They burned our homes, slaughtered our horses, and k-killed...." He glanced down at the hands fisted tight in his lap, swallowing forcefully.

"It's all right," Tam said quietly, touching him on the arm.

Vincent ignored him. "They killed almost everyone. And my sister...." There was another pause while he gathered his courage to speak. None of them interrupted him. "They raped and murdered her. I barely escaped. I think... I think they assumed I was dead when they left me there."

It was a long moment before any of them spoke.

"So you're saying Delafonte was the one who ordered the attack on Vincent's family," Tam said, turning back toward the Weasel.

"Of course it was. He'd just been elected, and he was eager to flex his newfound muscle. He's not the only one who's bigoted against gypsies; he has plenty of like-minded allies in the military, and you can be damned sure he's being very careful about who he appoints to his personal staff. Vincent's clan was only the first. He's been targeting the gypsy clans along the face of those mountains pretty regularly for the past few years; none of them dare to travel out in the open anymore."

"And the reason he's after Vincent is...?"

"Why else? He's the one who got away."

The thought disturbed Tam. He glanced at Vincent, but Vincent was refusing to look at any of them. The expression on his face was stony, eerily calm. It made Tam uncomfortable looking at him; surely he had to be having *some* kind of reaction to all of this.

Danny looked stricken. "So what you're saying is, we have the combined governments of Khatar and Vargess after us."

"That about sums it up." The Weasel looked amused.

"And there's no way to make them stop."

"Well, you could always hand over the gypsy."

Brand gave him an annoyed look. "That is out of the question." The absolute certainty in his voice reassured Tam. "The thing we have to be worried about is whether they're after anything other than Vincent. Reiji said something about a client list."

Ander looked worried. "A list like that could have enormous blackmail potential in the wrong hands. Not that *I* have anything in particular to fear from exposure, but I'm sure a lot of those men have families, public images."

Tam snorted. "I wish them luck finding it, if that's what they're after. Those filing cabinets in Charon's office are filled with junk. I couldn't find any client information in them, on Aburon *or* anyone else."

"Of course not," Phoebe said, sounding amused. "You don't honestly expect the boss to leave that kind of information lying around where just any fool can find it, do you?"

Tam locked gazes briefly with Vincent, his face heating.

"Aburon," the Weasel said in a casual tone of voice that instantly made Tam wary. "Francois Aburon? He's an interesting one, isn't he?"

Tam frowned. "You know who Aburon is?"

The Weasel grinned at him. "I might have heard a few things."

Brand looked exasperated. "If you don't have anything further to tell us, we're going to go."

The Weasel cocked his head to one side, contemplating the question. "I think that about covers it."

"Who in our government is backing Delafonte?" Phoebe asked. Her eyes were narrow when she said it.

"I don't know." The Weasel shook his head, looking honestly regretful. "If you happen to stumble across that bit of information, I'll be willing to pay quite a bit for it."

Brand looked disgusted. "Let's go." He pushed himself up from the counter and turned to leave.

There was a general furor of movement as the others got up to follow him. Tam hesitated, feeling the Weasel's eyes on him.

"You guys go on ahead," he said. "I'll be out in a minute."

He could feel the question in Brand's eyes and ignored it. Vincent met his gaze briefly before turning to go.

Finally, Tam was the only one of them left in the room. "Who is Aburon?" he asked, getting straight to the point.

"Ah," the Weasel said, sounding interested. "You want to trade."

"I do."

"What have you got?"

"Nothing more than I had two years ago." He held his arms out to either side in demonstration of his penniless status. "Take it or leave it."

"Oh, I don't believe that for a second, Mr. Temetria. A man of your colorful background, not having anything to trade?"

Tam gritted his teeth. "Unfortunately all of my earnings for the week are back at the House of Silence," he said, deliberately misunderstanding him.

The Weasel's eyes turned cagey. "Perhaps a quick visit to a local bank...?"

"They are going to come back in here any second now to see what's so interesting about our conversation. And *you* are talking yourself right out of a deal."

The Weasel chewed on his lower lip for a moment, looking thoughtful. "I believe I may be able to accommodate you," he said at last.

"How generous of you."

He got up and moved around behind the counter while the Weasel held the hinged bar top there open for him, and followed him into the back room.

The room had the musty, vaguely unpleasant odor of a storeroom, with walls lined in shelves filled with dusty glass bottles of various shapes, sizes, and colors. A narrow doorway with a swinging half-door led further back into the kitchen area.

"I assume your talents would have improved over the past couple years, given your recent place of employment," the Weasel said, reaching for the zipper of his pants.

"Practice makes perfect," Tam said with a shrug, and dropped down to his knees.

As many times as he did this, it never stopped feeling demeaning. Not that that bothered him unduly, but it was yet another annoyance to add to a life that had already become more chaotic than he generally cared for. He skimmed the Weasel's jeans down his thighs one-handed, using the other to knead through the thin boxers at the rapidly firming erection underneath.

"Ah," the Weasel said, curling a hand in his hair.

Tam winced when the hand gripped a little too tightly, but voiced no protest as he leaned in to take the hardening cock into his throat. Obviously, the Weasel approved of what he was doing. Tam firmed his lips and pressed with his tongue, and tried not to gag when the hips in his hands jerked forward, catching him by surprise.

The little bastard had done that on purpose. Narrowing his eyes, Tam sucked on one of his index fingers to wet it, then groped around behind the Weasel's ass and probed for the entrance there. Once he found it, he shoved the finger unceremoniously inside.

"Fuck," the Weasel breathed, his fingers tightening in Tam's hair. He was always a bundle of energy, but his body was *vibrating* now, all of the energy in it racing forward toward one very specific destination.

Tam pulled the neglected cock into his mouth again, pushing deep with his finger while he added another. What the Weasel *really* needed was to be bent over a convenient tabletop and taken for a ride, but his pride would never allow it. Tam didn't bother to suggest it to him; after all, it wasn't like the guy was a client or anything.

He got a good rhythm going, sucking hard in time with the gliding movement of his fingers in the other man's ass. There were two hands in his hair now, clenching so hard it brought tears to his eyes. The Weasel's body was hunched forward over him; his breaths heavy with a kind of hissing whine at the end of each one that told Tam he was doing it exactly right.

The cock in Tam's mouth was surprisingly thick for such a thin man, making his jaw ache a bit. It was a relief when the Weasel's hips snapped forward one final time, his head falling back with a yelped, "Fuck, yes!" as he spilled himself down Tam's throat.

Tam disengaged himself from the fingers coiled in his hair with an effort. "So," he said, wiping a hand over his mouth and sitting back on his heels. "Who *is* Aburon?"

Still breathing hard, the Weasel told him.

Chapter 28

Enemy Occupation

There were, Charon thought, far more annoying circumstances he'd had to live through since he'd taken ownership of the House of Silence.

At the moment, however, he could not think of a single one. He looked around his decimated office, taking in the storm of loose papers lying everywhere, the books thrown in heaps beneath the empty shelves, and—most vexing—the shattered crystal of the cognac decanter some of the boys had given him as a joint gift last year for his birthday. Somewhere, he knew, Montgomery was laughing.

"Bastards," Jacob said behind him, looking coolly dangerous in his black pinstriped suit.

"Hmm." Charon moved forward through the debris that littered the office floor and bent to retrieve the broken head of a heavy glass statue from underneath the twisted spine of a book. The statue's twin, oddly enough, was still sitting undisturbed on the shelf above it. He was at a loss to guess why the officers had found this particular bust so offensive, and not the other.

"Any other damages?" Arber asked from the doorway.

Jeremy looked up from where he was attempting to lift a filing cabinet that had been knocked sideways onto the floor. "Some doors have been forced throughout the House, and there's been a bit of ransacking here and there. Mostly that was confined to the rooms on the ground floor, although the music room will never be the same. No significant damage to any people, though." He paused. "Not on our side, anyway."

Charon looked up at that. "Explain."

Jeremy's expression darkened. "Someone tried to get a little too friendly with one of the boys, against the kid's express wishes. Bran ended up breaking the bastard's wrist."

"Good," Charon said coldly. Branwyn deserved a raise once all of this was done. "Any word on Vincent?"

"Nothing recent." Arber's expression was grim. "The last we heard, Phoebe was tailing him."

If Phoebe was with him, then Charon was willing to bet he was okay, at least for the time being. That gave them some breathing room.

"Boss." Harold, one of the newer guards on the estate, poked his head around the corner of the doorway. "A Sergeant Krantz is asking to speak with you."

Charon guessed that the request hadn't been worded anywhere near that politely. "I'll be right there, Harold. Thank you."

He dusted his hands off on his pantslegs and pushed himself to his feet, wishing he'd been able to finish his breakfast that morning. He gave curt orders for them to continue with what they were doing before heading out to the lobby.

"Mr. Marque," Krantz said with exaggerated politeness as soon as Charon stepped into the room. "You must think you're pretty clever."

"I've been known to be, on occasion. To what specifically are you referring?" His eyes swept over the room, taking in the group of boys standing huddled together at the base of the stairs. They looked frightened, but unharmed. He was relieved to see that there was one of his guards here to keep an eye on them.

"I'm talking about that tower of yours. My men haven't been able to get into the upper floors of it."

"That's surprising. They certainly haven't been shy about breaking down any other doors that have been in their way."

"They tried." Krantz's tone was dark. "And let me point out that you don't seem particularly surprised."

The man really shouldn't try sarcasm; it wasn't becoming at all on him. "And your people's inability to break through a door is my fault how, exactly?"

Krantz glared at him. "Your security guards tell me that none of

235

them have keys to those upper rooms. I find that very hard to believe."

Charon supposed Krantz would find it shocking how little he cared what the man believed at the moment. "Are you saying you still haven't found any evidence of this supposed tax evasion? I assure you, I have been quite fastidious in my civic duty and have been paying my taxes dutifully every year." Which was, incidentally, entirely true. "Unless there's something else you're looking for other than tax documents?"

The question hung in the air for several seconds before Krantz said, "You have an employee here that we need to talk to. A kid with an eyepatch, by the name of Vincent Michaelis."

Ah. Finally, they were getting somewhere. "What is it you suspect Vincent of having done?"

"It's nothing he's done, exactly. We think he might have been witness to a murder, and we want to ask him a few questions about it."

Interesting blend of half-truths. Vincent had, as Charon well knew, been witness to the brutal slaughter of his entire clan.

"My boys are under no obligation to report their whereabouts to me while they're off-duty," he said. "He might not even be inside the House at all."

Krantz's eyes glittered. "I *will* send someone out to get some explosives to blow down that fucking door of yours. Don't think I won't."

Charon was still contemplating possible ways to reply when one of the boys at the base of the stairs shifted. "Vincent's not here," the boy said, sounding frightened.

Every eye in the room turned toward him. "What did you say?" Krantz said with lethal softness, stepping toward him.

Charon's eyes narrowed. It was Meron, one of the House's newer boys. New enough, apparently, that he didn't know when to keep his mouth shut. It occurred to Charon belatedly that Meron had seen Vincent recently and might have some idea where he was right now. He wished there was a way to bring the boy out of the room and question him privately, but any attempt to do so would very likely result in his own arrest and incarceration, since Krantz was so clearly chomping at the bit to find an excuse to take him into custody.

"I—" Meron looked around with wide eyes. The single earring in his ear jingled.

"It's okay," Krantz placated in a voice that was surprisingly soothing. No doubt the man was an accomplished politician. "Just tell us where he is. His life might be in danger if we can't get to him in time."

Charon tried telling the boy with his eyes to shut up, but Meron wasn't looking at him.

"He left," Meron said in a rush, staring up into Krantz's face anxiously, "through the kitchen."

"I see." The words were even. "Was he alone?"

"Meron, shut *up!*" one of the other boys snapped, giving him a hostile look.

Meron caught Charon's gaze at last and swallowed hard, seeming to finally realize that he'd done something wrong. But it was too late for him to back out now.

"Um..." he said, wetting his lips uncomfortably. His gaze flickered back and forth between the two of them.

"Don't look at him," Krantz said sharply, making a laughable attempt to take command of the situation. "If you're withholding information, I'll have to have Officer Greene here arrest you and take you down to the jail. You don't want that to happen, do you?"

Over Charon's dead fucking body. A glance at the aforementioned Officer Greene showed him a man who looked disturbingly eager to have a young, attractive, impressionable boy of an obviously submissive nature under his sole and unsupervised control.

Of course it could be informative at this juncture to find out just how far Krantz would be willing to take this. What exactly were the orders he'd gotten from Montgomery, or whomever it was Montgomery had bribed to put these events in motion? Would he really allow one of his officers to assault an innocent bystander just to make a point? Not that Charon could allow him to actually harm Meron, but a cautionary tale about the hazards of acting against the Head of the House's wishes might not be amiss for the boy at this point.

Krantz advanced on Meron, using his superior size to its full intimidation potential. Charon watched through narrowed eyes, but didn't object when Krantz reached out to lay a hand on the boy's shoulder. He could feel the eyes of his security guard on him, alert but following his lead by not interfering.

"Vincent Michaelis," Krantz said, very softly. He didn't look away from Meron's eyes. "Where is he?"

Meron wet his lips and stared up at him. The poor boy was obviously terrified, and also very obviously regretted ever opening his mouth and drawing this man's attention. He glanced at Charon again and cringed visibly, apparently sensing the disappointment that Charon didn't bother to suppress.

Charon had to hand it to him, though; now that he was aware of his mistake, he was doing his best to find something resembling a backbone. It was too little too late, however, since the harm had already been done. Krantz was endearingly determined to unearth further clues about Vincent's whereabouts; Charon wondered just what the man had been offered in exchange for the information. A promotion? A house on the beach? A protectorate of his own to rule over? Montgomery's resources were pretty much unlimited when it came to persuading corrupt city officials to see his point of view about things.

When Meron didn't say anything further, Krantz shook his head in what almost seemed to be genuine disappointment and turned to look at Officer Greene. Greene gave a pleased sort of half-smile and stepped forward.

"Come on, kid," the officer said, reaching out to grab hold of Meron's arm. "I'm going to have to bring you in to the station for questioning."

Meron dug in his heels with a wild expression, trying to yank his arm away. Greene's grip on him tightened in response; he spun Meron around and pushed him face-first against the wall beside the stairs, holding his wrists firmly at the small of his back.

"Get the *hell* off of me," Meron snarled, the words trailing off into a whimper when Greene's hand clamped down on his shoulder in what had to be a devilishly painful grip. He turned to look at Charon again over his shoulder, his eyes pleading.

Charon watched dispassionately, his attention divided between Greene's manhandling of the boy and Krantz's alarmingly hungry expression as he watched it happen. Krantz, it seemed, had a bit of a sadistic streak to him, as well as a voyeuristic one. Charon spared a passing thought to be grateful the man had chosen to pursue a career in law enforcement instead of corrections; the idea of this man in charge of inmates inside the seclusion of a prison made his blood run cold.

Greene leaned low over Meron's ear, pressing forward against him full-length from behind with an almost imperceptible nudge of his hips. Charon was willing to bet he was letting Meron get a feel of just how thrilling he was finding this encounter.

"Think he's carrying any weapons?" Greene said, his voice deepening.

Krantz shrugged. "There's no telling what Marque lets the whores in this place get away with."

Which was permission enough, it seemed, for Greene to begin patting Meron's body down in a ludicrously contrived search for concealed weapons. Meron tipped his head forward against the wall and set his lips with a stony-eyed grimace as the officer's large hands smoothed over his ribs, his hip, and then reached down further, squeezing the flesh between his legs.

"You got any illegal substances on you?" Greene said with a small smile, brushing his lips over Meron's ear.

Meron was shaking visibly. He pressed his hands flat against the wall, his back arching as Greene continued to grope at him. Charon couldn't tell for sure from this angle, but it looked like Greene might have his hand inside the boy's pants now.

It was regrettable that Meron was being made to suffer like this, but he'd brought it on himself for his outburst earlier. Charon glanced at Krantz curiously, wondering how far he was going to let this go. Krantz seemed to have forgotten Charon existed, his gaze fixed on Meron and his officer with a kind of predatory focus that made Charon uneasy.

"Yeah, that's it." Greene's voice got seriously husky when he was aroused. He was using the weight of his body to pin Meron against the wall, his hands moving busily at the boy's groin area.

Meron stiffened abruptly, choking back a hoarse cry as his body spasmed. Charon winced in sympathy, guessing how difficult it must be to be forced to orgasm under these circumstances. Greene gave the boy's crotch a last hard squeeze before stepping away from him, letting him fall in a humiliated slump to the floor.

"No weapons," he reported with a grin, turning back toward Krantz.

Glancing around, Charon saw that while some of the officers in the room looked distinctly uncomfortable with what had just happened, most of them were flushed with the same greedy attentiveness that had characterized Krantz. He wondered with a twist of wry amusement if he should charge them for the show.

Meron sniffled, biting into his lower lip. He glared up at Greene with a sullen expression. "Bastard," he muttered under his breath.

Greene cuffed him hard across the side of the head. "You'll learn some respect, boy, if I have to fucking beat it into you." Clearly, he was looking forward to the opportunity.

Krantz glanced at Charon challengingly, daring him to intervene. Charon raised an eyebrow in response. He wasn't particularly impressed by either man's display of bravado. In his opinion, bullying those weaker than he was was a coward's game. Respect, like loyalty, had to be earned—not coerced. He was tempted to tell Krantz so, but decided against it. There was no point in attempting to educate men like him, no matter how strong the temptation to do so was.

Meron exclaimed sharply when Greene reached down to grab hold of his wrist, yanking him roughly up to his knees. He raised one arm over his head defensively. "Fucking all *right* already. *Damn* it!"

Instantly, Krantz's attention was focused on him again. "Tell me. Where is Vincent Michaelis hiding?"

The look Meron cast up at him was brimming with tears. "I told you, he's *gone*. Out of the House. Tam went with him, and Danny." His voice shook when he said it. "And Reiji, too, I think."

"Those are all whores who work here?" Krantz asked with characteristic bluntness.

Meron nodded, looking miserable.

"And who else was with them?"

"Some other guy; I don't know who he was. I think he was a guest. And one of the bouncers. And a guy in a uniform."

"A *police* uniform?" Krantz said incredulously. Meron nodded.

Apparently Charon's faith in Officer Chamberlain hadn't been misplaced after all. That was one bright point in a day that had so far been nothing but bad surprises.

"I think that's more than enough," he said, drawing Krantz's attention. At a glance from Charon, the security guard in the room stepped forward to rest a hand on Meron's shoulder.

"Enough?" Krantz echoed, sounding amused. "We haven't even gotten started, Marque."

"No, I really think we have." Now that he knew Vincent was safely off the premises, his own excuses for staying here were practically nonexistent. He'd learned everything he needed to from this little charade; Krantz was a man that needed watching, and no mistake. "I have business I need to attend to in the city, as it turns out."

"Now look, Marque, I'm not about to let you—"

"Unless," Charon said, talking over him smoothly, "you're planning to arrest me? In which case, we may have to wake up Judge Chaffee on his day off, which would be regrettable for all concerned." Judge Chaffee was, as it turned out, a longstanding client of the House of Silence, and would doubtlessly have a vested interest in keeping the House's internal business out of the public eye.

A flicker of uncertainty crossed Krantz's eyes. For a man of his obvious political ambitions, the threat of earning the enmity of a higher court judge was no small thing. "You're bluffing."

Charon smiled. "I think you'll find, Officer Krantz, that no matter who's holding the end of your leash, I also have friends in extremely high places."

Krantz glowered at him for a long moment before saying, "Fine. But don't leave the city."

"Wouldn't dream of it." Charon turned on his heel and walked toward the front door.

Arber seemed to materialize beside him, holding out his coat. Charon took it from him and shrugged into it without slowing.

"You're in charge while I'm gone," he said shortly, keeping his voice low. "Make sure someone keeps an eye on Krantz; that man is dangerous, and I don't want him fucking with my boys. Keep the boys safe, and if at all possible, keep those bastards out of my tower."

"Yes, sir." The quiet confidence in his voice was encouraging. "I think most of us are spoiling for a good fight."

Charon glanced at him out of the corner of his eye. "Don't push things. Let them smash up the building as much as they want; I don't give a damn what happens to the House. But not one of the boys gets injured. Got it?"

"Of course."

Charon nodded at him, mollified. One of the things he liked best about the staff he'd chosen was their dependability in a crisis. "Get to it, then." Arber nodded and disappeared down the hall.

Just as he reached the front door, his attention was snagged by one of his security guards gesturing from the hallway leading to his office. He made a quick detour, frowning a question as he approached.

"Phone call," the guard said without preamble. "It's Phoebe."

Charon's heart leapt at that. Doubtlessly, she'd somehow gotten off of the property and found her way to a public phone. He didn't spare a glance for any of the rubble littering his still-decimated office as the handset of a phone was handed to him.

"Ms. Grayson, hello," he said, deliberately keeping his voice calm. He knew that alone would tell her that things were more or less in control on this end. "How are things going where you are?"

"How the hell do you think they're going?" She sounded irritated.

Perversely, that made him relax slightly. Irritated was pretty much Phoebe's status quo, so if she felt secure enough to be annoyed about things, then everything was pretty much as it should be.

"Is everyone there with you?" he asked, keeping the question deliberately vague. There was no telling who might be accessing the records of this call later.

"Yeah, we're all one big happy family."

That was a relief, anyway. "I'm glad to hear that."

"I don't suppose we can come home yet?"

The strained longing in the words made him smile. "Not just yet, I'm afraid. What have you and the kids been up to?"

"Oh... sightseeing, wandering around, visiting some old haunts. The usual."

The Weasel, he identified immediately from her description. He couldn't think of anyplace else in the city she would refer to as an "old haunt" in that disgusted a tone. No matter how many times he impressed upon her the necessity of doing business with the man, she still maintained that he could not be trusted. Her opinion was a valid one, but Charon considered it entirely beside the point. The Weasel was a bottom-feeding user who would just as soon sell them on the open market as cater their business; the least they could do, in Charon's opinion, was use him in turn.

He wondered what kind of information they'd managed to obtain from their visit there. "We need to start organizing this little venture if it's going to be at all fruitful."

"*Agreed,*" she said tersely.

"Good. Get all the boys together and take them to the dog run. I'll join you shortly."

There was a moment's grudging silence before she answered. "*Fine. We'll meet you there.*" The line went dead, buzzing incessantly in his ear.

He smiled grimly as he set down the phone. Doubtlessly she was questioning the wisdom of this latest tactical decision, but the ease with which she'd complied showed that she was aware of just how narrow their choices were. Glancing briefly at Arber, he folded down the collar of his coat and turned to leave, feeling a renewed urgency to get out of the House as soon as possible.

There were those on his staff who had questioned his decision to make Phoebe his head of security. While her tactical skills were unmatched by anyone he'd ever met—either on his payroll or elsewhere—her people skills definitely left something to be desired. Even worse in the eyes of some people, she consistently failed to treat him with the awe and heavy-handed respect they considered his due.

Charon, however, had never felt particularly drawn toward fawning sycophants. One of the things he found most appealing about Phoebe was her willingness to slap him down, hard, when the situation called for it. He had no illusions that he was perfect, or that the world would instantly transform to his desires simply because he willed it so. He needed someone at his side with a down-to-earth viewpoint who wasn't afraid to voice opinions that were contrary to his. And, if necessary, call him to the table and declare him a damned fool when he was acting like one.

By the same token, Phoebe was also one of the most loyal members of his staff. She might argue with him, might fuss and growl and pull her hair out over what she openly identified as his moronic stupidity, but when push came to shove, she always obeyed his orders. Years ago, she had worked for one of the country's foremost cabals, second in command of the entire security force and personally in charge of protecting the cabal leader's son. She had a lover, also on the force, who ended up betraying her and making a play for a rival cabal. The man had used her to get information about their boss's itinerary; the ensuing violence had left the entire cabal in chaos, Phoebe's lover dead, and herself near death and discredited even though she had very nearly sacrificed her life to save the son she'd been tasked with protecting.

When Charon found her, she was unemployed and embittered, on the road to physical recovery but locked within a shell of animosity and self-reprisal that refused to allow her to trust anyone again. Charon had talked personally to several contacts from her former cabal and come to the conclusion that—despite the blame she heaped on herself for the perceived failure of her mission—only one security professional in a hundred would have been able to save her charge from the assassination attempt the way she had. He looked at her and saw a strength of character he admired, a dedication and a lethal skill that he knew instantly he had to have on his personal staff.

It had taken a long time to convince her to come work for him, but once he had succeeded in winning her loyalty he knew it was his to keep. At the core of their oddly balanced relationship was the heartfelt respect that each felt toward the other, even if that respect was often shown in unexpected ways. Right now, Charon was willing to trust her intelligence to identify the meeting place he'd specified for them. And her strength and fortitude to keep his missing boys safe until he could join up with them. That was a tall order to place on anyone's shoulders, but he had to believe she could handle it.

He paused at the front of the garage, glancing over his shoulder one last time at the towering, gothic silhouette of his House. The sight of it gave him a pang, as if part of him didn't believe he'd ever see it again. Sunlight caught like fire in its many windows, giving him the uncomfortable premonition that everything he'd worked so hard to build these past years was going up in flames. He wondered how many of his boys were looking down at him through those windows;

he wondered if any of them thought he was abandoning them.

Stay safe, he ordered them fiercely, and turned away toward the garage.

Montgomery had a hell of a lot to answer for.

Chapter 29

The Calm Before the Storm

Danny stared out the front window of the car with wide eyes as they pulled into the driveway of a large, extravagant-looking mansion with marbled columns. The lines of the house were sharp and clean, giving it a modern appearance that he found innately appealing. Unlike the House of Silence, this building had a lively feel to it, with large windows and a number of broad balconies decorated with small chairs and tables, suggesting that its owner enjoyed spending time in the open air.

"This is where Charon said he'd meet us?" Tam asked from the back seat.

Phoebe let the car's engine fall silent with a scowl. "He'll be here."

Danny climbed out of the car with a feeling of profound relief, stretching out limbs gone stiff from the lengthy drive. The relief he felt was only partly physical, however; just the thought that Charon might be joining them soon was invigorating, making the events of the morning seem not quite so overwhelming.

His gaze moved to Vincent, who was standing next to Tam at the other side of the car, looking up at the house with a frown. He couldn't imagine anyone wanting to hurt Vincent; the guy was quiet sometimes, and moody, but Danny had always gotten along well with him. The thought that someone in another country wanted to make him suffer or even *kill* him was incomprehensible to Danny. And the fact that the police in their own country were involved didn't make any more sense to him.

But that was reality, and they had to find a way to deal with it.

He'd learned a long time ago that the world wasn't going to make any particular effort to conform to his understanding of it; why should things change any now just because he was getting older?

Phoebe led the way up to the house's front doors and rang the doorbell. The bell sounded with a musical chime that seemed to echo throughout the interior of the house. She frowned, as if she found the cheerful sound of it somehow offensive.

Danny looked around as he waited, taking in the land around them. The grounds of the estate were expansive, dotted with dark green trees and foliage that gave the place a kind of woodsy, rural atmosphere that was at odds with the decadent nature of the house. The contradiction worked, however, giving the place a feeling of isolation, of enforced privacy, that seemed incredibly appealing under their current circumstances. From somewhere in back of the house, he could hear dogs barking.

The door was opened by a tall, elegantly dressed man in a long swallowtail coat and white gloves. His gaze swept over all of them briefly before finally settling on Phoebe.

"Ms. Grayson," he said, sounding as impassive as if this diverse a group of people showed up on his doorstep every day, "will Mr. Marque be joining us today?"

"Mr. Marque *will* be joining us today," she said, pushing past him to step inside. The rest of them filed in after her. "Please tell Lord Angelo that we're here, and that Mr. Marque is on his way."

The butler bowed slightly, a flicker of curiosity making its way through his stoic façade. "I will inform him immediately. You and your friends are welcome to sit in the foyer while you're waiting."

"Thank you." Phoebe watched him go, then walked stiffly into an adjoining entry chamber. She immediately took up a post standing in front of one of the large windows, staring outside at the front grounds with a frown.

"What *is* this place?" Danny asked, following her.

Brand had an odd expression on his face. "If I'm not mistaken, we're standing in the home of the infamous Lord Marcus Angelo."

"Really?" Reiji said, flopping back onto one of the room's low couches and crossing his feet over the arm of it. "What's he infamous for?"

"For being filthy rich, mostly. He's quite possibly the wealthiest man in the entire province, aside from Marque. He keeps pretty much to himself from what I hear, although he's known for breeding dogs and horses, and holding outrageous parties at different times of the year."

"Sounds like a fun guy," Tam said with a smirk. He glanced at Phoebe. "And Charon's friends with him?"

Phoebe hesitated before answering. "I don't know if 'friends' is the right word. But they've known each other for years."

Danny walked over to stand next to Ander. Ander was looking up at one of the elaborately framed paintings on the walls with a thoughtful expression, his brow furrowed. Danny wondered fleetingly if this house was anything like the one he lived in, or if these surroundings felt as alien to Ander as they did to him.

"Have you ever heard of Marcus Angelo?" Danny asked, crossing his arms over his chest.

"I've heard of him." Ander smiled faintly. "Usually not in a very favorable light, but then I come from a rather conventional crowd."

The thought made Danny smile. He couldn't imagine Ander throwing a lot of wild parties.

"Is Lord Angelo a client at the House of Silence?" Brand asked.

Phoebe snorted in amusement, not looking away from the window. "He doesn't need to pay for that kind of temporary companionship. He has his own harem."

That got Danny's attention. Judging by the sudden sharpening of Tam's and Reiji's expressions, they were having a similar reaction. Only Vincent seemed unaffected where he stood beside Phoebe at the window, staring outside.

Before Danny could give voice to the question hovering on his tongue, he heard a low clicking of claws on the floor of the hallway outside the room. He turned to see a stocky, dark-furred dog with a low-slung head come into the room, followed by a tall man holding a glass half-filled with what looked like an early evening cocktail.

This had to be the infamous Lord Marcus Angelo. He wasn't at all what Danny had been expecting; he looked to be in his late forties, with shaggy blond hair and a neatly trimmed goatee that accented the vulpine sharpness of his features. He was dressed in a colorful button-down shirt opened at the collar, the tails of which hung over the hips of comfortable-looking khaki pants. His feet were bare inside soft-soled loafers.

"Phoebe!" he said with a smile. "Abernathy told me you brought friends with you. How wonderful."

"Thank you for taking us in on such short notice," she said, turning away from the window. "Mr. Marque should be joining us shortly."

Danny eyed the dog warily, not liking the cautious way it was looking at all of them. The animal was *huge*, with enormous paws and jaws that looked strong enough to cut through steel. He couldn't quite place the breed; its fur was black fading to brown at the muzzle and lower legs, with a slightly lighter shading on the underbelly.

Angelo seemed to pick up on his anxiety. "Oh, don't worry about Josephine. I've been keeping her inside lately because she's about to whelp another litter for me. She's harmless." He grinned. "Mostly."

Wonderful. Danny shivered, sharing a long glance with Ander.

"So," Angelo said, clapping his hands together, "to what do I owe the pleasure of this visit? It's unusual company you're keeping these days, Phoebe." His gaze swept over each of them again, lingering on Brand's uniform.

"There's been a... situation." Clearly, she was uncertain how much Charon wanted her to reveal. "I'm sure Mr. Marque will explain everything once he gets here."

"Very mysterious," Angelo said, his eyes dancing. "You've gotten me curious now, dear girl." Thankfully, he didn't pursue the matter further. "But you all look half-chilled and starved. Why don't you come into the back room, and I'll have someone prepare some dinner for all of you."

Danny looked around the house in awe as they moved further into it, taking in the sweeping staircase leading up toward the second floor, the stained glass lamps that decorated the walls, the way the ceiling rose to a creamy apex at the top of the hall. He'd gotten used to extravagance over the past couple of months, but the sheer level of decadence evident here put even the House of Silence to shame.

They ended up in a large, airy dining area with tall windows and paned glass doors that opened onto the rear of the estate. The room was filled with fading sunlight, giving it a somber, calming ambiance. Danny sank down into a chair at the long table with Tam on one side and Ander on the other, and reached immediately for the bowl of fruit at its center. It was amazing how hungry escaping from one's home and being on the run from the law could make a person. He was *starving*.

More food arrived as the minutes slid past — hot, sweet rolls with a side of honey-flavored butter, some kind of creamy soup that tasted like it had real lobster in it, grilled fish, skewered shrimp, steamed vegetables of several different varieties. Everything he tried was absolutely delicious; the wine was particularly good, with a smoothness that eased out some of the tension he'd accumulated during the day. A servant showed up to stoke the fire in the large fireplace, which made the whole thing even better. Danny was just starting to feel relaxed for the first time since the whole adventure had started that morning when he noticed a boy with dark hair and a narrow, frowning face peering at them from around the edge of the room's arched entryway.

Brand seemed to have noticed him at the same moment. "Hello," he said, setting his napkin down in his lap. Of all of them, he was sitting the closest to the doorway. "What's your name?"

The boy looked startled at being addressed so forthrightly. His wide-eyed gaze flickered over each of them before he started to withdraw.

"Nao!" Angelo's voice snapped from across the room, freezing him in his tracks. "I'm glad you're here. Come in and say hello to our guests."

The boy hesitated for a moment before obeying, sliding around the edge of the doorway and stopping just inside the room. He was older than he had looked at first glance, delicately pretty with dark brown hair cut in an angled, feathery style that complemented the thin bones of his face. He was dressed in a pale shirt and loose cotton pants, his narrow feet bare against the cool ceramic tiles of the floor.

"This is Nao," Angelo said in a prideful tone similar to ones Danny had heard used to describe new cars their owners had recently purchased, "one of my boys. Nao, these are friends of Mr. Marque's."

"Hello," Nao said, dipping his head forward slightly. He had a timid, whispery voice that seemed somehow endearing.

Was this one of the harem boys who lived here? Danny was insanely curious about him. He couldn't imagine what it would be like to be a part of a rich lord's personal harem. He figured it must be something like his own job, only with a single client instead of the dozens Danny had to put up with. Did that make things easier or harder for him? Danny knew that if he ever had a customer he didn't like, he probably wouldn't have to see the man again after the morning. But Nao and Angelo were pretty much stuck together. Did Nao ever get bored with him? Or did he like the repetitive familiarity of it all?

His thoughts were interrupted when the front doorbell chimed. Phoebe looked up from her meal sharply and got up to stand at one side of the room's doorway, peering out into the hall.

After a couple of minutes, Danny was relieved to see Charon walking into the room, accompanied by the butler, Abernathy. Judging by the collective sigh that passed through the room, he wasn't the only one who was happy to see him.

Charon favored them all with a crooked grin. "Well," he said, "I can say very truthfully that it is *extremely* good to see all of you."

"Did anyone follow you?" Phoebe asked, holding out her hand.

He shrugged out of his coat and handed it to her. "Of course not," he said, sounding offended. "Give me a little credit."

She didn't look impressed. "They might have had an unmarked car tailing you."

"No one followed me," he said again. "And there are no tracking devices on the vehicle; I checked. You taught me well, Ms. Grayson."

"Tracking devices," Angelo said, perching on one corner of the long dining table. He had one arm around Nao's waist where Nao stood beside him, cradling the boy's head against his shoulder. "Unmarked cars? You have a lot to tell me, I think."

"Marcus." Charon gave the other man a tired smile. "I owe you for taking in my people unannounced like this."

"Yes, you do." Angelo grinned sharply. "You can start by telling me the story that's just dying to burst out of you. I'm sure it has to be a good one."

"It's certainly interesting." Charon moved forward and sat down at the table, reaching for an empty plate to fill once Angelo urged him to do so. He ate in silence for a couple of minutes before giving Angelo an abbreviated version of the events that had driven them out of the House of Silence that morning.

When he finished, Angelo's eyes were very round. "I can't believe it. The police have raided the House of Silence."

"Unfortunately, yes. They're being quite enthusiastic about it."

"And you just *left* them there? If it were my house, I'd have sicced the dogs on them and laughed while they had their faces chewed off."

Charon smiled slightly at that. "I didn't leave the place undefended. Plus, the boys' safety comes first."

"Ah, yes, your notorious boys." His eyes moved to glance at the rest of them, crawling over Danny in a way that made him uncomfortable. "These are some of them, I take it?"

"Reiji's one of mine," Charon said, gesturing toward each in turn. "And Tam, Danny, and Vincent. The rest are just along for the ride."

"You have a definite type you prefer," Angelo mused, eyeing them evaluatingly. "Young and pretty, with a touch of attitude. But I knew that already." He grinned.

Charon looked amused. "You might be surprised. All different kinds of people come to work at my place."

"Hmm." He ran his hand along the underside of Nao's throat, petting him absently. "I don't suppose you'd let me borrow any of them?" His eyes lingered on Danny when he said it.

"None of them are on duty at the moment," Charon said with a shrug. "They can do whatever they want. But we won't be able to stay long."

"Just till tonight, surely? Whatever you're planning to do, wandering around the city in broad daylight can't be a very good idea."

Charon hesitated at that, turning to look at Phoebe. They seemed to have a kind of unspoken conversation for a few moments before he nodded. "Till tonight," he said with a sigh. "It'll give us some breathing space, anyway."

Angelo's grin turned decidedly predatory as he stood up and walked toward Danny's chair. "How about it... Danny, did he say your name was? Do you want to play with us since you're stuck here for the time being?"

Danny stared up at him, not knowing what to say. His gaze moved to Nao, who still stood leaning against Angelo's side. The boy's eyes held his; there was a faint edge of inquisitiveness in his expression, as if he were curious about what Danny would do.

Phoebe snorted and pushed back from the table. "I'm going to go outside and keep an eye on the grounds." She threw her napkin down on the table and stalked out of the room without another word. No one offered to go with her.

At first Danny had thought Nao might be resentful at the offer of having an outsider join them, but that apparently was not the case. He wondered what it would be like to have sex for the fun of it, and not because he was being paid. The idea had a refreshing sort of novelty to it.

As if he sensed Danny's thoughts, Angelo gave Nao's shoulder a light nudge. Instantly, Nao moved forward and lowered himself to his knees in front of Danny's chair. Reaching up to cup Danny's head in his hands, he pulled Danny's face down for a kiss.

"Oh," Tam said from the other side of the table. "That is *very* nice."

Nao's mouth was smaller than Danny had been expecting, but it was wet and nimble and very good at what it did. He tipped his head to the side and sighed into the kiss, shivering when Nao's tongue flickered into his mouth, subtly urging his own tongue to follow.

He felt dizzy when Nao pulled away. He wasn't used to being on the receiving end of this kind of attention; his face heated slightly as he glanced up at Angelo, figuring it probably showed.

Angelo's eyes were focused on him with an intensity that made him shiver. "You, my boy, must make your employer a great deal of money."

The offhanded compliment made the heat in Danny's face deepen. "I don't know. I mean, I've only been there for a couple of months."

Charon was smiling where he leaned back in his chair at the end of the table. "He's also extremely modest, and has absolutely no idea about how attractive he is to the right kind of customer."

"All a part of his charm, no doubt." Angelo reached down to cup his hand under Danny's chin, tipping his face upward. "How about it,

Danny?" he asked softly. "Do you want to play?"

He could feel the others in the room looking at him, wondering what he was going to say. The scrutiny made him swallow uncomfortably.

"Yeah," he said, his eyes moving to Nao again. "I do."

Angelo's grin sharpened, the light in his eyes glittering. "Wonderful. Then come with me."

Chapter 30
A Time for Play

Tam chortled inwardly as he watched Danny leave the room, flanked on either side by Nao and the esteemed Lord Angelo. He had a feeling that the poor boy had absolutely no idea what he was in for.

"Go on," he said, nudging Ander on the side of the arm. He hadn't missed how interested the man had gotten while Nao had been kissing Danny. "I'm pretty sure that offer was open to everyone. You can go play with him, too, if you want."

The look in Ander's eyes was uncertain. "I...."

Ander just about jumped out of his skin when a hand fell on his shoulder, squeezing lightly. Glancing up, Tam saw a slim, attractive boy with the look of a nymph about him—slender and long-limbed with silky blond hair and round, startlingly green eyes. He was dressed in cut-off shorts and a soft, short-sleeved shirt that was a couple of inches too short to cover his belly completely. A jeweled ring winked in the concavity of his navel.

"Your friend's right," the boy said, giving an impish smile. "Lord Angelo sent us in to get you. You're all welcome to come play with us, if you'd like."

"An orgy," Reiji said, sounding impressed. He thought about it for a moment. "Why the hell not?" He rolled to his feet and turned to give Brand a piercing grin. "What about it, Mr. Officer? Are you planning to come play, too?"

Brand looked decidedly uncomfortable. "No. Thank you."

Reiji shrugged. "Suit yourself." Linking an elbow around the arm of the brown-haired boy standing next to him, he sauntered out of the room through the archway Danny had disappeared through.

255

Tam counted four harem boys in all, including Nao. Lord Angelo obviously favored a very specific type. All of them were in their teens and heart-breakingly beautiful, with slender limbs and hair cut at about chin-length. Many of them wore jewelry of some kind or other — an earring, a belly ring, and perhaps other kinds of rings in more private places. Their personalities seemed to range from the shy, self-effacing Nao to the impish beguilement of the blond boy who was even now leading Ander out of the room by the hand. Maybe Angelo liked to have a variety of them to choose between, depending on his mood. Or maybe they each served a different function when they all lay together. Just what was the relationship like between an eccentric, rich lord and the members of his harem?

Tam could understand Danny's curiosity about them. He chewed on the inside of his cheek, glancing at Brand. "You really should go with them, you know."

Brand's eyes narrowed. His posture was stiff. "I don't think so."

"Why not?" Tam was honestly curious. "Do you not like men?" That, from what he surmised from Brand's expression, was not the case. "Or is it that you don't like whores?"

"Officer Chamberlain," Charon said from the other end of the table, "suffers from a deplorable excess of morality. He feels that selling sex for money is dishonest."

An interesting point of view. It wasn't one Tam particularly understood, but he chose not to comment on it. "But there's no money involved right now," he pointed out. "It's just a group of people having fun together. Aren't you even just a little bit curious?"

He could feel the intensity of Charon's attention on their conversation, even though he had apparently turned back to his meal. Brand turned to look at the room's doorway, his expression turning uncertain.

"It's not that I think there's anything wrong with what you boys do. You're free to sell whatever you need to in order to make a living." Clearly, the admission was difficult for him. "It's just that...." He shook his head, looking rueful. "I think you're all a bit more used to this kind of thing than I am."

Tam smiled. "Maybe a private room, then?" he asked softly.

Brand stared at him, his eyes narrowing once he realized what

Tam was offering. "Look, I don't know what you—"

"It's not a bribe," Tam said firmly, pushing himself up from his chair. "It's not a trick, or a trap, or a hoax." Egad, the man had to be making this deliberately difficult. Anyone with half a brain could see that he wanted to get in there and join them, but was feeling too inhibited to do so. "You're a part of us now, whether you want to be or not. Don't tell me you haven't felt that."

Brand's eyes were very round. He didn't object to Tam's evaluation of the situation, however, which Tam took to be a very good sign.

"Come on." Tam reached for Brand's hand and tugged lightly. "Let's just go see what they're up to. If you don't like it, I promise we'll leave."

He held his breath, not knowing if Brand's fear of the unknown would outweigh his very healthy curiosity. After a moment, Brand slowly stood up from his seat.

Tam cheered silently. "All *right*," he said, unable to hold back his grin. "Let's go."

The others had retired into one of the inner rooms on the ground floor, a large, windowless chamber warmed by a huge fireplace, with multiple couches and all kinds of soft furs and throw rugs scattered across the floor. Tam remembered Brand's comment about the kinds of parties Angelo liked to throw and considered the possibility that this wasn't the first orgy to be held here.

Danny was already half-naked, stretched out on his back in front of the fire. Nao was bent over him, kissing him deeply, while Angelo had a hand moving busily between his spread legs. Tam couldn't see what Angelo's hand was doing at this angle, but judging by the expressions Danny was making, he could guess.

Reiji was curled up with two of the harem boys on one of the couches nearby; one of them had Reiji's pants open and was currently going down on him with a blissful expression while the other pushed up his shirt, tonguing at his nipples. Reiji glanced down at them with a slit-eyed expression, breathing shallowly as he petted at the hair of the one bent over his groin.

Ander was locked in an embrace with the fourth of Angelo's young nymphs, shivering visibly as fingers moved reverently through his long hair. Tam watched him with a smile, pleased that he had managed to open himself up to these kinds of experiences. Now if only he could get Brand to stop denying himself and give in to the pleasures his body so evidently wanted.

"See?" Tam said, rubbing a hand slowly up Brand's arm. "They look like they're having fun, don't they?"

Brand laughed under his breath; it was a nervous sound. "Yeah. I can't argue with that."

Danny made a small sound that went straight to Tam's groin. Glancing in his direction, Tam saw that Angelo had produced a dildo of some kind and was currently putting it to its intended use. Danny bit down hard on his lower lip and squeezed his eyes shut, his back arching off of the floor.

Tam's smile took on a wicked cast. "Come on," he said, nudging Brand toward that end of the room. He didn't give him a chance to protest, urging him down onto his knees at Danny's side.

"See?" he murmured in Brand's ear, bending down over the officer's shoulders. "No one's getting hurt here."

He could see that Brand was staring at Danny's naked form, his mouth hanging open slightly. His eyes were wide and unblinking, taking in every twitch and movement Danny made.

Tam could feel a slight vibration in his shoulders. He smiled, squeezing his fingers around them encouragingly. "It's all right to look at him. He *wants* you to look at him. He's beautiful, isn't he?"

Angelo gazed up at them with a lazy grin, giving the dildo in Danny's ass a sharp twist. Danny responded beautifully, lifting his hips with a small cry.

"Fuck," Brand said under his breath.

Tam settled his chin onto his shoulder from behind, grinning. Nao's expression was composed as he reached for Danny's hands, twining their fingers together above Danny's head to expose even more of him to their admiring view. Bending down, he trailed his open mouth along the underside of Danny's arm, laying down a glistening trail with his tongue.

Danny was very obviously erect, even though no one was touching him on that part of his body. The deep line etched between his brows gave evidence of how uncomfortable it was for him.

"Poor thing," Tam said with mock sympathy, petting at Brand's arm. "Look at him. He's so aroused, and no one is doing anything about it for him. He can't even touch himself now the way Nao's holding him."

Brand let out his breath in an explosive sigh.

"You can't tell me you don't feel for him," Tam said. He slid his fingers down to close around the back of Brand's hand and lifted it carefully, guiding it toward Danny's bare torso. He felt the jolt that passed through Brand's entire body when his fingers brushed the side of Danny's ribs. "You can feel his heartbeat, right here."

He pressed Brand's palm flat against Danny's chest, enjoying himself immensely. Brand was shaking like a leaf now, but there was nothing that could remotely be considered resistance in him.

"It's fast, isn't it?" he whispered, brushing his lips over Brand's ear. "He's so excited. He likes it when you touch him like this."

He moved Brand's hand downward, skirting the edge of Danny's navel until Brand's palm rested firmly over his erect cock. The sound Danny made at that was pained, but his hips thrust upward beseechingly.

"See?" Tam breathed, curling his fingers around the back of Brand's hand to tighten his grip. "Didn't I tell you he was suffering? You can make it better for him, Brand. Or maybe you like to see him suffer? He does look good like this, doesn't he?"

Brand made a wounded sound of his own, his hand twitching. He was staring down into Danny's face now, drinking in the desperate entreaty in the younger man's expression.

"It's a feeling of power, isn't it?" Angelo said quietly, looking up at them with darkened eyes. He was sprawled out on his side next to Danny now, propped up on one elbow. His shirt was opened, the slim hands of one of his harem boys sliding sensuously across his chest where the boy knelt behind him. "You can either indulge him, or deny him. It's entirely your choice."

Brand remained frozen for a moment longer before his hand started to move. Danny closed his eyes with a drawn-out sigh, his hips rolling sinuously with the movement. Angelo pressed hard on the dildo in his ass, drawing out a thin wail from him as he moved.

Brand was sweating now. Tam pulled the stiff collar of his uniform down and mouthed at the side of his neck, biting lightly with his teeth. He heard Brand's breath hiss inward sharply, but his hand did not slow on Danny's cock.

Grinning, Tam moved to unbutton the front of his shirt. He could feel Brand grow tense when he neared the side where his weapon was holstered and steered well clear of it, not wanting any concerns about officer safety to get in the way of the mood they were building. He allowed Brand to reach down and eject the ammunition cartridge from the weapon; that seemed as much like permission to proceed as anything else he could have said or done. Tam slid a hand down between the other man's legs and squeezed, feeling the impressively large bulge that was hardening there.

Danny was panting now, his eyes squeezed shut as his body moved in the rhythm Brand was setting for him. He really was such a sensuous little minx, despite his youth and his relative inexperience in these matters. Tam's personal opinion was that Charon was very lucky to have found him. Once he gained some confidence in his abilities, he was going to be one of the most sought-after boys in the entire House.

Nao wasn't making it any easier on him, his mouth moving from Danny's neck down to his chest with deliberate, indomitable purpose. His eyes, exotically dark and filled with good-natured mischief, flickered toward Danny's face briefly. He brushed his fingers across Danny's balls just as he bit down on one pert nipple, smiling slightly to himself at the cry Danny made in response to the action.

Watching the two of them, both dark-haired youths of incomparable beauty and intensely focused sensual appetite, Tam could understand why Angelo had wanted to see them together like this. It made Tam long, for a brief moment, for some of that kind of attention himself. Angelo's boys had doubtlessly received extensive training to be able to do the jobs they did, and were exquisitely skilled at it. Maybe someday, if he ever tired of the thrill of throwing himself on the mercies of uncounted strangers, he would retire and purchase a harem of his own; the thought made him grin.

Danny's breath caught in the back of his throat in a high, thin whine, and then he came with a harsh cry, his entire body arching. Brand's expression was wild, touched with equal parts arousal and sheer, naked incredulity, as if he couldn't quite believe just what it was he'd done.

He was so damned cute. Tam was apparently doomed to be surrounded by adorable, emotionally stunted men who needed to be coaxed past their intimacy issues. There were definitely worse lots a man could have in life.

Danny pulled himself upward and folded his arms around Brand's neck, kissing him deeply. Tam, free now to turn his attention elsewhere, was surprised to see that Charon had joined them, sitting in a plush armchair at the far end of the room with one of the harem boys curled up in his lap. The boy had his arms wrapped around Charon's shoulders, his body shaking visibly as Charon's hand smoothed over his back.

Tam glanced over at Reiji, frowning. Reiji was alone on the couch now, his feet tucked underneath him. His gaze was fixed unblinkingly on Charon, his mouth pressed together in a hard-edged frown.

With a sigh, Tam pushed himself to his feet and went over to sit with him, settling down beside him on the couch.

"You know," he said casually, "you could always go over there and join them."

Reiji shot him a glare so fierce it should have been physically painful. Tam, however, was used to being the subject of those kinds of expressions from him and barely felt it.

"Fuck off," Reiji told him tersely.

Tam nodded, having expected that kind of reaction. He sat watching Charon make out with the harem boy for a moment longer before saying, "You're going to have to make a move sooner or later if you want him that badly."

Seeing Reiji tense out of the corner of his eye, he wondered fleetingly if the other man was going to haul off and hit him. That would certainly be the cap on an already shitty day.

But Reiji, surprisingly, managed to keep himself under control. "You don't know what you're talking about."

The quiet misery in his voice made Tam's heart ache for him. "You might be surprised. We always seem to want the things we feel we can't have." He was thinking of the approval his father dangled so enticingly out in front of him when he said it.

Reiji didn't say anything for a long minute. At the other end of the room, the boy in Charon's lap threw his head back in reaction to something Charon had done to him, his arms tightening around Charon's shoulders.

"I'm just a whore," Reiji said finally. "That's all any of us are to him."

Tam gave him a censuring glance. "You don't honestly believe that."

A pause. "No. But he doesn't touch whores. Not after he hires them."

"You mean he never has before. Maybe you'll be the exception." Tam remembered his own "audition" with Charon with a fair amount of fondness, but he personally felt no particular desire to repeat the experience. It was clear from Reiji's reactions, however, that Reiji felt a great deal more for their boss than just respect for a trusted pseudo-father-figure.

Reiji stood up abruptly. "You're right. What's the worst that can happen?"

"That's the spirit." Tam was relieved; he was getting a bit tired of playing counselor. He was fairly worked up after that session with Brand, and he was looking forward to getting some attention himself in the near future.

Reiji's expression looked anything but confident. A moment later, however, his face hardened. *'When in doubt, get angry'* was apparently his motto. Tam had to admit that it seemed to have been working for him so far.

He stalked off toward Charon with his fists clenched at his sides. Tam watched him go, silently wishing him luck and hoping they both managed to survive the coming confrontation. Sighing heavily, he pushed himself up from the couch and wandered over to where Ander had his own young harem boy pressed down against the floor.

This kind of life, he thought with a grin, was one he could easily get used to.

Reiji listened to the dull thud of his heart pounding and wondered what the hell he was so scared of. He hated feeling scared. It wasn't something he'd had occasion to feel very often in his life; fear was something you could only really experience if you had something to lose, and he'd had precious little of that in his lifetime.

Just what was it he felt he was in danger of losing now?

Pushing the uncomfortable thoughts aside, he focused on the rage glowing warmly in his chest and stepped up beside the chair Charon was sitting in. The whore in his lap was curled over his chest, face pressed against the side of his neck. Reiji narrowed his eyes at the kid, disliking him instantly.

"Reiji." Charon smiled up at him in a lazy sort of way. "What can I do for you?"

The calming hand he placed on the whore's shoulder pissed Reiji off. He stood shaking for several seconds before sinking down slowly to his knees and resting one hand on Charon's bent knee.

One of Charon's eyebrows rose in question. Before he could say anything, Reiji leaned in to kiss him.

Maybe it was because he was caught up in the moment—having a young, attractive, willing whore curled up in one's lap tended to do that to a person—but Charon responded instantly, kissing him back. Reiji shivered straight down to his toes, leaning forward and sliding his hand further up Charon's thigh.

A firm grip around his wrist stopped him. "Reiji," Charon said again, in a gentle tone that made Reiji seethe inside. "What are you doing?"

Reiji closed his eyes. "Why won't you let any of us touch you?"

It was a moment before Charon answered. "I'm your employer."

He smiled grimly. "And we're just whores, I know. Do you really think so little of us that you can't even stand to have us near you?"

"You know that's not it, Reiji." The sharpness in his voice made Reiji flinch. His hand settled on Reiji's head in apology. "I can't take advantage of the position of authority I have over you. If I did, I wouldn't be any different than the men who've abused you in the past."

Images flashed through Reiji's mind of the encounters Charon was referring to, all the nameless, faceless sons of bitches he'd degraded himself for on the streets with the intention of obtaining a scrap of food, some training, or just in the hopes of getting a kind word. It pissed him off that Charon would compare himself to any of those bastards; he was so obviously above them, he was absolutely nothing like them. All they'd ever done was make Reiji feel ashamed, used. All Charon made him feel was warm and protected. Why couldn't Charon see that?

A brief tug on his wrist urged Reiji to climb up into the chair, curling up on Charon's lap. He recognized dimly that the whore who'd previously occupied that position had disappeared, but then his mind was caught up in the sensation of having Charon's arms wrapped around him, one hand stroking soothingly at his hair.

"I love you, Reiji," Charon said in his ear, but he meant it the same way he loved all of his boys, as a part of his family. "You know that. I'd never do anything to hurt you."

Reiji closed his eyes and burrowed into the warmth of the embrace, giving in to the comfort of it and hating himself for needing it so badly. It occurred to him that he was well and truly lost now; he'd been refusing to admit it for a long time, but there was no denying it any longer. Maybe it had started all the way back when they'd first met, there on the streets of Aechestan. He wanted Charon so very badly, and it was eating him up inside that Charon wouldn't let him have him.

But Charon loved him. He'd said so.

He told himself that that would have to be enough.

Chapter 31

Sensorium

There were countless reasons, Brand thought hazily, why all of this was an incredibly bad idea.

At the moment, however, they all seemed to be escaping him. He'd lost his shirt somewhere over the past several minutes, and slender hands were currently making their way over his bared chest, brushing his nipples in passing. It felt surprisingly good in his presently aroused state. He caught himself making a small sound in the back of his throat that brought a rush of heat to his face, but the embarrassment he felt couldn't eclipse the sheer, undeniable bliss of being touched this way.

"That's it," Danny's voice murmured in his ear. The boy was all but straddling his lap now, slender thighs moving to press tight around his hips. Danny's nails left little sparks of pleasure behind them where they trailed over the skin of his arms. "It's all right to let yourself feel good."

Brand's breath caught in his throat as teeth pressed briefly at the lobe of his ear, hot breath wafting across the skin of his neck. There was another body pressed up against him from behind; one of Angelo's harem boys, he thought, but it was difficult to be sure. It didn't seem to matter. Everywhere he was being touched felt good, felt *incredible*, and even as his body drank up the pleasure of the touches it still somehow wasn't *enough*.

"Mmm." Danny's voice was a deep-throated purr of contentment as he rubbed their bodies together. There was a lazy kind of satiation to his movements that made Brand's hands tremble, remembering that he had been the one to do that to him. "Feels good to let go once in a while, doesn't it?"

Brand squeezed his eyes shut. "Yeah," he said hoarsely. It was impossible to be anything less than honest with this boy. "It does."

He could hear the smile in Danny's voice. "What do you want me to do for you?"

Another low moan escaped him when a hand settled over his groin, squeezing firmly. He was already hard, painfully so, and that ratcheted him up just that much more. His hips moved without his conscious volition, pressing forward into Danny's touch.

"I don't...." He bit hard on his lower lip. "Look, Danny, maybe this isn't such a good—"

"Wrong answer." Deft fingers pulled open his belt and slid down his zipper, still kneading him through the fabric of his trousers.

Brand was panting openly now, unable to think of anything beyond the heat of the body pressed so willingly into his arms. He slid his hands down Danny's back, feeling the smooth heat of him, and mouthed blindly at the curve of his shoulder. The boy tasted like soap and clean sweat, and he smelled like the winter wind.

"Gods," Danny breathed, arching forward against him. There was a little hitch in his breathing now that made Brand's chest tighten. The hands at his groin squeezed the tops of his thighs briefly as Danny shimmied forward to seat himself more firmly on top of him. "Just hold yourself still, right like that."

Brand tipped his head backwards when Danny lifted up onto his knees and then lowered himself again, steadying the base of Brand's cock with one hand and easing him inside. Tight, slick heat engulfed him, taking his breath away as Danny sank down onto his lap, thighs trembling slightly where they bracketed his hips.

"Fuck," he said on an explosive sigh, his hands tightening around Danny's back. The body behind him pressed more firmly against him, surrounding him with molten heat both in front and behind. Twin mouths trailed along his neck, his shoulders, teeth scraping wetly across his skin. He felt like he was being devoured alive, and he *loved* it.

"That's the way, Brand," Danny said, his voice shaking. He was moving now, falling into a steady rhythm that spoke eloquently of his extensive experience in these matters. Brand couldn't find it in him to mind, though, not when the results made him feel this good.

"The two of you look amazing together." That was Nao's voice behind him, timid and breathless. Lips trailed across Brand's ear, a small tongue leaving a shocking stripe of wetness in their wake. The hands on his chest dipped lower, slim fingers spreading out across the bones of his hips.

He couldn't find the breath to respond. Pleasure coiled at the base of his spine, sending pulses of sensation out through his entire body as Danny continued to move over him. He moved his own hips in steady counter-rhythm, rocking gently in between the two bodies that held him.

Danny's hand was moving at his own groin now, stroking himself in time with their movements. Once Brand saw that, he couldn't look away. Danny's face was flushed, his hair curling damply against his forehead; he was a perfect picture of desperation and lust, but there was nothing lewd or obscene about him. He looked beautiful in a way that made Brand's mouth go dry, angelic and perfect and *his*, for however long this communion between them lasted.

There was no way it could possibly last. Pleasure exploded like hot shards of broken glass through every part of Brand's body, making him cry out. He tightened his hands around Danny's hips and thrust upward, his muscles seizing up with the force of the orgasm that ripped through him.

"Beautiful," Danny sighed, mouthing at his ear. Brand shuddered and wrapped his arms around the younger man's shoulders, crumpling forward against him.

A shadow flickered at the corner of his vision, making Brand raise his head sharply. He frowned when Angelo reached for Danny's hand, curling their fingers together.

There was an edge of amusement in the older man's eyes. "He's exceptionally well-trained, isn't he?" The words were approving. "He's already come once this evening, though. I think that's enough for the time being."

Brand was still breathing hard. He held Danny's waist to steady him as the two of them separated. He could tell by looking that Danny was more than ready to come a second time. A glance at the boy's eyes showed a glimmer of apprehension there.

Self-consciousness returned in a rush now that the adrenaline of the encounter was fading. Reminded of the fact that they weren't alone, Brand glanced around the room uncomfortably. His heart was pounding, expecting more eyes than just Angelo's to be on them, but from what he could see, the others were all occupied in matters of their own. The realization made him relax slightly.

Angelo trailed his knuckles over the side of Danny's face, leaning in to nuzzle at the hair in front of his ear. "You're a very selfish boy, Danny," he chastised lightly. He was smiling. "Taking all of this attention for yourself, when poor Nao is sitting neglected."

Brand turned to look at Nao. The boy knelt behind him with his eyes downcast, dark hair falling feather-soft across the skin of his brow. His narrow face was slightly flushed, giving proof of the fact that he hadn't been unaffected by what had been going on around him this evening. He looked submissive, and obedient, but with a core of quiet hunger to him that was doubtlessly one of the things that had drawn Angelo to him in the first place.

"Ah," Danny said, sounding contrite. He moved toward Nao with a smile of his own, his own aroused state apparently forgotten. Tugging gently on the other boy's hand, he pulled him forward and laid him back against Angelo, pillowing his head on the older man's lap. Angelo slid a hand over Nao's forehead to soothe him.

Brand stared, his heart pounding. For a moment he'd been afraid that Angelo might turn his attention to *him* now, but apparently that wasn't something he had to worry about. Danny and Nao were much more this man's type. Brand himself preferred a bit more bite in his relationships, although he had to admit that there was something undeniably attractive about being here with these two ethereally beautiful young men.

Danny leaned down to kiss Nao, twining his fingers deep into the other boy's hair. Brand made a small sound at that, feeling flushed. Danny pressed a kiss to Nao's cheek, his chin, the side of his neck, and skillfully opened the buttons of his shirt as he made his way down his chest. He tongued at one nipple in passing, making Nao's head tip back with a low hiss.

Brand was beginning to see where this was going. The thought made him dizzy; he thought about what it would feel like to have

Danny's mouth moving so reverently over *him* and wondered feverishly if he'd ever have the chance to find out. Obviously, his morals had taken a severe turn for the worse since he'd joined up with this group. Not that there was anything technically *wrong* with anything they were doing. It wasn't like he was paying for sex. They were all here quite willingly, just a group of friends indulging in the pleasure of each other's bodies, and no matter how embarrassed or confused or uncomfortable it made him, he couldn't bring himself to pass up the opportunity to indulge right along with them.

Nao gasped when Danny opened the front of his pants, teeth trailing lightly across the skin of his stomach as the clothing was eased down over his narrow hips. Angelo's hands held Nao's upper arms firmly, holding him down lazily as Danny pleasured him.

Internal turmoil or no, there was no way Brand could look away from this even if he tried.

The blond-haired boy's name was Nero. Ander had learned that much. He looked like an angel, all slender limbs and beguiling smiles, and he kissed like a demon. Already, Ander was so hard he felt he could die from it, and he still had most of his clothes on.

There had been a time, he mused, when he would have felt self-conscious about engaging in these kinds of activities, particularly in the middle of a crowded room. But there was something thrilling about the forbidden nature of it that set his heart pounding, filling him with a warmth and a passion he hadn't felt outside of his rare assignations inside the House of Silence. It was heady, addictive, like getting drunk on expensive wine.

"You two look good together." That was Tam's voice, settling in behind him. The sound of it made Ander smile. "Mind if I join you?"

"Please." Ander liked Tam immensely. He felt comfortable around him, which was rare enough for him to feel toward anyone recently. There was something down-to-earth about Tam that Ander felt innately drawn to; this was a man who understood the darker side of life, but had made the decision not to bow to it. He was strong, and capable, but more than that, he cared deeply about people and it showed.

Tam had grabbed a heavy blanket from the back of the couch and spread it out over them as he lay down on the floor, molding himself against Ander from behind. "Don't mind me," he said, breathing out warmly across Ander's ear. "Just continue with what you were doing."

Smiling, Ander bent down to kiss Nero again. Nero seemed grateful for the attention, his hands sliding up Ander's arms to tangle in his long hair. This boy had an enormous sexual appetite; he kept urging Ander on with subtle touches and low moans to move faster, to touch him in more varied and provocative ways.

It was impossible not to feel just a little ribald with that kind of encouragement. Ander was breathless now, his heart beginning to pound as Tam's teeth pressed against the side of his neck, trailing hot kisses down to the curve of his shoulder. A strong hand smoothed over Ander's waist, squeezing briefly before moving down to clutch at his hip. Tam's hips ground against him from behind; Ander could tell that he, too, was aroused by all of this.

"Feels nice," Tam sighed, rubbing his cheek against Ander's. He slid his fingers underneath the front of Ander's shirt, tickling his stomach briefly before dipping down to tug at his belt. "You mind if I...?"

"Uh, no. Go right ahead." Ander was finding it difficult to breathe now. Nero's hand had worked its way underneath his shirt and was currently playing with his nipples in a way that made him *really* want to feel the wetness of a mouth there. He trailed a finger across Nero's lips absently; smiling, Nero reached for Ander's shirt and began pulling it off over his head.

Tam had worked Ander's pants down over his hips now. Palming his ass with one hand, he bent to bite at the juncture of Ander's neck and shoulder.

Ander's breath left him in a ragged sigh. His hips twitched when Tam's middle finger pressed in between his legs, curling in to touch his body's opening.

"Can I?" Tam said. He sounded breathless.

Ander squeezed his eyes shut briefly, then nodded. He thought he should probably be mortified at how eagerly his heart leapt at the question, but Tam had assured him last time that there was nothing to be ashamed about. It still surprised him how much he had responded to having Tam inside of him; just the thought of it was enough to make his skin go hot and prickly, and his chest to constrict in sudden desire.

He allowed Tam to pull his pants the rest of the way off, and then he was naked underneath the blanket. The feel of it was electrifying; Nero was a fluid heat in front of him, hands splayed across Ander's ribs as his agile mouth applied gentle suction to one of his nipples, tongue lashing across his skin. Tam was pressed up full-length behind him, spooning his body from behind.

It felt surreal when Tam's finger slid into him, coated in some kind of lube. Trust someone of this man's profession to never go anywhere unprepared. The thought brought a flash of amusement with it. That troubled him for some reason, until he realized it was because he wasn't used to associating joviality with sex. Sex was pleasure, and pleasure was happiness, and either of those things had equated with guilt in his mind for a very long time. But the truth was that here, now, on the run from the law, in fear for his life, surrounded by warmth and the comfort of friends, he felt happier than he could remember being in a good long while.

"Good?" Tam whispered, his voice hoarse. Ander could feel him shimmying around behind him, opening the front of his own pants and pushing them down his thighs. His finger didn't stop its steady stroking inside Ander's ass as he slid out of them.

"Yes," Ander replied, gasping as Nero's teeth nipped at his right nipple, teasing the hard little nub.

Two fingers now, and that made the whole thing feel even better. Ander tugged at Nero's shirt, trying to get it off of him, a plan with which Nero eagerly complied. The boy wriggled out of the rest of his clothes with impressive agility. His breath hitched when Ander's hand closed around his cock, which was smooth and hot and delightfully hard against his palm.

It was a curious harmony as the three of them moved together. Ander strongly suspected that he was the only one unfamiliar with this kind of group intimacy, but the thought of it only inflamed him further. Even the knowledge that there were others in the room with them failed to quench the passion he felt. On the contrary, the sound of other voices moaning, other bodies moving in indistinct shapes around him, made him feel even lustier.

You, my dear Lord Delacroix, are a hopelessly ribald man. The thought made him smile.

Tam groaned low in his chest as he slid his thigh up over Ander's hip, leaning forward against him. Ander could feel the hardness of him pressing from behind, moving against him in small, impatient little thrusts.

"Tell me you're ready for this," Tam said, a note of pleading entering into his voice. He knotted his fingers in Ander's hair, pulling his head back to expose his throat to Nero's adoring mouth. "Gods, you look so good like this...."

Ander made a strangled sound and pushed his hips backward, hoping Tam would get the message that he was entirely on board with the plan he was proposing. In front of him, Nero gave a keening moan as Ander stroked him harder and faster toward orgasm.

"Yes," Tam whispered in his ear, pulling his fingers out of him.

Yes, Ander agreed, panting harshly. *Yes, yes, yes....*

Chapter 32
Consummation

This was, Reiji thought, the closest he might ever have been to heaven.

Having a pretty whore bent between his spread thighs, mouth moving busily at his groin while Charon supported his body from behind. He was sitting on Charon's lap now, back nestled against the older man's chest. Charon's hands were on his knees, holding his legs open to give the whore better access.

"You look incredible like this, Reiji." Charon's breath was hot on his neck. For a moment Reiji thought he was going to kiss him there, then reason reasserted itself.

Reiji refused to show how much the words warmed him. "The whore's good at what he does," he said, panting only slightly.

"Ian's pretty talented," Charon agreed. He sounded amused.

Ian? Was that the bastard's name? Reiji twisted his fingers in the kid's hair and squeezed, thrusting his hips upward.

"Easy," Charon chastised, closing his palm over the back of Reiji's hand. "He's younger than you are, you know."

Like that mattered. He was obviously old enough to have chosen this profession, which meant he was old enough to handle whatever his clients dished out. Reiji wondered suddenly if Charon had been gentle when he'd fucked him in the past. He probably had been, the bastard.

"You're not doing it right." He pushed Ian away from him with a sudden surge of anger, rocking him back onto his heels. He felt a flash of bitter satisfaction at the resentment the kid couldn't quite manage to hide when he glanced up at him.

"What would you like me to do for you?" Ian asked.

Oh, that question opened up so many possibilities, none of which Ian would find at all pleasant. Reiji wondered at this sudden sadistic streak inside himself. He didn't have anything against Ian per se; the kid was nothing to him, little more than an unexpectedly talented mouth to pleasure himself with. It was the thought of Charon putting his hands on the kid that angered him, when Charon wouldn't give *him* so much as the time of day. What was so fucking special about this kid, anyway?

Charon leaned forward slightly, his chest pressing against Reiji's back. Reiji shivered at the feel of breath ghosting across his ear. "This is supposed to be fun," Charon said, rubbing his thumb over the back of Reiji's hand.

Fun? When had sex ever been fun? Reiji scowled, glaring down at the whore framed between his knees. Sex was a job, and an obligation, and at times it could be a necessary physical release, but it was nothing more than an onerous duty. Something to be gotten through so he could get the reward at the end, be it a paycheck or the endless quest for orgasm.

Although he did have to admit that it felt nice having Charon's arms around him like this. He allowed himself to lean back when Charon's hands urged him to do so, settling the two of them further back into the chair. He closed his eyes at the feel of strong fingers massaging into the tops of his thighs.

"Relax," Charon said, his voice a low purr. "That's the way." His hand slid up Reiji's chest to cup his throat, tipping his head back against his shoulder.

Reiji felt boneless. Charon was surprisingly good at this. The room seemed to go hazy as Charon continued to rub his leg, encouraging the muscles there to loosen. He watched through slitted eyes as Ian leaned forward to nuzzle at Charon's knee.

Reiji was just about to tense up again when Charon gestured sharply with one hand. Ian responded instantly, climbing up onto the chair and settling down over Reiji's lap.

Oh, that *did* feel good. Reiji arched his back slightly, closing his hands over the kid's hips. Charon's body was warm behind him, cradling him in heady heat. Ian knew better than to try to kiss him; he cupped Reiji's shoulders in both hands as he began to move, slowly grinding their hips together.

"How does that feel?" Charon's voice was a rough whisper, warm and intimate. Reiji *really* liked the sound of it.

"Mmm," he said contemplatively, considering the question. To be honest, he wouldn't object if Ian decided to keep moving just like that. There was a seam in his pants that was pulling... pulling just right.

"You want more?" The words seemed to rumble up through Reiji's back and into his head, where they set up a low buzzing inside his ears. He knew what Charon was really asking, that he wasn't really offering up himself as any part of this rather bizarre equation, but that didn't stop Reiji from fantasizing, just a little.

"Yeah," he panted, turning his head to nuzzle against Charon's cheek.

Ian withdrew slightly. Reiji watched as the clothes seemed to melt off of him, and then he was back, kneeling down to straddle Reiji's lap.

"Fuck, yeah," Reiji sighed as the front of his leather pants was opened. Charon's hands moved restlessly over him, drawing little shivers of sensation to the surface of his skin. They moved down his arms, over his sides, cradling the underside of his chin. Reiji gave himself up to them, feeling more aware of them than he did of the hands that were curling around his cock.

Ian's body sank down over him, drawing him inside. Reiji hissed low between his teeth and tightened his fingers over the kid's hips, thrusting upward sharply. Had Charon fucked him like this? Maybe in this very chair? The thought made him angry again, but there was a touch of despondency to it now. He knew by now that Charon would never look at him as anything other than an employee to order around, or a charge to be cared for.

It made him less kind, maybe, than he would have been otherwise. He tightened his hands around Ian's hips as he thrust upward, knowing he was leaving bruises and not caring. Ian folded over him, letting his body be used in whatever way Reiji desired. Reiji was rather glad he wasn't trying to fight him, because in the mood he was currently in, he might have tried to hold him down and that would have been a mess for everyone concerned. The last thing they needed was for the esteemed Lord Angelo to think they were mistreating his whores.

"You're beautiful," Charon whispered, nuzzling against Reiji's ear.

Closing his eyes, Reiji tried to pretend that the words were for him.

Nao came with a hoarse shout, his back arching and his hands clenching white-knuckled in the rug to either side. Danny swallowed the resultant flood with ease, drawing back to sit on his heels.

He could feel Brand's wide-eyed gaze boring into both of them. The poor guy really wasn't used to this. Danny flashed a grin at him and sidled toward him as Angelo scooped a breathless Nao up in his arms.

"Beautiful, isn't he?" Danny said, curling his hand into Brand's and squeezing tightly.

Brand's eyes were troubled. "You're all beautiful."

Danny remembered what Charon had said about this man suffering from an excess of morality. All of this had to be difficult for him.

"So are you." He leaned in to lick at Brand's ear, feeling heartened when the other man let him do it. He pressed down with his teeth lightly in reward.

Brand shivered against him. "I'm not," he said, sounding uncertain.

"Are, too."

"No. I'm—"

"A god," Danny finished for him, leaning in to kiss him on the mouth. He wasn't being flattering, either. Brand had a delightfully strong body, long and lean with a kind of runner's grace. His face was clean-lined with strong features, and that dark blond hair gave him a rakish look that appealed to the bad boy in Danny's soul.

They were just getting into the spirit of the kiss when arms closed around Danny from behind. "Are you planning to share any of that affection with me?" a low voice murmured in his ear.

"Mmm," Danny said in reply, tipping his head backwards. A hungry mouth fastened onto the side of his neck, marking him. The soft fringe of the goatee there tickled his skin.

He'd known from the moment Lord Angelo had laid eyes on him that the man wanted to fuck him. The thought made him shiver. He was still a bit sore from having sex with Brand earlier, and from that damned dildo. He wasn't sure his body could take much more. Angelo gave him the impression of being a man of tremendous sexual appetite, especially considering that he needed four harem boys to service him.

Twisting around in Angelo's arms, Danny met the man's mouth in a kiss. Nao was kneeling with another of the harem boys behind Angelo's shoulder; the two of them were starting to fool around together now that it was clear their lord's attention was turning elsewhere. Nao met Danny's eyes with a rueful smile before turning away from them.

Angelo was starting to press Danny down toward the ground now. Danny reacted quickly, reaching for his groin and kneading a low groan out of him.

"That's it," Danny said encouragingly, pulling open his belt. He kissed Angelo once on the side of the neck before dropping down to his elbows and nuzzling at the older man's crotch. It was a relief when Angelo allowed it, settling back on one hand and entangling the fingers of the other deep in Danny's hair.

Oral sex was a lot less demanding than actual intercourse, and in Danny's experience, a lot of clients found it just as satisfying. He mouthed at Angelo's cock through the fabric of his boxer briefs, putting honest enthusiasm into it. It was the least he could do since the man had been kind enough to let them play with his harem.

A hand on his back startled him. A quick glance to the side showed him that it was Brand. The sight made Danny smile; shirtless with his belt hanging open, with those amazingly intense eyes of his, he looked like a wet dream come to life. Danny arched his back under the caress with a low hum of pleasure, doing what he could to encourage him.

Angelo's cock was thick and heavy inside Danny's mouth. He petted one hand over the back of Danny's head lazily, leaning back against the two members of his harem and accepting the service like the lord he was. The thought amused Danny; it wasn't every day he got the chance to service someone who acted with such high-handed panache who was actually entitled to do so.

Danny shivered when Brand moved in from behind him, large hands bracketing his hips. Brand seemed to enjoy touching him, which was entirely okay in Danny's opinion. He wondered if Brand was planning to fuck him again. If so, Danny wouldn't mind; he *liked* Brand, and he wanted to help him get over that endearing inhibition of his. He had a feeling that the man would be a hell of a lot of fun if he ever learned to cut loose a little.

Hands smoothed over his sides and back, sliding teasing trails of sensation up to his shoulders and then back down again. Danny wrapped an arm around Angelo's waist to brace himself as Brand eased in between his thighs. There was a charming hesitation to his movements, as if he were waiting for Danny to tell him to leave him the hell alone. Instead, Danny pressed his hips backwards in encouragement, humming low in his throat.

Finally, Brand seemed to get the message and leaned down to drape himself over Danny's back. The heat of him made Danny's breath catch, his upper arms trembling where they held his weight up against the floor. The feel of a hard cock sliding into him was deliciously welcome, taking the edge off the arousal that buzzed like an angry insect just underneath his skin. Brand, he knew, would be faultlessly gentle with him, which was just the kind of loving he needed right now.

Angelo flexed his hips, reminding Danny of his primary purpose. Closing his eyes, Danny concentrated again on the task in front of him. Brand leaned against his thighs from behind, filling him entirely, the tentative thrusts he made deepening as the moments slid past. Danny whimpered in approval and sucked hard on the cock in his mouth, trying to give Angelo as much pleasure as he could.

Excitement crawled over Danny's skin, making him sweat from exertion. He was so damn hard now, even though he'd already come once this evening. He was going to die if Angelo refused to let him come again. His jaw ached from the work he was requiring of it, and his thighs were trembling. He felt dizzy; kneeling with his head down like this was making the blood rush to his head, and Brand thrusting behind him was moving him in a steady rocking motion that made the whole thing seem somehow unreal.

Finally Angelo's fingers clenched tight in his hair, and his cock pulsed once before spurting into Danny's mouth. Danny moaned low in his chest as he swallowed, the strength of the grip bringing tears to his eyes. It felt good, though, the same way the ache in his jaw and his thighs felt good. Still the hard edge of his own unfulfilled need sang through him, making it increasingly difficult to think of anything aside from the signals his body was sending him.

"Danny," Brand said behind him, his breathing ragged. He held Danny's hips firmly, leaning over him as he thrust with increasing urgency. Danny arched against him and pressed his forehead against Angelo's thigh, biting back the keening wail that wanted to escape his throat.

The feel of Angelo's hand brushing his hair back from his forehead was both soothing and aggravating all at the same time. Danny could imagine the man's indulgent smile; ignoring him, he reached down between his legs to take his own cock in hand, working it with hard, short jerks that left him gasping.

Brand thrust a final time and pressed hard against Danny's back, the weight of him taking Danny's breath away. Danny continued to stroke himself, squeezing his eyes shut as colored lights began to dance behind his closed eyelids. Then, finally, the pleasure whiplashed through him, pulling a ragged shout through a throat that felt raw and used.

Trembling, he sank down onto the rug with Brand curled around him. Angelo had fallen back into the arms of his two harem boys, kissing one of them while the other massaged at his shoulders and chest. Danny watched them for a while, contentment and satiation slithering through him. Brand's hand was warm and heavy where it petted at his hair, calming both of them while their heartbeats settled.

All in all, Danny was ridiculously happy that Charon had sent them here.

Ander bit hard on his lower lip while Tam slid inside of him, his hips shaking slightly where Tam held them in both hands. It didn't hurt as much as it had the first time they'd done this, but there was still a fair amount of discomfort involved.

"Just ride it out," Tam whispered to him, nipping lightly at his ear. "Breathe for me, okay?"

Breathe. Right. Ander sucked in a deep breath and then let it out slowly, his breath stuttering as Nero's teeth scraped across his chest. It was certainly distracting being with two men at the same time. Even as the thought crossed his mind, Nero's slender fingers wrapped around his cock, coaxing him back to full hardness.

Ah, that was very nice. He breathed out again, more easily this time. Tam licked at the inner curve of his ear in reward, his breath turning cool and then warm as it wafted over the dampened skin. Ander shivered, flexing his hips slightly as the unfamiliar sensation of being filled rolled through him.

"Feels good, doesn't it?" Tam said on a small huff of laughter, settling himself more firmly against Ander's back.

"Yes." Impossible to say anything other than the truth. "It does."

Tam's hand curled around the underside of his chin, tipping Ander's head back against his shoulder as he thrust in more deeply. Ander bit back a moan at that, closing his eyes tightly. Ah, gods, that felt good, especially once Tam touched that place inside that made his chest constrict and his hands tremble. He reached out to Nero just so he'd have something to hold onto; Nero melted against him obligingly, still stroking at his cock. Not wanting Nero to be left out, Ander reached for the younger man's cock again and started giving it a determined working-over. Nero nipped at the side of his neck in gratitude, his breaths deepening.

Pleasure seemed to roll back and forth between the three of them, from one to the other and then back again. Ander rolled with it, letting Tam set the pace. All of the sensations he felt were overwhelming, from the cock sliding with increasing urgency inside his body to the molten hot cock in his hand, an arm wrapped reverently around his shoulder while other hands clawed at his hips, his own cock encased in a tightly sliding grip that took his breath away. Bodies surged with breathless excitement both in front and behind, making it impossible to think of anything other than what was being done to him, of what he was doing to them.

Orgasm hit him with the weight of a freight train, which seemed to be the spark that sent the other two off as well. Nero stiffened in his arms, crying out sharply as he spurted over Ander's hand, and a moment later Tam came with a final thrust that Ander knew was going to leave him aching. It felt good and hot and right and he wasn't quite sure how he'd ever lived without this kind of sweaty, groping, visceral communion in his life before.

"That was incredible," he said, still feeling somewhat shell-shocked. He wrapped an arm around Nero's shoulders as the boy curled in against his chest.

"Hells, yeah," Tam said with a grin in his voice, and collapsed in a sweaty slump against his back.

Reiji came with a low curse, pressing his face against the side of Charon's neck. Charon's arms closed around him, holding him tightly as the sensations tore through him. Reiji held himself stiffly, clenching hard around Ian's hips with both hands as his cock emptied itself into the body above him.

It was physical release, nothing more. Too intense and edgy even to be called pleasure; nevertheless, there was definitely something appealing about being cradled in Charon's arms like this as he came down off the edge. He could smell the scent of him, clean skin and wool and the lingering spicy scent of his cologne. Reiji resisted the urge to taste him or, barring that, bite him.

"Beautiful," Charon sighed. He tightened his arms around Reiji's waist. "But you've got to finish what you started, Reiji."

Reiji narrowed his eyes when Charon's hand snaked forward to clasp hold of Ian's hard cock, giving it a strong, proficient twist from root to tip. Ian's entire body jerked, a low cry escaping him as he bent forward, bracing himself against Reiji's shoulders.

Reiji wanted to hate the kid, but he just couldn't muster up the energy at the moment. So he settled for slouching back and letting Charon do what he wanted. It was actually kind of amusing; Ian's face was scrunched up in an admittedly pretty way, his body moving with a kind of liquid grace that was almost hypnotic to see. Even more interestingly, Charon's breath rasped right next to Reiji's ear, giving proof—however circumstantial—that he was actually being affected by this.

Ah, the trials of having two willing, greedy whores in one's arms. Reiji grinned, wondering if Charon considered it an imposition to indulge the two of them like this. The tolerant master giving in to the whims of his voracious minions; or the lord descending from on high to appease the vassals that were bond to him. Not that Charon was a lord; he didn't have any ranking at all as far as Reiji could tell. Aside from his obvious wealth, he was just as common as the rest of them. Which was just fine as far as Reiji was concerned; he hadn't met many lords who didn't think they were a superior breed of human being solely on account of their family's status.

Ian's hands tightened over Reiji's shoulders, and he came with a low cry. Reiji watched him with absent-minded interest, wondering if he looked that wanton when *he* came. Somehow, he doubted it.

"There," Charon said, sounding pleased. "That's better now, isn't it?" Ian gave him a grateful smile and then slid back off of Reiji's lap, slinking away to curl up next to Ander and Tam under a blanket on the floor.

Reiji resisted the urge to turn around and look at him. "I suppose you want me to thank you?" he said caustically, watching as Tam lifted up a corner of the blanket to invite Ian in to lie beside them.

Charon snorted in his ear. "Hardly."

They sat together in companionable silence for a while. At the other end of the room in front of the fireplace, Danny and Brand were settling down with sleepy murmurs with Angelo and another couple of the harem whores. Everyone looked sated and tired and spent, and quite ready to indulge in some much-needed rest before they had to leave later tonight.

Reiji fought back a yawn of his own, only half-successfully. "What about you?" he asked at last.

"I beg your pardon?"

"Don't be stupid. You know what I'm talking about. You're the only one in this room who hasn't come at least once tonight."

He could feel Charon smile against the side of his face. "Don't worry about me. I've got a lot on my mind this evening."

Which was utter bullshit, because Reiji had been able to tell clear as day that Charon was hard when he and Ian were fucking on his lap. If Reiji hadn't come over and interrupted them, would Charon have been the one fucking him?

The thought made Reiji's mouth turn down at the corners. He

thought about pushing the matter, but decided against it. Charon was being amazingly lenient by letting him cuddle on his lap like this, and he wasn't about to risk having that taken away from him.

"You can go join them, you know," Charon said after a while.

Reiji gave him a puzzled glance. "Who?"

"Tam and Ander. Or Brand and Danny, if you wanted to move closer to the fire."

In other words, he was being invited to go take his place among his fellow whores. Reiji frowned, deciding that if Charon wanted to get rid of him, the man would have to come right out and say so.

"I'm too tired to move," he lied. He was relieved when Charon didn't call him on it.

Together, the two of them settled back more comfortably into the chair. The warmth of the fire was soothing, the low popping of its embers creating a steady counterpoint to the subdued rustling as one body or another shifted into a more comfortable position on the floor around them. The air was thick with the scents of sex and damp wool and lingering woodsmoke, with a subtle undercurrent of Charon's cologne. It was a combination that Reiji could definitely become addicted to.

Relaxing into the heady comfort of the arms that held him, Reiji drifted off to sleep.

Continued in Volume 2: Ricochet

If you enjoyed this story, you can sign up for a free membership at ForbiddenFiction.com and discuss it with other readers and the author at the *Exodus* story page at
http://forbiddenfiction.com/library/story/JAJ-1.000001.

We do our best to proof all our work, but if you spot a text error we missed, please let us know via our website Contact Form at
http://forbiddenfiction.com/contact.

About the Author

J.A. Jaken has been writing homoerotic fiction for more than ten years. She got her start in the profession writing slash fanfiction, where she has published numerous stories under the pen-name Rushlight. Over the years she has written erotic short stories and novels in genres ranging from science fiction/fantasy to gothic horror to modern detective mysteries. Outside of writing, her interests include studying foreign languages, practicing martial arts, riding horses, and collecting medieval weaponry.

Other works by J.A. Jaken:

The House of Silence: Exodus (Volume 1)
The House of Silence: Ricochet (Volume 2)
The House of Silence: Consort (Volume 3)
Entering The House of Silence (anthology)

Pathfinder

The Charming

Nicholi's Vengeance

His Whipping Boy

About the Publisher

ForbiddenFiction.com is a publisher devoted to writing that breaks the boundaries of original erotic fiction. Our stories combine intense sexuality with quality writing. Stories at Forbidden Fiction.com not only arouse readers through sensations, but also engage them emotionally and mentally through storytelling as well-crafted as the sex is hot.

ForbiddenFiction.com is also designed to be a social reading environment. You'll have fun even if just reading the latest post each day, yet you will have the chance for so much more. Readers and authors can be part of ongoing discussions of specific works and individual authors as well as more general topics.

Sign up for a FREE Membership today at ForbiddenFiction.com

www.ingramcontent.com/pod-product-compliance
Lightning Source LLC
Chambersburg PA
CBHW060541180626
46817CB00002B/680